PROMISED LAND

How the MIDWEST was Won

"With God, all things are possible."
– Ohio state motto[1]
MATTHEW 19:26

"No people on earth, in similar circumstances, ever
acted more nobly or more bravely than they did.
No people of any country, or age, ever made greater
sacrifices for the benefit of posterity than those which
were made by the first settlers of the western regions."
– *Notes on the Settlement and Indian Wars,*
Joseph Dodderidge, 1824

---

1   Chosen by 12-year-old Jimmy Mastronardo of Cincinnati in a 1950s statewide contest.

Dedicated to my grandchildren,
Audrey and Robbie Rosenau,
who love books.

CONTENTS

INTRODUCTION

"As a writer, you should not judge, you should understand."
—Ernest Hemingway

In his historic 1885 book *Democracy in America*, the Frenchman Alexis de Tocqueville wrote, "In countries where associations are free, secret societies are unknown. In America there are factions, but no conspiracies."

His flattering portrait of the American spirit was correct about many things, but not about secret societies and conspiracies. With each incremental expansion of government, freedom was fenced in like the Western prairies after the invention of barbed wire. New rules, regulations, taxes and bureaucrats nibbled at the edges of American Constitutional liberties like mice in a museum.

And wherever freedom was smothered, the weeds of conspiracies and secret societies sprouted like crabgrass.

One of the most dangerous secret societies in American history began in Cincinnati. The Knights of the Golden Circle was started by a failed writer and quack doctor, George Washington Bickley. The KGC had secret meetings in "Castles," secret handshakes and passwords, oaths of allegiance and chapters we would now call "sleeper cells." Thousands of members met in dozens of states, including Ohio, Indiana and Kentucky.

It all began with "filibusters"—which in those times meant private invasions of Mexico and Central America to seize land and expand the borders of the United States. They were illegal under the Neutrality Act of 1794, but the federal government often winked and nodded "go ahead." As the Civil War approached, the KGC picked up the sword of secession and swelled with supporters in the North as well as the South.

Promised Land brings to light the long-forgotten plots, schemes and conspiracies of the KGC.

The story begins farther back in time, with the courageous Revolutionary War veterans who settled Ohio. They risked their lives and their families and came to the "Miami Slaughterhouse" wilderness on crowded flatboats with all their paltry property and livestock. Almost immediately, they had to fight a new war. Shawnees, Miamis and other tribes terrorized and tortured the white settlers the way the tribes had terrorized each other for thousands of years.

There were massacres and scalpings on both sides of that brutal battle. The barbarity of the Indians increased as their hunting grounds were crowded back by the smoking chimneys of pioneer log cabins. In *Notes on the Settlement and Indian Wars*, Joseph Doddridge described the Indians in 1824 from personal experience: "They foresaw the loss of their country and the downfall of their people, and therefore resolved on vengeance for the past and the future wrongs to be inflicted on them."

The tough pioneers and their sons and daughters overcame many devastating raids and discouraging defeats before they finally tamed Ohio by routing the Indians and their British allies at Fallen Timbers in 1794, and again in the War of 1812.

To win the Indian War, President George Washington created the first US Army, which was headquartered at Fort Washington in Cincinnati.

Then in 1836, Cincinnati's leading families who had won the Midwest, played a key role to win the West: They defied the federal Neutrality Act to support Texas in its war for independence from Santa Anna's Mexico. Few remember it today, but Cincinnati saved Texas. And that private "filibuster" planted the seeds of the KGC.

Later, during the Civil War, the Queen City's valiant defense in 1862 thwarted a siege that might have destroyed the Union if the city was lost.

Today, Ohio's slogan is "The Heart of it All." It's a good motto for a place where so much American history was born. Without Cincinnati in 1794, 1836 and 1862, there might be no United States as we know it.

This was the Promised Land—an emerald Eden of rich black soil, towering trees, abundant game, beautiful rivers and infinite possibilities for free people. It's a region blessed with an exciting, rich history. But much of that history has been lost under the silting sands of time. Too often it is presented as boring dates, numbers and names as dry as dead sticks—when it is more thrilling than fiction.

To quote Doddridge: "National history is all important to national patriotism, as it placed before us the best examples of our forefathers. ... Our youth ought first to be presented with the history of their own country and taught to believe it to be a greater importance to their future welfare than that of any other nation or country whatever."

A few notes on the book:

Promised Land is faithful to the people and their times and relies wherever possible on primary sources. There is no shortage of books that power-wash the Wolly Mammoth hide of history until it shrinks to fit modern fashions.

For example: It is popular to call Indians "indigenous peoples" or "Native Americans." But those "cramp words" are not how people spoke in the 1790s or the 1860s. For better or worse, they were "Indians" for 200 years, and that's how they are described here.

Sanitizing history disrespects the ferocity of the tribes and belittles the courage of the pioneers. Only one side in that war made a routine sport of torture. Doddridge, whose family experienced that horror, had this advice for anyone who accused the pioneers of barbarism: "Let him hear the shrieks of the victims of the Indian torture by fire and smell the surrounding air...." And if those victims were wife, brother, sister, mother or father, "After a short season of grief he would say, 'I will now think only of revenge.'"

Such vivid descriptions are disturbing. But unless we can imagine the barbaric "depredations" we can't understand the merciless response and the depth of hostility in those times. Pretending the Indians were peaceful, nature-loving innocents is a gross distortion and an insult to both sides.

To add realism to the history, I unearthed some "ramstuginous" (rowdy) words and phrases from the past.

And as in my previous books, I used a small cast of fictional characters to bring black-and-white history into living color, a technique common to historical novels. Duffy, Nehemiah, Amos, Klaus, Butcher and Emmaline are fictional. All the others are real.

Footnotes are used to cite sources, explain obscure customs and words, expand details, add depth to the story and map places where exciting events took place.

Readers who have already read *The Man Who Saved Cincinnati* will notice that this book is both a sequel and a prequel. It brings along some of the characters—Amos, Nehemiah, Lew Wallace—but also reaches back to the previous century to introduce the brave families who settled Kentucky, the Miami Valley and Ohio.

These stories set in the 1790s and the 1860s are connected by American history and the people whose amazing faith and courage created it. Both turn on the axle of a debate that began as soon as the United States won its independence: What is the ideal balance between government and liberty?

Tocqueville may have been wrong about secret societies, but he predicted the isolation of the individual, social materialism and the tyranny of the majority over thought—all very relevant today.

He also warned that governments absorb power as surely as sharks swim and bacteria multiply. Liberty must be vigilantly protected, he said, because "centralization will be the natural government."

President Washington expanded central control to create a standing army in 1792 that opened the Northwest Territory. Almost a hundred years later, the South rebelled against that growing central power over the states. President Lincoln answered by welding the Union together with the white-hot flame of war. That forged a federal government that now spends more than $6 trillion per year and has nearly three million employees—more than the entire population of Ohio in 1860.

Washington and Lincoln would shake their heads in dismay. The ramstuginous debate continues.

September 2024

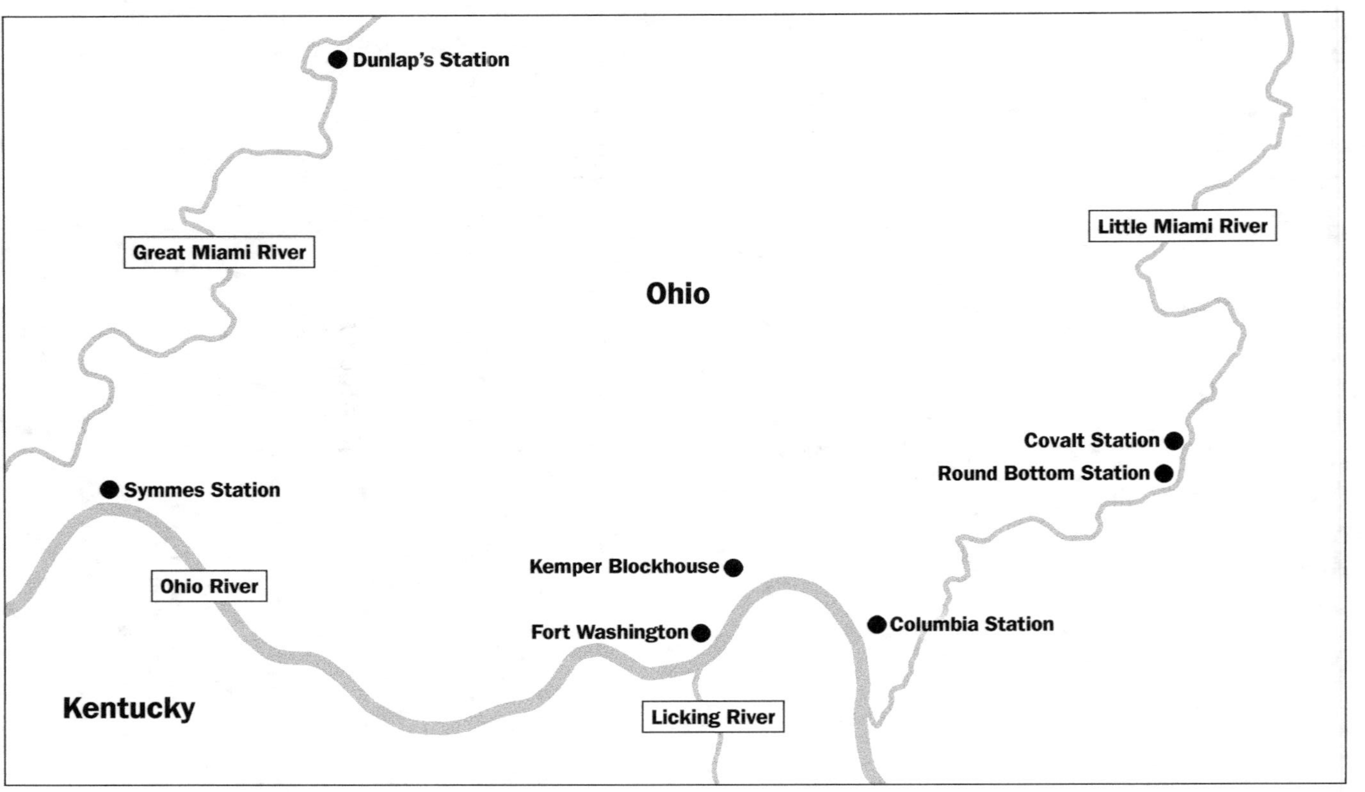

Map 1 - Ohio Stations

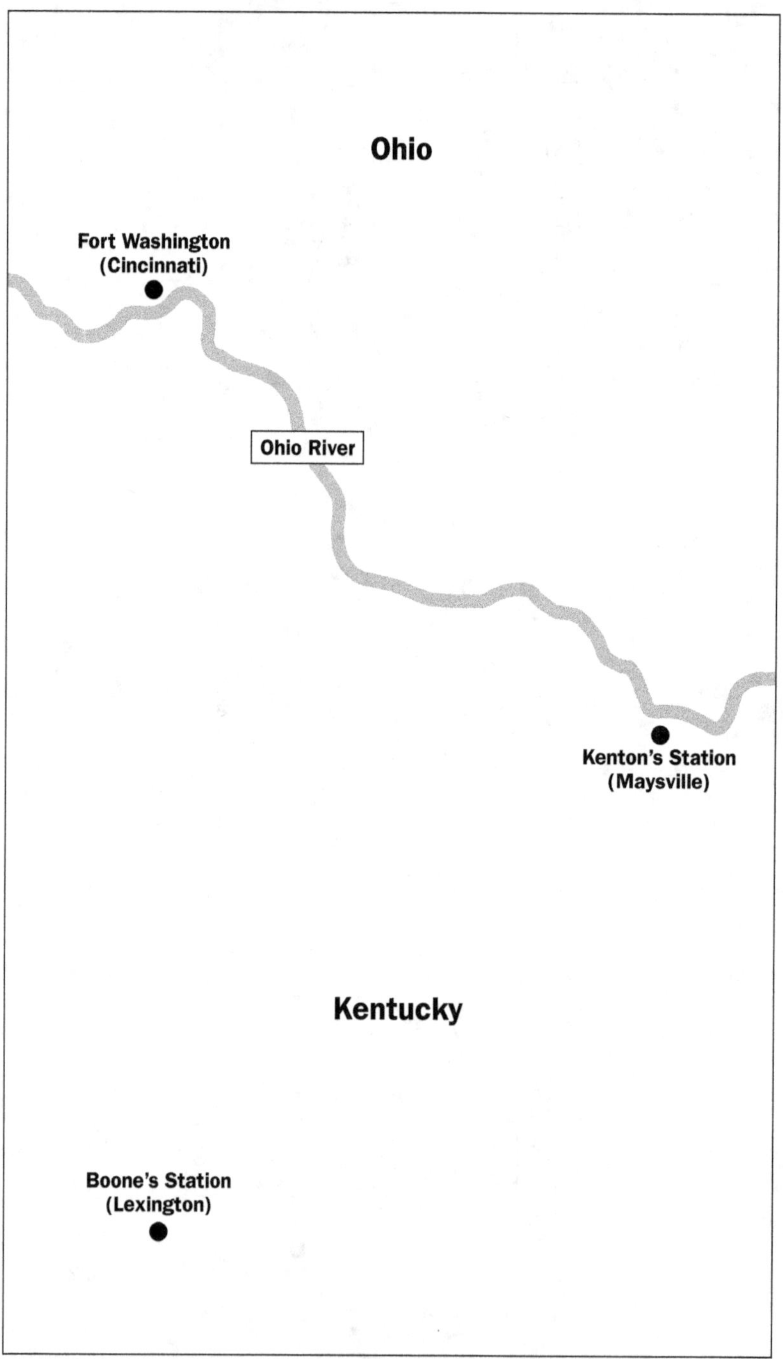

Map 2 - Kentucky Stations

Toledo
Maumee River
Camp Deposit
Fort Defiance
Fort Wayne
Auglaize River
Indiana
Ohio
Fort Recovery
Great Miami River
Fort Greenville
Mad River
Fort Jefferson
Fort St. Clair
Dayton
Little Miami River
Fort Hamilton
Fort Washington
Ohio River

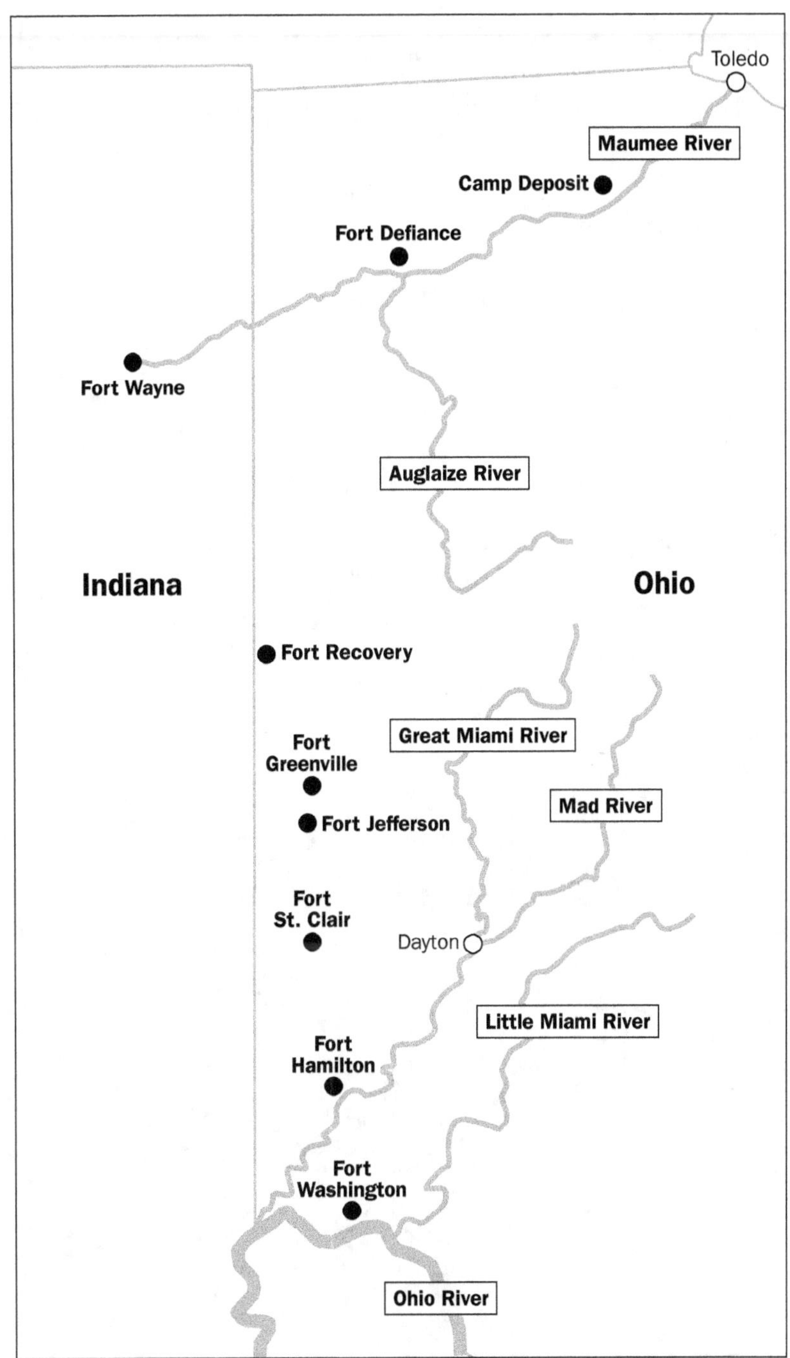

Map 3 - Forts

Map 4 - Battles

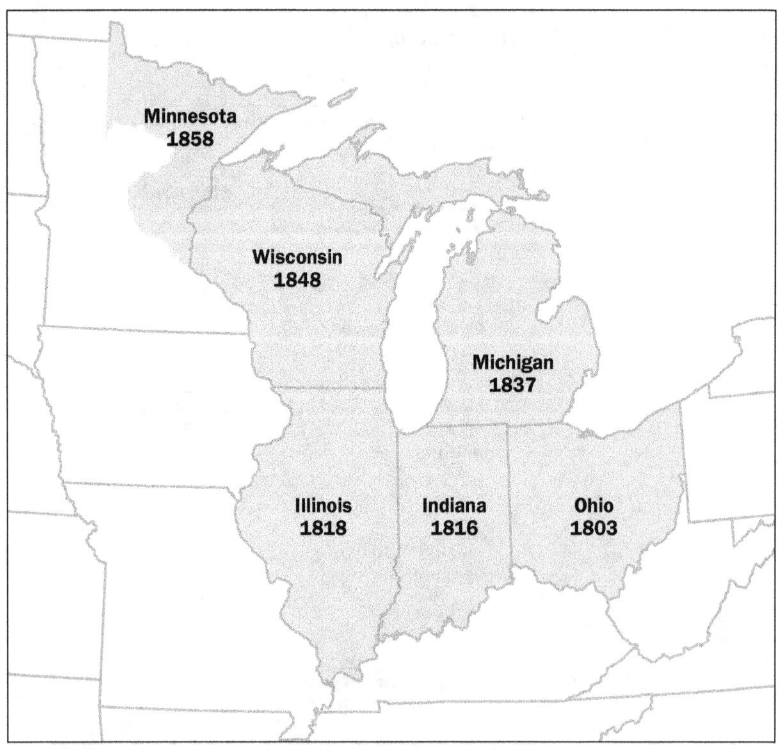

Map 5 - Northwest Territory

SEPTEMBER 11, 1862

The Siege of Cincinnati

They were stalking a whitetail buck in the shadowed, tangled woods about a half mile south of Battery Kearney—still within cannon range—when Nehemiah stopped suddenly as he ducked under a drooping hickory limb and touched his ear for silence. Amos saw the signal, and both froze to listen.

The seconds ticked by. Then faintly, something that sounded like a distant moan could be heard under the chirping cardinals and scolding jays in the trees above. A breeze from the northwest lifted the maple leaves to show their silver backsides and the sound became a little bit clearer.

Cheering.... Thousands of men throwing their hurrahs to the skies in a heavenly chorus of joy—rising and falling like surf on a far shore.

Nehemiah and Amos looked at each other with raised, shaggy eyebrows that were the same coal-and-ashes color of their long, graying beards. They waited. Listened again. And there it was, taking shape in a staggered rhythm.

Amos smiled. In an airy stage whisper that mimicked the voices that floated on the wind he said, "Huzzah! Huzzah! Huzzah!"

Nehemiah nodded once and looked as if he would almost smile. "I reckon our great adventure in the sacred hunting grounds of Old Kaintucky may have come to an end," he said softly.

Their small camp was nearby. They didn't have to walk far to hunt game in the rolling hills of Northern Kentucky. Deer, rabbits, raccoons and possums were as plentiful as fleas on a farmer's dog—though still a far cry from the days when this land south of the Ohio River was shared by the Shawnee, Cherokee, Pawnee, Wyandot, Iroquois and other tribes.

They had chosen a campsite about a mile in front of the defensive lines of cannon batteries and rifle pits that wrapped a prickly necklace along a seven-mile arc, just south of Covington and Newport. They were woodsmen from the still untamed wilderness of Ohio, uncomfortable with crowds, soldiers, morning bugle-calls and toy-soldier officers. They kept their distance.

Unlike the regular troops and local militia commanders who shied like startled birds when they heard gunshots, they were unworried about being caught sleeping by the invading Rebel horde. They had lived in the wild too long and fought Indians too many times to be taken by surprise by a clanking, creaking, shouting army of thousands, or even its stealthy cavalry scouts.

So while the Union soldiers prepared for an invasion, drilled with the local militias and accidentally shot at each other more often than they shot any Confederates, the two Squirrel Hunters, as they were called, did what they enjoyed most: they hunted, fished in the Licking River about a half-mile west, spun their yarns around the campfire and waited.

The huzzahs drew closer like a brushfire pushed along on the breeze, rolling east from Fort Mitchel, where the Rebel camp had been found deserted just that morning. Amos nodded, reached into a soft deerskin pouch on his belt, and withdrew a clear pint bottle that contained a liquid as colorless as water, uncorked it and offered it to the sky in a salute: "To the Union."

Nehemiah actually did smile behind his beard, took the bottle of 130-proof "fog-lifter" and nodded, "To Major General Lew Wallace and the fair Queen City that he has rescued. Confusion to the enemy."

Even as they spoke, nearly 10,000 Confederate soldiers who had threatened to burn, loot and lay siege to Cincinnati were marching back to Lexington with slumped shoulders and leaden boots—ordered to retreat by nervous Gen. Braxton Bragg, who had an uncanny talent for turning victory into defeat and turning his own soldiers into his worst enemies.

Bragg had sent orders the day before, calling off the Siege of Cincinnati and summoning Gen. Henry Heth to Lexington. Heth was ordered to join his immediate commander Gen. Kirby Smith. Both were summoned to reinforce Bragg's army in western Kentucky, where Bragg's troops were outnumbered two-to-one by Gen. Don Carlos Buell's Union troops. A battle was said to be looming like thunderheads over the horizon. And it was certain the lightning would strike Louisville, not Cincinnati.

But the nervous Confederate general would have been surprised to learn that Buell was even more antsy. Like so many generals on both sides during the war, Buell had more fear of defeat than appetite for victory. Even with his superior numbers, Buell refused to commit his troops for decisive victories and missed no opportunity to hesitate. The two generals hunkered down, uneasy as cats indoors on a rainy day.

Both still wore the mental scars and physical wounds of Shiloh, where they ordered thousands of young men to march into death like livestock herded into a slaughterhouse. That was only five months ago. They and their soldiers had been given no chance to recover from it, as they fought again at the Siege of Corinth, Mississippi, and other battles that history would call "minor" to everyone except the men who were wounded, maimed and killed.

If Bragg had only known that Buell would stay glued to Louisville, exaggerating the Confederates' strength the way the late afternoon sun stretches shadows of children into giants, he could have ordered Smith to reinforce Heth, as planned. Together, Heth's 10,000 men and Smith's reserves of almost 10,000 could have taken Cincinnati. That would have cleaved the Union in half like one of Abe Lincoln's split rails. The North would have been forced to negotiate or surrender, and the re-election of President Lincoln would have been doomed, finally giving the South what it wanted: to be left alone as a separate Confederate nation. The violent divorce would be final.

At minimum, the Confederates could have looted the city's stockpiles of uniforms, boots, weapons, wagons, mules, horses, cattle and gold, to give the Confederacy a desperately needed transfusion of supplies while bleeding the anemic morale of the North. And if hit by cannon fire, the riverfront tinderbox of boatyards, riverboats, warehouses and businesses would burn like a box of kitchen matches.

But that opportunity to take a Northern city was lost.

As it turned out, there was no battle of Louisville. Nothing would happen until October 8 in Perryville,[2] Kentucky, and then only by accident.

But on the morning of September 11, 1862, all that was still in the future. Newspapers and panicked citizens in the Queen City all agreed: The next big battle was certain to be in Cincinnati, and Union cavalry scouts in Covington were eager to resume the gunbattles and skirmishes of the day before.

As they rode south from Covington to spy on General Heth's Confederate camp in Forth Mitchell, a patrol of Union scouts was shocked to find it empty. Nothing was left but the litter of 10,000 soldiers: full latrines and empty campsites, smoking fires, chicken bones, broken equipment and scraps of paper skittering crablike in the morning breeze. A dust cloud rising just over the horizon down Lexington Pike, raised by thousands of Confederates marching south, told the rest of the story.

Two of the scouts split up to scour the area to the east and west, while a third rode after the retreating Rebels. The fourth reined his horse around hard, and spurred north in a whirlwind of dust, pounding hooves and divots of dry earth. Lathered and sweaty, he dismounted at a run in front of the headquarters of Maj. Gen. Lew Wallace, in an old brick winery in downtown Covington.

"Sir," he reported breathlessly, with a salute, "the Rebs are gone!"

The good news seemed to fly through the Union lines like lightning on horseback. A few isolated cheers outside the headquarters spread and swelled until the whole city was shouting as if to chase away its knee-knocking dread of the Confederate attack, purging weeks of fear, nerves and nightmares in convulsive "Huzzahs."

Wallace also heaved a heavy sigh of relief. He knew from sleepless

---

2   Perryville, on October 8, 1862, was the largest battle in Kentucky. 55,000 Union troops fought 16,000 Confederates. But the Union lost 4,241 killed, wounded and missing; Confederate casualties were 3,396. It was among the bloodiest battles of the war.

nights that his defenses were only a coat of thin whitewash: untested soldiers backed up by a paper army of store clerks, teachers, rivermen, Squirrel Hunters and farmers who were led by lawyers, merchants and politicians. None had seen bullets fly. None had "seen the elephant"[3] the way Wallace had seen its red-eyed rage in the storm of deafening chaos and killing at Shiloh.

Would they stand and fight when the first Southern cannons coughed death and thousands of rifles rained a hailstorm of lead? Or would they catch "vamoose fever" and run to clog the only bridge—a narrow, improvised span of coal barges across the Ohio River. He could imagine them milling in panicked herds, corralled against the riverbanks like sheep, helpless targets to be massacred as Cincinnati watched in horror from the north bank.

'Y'all shot first'

As Wallace mounted his spirited war horse, "Old John," to ride out and confirm the reports for himself, a couple of miles to the east Nehemiah Woods and Amos Breyer stood as still as tree stumps, their heads lifted to the distant sounds. Out of the corner of his eye, Nehemiah saw something move. The buck had been almost invisible when it stood still, perfectly matched to the forest background. But now it raised its head to listen to the strange sounds and became a vague leaf-brown ghost, stepping as soft as moth wings through the undergrowth.

He began to raise his Kentucky rifle to his shoulder slowly, so slowly it seemed as if it would never get there, his eyes never leaving the target. The deer stopped. Lifted its head again, sniffed the air. Nehemiah froze too. The buck looked his way. Snorted quietly. Twitched its ears and seemed to look right at him.

Then its head dropped again, and it took another step, nuzzling the ground for late-summer mushrooms and hickory nuts.

Nehemiah squeezed the trigger—the flint sparked with a sharp snap, followed by a boom that woke the whole forest from its quiet slumber.

---

3   Civil War soldiers who had been in a battle said they had "seen the elephant," comparing war to a traveling circus.

Birds beat the air, crows cried hoarse alarms and a heavy thud cracked branches and twigs as the buck collapsed and fell like a sack of corn.

Nehemiah peered through drifting gun smoke to confirm his shot and had just opened his mouth to tell Amos when a smaller "crack!" answered his rifle's deep voice and something whistled through the leaves just over his head before hitting a tree trunk with a solid whack like the sound of an axe.

"What the—" Amos cursed.

"Down!" Nehemiah growled.

The woods went silent. They waited, lying in the forest mulch, peering through the tangled leaves. Finally, Amos whispered, "You ever known the critters in these parts to shoot back?"

"Raccoons can be quite ramstuginous when chivvied into a corner, but I've never known any to carry pistols. I'm afeared someone on two legs did not get the news that the big battle has been called off."

"I hear y'all," a voice shouted. "Y'all shot first."

"Unless you are an eight-point named Buck, I did not shoot at you," Nehemiah shouted.

There was a long pause. Then, "I ain't no deer."

Nehemiah rolled onto his back and began reloading—powder horn, ball, then ramrod. Amos shouted, "No cause for shootin'. Can you hear that cheerin'? It's all done. The Rebs is gone."

"Not all of 'em is gone," the voice replied, defiant.

Nehemiah gave Amos a look, eyebrows raised. "So what's your play?" he called out. "Are you gonna shoot at us if we dress out that buck?"

"Are you soldiers?"

"Not if we can help it," Amos said.

"I didn't think so. From what I could see, more like a talking bear and—I cannot tell what. Maybe an Indian. Are y'all fixin' to shoot me? I can hear you reloading over there."

Nehemiah chuckled. "Just being prudent. I have learned that a loaded rifle can be serendipitous when lead is being throwed in my direction." He nodded to Amos, who nodded back and raised his own rifle. Nehemiah shouted again, "Listen here, Buck. I'm about to stand up. If you can see me, you will know my hands are empty. But Amos here, he is not at all emptyhanded. And if you shoot at me, it will not go well with you."

The reply sounded uncertain. "I told you I ain't no deer named Buck. But well... yeah... I reckon you can stand if you've a mind to."

Nehemiah slowly rose to his feet, all six foot three topped by a floppy brown hat that looked older than Noah's grandfather. He wore buckskin pants that were grayish black from years of grime, and a buckskin shirt with a faded blue bandanna around his neck. His chest was crossed with belts for his powder horn and gamebag. A few strings of buckskin fringe hung from his chest and arms where they had not been torn off to tie his bedroll together or make a snare for small game. He leaned his long Kentucky rifle against a tree and extended his huge arms out to the sides.

"Dang me," the voice in the woods said. "It *is* a bear. Or maybe one of them squirrel men I heard tell of. Now I see why General Heth skedaddled. You're a fright."

"Watch that mocking tongue, son," Amos said. "You don't want to make the squirrel man angry. I saw him thrash a big Irishman so bad the man gave up drink. He left that man catawamptiously chawed up."

The man with the pistol laughed. "Then I am right sorry," he said. "I would give up drinking too if I was thrashed by a squirrel man."

They heard the soft click of a hammer being eased down, then leaves rustled and a slim body took shape through the trees. "Corporal Caleb MacDuff, Thirty-Second Texas Cavalry," the young man said as he emerged through the trees.

Nehemiah's flinty eyes softened. The poor boy was emaciated, a butternut and gray scarecrow of torn, dirty rags that were once a uniform. His sword was the only thing that looked moderately clean. But through the dirt and his dark, sunken eyes of hunger, a once-dashing young man could be glimpsed. It was in his posture, his wild, shaggy blond hair and his twinkling eyes that showed intelligence and good humor.

His boots were dusty and rundown in a way that suggested the soles had been worn through from heel to huckleberry. The curved-up sides of his slouch hat said Texas, but the crossed swords in tarnished brass on the front said CSA. His jacket looked as frayed as a battle flag and his trousers were patched with crude, hand-stitched scraps of mismatched colors.

"You are quite a fright yourself," Nehemiah said. "I can see now why you were able to conceal yourself so well. You're as scarce as a whittled twig. There's not enough between your ribs to fill a can of snuff. Where's your horse, cavalryman?"

"We've been dismounted since Richmond. Which we won. Brazos— that's my horse—or was. My horse is pulling a wagon, I hope. More likely been et. I may not be much to look at, but what you see is all fight."

Nehemiah turned, "Amos, you got any of that rabbit jerky we made?"

"My thoughts zactly," Amos replied, offering a deerskin pouch to the Confederate, who mumbled grateful thanks as he stepped forward and scooped out a handful.

"It's true?" Amos asked. "You-uns all gone back south?"

"I guess it can't hurt none to acknowledge the corn now," the soldier said. "It's true. General Heth was fitten' to spit nails when he got the orders."

Nehemiah and Amos shared a look. *So that's how it was.*

"And you, Corporal MacDuff?" Nehemiah asked. "How'd you get left behind?"

"Duffy. Call me Duffy." He looked at his boots. Then he raised his chin, defiant. "I met a girl."

There it was again. Something that made Nehemiah like the young man. Something good. He looked nothing like Nehemiah's son, who was last heard from at Corinth, but Duffy somehow reminded him of the boy anyway.

"For everything, there is a season," Amos quoted from *Ecclesiastes*, surprising Nehemiah.

"A time to kill and a time to heal," Duffy replied.

"A time for war and a time for peace," Nehemiah finished. Then he smiled. "And a time to dress this fine buck and roast us some venison. We'd be honored if you would partake."

"You're not gonna turn me over?"

Nehemiah shook his head. Amos chuckled and said, "Turn you over for what? I reckon the other side looks worse than this one. Besides, squirrel men don't take prisoners. We only shoot what we eat and there's not enough meat on your bones to make stone soup."

They dressed the buck and headed back to their camp as the thready thump of drums and bleating trumpets joined the distant chorus of cheers. The victory parades had begun. Cincinnati was safe again.

As they made their way around fallen trees, Amos pointed with the barrel of his Hawken rifle to a spot about ten feet high on the side of a large oak, where there was a scar in the bark like an unhealed wound. "Another one up there," he said. They all stopped and laid down the deer haunches.

"Looks to me like a letter 'K,'" Duffy said. "Why would someone put their brand on a tree? Do y'all have tree rustlers in Kentucky? And what manner of Goliaths do you grow hereabouts to make a mark up so high?"

Nehemiah nodded to Amos, "Yep, another one. Simon was busy in these woods."

"No wonder these woods is haunted," Amos said.

Duffy looked from one to the other, puzzled.

"This here is the Miami Slaughterhouse," Nehemiah said, finally answering Duffy's frown. "Or used to be called such. Those marks were left there by a man named Simon Kenton. One of the greatest Indian fighters and scouts ever lived."

"How big was the man?" Duffy asked. "I couldn't reach that mark standing on my saddle."

Amos answered, "He was bigger than Mr. Woods here, they say. But those marks were made nearly a hundred years ago. They have grown up along with the oak tree."

"What y'all mean by haunted?"

Nehemiah shook his head. "Sad stories of the kind that would trouble your sleep. Many a man, woman and child were murdered, tortured and scalped here in these woods, along both sides of the Ohio River. The

Shawnee and Miami tribes, among many, claimed the north shore. It was promised to them in treaties. This side was their sacred hunting ground. When white settlers moved in, all hell broke loose."

"And all its devils," Amos added.

"Now that's something I can picture a mite," Duffy said. "Where I come from we've had mucho problemos with the Comanches since the war began. Looked to us like the government punished Texas by pulling soldiers out of Fort Parker, leaving our families on their own."

"We've seen things like that in Ohio," Nehemiah said. "Our own sons were taken off to war. And what Indians that are left have noticed too. Where we come from north of here," he tilted his head at Amos, "we keep the door barred and leave a dog out at night."

This time it was Amos who held up a hand in warning, then pointed to his ear. They listened. After a pause, he said softly, "Somebody out there. More than one."

Nehemiah and Duffy heard it too—twigs snapping, leaves rustling, as soft as grazing does. To a trained ear, it was the sound of men moving silently in the woods. Then came a soft curse, muttered and overlapped by a muffled laugh.

"Sounds like they's in our camp," Amos said.

Duffy's eyes widened as he looked at both men, asking a silent question.

"Here," Nehemiah said softly, "Put this on until we know who they are." He snatched the Confederate cavalry hat off Duffy's head and handed him his own floppy, stained hat, which slid down almost over his eyes. Nehemiah reached up into the lower limbs of a maple and hid the cavalry hat behind the leaves.

"Hand me that sword," Amos whispered. He laid Duffy's sword at the base of the maple and kicked leaves over it until it was covered. Then both men looked at Duffy, frowning.

"Ya reckon?" Amos asked quietly.

"Worth a try," Nehemiah said. He looked pointedly at Duffy's pistol.

"No sir," the corporal whispered, shaking his head.

Nehemiah thought about taking it, shook his head and said softly, "Then at least stuff that colt pistol into your pants under what's left of your shirt."

"Who goes there?" a voice bellowed. "Show yourself or we will shoot."

Amos and Nehemiah took a survey of Duffy, then Nehemiah said in a deep rumble that could cross the river through dense fog, "Mad River Volunteer Militia. Who goes there?"

There was a pause, then indistinct conversation. Finally, a voice said, "Burnet Rifles. I repeat, show yourself, sir!" This time it sounded like an older man.

Nehemiah got the flinty look in his eyes again and shouted, "That's the second time today someone has threatened to shoot me. Most don't live after the first mistake. So put your guns up. We won't shoot if you don't. But if you make a move...."

He left the rest to their imagination and stepped forward with his loaded rifle held angled upward, high enough to look peaceful, low enough to use in a hurry.

Amos waved Duffy ahead and moved to his left, using the footsteps of the other two to cover his own. As they stepped into the clearing, three men were waiting. The man clearly in command was in his mid-50s, with groomed, graying hair and a fine Union uniform over polished black boots. He was slim and stood straight, with one hand on his sword hilt and a pistol in the other hand, pointed at the ground. The other two wore uniforms Nehemiah and Amos had seen on the Cincinnati Police, who had been drafted into the defense works on the orders of General Wallace.

One was hardly more than a teen, pock faced, with bad teeth and darting eyes. He looked scared. The older one was stocky and was spoiling for a fight, as if he was itching to make up what the other one lacked. Both carried Army-issue Springfield rifled muskets with bayonets attached. Duffy thought that was odd. Genuine soldiers wouldn't attach bayonets in the woods where they were just one more thing to get tangled or cause a careless stab wound.

The clearing was silent as the men sized each other up. The stocky policeman paid special attention to Nehemiah. Finally, the old man spoke.

"I'm Lieutenant Robert Wallace Burnet of the Burnet Rifles," he said. "We're here to inform you the Confederates have retreated. I take it you are among the volunteers who came to the aid of our city? Forgive me, but I have not heard of the Mad River Volunteer Militia. To whom do I have the pleasure of speaking?"

Duffy started to speak but Nehemiah cut him off. "Nehemiah Woods, sir. This is my son Caleb. We heard the huzzahs and reckoned it was good news."

"Mebbe we oughta haul 'em in," the stocky one said. "Something about that big one... I think I know him from—"

"No, Sgt. Butcher, stand down. That would be a fine way to show our gratitude for these men's efforts to defend our city." He turned back to Nehemiah and bowed his head a dip. "Apologies for the sergeant, he has been disappointed that he was unable to singlehandedly whip the Confederate Army."

"How do we know they ain't Rebs?" the sergeant spoke up again.

Lieutenant Burnet smiled. "Are you Rebs, gentlemen?"

Nehemiah gave a rumbling low chuckle that stopped abruptly as he turned a cold eye on the sergeant. "Where I come from, them's fightin' words. If you put down that hog-sticker I will lay down this rifle and show you what kind of hell and brimstone men on the Mad River are made of."

The sergeant began to lift his rifle but was stopped by the distinct sound of a hammer being pulled back. "Best not do that," came the flat voice of Amos from somewhere nearby in the woods.

"None of this is necessary," Lieutenant Burnet said, stepping between Sgt. Butcher and Nehemiah. "I am addressing *you*, sergeant," he barked in a parade-ground order. "I ordered you to stand down. If you disobey again, I will arrange your court-martial and flogging. Am I clear?"

The sergeant turned as red as an October maple and looked as if his face would burst, but finally muttered, "Yes sir."

"I am curious," Nehemiah turned to Burnet, "am I to understand that the Burnet House Hotel has its own militia?"

"Not quite," the commander smiled. "My father, Judge Jacob Burnet, owns the hotel. I am a banker. West Point class of 1829, graduated with Robert E. Lee. I organized, armed and trained the Burnet Rifles by recruiting members of the Cincinnati Literary Club."

Duffy made a soft noise through his nose. Nehemiah heard it and shot him a look. "As I heard tell, the Cincinnati Literary Club has produced some fine generals for the Union cause," he said.

"You have heard true. I have the honor to be president of the club."

"Well, sounds like all of us can pack up and head for home," Nehemiah said loudly toward the woods. "It has been an honor, sir," he said, crossing to shake the hand of Lieutenant Burnet.

"My honor, sir," the commander said. He cocked an eyebrow and tilted his head slightly. "Mad River Militia?"

"Battle of Fallen Timbers, 1794. My father wore this very hat"—he reached for his head then caught himself—"that my son now wears."

"And the tomahawk?" Burnet asked.

"Yes sir, that too," Nehemiah said. He reached for his belt, lifted the weapon and handed it to Burnet, who examined it closely.

As Burnet handed it back, he said, "Thank you. I have held history in my hands. Ohio owes an incalculable debt to your father and the men who fought there."

The sergeant interrupted, "I know now... it has come to me. This is the Squirrel Hunter who busted up Captain Riley over near Battery Hatch!"

"Is that correct?" Burnet asked Nehemiah.

"If you mean a drunk Irishman who had abused one of my friends in the Black Brigade, I believe so," Nehemiah said. "It was my pleasure."

"Then my compliments, Mr. Woods. Captain Riley is a bushel of trouble. You will be glad to hear his broken arms are on the mend." The last was with a hint of a smile. "My apologies for the manners of Sergeant Butcher. He is dyspeptic from missing the whiskey and revelry across the river."

"My own manners fall short of perfection," Nehemiah said, "but I will be glad to give him some lessons the next time we meet."

Sgt. Butcher stared daggers and his bandy legs twitched, but he said nothing. Lieutenant Burnet smiled.

He turned and addressed the other two: "We're done here. They are informed, perhaps better than some of us. And Mr. Woods," he said, turning, "I sincerely hope your son also recovers. I haven't seen a man so skeletal since Florida. We lost many a man to dysentery in the Seminole Campaign. I hear castor oil and turpentine can have salubrious effect."

"Thank you, sir," Duffy said with a Texas drawl that sounded just enough Kentucky. "I was lately at the Siege of Corinth."

Nehemiah had to stop himself from staring at Duffy in surprise. Burnet shook his head sorrowfully. "God bless you, son. By all accounts I have read it was grievously tragic." He touched his hat brim and turned, "Sgt. Butcher, Private Wheeds, let's move out. We have miles to cover before we can join the parade across the pontoon bridge."

● ● ● ●

Later, as they sat by the campfire and dined on fresh venison that Amos had skinned, spitted and roasted, Nehemiah carved off another slice with his big skinning knife and warned, "Texas, you had best slow down or you will be returning that deer to the forest, much the worse for wear."

"Boy eats like his stomach thinks his throat was cut," Amos said. "Tell us how you come to be here. Something about a girl?"

The young man dragged a dirty gray sleeve across his mouth and nodded. "I was attached to Morgan's Raiders on the first tour of Kentucky last July. I had scouting experience in Texas so they ordered me to volunteer."

"We heard aplenty about that," Amos said. "Folks was panic-struck as far north as Dayton. But we heard that raid never got closer'n thirty miles south of here."

"You heard true. But I was sent downrange to scout the defenses of Cincinnati," Duffy explained. "I have family on my mother's side in Covington and east of Cincinnati in Goshen."

He told them how he passed himself as a cousin from Lexington in a pair of borrowed trousers and met a girl named Sarah Mason at a barn dance in Goshen. Nehemiah saw how the young man's eyes glowed when he said her name, and remembered courting his own late wife, long ago.

"So, it's Goshen you're bound for?" he asked.

Duffy nodded. "I have got to a place where I cannot abide more killin' and blood," he said. He paused.

The fire crackled. The birds sang their evening songs. Amos and Nehemiah were silent, both thinking of their own sons gone off to war.

"Sarah...." Duffy paused again. "A man has got to know there is something beautiful and kind left in this world, something...."

After a long silence, Amos said, "Nehemiah, tell him about them hoop snakes."

Nehemiah's eyes twinkled and a smile moved his thick curtain beard. Duffy looked up, curious and puzzled. "*What* snakes?"

And the yarns began. Hoop snakes that bite their own tails and roll down a hill fast as a scared rabbit. Snakes with poison stingers in their tails that can kill a largish bear. Then Amos told of horned snakes that could launch through the air like a muleskinner's whip.

Duffy chuckled and answered with Texas tales of winged rattlesnakes that would fall out of the trees on a man. Hairy spiders as big as a frying pan. Scorpions that crawled into your boots and paralyzed a man's leg with one sting.

That led to stories about a deeper, colder fear they shared, far more deadly than snakes and spiders: Indians.

Duffy soon learned that the cruelty of the Apaches and Comanches had been matched long ago in Ohio and Kentucky by the Shawnee and Miami tribes, whose decades of brutality still could make a man shiver on a hot day in July. The Confederation of Tribes was finally defeated at the Battle of Fallen Timbers, and they were forced to move west to Oklahoma and Texas. But the terror still haunted the woods, as real as the worn trails they left behind.

Duffy had seen his share of cruelty on both sides of the Indian wars in the West. "The Apaches are bad. Very cruel. But even the Apaches would cross a waterless desert to avoid the Comanches," he said.

Nehemiah and Amos had grown up steeped in the frontier legends told by their fathers and grandfathers, who had carved out their homesteads under constant threat of seeing their families scalped, raped, murdered, raided, tortured or sold as slaves to the British in Detroit.

"We were not the first to bring slavery to this land," Nehemiah said.

"Well I know it," Duffy replied. "The Comanches and Utes are the biggest slavers in the West. They started selling Apaches to the Spanish more than a hundred years ago."[4]

"I have little book-learnin'," Amos said, "But even a fellow like me knows a man was meant to be free. Chaining a man like a dog is evil."

Nehemiah nodded. "Some men choose freely to wear the collar and leash, sleep in the barn and be fed regular. I'd druther be the coyote and run free like Boone and Kenton. What would you say, Reb?"

"I would say," Duffy replied, "that I would like to learn a mite more about this giant named Kenton."

---

4 Hämäläinen, Pekka. *The Comanche Empire*. Yale University Press, 2008.

August 1792

Ambush

Simon Kenton was hot, angry and frustrated. He pulled his tomahawk from his belt and chopped his trademark "K" into the trunk of a healthy young oak tree. But as he marked another section of the land he loved—claiming land for himself, his family and for others who would follow him into the wilderness—he wondered who would ultimately own it.

Already, his "tomahawk improvements" marking thousands of acres south of the Ohio River were being dragged into court and contested by anthills of lawyers from Philadelphia, Connecticut, Pittsburgh, New York and wherever decaying heaps of compost spawned them.

The man who was feared and respected by the fiercest Shawnee and Miami warriors, the man who had bested Blue Jacket, the man who had saved countless lives of white settlers and taken countless lives of Indian raiders, feared nothing in the wild frontier. But lawyers made his palms sweat and itch for his tomahawk.

I'd almost run the Shawnee gauntlet again in Chillicothe to spare being caught in their briars of breakteeth words and no-see-um print, he thought.

He paused, tomahawk in midair. Something had alerted his senses—a sound, a scent, maybe just a feeling or instinct that he had almost missed while lost in thought about the dozens of court cases that wrapped around his ankles like creeper vines.

Something...

There it was. The tiniest rustle of a dry leaf. The forest was suddenly silent. The birds had stopped singing. The hair on the back of his neck stood up. He was being watched. He could feel it like he could feel sun on his neck.

He very slowly shifted his rifle from his left hand to his right, resisting the urge to turn his head and search the forest. He casually slipped the tomahawk back in his belt. And then, at the same instant he heard the soft twang of a bowstring being released, he bolted and ran as fast as his long legs could churn. The solid thwack of an arrow hitting that same oak where he had been standing confirmed it. Ambush.

At six foot five, Simon could run like a startled deer, leaping fallen logs, vaulting low bushes, sure-footed and fast. But was he running into or away from the ambush? How many? Would he have to break through? He lifted the tomahawk again into his left hand just in time to see a young Shawnee step from behind a tree in his path, not more than five yards away. Both were surprised. Only one was fast enough to live. Simon was on the warrior before he could react, and hardly broke stride as he slashed him across the throat with his tomahawk—killing quietly and saving the load in his rifle.

The body thumped to the ground, already far behind him, and gurgled, but did not cry out, giving Simon precious time. If they were on foot, he liked his odds. If the raiding party was mounted on stolen horses, he might be in trouble.

He ran down the side of a steep ravine and followed the bottom as it wound along an indifferent creek that could not make up its mind to pond or flow downhill. By the grace of God, he sailed over fallen limbs and jagged rocks without breaking a leg, twisting an ankle or cutting a foot. It was all or nothing. To be captured would be slow death. He used the stream in places to hide his path, climbed a steep ravine and emerged on more level ground. His moccasins churned the loose earth, but he had no time now to cover all of his tracks.

Once on level ground, Simon settled into an easy lope he could maintain all day, eating up long yards with each stride through the woods and out into an open meadow of tall waving grass. He didn't have to look back to know he was alone. He sensed it, just as he sensed the ambush. And he had learned to trust that sense above all others. He resumed his comfortable rhythm of running, and soon was hidden by the rolling hills.

Back in the clearing where his "K" stood white against the dark gray bark of the oak tree, the leader of the raiding party, Red Snake, stared at the strange English letter and shook his head. "Butlah," he said, his face going dark and worried. As he tried to yank out his arrow, the shaft broke, leaving the stone arrowhead embedded.

Fifty yards away in the woods, one of the raiders made a high trilling call. Red Snake ran to the sound and found the victim of Kenton's escape, his neck and bare chest painted with blood, eyes gone glassy and already glazed hard with death. Another young warrior, Licking Dog, who had found the body, stood nearby, his chest heaving with rage.

There would be no chase. "Butlah," the name given to Kenton by the Shawnees, had already proven too many times that he was magically blessed by the wrathful great spirit Moneto. He could not be killed. Moneto would surely punish anyone who tried. And he was more than a match for a party of seven—now six—raiders.

Red Snake fingered the scalps on his belt: a farmer, his woman and two children. One of the smallest was golden haired—a special prize. They had a string of five stolen horses and seven more scalps, including two on the belt of Butlah's victim, Crow Eye. Red Snake would have to carry his sister's son home for burial. He had died with honor, falling in battle against the enemy most feared by all the Indian nations in the Miami Valley.

The raiders had looted food, grain, powder, shot and a few rifles from the farms they attacked. In their code of honor, such violence was not only justified but celebrated. Their laws only applied to other Shawnee. Any cruelty or crime against the white people was a badge of glory in the tribe.

Red Snake told his men to tie Crow Eye to one of the stolen horses. It was time to return north across the Ohio River before Butlah came back with a raiding party of his own.

But first they went east to avoid the new stockade of the "Shemanese" ("long knives") at Fort Washington.[5] There were many tempting settle-

---

5   Between Third and Fourth Streets and Ludlow and Broadway in downtown Cincinnati. A marker on the side of the Western & Southern parking garage shows where the fort's ammunition

ments around Covalt Station,[6] a dozen miles east of Fort Washington. A few more scalps or prisoners would be worthy of a great victory dance when they returned to their village. Licking Dog had taken enough scalps from women and children to choose a new name more worthy of his courage in battle.

Two miles south, Simon Kenton stopped to listen and watch, his sharp blue eyes scanning the horizon for landmarks, his ears taking in every bird call, breeze and broken twig. He smelled the wild, musty scent of buffalo nearby. But he heard no pursuit from the Shawnee warriors.

Kenton was an unlikely savior for the settlements in Kentucky and Ohio. But he was a legend almost approaching mythology on both sides of the river, among Indians and whites alike.

Around their campfires, the Shawnee, Miami, Delaware, Ottawa and other tribes told stories of their encounters with Butlah. They remembered the time he was captured and forced to run the gauntlet three times, beaten, stoned and whipped almost to death, as everyone in the tribe turned out—young and old, men, women and children—to swing war clubs and fat sticks and hurl rocks at him as he stumbled and staggered between two long lines of Shawnees.

And all that was after he had been stripped naked, staked to the ground and beaten for hours with clubs until there was not room to lay a tomahawk on his body without touching an ugly purple-yellow bruise.

They had strapped him to a wild, bucking colt with his hands tied, and chased it into a dense growth of wild roses, where his body was ripped and torn until the colt finally came out, heaving with exhaustion. And there the prisoner remained for all the long miles back to their village.

On his final, third run through the gauntlet he had been knocked unconscious by a big rock hurled into his head. He collapsed and was beaten and stoned as he lay senseless. Finally, he was dragged into a lodge, where a young woman nursed him back to his feet. The mercy

---

magazine was found during construction in 1952.

6   At the east end of Terrace Park off Wooster Pike, on the property of St. Thomas Episcopal Church on Miami Avenue.

was cruel. He was revived so he could be forced to do it all again before he would finally be burned at the stake. But he had shown great courage, so if he was lucky, they would burn him alive quickly, without days of torture first.

The warriors told of how he had escaped as soon as he was able and almost eluded them all until he ran into the path of Blue Jacket on horseback, who had felled him with a war club that sank a knuckle deep divot into Butlah's skull. And still the amazing white man survived. When he finally recovered, a council was held and it was decided that he would be granted a reprieve for his courage. He would be adopted into the tribe.

For months, the captive they called Butlah seemed happy. Who would not be, given the honor to be part of the Shawnee family? But then he escaped again—running more than 150 miles back to Kentucky, where he became the most fearsome and relentless enemy of the Indian tribes that shared the Miami Valley. Now his name was spoken with fear and awe, used by mothers to frighten bad children, mentioned by warriors as a curse. The Shawnee saw symbols and meaning in all of the natural world they lived in—a clouded moon was an omen, a flock of geese on the wing could signal storms—and Butlah had become a word that described the relentless, invincible Shemanese, who kept coming no matter how many were killed, tortured, scalped and sold.

Among the settlers who lived in constant terror of the Shawnee raiders, Simon Kenton was a different symbol of hope and protection. Only a few knew how he had fled Pennsylvania as a fugitive and murderer, only to find out that the man he believed he had beaten to death over a woman was still alive back in his hometown.

As a fugitive from the law, Kenton had adopted the name of a man who was kind to him: Butler ("Butlah"). When he finally discovered that he was not wanted for murder, he took back his family name and made amends with the man he almost killed: a gift of land in the new frontier and a home in the settlements where Simon Kenton was an avenging angel of protection and justice.

Nobody in the new Indian Territory compared to him except his close friend Daniel Boone—whose life Kenton had saved from Indians. But now the same settlers protected and encouraged by Kenton were pouring into the paradise he had discovered, changing everything with towns, mayors, laws, lawyers and soldiers.

Even Boone was heading west, fed up with the encroachment of claim quibbling predatory lawyers who were robbing the men who settled the land by litigating overlapping "shingle claims."[7]

Together, Boone and Kenton had marked thousands of acres and established the boundaries of civilization in the new lands along the Ohio River. Thousands of new settlers owed their lives to those men and a few others. Thousands more never made it past the marauding Indians, who intercepted their flat boats in war canoes up to 30 or 40 feet long.

Kenton had no time for thoughts about lawyers now, though. He came to a clearing and paused to scan the surrounding woods and horizon. He knew the wilderness on both sides of the river the way other men knew every inch of their dim, cramped cabins.

He angled northeast toward Maysville, one of the largest settlements in the new state of Kentucky. He loped along at a steady pace, eating up miles, bounding over tangled treefall and vines that could break the legs of a deer. It did not take him long to discover that the raiding Shawnees had been there already. A small cabin in a clearing surrounded by tree stumps and a struggling garden gave him a bad feeling even before he crept close enough to see the door hanging loose on its leather hinges.

A little body was in the yard, sprawled in the unnatural position of someone who had fallen from a great height. But as he drew closer, he could see—it was not a fall that killed the little girl. Numerous tomahawk wounds left gaping rips in her blue gingham dress; she was lying in a pool of drying blood and a cloud of fat, buzzing blue-bottle flies. As he expected, the top of her head looked as if it had been shaved

---

7   Entries of these certificates were made in a way so loose that different men frequently claimed ownership of the same lands, with one title often overlapping upon another, and almost all the titles conferred in this way became known as "the lapping, or shingle titles." Boone, Daniel, and Francis Lister Hawkes. *Daniel Boone's Own Story & The Adventures of Daniel Boone*. Courier Corporation, 2012.

bloody—her scalp of fine long blond hair had been cut and ripped away, now hanging on some warrior's belt.

He found more bodies inside. It appeared the father had been shot and then clubbed to death as he came out of the cabin. A boy of about 9 or 10 had been tortured and scalped while he was still alive, judging by the bloody mess his kicking feet had made. The mother had been grotesquely mutilated, probably after prolonged rape and torture. All were scalped.

Kenton had seen it all so many times. He could easily imagine the scene: a sudden ambush; the father rushing for his gun; shots cracking from the woods; then the family helpless, at the mercy of the Shawnees.

He pieced together the path the Indians had taken back to the river where they almost killed him and nodded to himself. They would probably go east to cross the Ohio upriver rather than anywhere near Fort Washington or the village of Losantiville, now named Cincinnati. If his luck was good, he could round up men and catch the raiders as they returned north to Chillicothe.

SEPTEMBER 12, 1862

The cavalry arrives

"I Believe I heard an owl laughing at me last night," Duffy said, "unless it was one of those spirits in this haunted forest."

Amos took a sip of campfire coffee and squinted at the young man. "I heared some strange noises too, but they was coming from your bedroll. I imagine it was all that venison you ate?"

Duffy shook his head and studied the grounds in his cup. "I was a mite hungry, but it appears my innards were caught by surprise at such abundance."

"And you ought not to lark about this land and the spirits that watch over it," Amos said. "This here's bloody ground, once known as the Miami Slaughterhouse. I can surmise from what you told of last night you've seen a lot in Texas. But many is the poor souls who died hereabouts. And they did not go peaceful in their sleep. More like their worst nightmares."

Nehemiah said, "Some legends go back to the Shawnee, Miami and other tribes. They believe this land is troubled by bad spirits from ancient tribes that were here long before the white man and even the Indians came. I never put much stock in it until about a dozen years ago. I was helping a friend dig a foundation for his cabin on high ground across the river. We didn't get far down when we ran into bones. Lots of bones. It looked like the whole hill was a burial mound."

"For who?" Duffy asked.

"Can't say," Nehemiah said. "But they was big people, judging by the bones,[8] and some were too small to be anything but children. The

---

8   In 1927, an excavation of the Spearhead Mound by Willis Walker, W.H. Haber and B. Jewett

legends say they were sacrificed to some ancient dark gods. Buried alive."

"That part I understand," Duffy said. "The Apaches do that. Bury a man up to his neck, cut off his eyelids and let the ants and Coyotes go to work on him. I've seen the results of that."

"Is it true they skin prisoners alive?" Amos asked.

"Yep," Duffy nodded. "Not common, but not uncommon enough. The Comanches did that to a man who killed one of their women for sport. And they made the rest of the wagon train watch. It took several hours."

He seemed uncomfortable with the memories. As if to shake it off, he stood and walked over to the marked oak tree. Studying it, he asked, "What's that next to the 'K,' he made? Looks like something sticking out of the bark."

Nehemiah got to his feet, stretched his long arms and joined Duffy under the tree. He eyed the spot for a minute, then reached in a pouch on his belt and pulled forth a collapsible spyglass. He stretched it out, put it to his eye and grunted. "Hard to focus at this distance."

"Hard for you to focus at any distance," Amos laughed.

Nehemiah gave him a sharp look, stepped back five paces and tried again. "Huh," he said. "If I had to guess, I'd say it looks like a stone arrowhead. I reckon the Shawnee were not rolling out the welcome mat for Mr. Kenton."

Duffy asked to take a look, so Nehemiah handed him the glass. "Your young eyes are probably sharper than mine. Or so I have been told." He looked again at Amos. "Here, have a go."

Duffy looked, nodded and said, "From what I can see, you're right. Looks like many I've seen coming in my direction on raids in Texas. Stone-like, chipped and flaked to a razor edge. Buried about halfway in. Maybe the stump of a broken shaft still sticking out."

Amos dumped his coffee out and said, "Like I was sayin', this land has stories to tell, and most would give you sleepless nights. Nehemiah's

---

Jr. found bones in bark graves. They reported finding the bones of a "giant." The mound was destroyed in 1940. Murphy, James M., "Hamilton County's Spearhead Mound," Ohio State University Libraries.

daddy was captured by the Shawnee when he was just a pup, ain't that right, Nehemiah?"

"Then how's it he survived to grow up and have a son?" Duffy asked, turning to Nehemiah with raised eyebrows.

"Long story," the woodsman replied. "Ya see, he was taken from his family's cabin near Covalt Station by an Indian named Red Snake."

Amos stood suddenly and pointed to his ear. "Someone comin'," he whispered. They stood silent and listened.

Duffy nodded. He heard it too. "Quite a few and all around us," he said quietly. "I guess I didn't fool 'em none with these Dixie trousers," he added, pointing to his torn, patched and stained pants, still light blue in places. A gold stripe down the sides could be seen by sharp eyes.

"You men put down your rifles," a voice shouted from the woods. "We have a half-dozen guns on you."

Nehemiah looked at Amos, who nodded agreement. "Is that Captain Burnet?" he shouted back.

"That ain't none of your nevahmind," a second voice rasped from the woods.

"Sergeant Butcher," Amos said to Nehemiah and Duffy.

The first voice barked an angry command, "Stand down, Sergeant!" Then turned their way. "It's lieutenant. I haven't been a captain since the Seminole Wars. But thank you for the promotion, sir."

He stepped out of the woods. "I have orders to take you to headquarters. It seems Sergeant Butcher was unsatisfied with our last conversation and contacted Mayor Hatch."

"I ain't about to surrender to that Copperhead," Nehemiah said, gripping the tomahawk on his belt. Sgt. Butcher stepped into the clearing and aimed his rifle at Nehemiah.

"You won't have to," Lt. Burnet said. "I have arranged to introduce you to Major General Wallace. When I explained the situation and your, ahem, history with the police, he superseded the mayor's authority and ordered me to bring the three of you in for an interview. It is three, right?" he asked, looking pointedly at Amos.

Amos made no reply, so Lt. Burnet turned to Butcher and said, "Hand me your rifle, Sergeant."

"That big man's as deadly as a short-fused cannon," Butcher protested.

"*Sir*," the lieutenant said, holding out his gloved left hand as his right rested on the hilt of his sword.

"Deadly as a short-fused cannon, *sir*," Butcher corrected.

"That was not an invitation, it was an order. Hand me your rifle."

With a scowl like a July thunderstorm, Butcher slowly lowered the rifle and presented it to Burnet, who coolly removed the cap primer, lowered the hammer and handed it to one of the soldiers who had emerged from the woods to get a look at the Squirrel Hunters.

"The sergeant is not to possess a firearm until I say otherwise," he ordered. "Now, gentlemen," he addressed Nehemiah, "if you will gather your belongings and follow me."

• • • • •

"So, I finally make the acquaintance of the Thane of Fife," Maj. Gen. Lew Wallace said, standing behind his paper-cluttered desk to reach out a rough hand with ink-stained fingers.

To the astonishment of Nehemiah and Amos, Wallace ignored them and shook hands with Duffy, who replied, "Sergeant Gillespie sends his regards. Oh yes, the password: 'Double, double, toil and trouble.'"

"Fire burn and cauldron bubble," General Wallace replied, chuckling.

"Ah, sir," Duffy said, "allow me to introduce my companions, Mr. Nehemiah Woods and Mr. Amos Breyer."

"Step forward and let me shake your hands," Wallace said, "Thank you both for keeping this man safe. He is important to me, and even more important to our cause."

Wallace looked crisp in his clean blue uniform trimmed in gold braid, but his face was narrow and worn from the weight of command, giving him the appearance of a bird of prey. Nehemiah took off his misshapen hat, scratched his tangled gray hair and said, "If you will excuse me, sir, we're at a disadvantage. You evidently know who we are, and we certainly know who you are, General, but now we don't know

27

who in tarnation this young man is or what language you are speaking. It sounds like the palaver in books by Shakespeare."

"Aha, you are familiar?" Wallace smiled, delighted.

"I have little to keep me company through the winters," Nehemiah replied, "but my Bible and my late wife's worn volume of his tragedies."

"Then you may recognize Macbeth?"

"I may recognize Macbeth, but I no longer recognize MacDuff," the big man in buckskins replied, pointing a large finger at Duffy.

Wallace raised his eyebrows over piercing blue eyes and looked at Duffy, who guessed the question and answered, "Yes, sir, I trust these men. I would trust them with my life. Already have, in fact, and they did not fail."

"Then have a seat, gentlemen, while we conduct a briefing. Many of your questions will soon become clear. Even to you, Mr. Breyer," he chuckled, addressing Amos, who looked flummoxed, his brows pinched together in puzzlement like the top of a closed purse.

"You see," Wallace continued, "Mr. MacDuff, as you know him, is one of ours. You may have run across his name in your winter reading, Mr. Woods."

Nehemiah ran a big hand through his beard, thought for a moment and then looked up, his eyes showing sudden understanding. "Macbeth killed King Duncan of Scotland. Then it was MacDuff that separated Macbeth from his head, if I have the right story. Which I thought peculiar. It is usually kings what do most of the head separations."

"Exactly," Wallace said.

"Well… not exactly," Nehemiah replied. "I am still bewildered."

"Do you recall how Macbeth became King of Scotland?"

"His wife, Lady Macbeth, shamed him into murdering the king and taking his crown?"

"Mack-what?" Amos asked. "I'm more tangled up than a bucket of nightcrawlers."

Wallace said, "You have a remarkable aptitude for literature, Mr. Woods. Remind me to share my own work with you sometime. But for now, we need to conduct some business. As you listen, things should become plain."

Duffy turned to Amos and Nehemiah and said, "My heartfelt apologies for deceiving you men, but I had little choice. A lot is at stake, no less than the future of the Union, as you will discover. And allow me to properly introduce myself: Ezekiel Smith."

"Are you really from Texas?" Amos asked. "And what about them horned snakes you told of?"

"My grandfather was at the Alamo. I admit to embellishing the horned snakes, although the diamondback has horns of a sort and is more than enough real." He pulled up a sleeve to show two red puncture scars on his forearm, more than an inch apart.

Amos whistled.

"You go by Zeke, then?" Nehemiah asked.

"At home, yes, but I have come to like Duffy for the present."

General Wallace cleared his throat. "Let's get to the matter at hand, Lieutenant Smith."

As they listened, the woodsmen learned that Duffy was a Jessie Scout, part of the Union Army's branch of special agents—spies, scouts and rangers. He was among the minority in Texas who sided with the Union against the Confederacy. Before the war, he had joined the Rangers after his own father died and his mother and sisters were massacred by raiding Comanches.

He believed it was lunacy to leave other families at the mercy of Comanche and Apache war parties, unprotected by federal troops or local men after Texas called them all to join the Confederate Army.

"Lieutenant Smith is uniquely fitted to this task I have in mind. He has a connection to Cincinnati that he can explain to you men when you have more time," General Wallace said. "It is quite a story. I think you will enjoy it. Something involving a pair of twin sisters."

Nehemiah and Amos raised their eyebrows and took a fresh look at their new "Confederate" friend, who laughed and continued with his explanation.

He had fled Texas and enlisted in Indiana, where he joined the 11th Indiana Volunteer Infantry Regiment, commanded by Col. Lew

Wallace. Wallace, an excellent horseman himself, quickly recognized Duffy's scouting skills and horsemanship and promoted him to the cavalry. After fighting with Wallace's Third Division at the Battle of Shiloh in 1862, he was sent to scout the Confederate entrenchments at Corinth, Mississippi. His reports, relayed by Wallace, revealed that the Confederate army was slipping out of Corinth, but the dispatches were ignored by Gen. Henry Halleck, whose incompetence was exceeded only by his petty jealousy and self-promotion. By the time Halleck led the Union Army into Corinth, the Confederates were long gone to regroup, and the next bloody battle of Corinth was inevitable.

But the young scout's skills at infiltrating enemy encampments gave Wallace an idea: Lieutenant Smith was sent to train with the Jessie Scouts, then sent by Wallace to Texas to join the Confederate Army as an undercover agent. Eventually, he rode as a scout for Morgan's Raiders, which gave him occasional opportunities to make contact with Wallace through other agents on the general's staff, such as Gillespie.

Then, during the Siege of Cincinnati, he rode and marched with Gen. Henry Heth's army as far as Fort Mitchell before Heth was recalled on the brink of the assault by Gen. Braxton Bragg. The order was brought by a hard-riding courier—"Corporal MacDuff." And while Heth marched back south to Lexington, Duffy dismounted and disappeared into the woods alongside Lexington Pike, turning north to make contact with Wallace.

Wallace had sent orders to Duffy that he was needed for another assignment.

As Nehemiah and Amos listened with open mouths behind their bushy beards and tried to untangle the twisting grapevine of the story, Wallace gave Duffy his new orders: Infiltrate a secret society in Cincinnati, the Knights of the Golden Circle, identify their leaders— and, if possible, discover who was behind the plot to assassinate President Lincoln in Cincinnati on his way to his inauguration two years earlier.

"I think I'm beginning to get a handle on this," Nehemiah said.

Wallace nodded at him to go on.

"Macbeth killed a king. And MacDuff killed Macbeth. Here's

our MacDuff." He pointed a thumb at Duffy. "We just need to find a Copperhead Macbeth who tried to kill our president. And some knights standing in a circle."

"Correct, sir. Are you in?" Wallace asked. Nehemiah turned to Amos, who still looked bewildered but hardly paused before nodding once. "My son went off to war and has not come marching home again. Nobody is waitin' on me up on the Mad River," Amos said.

Nehemiah also nodded and said, "Yep. If'n you need us, we're here. I reckon Copperheads is about like Shawnees, but without being so honorable.""

"Will you need more men?" Wallace asked Duffy.

"No, sir. These men are the equal of my Texas Rangers. But please don't let any Rangers learn I said that."

"There is one I must recommend," Wallace said. "I would like you to speak to him." He handed Duffy a piece of paper. "Unlike a few who take orders from the Copperhead mayor, he is completely trustworthy, and he understands this city far better than any of us."

"I have one question," Amos said. The three looked at him. "What about that girl in Goshen? Was you butterin' our bread about her too?"

Duffy replied, "No sir, she is exceedingly real. I hope to marry her."[9]

Amos nodded. "One more. What about them bodacious big spiders in Texas?"

---

9   Such North-South romances were possible. John Anderson, who rode with Morgan's Raiders in July 1863, met Katherine Deerwester on her farm near Goshen, Ohio when she implored him not to take any of their horses. He agreed but promised to come back and marry her after the war. They were married and are buried together in Evergreen Cemetery in Miamiville, Ohio.

Death of Red Snake

**Fort Washington as it appeared in 1810 after many additions.
From *Cincinnati, the Queen City,* 1788-1912.**

Kenton headed east toward the settlements of Limestone and Maysville in
Kentucky. Along the way he spread the alarm, stopping wherever he found
chimney smoke. Along the way, four men grabbed their rifles and left
their families and cabins in the woods to join him, determined to punish
the war party of Shawnees and discourage attacks that could take their
own wives, children and horses next. It was a heart-wrenching decision:
They could leave their wives and children alone and defenseless, or stay
home to protect them and encourage more raids by showing weakness.

Most chose to stay; a few chose to fight.

The small party crossed the Ohio River and headed northwest,
to intercept the war party on its way north to the Shawnee village of
Chalahgawtha.[10]

---

10 Chalahgawtha (Chillicothe) was the name of one of the Shawnee tribes, and also the name of
many Shawnee villages in various locations where the tribes met for councils.

At Covalt Station, Kenton and his group found they were too late. A young girl and two boys were missing. The father of one of the missing boys insisted on coming. He was joined by another skilled Indian fighter and tracker, Reason Bailey.

When the distraught father asked Kenton if he thought the children were still alive, the woodsman only nodded slightly, "We pray so." He understood a father's anguish. His own first son, John Kenton, had just been born that year, the same year Kentucky became the 15th state in the young nation: 1792.

He had reasons to be hopeful. The captives were worth more alive than dead. The British in Detroit, still rankled by the loss of their colonies and determined to inflict grief and fear in the new settlements, offered $50 for each white scalp, but $100 for live captives.[11]

Kenton knew that captives who could survive the harrowing death march through hundreds of miles of wilderness to Detroit would be allowed to live, often sold as servants and slaves in Canada. Those who stumbled, lagged or fell ill along the way would be left to freeze to death in winter or more likely killed and scalped on the spot. It was still summer. If they were hardy, the captives might make it, and might even be ransomed from the British with gold, tobacco or horses.

Neither the British nor the Americans had any appetite to reignite the bloody war for independence that had ended only eleven years ago at the Battle of Yorktown. So the British were allowed to remain in Fort Detroit like unwelcome in-laws who refused to be evicted. Their commander, Gen. Henry Hamilton, used trading posts and his Indian agents to pay scalp bounties, collect prisoners and distribute knives, guns and powder to the tribes.

The British hoped to strangle expansion of the new United States with the bloody warclub of Indian raids and the olive branch of trade with the world's greatest empire, Great Britain.[12]

---

11   A $100 bounty in 1792 would equal thousands of dollars today.

12   The American Historical Review, Vol. 8, No. 1, Oct. 1902: From a document obtained from the English Public Record Office: English Policy Toward America in 1790—91: "...in a commercial

For the hardy and brave settlers who came to Covalt Station on the Little Miami River and nearby Columbia Station,[13] miles from protection by Fort Washington in Losantiville,[14] the policy ordained by distant Lords in the British Parliament meant constant fear and dread of savage attacks. Even the harshest starvation winters were a welcome respite from raids. But the beauty of Ohio springtime had a dark side: the creeping return of terror as the men had to leave their families undefended while they cut trees, planted crops, hunted fresh meat and traveled for trade. Even retrieving daily necessities such as salt and water could mean sudden death or capture by Indian raiders.

Just two years earlier, in 1790, the Shawnee chiefs had asked for a month to consider a peace treaty—then used that "truce" to kill and abduct nearly 200 settlers. In the seven years before 1790, more than 1,500 men, women and children were murdered, tortured or taken by the tribes. At one treaty conference the Indians purposely killed and drove away game for twenty-five miles around the pioneer village to starve the settlers through the winter.

Both sides made and betrayed treaties as often as the seasons changed. But since 1781, when the British began to incite more vicious attacks, it was the settlers who paid the heaviest price: thousands of men, women and children had been killed or taken prisoner for bounties or died slowly in the Indians' grisly sport of torture.[15]

Kenton had no illusions. He had been tortured, seen it done to others and heard many stories about prisoners tied to stakes and burned alive

---

view it will be for the Benefit of this Country to prevent Vermont and Kentucke and all the other settlements now forming in the Interior parts of the great Continent of North America, from becoming dependent on the Government of the United States, or on that of any other Foreign Country, and to preserve them on the contrary in a State of Independence, and to induce them to form Treaties of Commerce and Friendship with Great Britain."

13   Now Columbia Tusculum.

14   Named in 1788 to combine Latin words meaning "opposite the mouth of the Licking River." It was renamed Cincinnati, after the Society of Cincinnatus, by Governor Arthur St. Clair in 1790. St. Clair was a member of the club that was formed by veterans of the Continental Army in 1783, in the tradition of the Roman General who left his farm to save the Republic but refused to become emperor and went back to his farm. George Washington was a founder.

15   Boone, Daniel, and Francis Lister Hawkes. *Daniel Boone's Own Story & The Adventures of Daniel Boone*. Courier Corporation, 2012.

slowly for days, flayed alive or slowly scalded to death with boiling water. He was resolved, along with his men, to save the captives, if possible, and kill as many of the war party as he could.

Simon Kenton and his party set out on an August morning that whispered September as soft as a dove's wing. They quickly picked up the Shawnee trail of droppings from stolen horses and footprints of the prisoners on the way to Todd's Fork. The creek was named after Col. John Todd,[16] who was killed in one of the final fights of the Revolutionary War at the Battle of Blue Licks, southwest of Maysville. British Loyalists had led an attack with 300 Indians against fewer than 200 Kentucky Militia soldiers who fought for independence, including Kenton's good friend Daniel Boone. Boone's son, Israel, was killed in the battle.

Kenton himself had arrived leading reinforcements of nearly 500 men, but he was too late, the battle was already lost. Todd and many other good men were killed or wounded.

And now, he thought, he might have the opportunity to avenge that loss ten years later, not far from the stream named after the man he nearly rescued, John Todd. It seemed fitting. He thought of his own son. Then the little girl, only 7, taken from Covalt Station. His blue eyes lost their warmth and looked as cold and steely as the Ohio River on a winter day.

That night, long after dark as the other men slept, he touched Reason Bailey on the shoulder and was not surprised to find the young man wide awake, ready. They slipped away quietly and scouted the trail north. After a few hours, even the rhythmic chirping of tree frogs had ceased and all was quiet. An apple-wedge of moon lit the places where the trees parted, offering just enough silvery light to follow the trail. A few of the prisoners had left heel marks of their shoes in places where the ground was soft and uncovered.

Bailey pointed silently to one shoe print. It was so small it could fit into one of Kenton's big hands—made by a child. They looked at each other and nodded. And then they heard it. Something that sounded like

---

16   He was a pioneer, founder of Lexington and great uncle of Mary Todd Lincoln, wife of President Abraham Lincoln.

the dying shriek of a rabbit when it has been snatched by an owl. Then it became more like the mournful howl of a wolf. But it was neither. It was a man, hoarse with anguish, pouring out his soul in agony and despair.

They were close.

As the glow of a campfire began to light the woods ahead, Bailey tapped Kenton on his shoulder and pointed to his left, and Bailey disappeared into the darkness. Kenton crept closer, slowly. The wails were louder now, covering the sound of his approach, but he was taking no chances.

As he reached the clearing, the scene unfolded in the jumping shadows of a roaring fire that sent hot red embers to the heavens like prayers. He saw the string of captives, tied together with a long rope that looped around their necks and was knotted on a tree limb overhead. Some hung their heads and wept. Others stared with glazed eyes, lit scarlet by the fire. Nearby was a stake in the ground. A man was tied to it, stripped bare, lit by a smaller fire that circled his bare feet. He stood on glowing coals.

His beard smoked from the intense heat. His eyes were squeezed shut—in prayer or in desperation. But his mouth was gaping open, stretched by a moaning, growling, choking scream. Around him, the Shawnees had placed long hickory sticks, sharpened on the ends. These were left in the fire until the sharp ends glowed like a blood moon. They were using the sticks to burn him, jabbing the ends in his groin, his bare stomach. His body was dotted with black charred circles where the sharp, flaming sticks had done their work.[17]

Kenton loosened his tomahawk and then raised his rifle. And he waited. He did not have to wait long. Bailey had seen it all too. Suddenly,

---

17   "Sometimes the poor prisoner would be tied to a stake, a pile of green wood placed around him, fire applied, and the poor wretch left to his horrible fate, while, amid shouts and yells, the Indians departed. Sometimes he would be forced to run the gauntlet between two rows of Indians, each one striking at him with a club until he fell dead. Others would be fastened between two stakes, their arms and legs stretched to each of them, and then quickly burnt by a blazing fire. A common mode was to pinion the arms of the prisoner, and then tie one end of a grapevine around his neck, while the other was fastened to the stake. A fire was then kindled, and the poor wretch would walk the circle; this gave the savages the comfort of seeing the poor creature literally roasting, while his agony was prolonged." Boone, Daniel, and Francis Lister Hawkes. *Daniel Boone's Own Story & The Adventures of Daniel Boone.* Courier Corporation, 2012.

across the clearing Kenton saw the flash and heard the spark and blast of Bailey's rifle. Before one of the capering tormentors even hit the ground, his own rifle took the second one through the head and Kenton was on the move, dashing into the clearing.

Bailey used a pistol to shoot a third Indian through the stomach and there were three left. Red Snake, hearing shots from both directions, reached for his own tomahawk and ran to meet the white giant who had haunted his dreams. Red Snake was a strong man, made agile and lethal by years of training and battles from the time he was a boy, when his face was painted black by the tribe to send him on his first hunt—kill or die. His name, earned by acts of courage and speed in battle, honored his ability to strike like a rattlesnake.

But Kenton was also hardened by war, wise with the deadly experience of more than a dozen years of battle against the tribes. He had been with the Shawnees long enough to learn their ways. And though he looked more bear than snake, he was faster.

Red Snake feinted with the knife in his left hand and swung the tomahawk low, to strike below the ribs where the blood would flow fast, unstoppable. But his murderous scowl of anger turned to surprise as Kenton blocked the knife with the long barrel of his rifle, knocking Red Snake's arm back in a bone-cracking sweep, while he reached out his left hand and caught the wrist that was swinging Red Snake's tomahawk in midair. Red Snake felt as if he had tried to swing his arm through the trunk of a tree. Kenton bent the wrist backward and the right arm followed, the left arm now useless.

Red snake kicked out to dislocate Kenton's knee, but he realized too late that it was a fatal mistake. That move was anticipated, and he found himself instead off balance, being swung like a rag doll over Kenton's hip into the bonfire. As he landed in the fire he frantically tried to roll away, but felt the huge blow of a tree limb that pinned him to the coals. Kenton had grabbed the unburned end of a log that was feeding the flames, pulled it from the fire and slammed it on the writhing figure on the hot coals.

As Kenton stood back, he heard the wet slapping thunk of a tomahawk hitting flesh and turned to see Bailey standing over a warrior. Another lay dead nearby, with Bailey's long skinning knife buried in his chest.

Both men spun and looked around quickly. That was six. If there were others, they had fled. Kenton and Bailey looked at the terrified prisoners who were crying and begging for help or standing dazed, numbed by shock from what they had witnessed. The two Indian fighters looked at each other, trading a silent understanding of what needed to be done next. Kenton thumbed at his chest. Bailey nodded once again and hurried to untie the captives as Kenton quickly reloaded his rifle.

Bailey cut the rope and hurried the children out of the clearing. When they were gone, Kenton crossed himself and turned to the mutilated man at the stake. The man's mouth made an "O," but no sound came out. The words were written in his tortured eyes: "Please! Please!"

Kenton raised his rifle and ended the misery. He turned then to the gut-shot warrior, who glared at him with the bright, seething menace of a panther. There was no time for burials or scalps. He loaded again quickly and saw a flicker of hope in the Shawnee's eye. It was Licking Dog. He wanted death, too, but would never beg for it. Kenton shook his head.

You wanted torture and suffering, he thought. *Now you have your share and you are welcome to it.*

He turned his back on the dying man and found Bailey as he was putting the prisoners on the stolen horses. When all were mounted, they rode south, Kenton loping ahead to scout the trail, Bailey behind to cover their escape.

'Your demon is here'

"That was my pa who watched that man being tortured by those hellish monsters. He was hardly eight years old."

Duffy quoted, "Hell is empty and all the demons are here."

Nehemiah looked at him. "I have often paused on that line," he said. "Do you reckon William Shakespeare had seen the elephant?"

Duffy shook his head. "As far as I know, he was just a poet, not a fighter."

"I don't know nothing about this spear shaker you-uns blather on about, but I reckon it was pretty hellish on both sides," Amos said. "When my pappy died, I found quite a collection of Indian scalps in his trunk. Kindness and mercy was harder to find than a catfish climbing a tree." He turned to Duffy. "Much the same in Texas, Mr. Zeke MacDuffy Smith?"

Duffy chuckled. Nehemiah rumbled a laugh. They were in Arnold's Saloon on Eighth Street, seated at a table where they could keep their eyes on the door and watch the line of men who leaned on the long bar. Duffy was now dressed as a civilian gentleman, with a white shirt, dark blue vest and blue slacks that covered the tops of his Texas boots. A bloused neck scarf in the pale blue-gray of Confederate cavalry was his only hint of the South—at least until he spoke.

Nehemiah and Amos also looked "remarkably spruce in new shop-mades," Duffy said after they had bathed and put on new city feathers. "I had no inkling that there were human beings under all that hair, dirt and buckskin."

The Squirrel Hunters were not amused. "This choke-strap is starvin' my air," Amos said, yanking off his black ribbon tie. "I don't know how that flannel mouth clerk jawed me into wearin' this hangman's noose."

They were waiting for the man whose name had been written on a scrap of paper by General Wallace. Wallace's precise, graceful handwriting said, "Detective William Reany."

"There is not a lot the Apaches and Comanches could learn from the Shawnee when it comes to writing operas in agony," Duffy said. "That story you told reminds me of Mathilda Lockhart," he said to Nehemiah. "In 1838, she was captured by the Comanches along with four other children of the Putnam family while they were out gathering pecans. She was finally reclaimed several years later as part of a treaty, but the poor child was only a shadow of the bright light she had been. She died when most women's lives are just beginning, only seventeen."[18]

Duffy told how the women who examined Mathilda found no place on her body more than a hand apart that had not been burned with hot irons. She had been flogged every day and used as a slave. "To keep her from running off, they burned the soles of her feet. One of the other girls was sold several times to trappers and traders. When her family finally found her, she could remember nothing of her life before her capture."

The men sat without speaking, a small island of silence in a tavern humming with loud talk, shouts and outbursts of laughter. Finally, Nehemiah heaved a sigh and said, "I think I'll have another."

"On me, gentlemen," Duffy said. "The general has blessed us with abundant resources to stage our play." He waved his arm to the bartender who nodded his big handlebar mustache briskly and turned to the ale taps with three fresh beer steins held in one hand.

"If I may ask," Amos said, "was Mathilda any kin to you?"

"No, she was not. I pray that my own sisters died quickly if they were murdered. But I always hoped to see their faces among the prisoners we rescued when I was riding with the Rangers." He cleared his throat and changed the subject. "On a lighter note, when I was with the Rangers, I had the honor to meet a true legend of the West. He was a man who would even put Mr. Woods in the shade for size. Big Foot Wallace. His

---

18   Wilbarger, John Wesley. *Indian Depredations in Texas.* Eakin Press, 1889.

partner in devilment was Ben Wade, known as the eatenest, sleepinest man to ever lift a spoon of Pecos strawberries."

He noticed the puzzlement on Amos's face and added, "Beans. Pinto beans. We lived on those for days and weeks. Might explain why the Apaches never troubled long to track us or know we was a-comin'." He smiled and continued.

"Bigfoot liked to say, 'Ben Wade could eat more and sleep more than any man I ever saw. When he was out on the plains, he would eat forty times a day if he had the chance.' And Ben says back to him, 'It may be forty days before we will get any more, and in this way, by being sure to keep eating while I have it, it enables me to go without a long time.'"[19]

"I believe I'm getting hungry," Amos said.

Duffy told how Bigfoot and Ben were caught one night spying on a Comanche camp and had to run for their lives. As they passed a lodge, Ben saw a side of buffalo ribs roasting over a fire and said to Bigfoot, "Cap, let's stop and take a bite, there is no telling when we will get another chance."

With Indians hot on their heels, chasing and yelling like hungry wolves, Bigfoot replied, "Well, Ben, if you are willing to sell your life for a mess of pottage you can stop, but I set a higher price on mine and can't tarry just now."

With the pursuers just 100 yards away, Ben said, "If you won't wait, I must take the ribs along with me."

They tore on through the night and when they finally reached a place of safety and caught their breath, Bigfoot turned to Ben and said, "As you would bring the ribs along, I believe I will take one of them now, my run has given me an appetite."

"I am sorry, Cap," Ben replied, "but you spoke too late. I've polished them all."

Nehemiah and Amos broke out in laughter, drawing the attention of men at the bar. Duffy continued, "Bigfoot said, 'While we were running for dear life, Ben had plucked the ribs as clean as the ivory

---

19   Ibid.

handle of my six-shooter.'"[20]

They laughed again and tipped their beers. Amos said, "Do you reckon they serve ribs here? They sounded quite tasty—except for all that runnin'."

"Cracky, they do," Duffy said. "How many buffaloes would it take to feed Mr. Woods?"

"Not more than three or four if they're largish ones," Nehemiah answered. "Maybe washed down with—"

"Hell is empty," Amos interrupted. "Your demon is here."

They looked up at the door to see Sergeant Butcher coming in with a well-dressed man. Butcher scanned the room, saw Duffy and frowned, then saw Amos and Nehemiah in their new suits and recognition slowly dawned.

Nehemiah stared back, eyes locked on the police sergeant in uniform. Men at the bar near the door also saw the uniform and the big sergeant in it, and were suddenly subdued, checking pocket watches, tipping up their drinks to make an exit. The uneasy chill radiated like a bad odor and the saloon went quiet.

"That will be all tonight, Sergeant," the man in the black bowler hat said. "You're dismissed. Thank you for your assistance."

Sergeant Butcher retreated grudgingly, never taking his eyes off Nehemiah, who returned a glare that could start a fire in wet kindling. When the door to the street closed at last, he belched loudly and said, "Just like staring down a polecat."

Duffy smiled and stood, extending his hand, "Detective William Reany?"

"At your service." Reany was a stout and solid man in a black vested suit with a watch chain at his waist and the butt of a pearl-handled pistol peeking from a shoulder holster behind his open suitcoat.[21] "You

---

20   Ibid.

21   Reany was a private detective and Cincinnati Police detective. He served with the 7th Ohio Volunteer Cavalry during the war and fought in three battles with Morgan's Raiders. Kramer, Stephen, "Detective William Henry Reany (1822-1874)," the Greater Cincinnati Police Historical Society.

gentlemen match the description I was given. Excuse the lack of courtesy, but Sergeant Butcher had somehow learned of our meeting and volunteered very adamantly to introduce us."

He put a card on the table that was signed by General Wallace. "We cannot be too careful. There are many like Sergeant Butcher in our city."

"Then perhaps we should retire to a place more appropriate to the nature of our conversation," Duffy said, standing. He turned to Nehemiah and Amos. "Enjoy your dinner," he said, laying five dollars on the table, "and whatever amusements that follow."

"At our age, that menu is short and as dull as a turnip," Amos said. "But much obliged to you and the general."

Nehemiah said, "Let me know if Sergeant Butcher becomes a nuisance."

Detective Reany sized up Nehemiah with a professional eye, smiled and said, "I believe you may have the chance to get better acquainted with him. I would like to be there to witness the ruction when it takes place."

•　•　•　•　•

The next morning the three men met for breakfast in Duffy's suite at the Burnet House.[22] "The general was right," Duffy said, pouring coffee. "Detective Reany was very helpful. He has policed the most hazardous neighborhood in town, the Bottoms along the riverfront. He's also a specialist in exposing and arresting counterfeiters, who are often connected to the Knights of the Golden Circle. He suggested we should meet with a Mr. J. W. Pomfrey of Covington this afternoon. Detective Reany believes Pomfrey will be very helpful. He also provided extensive background on his own investigations of the Knights of the Golden Circle in Cincinnati, Indiana and Kentucky."

"What have they done to these eggs," Amos asked. "They taste good but look distressed."

"They call those 'poached' eggs," Duffy replied. "It's a specialty."

---

22 At the corner of Third and Vine in downtown Cincinnati, from 1850 to 1926.

"Now why would a fancy hotel like this need to steal eggs?" Amos wondered.

Duffy started to explain, but Nehemiah said, "We'd like to learn more about those gold knights."

"And what about those twin sisters the general mentioned?" Amos added with a wink. "Were they 'poached' as well?"

"I fear one topic will dismay you and the other will disappoint you. Which would you like to hear first?"

"Twin sisters," they said together.

1836

HOW CINCINNATI SAVED TEXAS

'Liberty or death!'

Replica of one of The Twin Sisters cannons at Booneville Heritage Park in Bryan Texas. Photo by Larry D. Moore, Wikimedia Commons.

If time is like a river, some years are floods that spill over the riverbanks and reshape the landscape of history. For America in the mid-19th century, one of those years was 1836.

It began with a border war between Ohio and Michigan, which rose to its peak of hostilities when an Ohio man named Two Stickney stabbed a Michigan sheriff with a penknife.[23] Congress and President

---

23   Two Stickney had a brother named One Stickney. Their father was Major Benjamin Franklin Stickney of Toledo. The sheriff's wound was minor, and the border war was averted when Michigan gave Toledo to Ohio for the consolation prize of the Upper Peninsula—which seemed like a raw deal at the time but turned out to be a jackpot of resources for Michigan. One of the men who helped avert the war was Congressman David Disney of Cincinnati. The Army Lieutenant from West Point who was sent to survey the new border was Robert E. Lee. Michigan won statehood in 1837. Border war hostilities are reignited each year during football season.

Andrew Jackson had to intervene to prevent America's first war between the states over possession of Toledo. The Territory of Michigan was pacified with a gift of the Upper Peninsula, and Ohio kept Toledo.

Borders were deadly serious business as the new nation mapped its future. Everything west of Illinois, Missouri, Arkansas and Louisiana was marked as wild Indian Territory, empty Northwest Territory or Property of Mexico. The United States had only twenty-five states, with a population about the size of greater Los Angeles today: 13 million.

There were no Dakotas, no Nebraska, Kansas, Colorado, Wyoming, Montana, New Mexico, Utah, Idaho, Nevada, Arizona or California. Oregon and Washington were called Oregon District, claimed by Great Britain as part of Canada.

The term "manifest destiny" had not yet become the national gospel,[24] but young America—an adolescent compared to arthritic Europe—was itching to stretch its legs out from the rocky shores of the Atlantic to the deep Pacific. President Jackson, a hero of the War of 1812, believed America could hardly grow fast enough.

It was also the year new technology arrived that would play a key role in westward expansion: The first practical steam locomotive and the Colt Revolver were both patented in 1836.

And 1836 was the year all eyes of the young republic turned west, riveted by reports that rumbled like the grinding train wheels of manifest destiny itself. The whole nation watched a dusty, sunbaked little cowtown called San Antonio, where a ragtag army was fighting for its life behind the thick walls of an old Spanish mission called the Alamo. Compared to what happened at the Alamo, Ohio vs. Michigan was slapstick.

About 300 men were trapped behind the ancient adobe walls of the Alamo. They called themselves "Texians"—residents of Mexico fighting for the independence of Texas. Standing alongside them were

---

24   The term was coined in 1845 to describe the God-given mission of the United States to expand its borders and spread freedom, civilization and independence. It was used for the first time by an editor at *The United States News, and Democratic Review*, John O'Sullivan, writing about the annexation of Texas.

Tejanos (Mexicans) who resented Mexico's heavy taxation without representation. What would later become Texas was then the Mexican state of Tejano—treated like an unwelcome, misbehaving stepchild.

Mixed among the Texians and Tejanos at the Alamo were a gumbo of freedom-loving romantics and adventurers who came from Tennessee, Louisiana, Kentucky, Ohio and other states, drawn to glory like moths to a flame.

National hero Davey Crockett joined the fight and offered to give his life for Texas independence. After losing his bid for re-election to Congress in Tennessee, the famous frontiersman told his ungrateful constituents, "You all can go to hell. I'm going to Texas."

Jim Bowie was there too. A brawler and killer who had a quick temper and an even quicker knife that was as long as a man's arm, Bowie had bounced around from his native state of Kentucky to Louisiana, where he killed a sheriff *after* he himself had been shot and stabbed. The "Bowie Knife" he used became legendary.

Col. William Travis led what little there was of the Texian (Texas) army. He was a failed lawyer, newspaper publisher and businessman who also said "the hell with it all" and ran off to Texas, leaving behind his wife and children, large debts and a warrant for his arrest for unpaid debts.

To the government of Mexico, they were insurgents, revolutionaries, rebels and outlaws. Mexico had seized ownership of Texas in 1824 after the Mexican War for Independence from Spain; Texas was the Mexican state of Coahuila y Tejas. But a flood of new settlers, mainly from the Southern states, tipped the scales against Mexico and sparked demands of independence for a new nation: the Republic of Texas.

When Mexico outlawed slavery in 1829, more fuel was added to the sagebrush rebellion, especially among the southerners who had brought their slaves to Texas to raise cotton. Their militant resistance was a preview of the American Civil War.

On December 5, 1835, a volunteer force of 300 Texians and Tejanos drove the Mexican Army out of San Antonio and seized the Alamo fort there, including several cannons the Mexicans left behind. Mexico's El Presidente himself, Generalissimo Antonio Lopez de Santa Anna, strapped on his ornate brass eagle-hilted sword and announced that he would personally lead the Mexican Army to take back the Alamo and crush the rebellion.

As Texians rushed to reinforce the Alamo, the dictator Santa Anna marched north and crossed the Rio Grande. Then on February 23, 1836, the Texians watched with sinking hearts from the walls of the Alamo as Santa Anna arrived with more than 2,000 soldiers, several cannons and a long train of supplies. The siege had begun. General Santa Anna moved into the San Fernando Church near the Alamo and had his men raise a red flag. It was a signal to the Texians: No prisoners, no mercy.

The Texians replied with a blast from their biggest cannon, an 18-pounder. The battle was on.

Day after day, the Mexican Army sledge-hammered the walls and interior of the Alamo with cannon fire, but casualties inside the fort were low. And the Texians had an advantage: Their Tennessee Rifles were far more accurate at much greater range than Mexican muskets. Similar to Kentucky Rifles and Pennsylvania Rifles, they were up to six feet long from buttstock to muzzle. They were muzzle-loaded, usually firing hand-molded balls of .48 caliber at a rate of two per minute. The Texian sharpshooters could knock down a man at 200 yards—twice the range of the Mexican infantry.

On the second day of the siege, Colonel Travis sat down amid the choking dust and deafening crashes of cannon fire to write a letter that became a legend in Texas and American history. Calling desperately for reinforcements, he closed with the line, "If this call is neglected, I am determined to sustain myself as long as possible and die like a soldier who never forgets what is due to his own honor and that of his country—Victory or Death."

Those words rang across America like the Liberty Bell, bringing back echoes of Patrick Henry: "Give me liberty or give me death."

The reinforcements would never arrive, but the letter was published in a handbill that circulated throughout Texas, the United States and worldwide. Headlines in Ohio and as far away as London quoted the undaunted, outnumbered, heroic Texians who were holding out against thousands of Mexican soldiers commanded by the president of Mexico, who was known as "the Napoleon of the West."

If prayers were armies, the Texians would have crushed Santa Anna, and nobody would remember the Alamo. But on the twelfth day of the siege, Santa Anna made his move. The Mexican artillery suddenly stopped raining deafening fire on the Alamo. The men in the fort began to hope the Mexican Army might withdraw. They welcomed the sudden quiet to finally rest. Then, before dawn the next morning—Sunday, March 6, Day 13—they were suddenly awakened shouts of "Viva Santa Anna!" Hordes of Mexican soldiers assaulted the old mission, poured over the walls and took the Alamo with sheer numbers.

The Texians fell back and made a valiant stand in their barracks, but they were soon overwhelmed. None of them lived to see the morning sunrise. A handful who surrendered were shot to death on orders of Santa Anna.

A dispatch from Sam Houston, commander in chief of all armies in the Texas Revolution, described how Santa Anna burned the bodies of the Texians. Newspapers vividly described massacre, cruelty and mutilation.

Readers all over America read the report from Gen. Houston: "Lieut. Dickinson, who had a wife and child in the fort, after having fought with desperate courage, tied his child to his back and leaped from the top of a two-story building—both were killed in the fall. The wife of Lieut. Dickson is now in possession of one of Santa Anna's officers. ... We regret to say that Col. David Crockett (was) among the slain. ... Colonel Bowie was murdered in his bed, sick and helpless." And "the face and limbs" of the body of Colonel Travis were mangled with a sword.

Santa Anna had delivered his merciless warning to the state that called itself Texas: Surrender or face total annihilation. While the dark smoke from burning bodies curled into the empty Texas sky, he sent word to General Houston that the Texians would be granted amnesty if they laid down their weapons and vowed to submit to him and his government.

General Houston replied, "True, sir, you have succeeded in killing some of our brave men, but the Texians are not yet conquered."[25]

Many initial reports were exaggerated, but the cruelty of Santa Anna could not be overstated. Three weeks after the Alamo[26] fell, Santa Anna and his army massacred more than 300 Texian prisoners at Goliad, Texas. One of the men killed in the Goliad Massacre was Richard Disney, editor and owner of the *Cincinnati Republican* newspaper, who had joined the patriotic crusade to save Texas.[27]

The Texian commander at Goliad, James W. Fannin, was assured that his men would be treated fairly if they would surrender. His situation was hopeless, so he agreed. As the men laid down their arms, they were promised freedom in eight days.

But President Santa Anna ordered his officers in Goliad to kill them all. As the sun came up on Palm Sunday, March 27, 1836, all of the Texians who were able to walk were marched out at gunpoint and told they would gather wood. They were separated into three groups. Suddenly, on command, the Mexicans raised their rifles and opened fire at close range. The prisoners were mowed down. Back at the presidio, the wounded were also executed. Fewer than thirty escaped; another twenty doctors and interpreters were spared to tell the story. The bodies of the dead were left rotting in the sun, unburied for weeks.

Santa Anna had legal authority to execute prisoners under a law he had demanded from the Mexican Congress, declaring that prisoners could be shot as pirates. But his barbaric massacres of unarmed prisoners inflamed the United States.

First, Americans were shocked by the Alamo. Then came the tragic news of Goliad. The Texians were galvanized and enraged. The rest of

---

25   New Orleans Free American, Carrolton (Ohio) Free Press, April 22, 1836.

26   Santa Anna gave the Alamo widows who survived two dollars and a blanket. The few Texian prisoners who surrendered were slashed to death with sabers. The Mexicans lost more than 600 men in the battle. One Mexican captain wrote in his journal, "With another victory like this one, we may all end up in hell." It was prophetic. Hutton, Paul Andrew, "Mexico's Napoleon: Who Was Santa Anna, the General who Defeated the Texians at the Alamo?" History Net, Feb. 19, 2018.

27   Preston, Steve, "Our Rich History: In March 1836 the Alamo fell: More to the story on our region's connections to Texas." *Northern Kentucky Tribune*, March 5, 2018.

the nation was outraged and angry. Recruits for the Texas Revolution poured in.

Richard Ellis, president of the Convention of 1836 that wrote the Texas Declaration of Independence from Mexico, sent out a cry for help in the form of an appeal published across the nation: "Our numbers are few, but our hearts are firm, and our nerves are strung to the high resolve of *liberty or death*. Will you brothers and friends ... calmly witness the destruction of your kindred and the triumph of tyranny and make no effort to save the one or arrest the other? It cannot, it will not be. The sainted spirit of Washington would rebuke your apathy."

Most states and cities talked about Texas but did little. But in Cincinnati, the Queen City of the West, the sixth largest city in the nation was already waving the flag for Texas.

"The story began in November 1835," Duffy told Nehemiah and Amos, "when Texas secret agent William Francis 'Picayune' Smith arrived in Cincinnati to meet with a group of Cincinnati patriots called The Friends of Texas."

The group was led by the most respected men in Cincinnati, including Robert Todd Lytle, a lawyer and member of Congress; David T. Disney, speaker of the Ohio Senate, future member of Congress and brother of Richard Disney, who would be killed at Goliad; and Nicholas Clopper, who had big investments in Texas.

"The Cloppers are well known along the Brazos," Duffy said. "They own a big piece of Morgan's Point in Galveston Bay. But they have paid a steep price, as you will see. The Queen City has been like an older sister to young Texas."

"How is it you come to know of all these things if they was secrets?" Amos asked.

"It was not secret at the outset. But secrecy soon became necessary, as I will explain. And allow me to mention another man who would be influenced by The Friends of Texas. His name is George Washington Bickley—a scoundrel who could not be less deserving of being named after the father of our country. Remember the name, gentlemen. We will get to know him later."

Duffy refreshed his coffee from a pot on the table and continued the story.

"The Friends of Texas had to be very careful," he said.

Aid to Texas was illegal under the federal Neutrality Act of 1818, he explained. If caught, violators could be fined $3,000 and sent to prison for three years. Official US neutrality in the battle for independence from Mexico would change violently ten years later in the Mexican-American War of 1846-48. But in 1835, sending money, troops and weapons to the Texians could be treason, especially for elected officials such as Lytle and Disney.

The initial meeting on November 19, 1835, was announced by the *Cincinnati Republican* newspaper, which was published by David Disney's brother, Richard. The item said Mr. Francis Smith of Texas would visit to describe recent events there.[28]

The crowd that came to hear him was among the largest ever assembled at the courthouse. As Picayune Smith rose to speak, the chattering hum was hushed like birds in the woods when a hawk flies by. A man coughed. A chair scraped. And then Rev. Dr. Elijah Slack rose to introduce the guest speaker. Dr. Slack was a former vice president of Princeton College of New Jersey, president of Cincinnati College and founder of the Medical College of Ohio,[29] where he was a professor of chemistry.[30]

"The object of this meeting is to take into consideration the situation of the people of Texas," Dr. Slack said. "Please welcome Mr. Francis Smith, an agent of the Secret Service of the Republic of Texas, sent to us by the Father of Texas, Stephen Austin,[31] to speak on his behalf.

---

28 Clark, Kirk. "Origin of the Twin Sisters Cannon." Origin of the Twin Sisters Cannon, 2021.

29 Both were founded in 1819 by Daniel Drake and William Lytle, who became the first president of Cincinnati College, which became insolvent and closed six years later.

30 The Medical College was on 6th Street, between Race and Vine. It closed in 1839 for lack of funds and was destroyed by fire in 1845. Slack Street in the Liberty Hill neighborhood is named for Dr. Slack. Jenson, William, *Elijah Slack*, Notes from the Oesper Collections, Department of Chemistry, University of Cincinnati, Museum Notes, January 2011.

31 Austin led the Texian forces to victory over Mexico at the Siege of Bexar, which was still in doubt as Smith visited Cincinnati. He ran for president of the new Republic of Texas but was defeated in a landslide by Sam Houston.

Mr. Smith's recent experiences could entertain and astonish us all for several evenings, but tonight he is here to communicate the plight of the Texians, as they are called, and seek whatever help may be proper in so worthy a cause."

The tall Texan known along the Brazos River as Picayune Smith rose and nodded his thanks to Dr. Slack. As the crowd appraised Mr. Smith, they saw a man who looked pale and drawn, gaunt and worn—not a swashbuckling Texas Ranger, Indian fighter and fearless warrior in the battle for Texas independence.

But he was all of that and more. Many years later, his daughter, Emeline D. Smith, described her father in an autobiography. In 1826, he had been arrested by the Mexican federales for speaking against the government. Emeline described his treatment.[32]

Picayune Smith

"I shall charge my memory as far back as 1826, when he laid in prison in Victoria, Texas. He was ironed down on the ground by his ankles, and his head was between two great huge logs, for what time, I do not know. But I used to carry his meals to him that mother sent him while in confinement. The Mexicans then took him away, I was told, to the mines. He was absent for several years.

"In his absence his only son, Augustus, died and I was left his only heir. My mother, being left with two small children and no protector, remarried."

By the time he was recruited by Stephen Austin to go to Cincinnati, Picayune Smith lived alone on the wildest outskirts of the Texas frontier, trading with the Indians, who were his friends. "About 1830 my father was carrying on a trading business with the Indians and Mexicans at the Falls of the Brazos River," his daughter recalled. "He had purchased several leagues of land lying near the river. At this trading post, there was but few whites. He principally traded with the Indians and Mexicans. He bought furs and buffalo rugs, beautiful dresses, painted and beaded,

---

32 Clark, Kirk. "Origin of the Twin Sisters Cannon." Origin of the Twin Sisters Cannon, 2021.

and would swap, as the Indians would say, bed blankets, looking glass, beads of all colors and shapes and sizes, brass earrings, red handkerchiefs, buttons. And here my father built him a large stone store opposite the town of Viesca, which has long since been burnt."

She added, "He was deeply interested in behalf of his country."

"Gentlemen," Picayune Smith said, addressing the city's most respected leaders in the front rows—captains of business, members of Congress, the mayor, judges, doctors, newspaper editors and publishers, reverends, lawyers, industrialists and wealthy benefactors who held the fate of his beloved Texas in their hands.

"I appear before you this evening for the purpose of calling your attention to the present situation of your brethren in Texas, with the expectation that you will assist me in raising funds to purchase a pair of field pieces to take to Texas to assist in maintaining the rights and privileges you here enjoy."

The editor of the *Cincinnati Gazette*, E.C. Hammond, drew a sharp breath. *Field pieces?* he thought. *That's cannons. And that's a violation of the federal Neutrality Act. What are these men doing? This is criminal!*

Not far away, Richard Disney, publisher of the *Cincinnati Republican*, noticed Hammond and thought, *It was a mistake to let him in here. The man is a ninny. He will betray us all. He would never do anything because he only knows how to belittle others who dare to do what has to be done.* And then he thought: *And what will I do…?*

"The well-known enterprise and perseverance of Americans, has, in about fourteen years, changed Texas from a hostile wilderness into flourishing villages and beautiful farms," Smith continued.

"We immigrated to Texas when a free republican government invited us to take the then wilderness for our homes. That government guaranteed to each individual emigrant one league of land—a small premium for the hardships that had to be braved by the first settlers."

Many in the crowd nodded. They were the descendants of the first settlers of Ohio when it was known as the Miami Slaughterhouse, where every day's existence had to be wrestled from the wilderness under constant threat of murder, kidnapping and torture by Indians.

One small parcel of land was, indeed, small compensation—not unlike the acres granted to their grandfathers who were given land as payment for their service in the Revolutionary War against Britain.

"Yet no hardships, privations or danger, have we thought too great to undergo for Texas. Tho' we have often been under the necessity of living on horseflesh, panthers and alligators; and eating the bloodshot quill of wild turkeys without bread. Myself, for one, when water could not be had, have had to drink the blood of animals, as it flowed after my knife."

Some shuddered, others nodded knowingly. Starvation cures the squeamish.

"For years in settling and driving the savages from Texas, we have had to sleep on the naked earth, open to the doors of Heaven; with our horse tied to our arm, our shot bag and powder horn for our pillow, and in our arms our rifles."

As he listened, Congressman Robert T. Lytle thought of his late father, William Lytle, passed just four years ago. "The General," as he was known and loved by settlers in the Miami Valley, was the son of one of the first settlers in Kentucky. He had joined expeditions against the Shawnee and risked his life in the early Ohio wilderness to survey Williamsburg, New Richmond, Point Pleasant, Port Clinton and Sandusky. His quill had drawn the boundaries of Clermont County before it was divided to create Brown County. William Lytle had been one of the original founding fathers of Cincinnati, a respected leader, gentleman and devout Christian who ingrained in his sons an obligation for public service and improvement of his city and his country.

Robert was just thirty and had nearly been barred from Congress for being too young. He had been defeated in his bid for re-election just the year before. His friend President Andrew Jackson would soon appoint him Surveyor General of the Northwest Territory, the same post his father had held. He was a lawyer, a politician and a romantic, whose future was clouded with illness, plagued with "consumption" (tuberculosis). He would die just four years later. His son William Haines Lytle would become a nationally famous poet and hero of the

Civil War.33 But in 1835, Robert Lytle knew none of that, and thought only of the stories from his father about the sacrifices in blood, pain and grief to make Ohio safe for everyone who was at the courthouse that evening, and all the families like them.

And now that story was being written again in Texas. *And once again, here we are*, he thought, *risking our fortunes, our property, our reputations and our lives, like Washington and the signers of the Declaration of Independence.*

Smith was saying, "We have but just removed our families from camps and shady oaks into our new dwellings to enjoy the fruits of our labor and the comforts the excellent soil and serene climate affords. Our prosperity has excited the jealousy of the Mexican government. Many obstacles have been thrown in our way to prevent our advancement.

"We have by indefatigable perseverance made Texas what it now is, and what the fate of Texas is to be, is ours."

Use of the courthouse for the meeting had been arranged by Judge Jacob Burnet. His brother Isaac was the popular longtime mayor of Cincinnati. Both sat in the first row and listened intently. They had good reason to be concerned: Their half brother, David Burnet, was one of the leaders of the Texas rebellion and would become the first president of the Republic of Texas the following March 17, 1836. Their father, Dr. William Burnet, had fought Indians in Ohio and bore the scars to show for it. Dr. Burnet had been a veteran of the Continental Army in the American Revolution and had served in the Continental Congress.34

"That Republican government which sole cited us to our chosed spots is no more," Smith said in his Texas drawl. His voice rose with

---

33   When William Haines Lytle was killed at the Battle of Chickamauga in 1863, a Confederate honor guard protected his body until it could be presented to a delegation of Union officers who arrived under a flag of truce. The spot is called Lytle Hill in the Chickamauga National Military Park. His funeral was the largest ever in Cincinnati at the time.

34   The Burnet House hotel became famous nationally for its beauty and luxury and as a symbol of Cincinnati's success at civilizing the frontier. It was named after land donated for the project by Jacob Burnet. It opened in 1850 and was used as military headquarters during the Civil War. Famous guests included Gen. William Sherman, Gen. Ulysses Grant, Abraham Lincoln, Gen. Ambrose Burnside, Jefferson Davis, Henry Clay, actor Edwin Booth (brother of Lincoln's assassin), Daniel Webster and President James Buchanan.

emotion. "A tyrant now reigns. He has armed the savages and sent them against us. They have already commenced scalping our neighbors!"

Many shook their heads in anger and disgust. Memories of the Indian depredations against Ohio—brutal attacks that were armed, encouraged and funded by British bounties for scalps and prisoners—still lingered like the bleached bones at St. Clair's Defeat and Fallen Timbers.

"He has sent his troops against us, to take our arms from us and subject us to his will, or drive us from our homes," Smith said of Mexican President Santa Anna. "Oh, what a harassing thought for free men! Will we give up our arms, that hard necessity has taught us to use so well, that we have so long supported ourselves and families with, and have driven the savage out of Texas with?

"No! Thrice no!" Smith shouted. "Not as long as we can see an object through their sights.

"Will we be subject to a tyrant's will? No, the blood in our veins of our fathers of '76 boils high at the thought!"

Isaac Ludlow wanted to stand and cheer and shake his fists. His father, Col. Israel Ludlow, had surveyed the Miami Valley and a great deal of Ohio while working for John Cleves Symmes, a Revolutionary War veteran who had fought for independence and been a delegate to the Continental Congress that signed the Declaration of Independence. The spirit of '76 still inspired the young nation. He thought, *Our fathers fought in that war so we could be free from tyrants!*

"Will we go leave our hard-earned homes, when the tyrant's troops approach us? No, no, no. Before we will go and leave them, our blood shall enrich the soil of Texas. Then our children will have a fruitful foundation to build their independence upon; and the tyrant shall see, feel and know, that we are worthy of the land of our birth, and that we are at home."

Just two months later, in January of 1836—the most fateful year in Texas history—Smith's own family would be forced to flee their home and run for their lives from Mexican soldiers and Comanches. Smith himself would not live to see that terrible day or witness how his speech would change history. He had already visited Cincinnati doctors for help with a severe stomach ulcer. They told him to go home and put his affairs in order. They gave him six weeks to live. He returned home outfitted with new pistols, ready to go to war, but died a few days later, on March 20.

"The light of freedom has been extinguished by him in all the Mexican states, with the exception of Texas. And a cloud of his troops has begun to pass over that bright star, and darkness begins to prevail in the American settlements."

The editor E.C. Hammond scoffed loud enough to draw glares from the people around him. He avoided their sharp looks and thought, *Settlements, indeed. That's what it's all about. Speculation by the Cloppers and others. Land brawlers, raising weapons for a war to protect their property.*

The next day, Hammond wrote a column in *The Gazette* that accused The Friends of Texas of being criminals and called them "Land Brawlers." Ohio State Prosecutor N.C. Read and others responded with angry letters to the editor, setting off a skirmish of ink. In his scorching letter, Read wrote, "Now you denounce me as a criminal and threaten that you yourself will become the informer, because I have said no law, either human or divine, except as such are formed by tyrants, and for their sole benefit, forbids our assisting the Texians, and such law, if any exists, we do not, as Americans, choose to obey."

The editor Hammond used his abundant supply of ink to have the final word, writing again that they were "Land Brawlers" and "I cannot take it back." He also informed on The Friends of Texas, but a US grand jury was unenthusiastic to prosecute them and issued an opinion that the Neutrality Act only applied to "military expeditions." Hammond was bitterly disappointed and wrote that "we doubt the soundness of the opinion."[35]

Smith's speech continued:

"But the free men of Texas are determined that the light of freedom shall emerge from the present darkness and enlighten the whole

---

35   The Neutrality Act was selectively enforced according to the policy aims of the US Government. Clark, Kirk. "Origin of the Twin Sisters Cannon." Origin of the Twin Sisters Cannon, 2021.

Mexican nation. The light of freedom that now shines in Texas carries conviction of success with it.

"The bright flash of rifles now dazzles the eye like fireflies in a warm summer's evening. O that I were ready to embark with a pair of six-pounders to increase that light!"

Jacob W. Piatt thought, *Exactly. And we have the means at our fingertips!* He was the son of American Revolution veteran William Piatt, who was killed at St. Clair's defeat by Shawnees.[36] Jacob Piatt was a successful lawyer and city councilman who fought a long battle to establish the first professional fire department in the US in Cincinnati in 1853.[37] And as Picayune Smith spoke, Piatt's thoughts turned to the local foundries and the Federal Arsenal across the river in Covington. *Miles Greenwood has a foundry, and he is sitting just over there, listening. I think we will have a talk.*

Meanwhile, Smith scanned the crowd and found the eyes of the men who were with their wives. "And think of the fair ladies of Texas, who are mothers, sisters and daughters from your own firesides," he said. "What insults and abuse they will have to endure, if the Americans should not prove victorious? What would be your feelings to hear that the Texians lost all for want of arms and ammunition to keep up the contest, and their wives and daughters are forcibly embraced in the arms of ruffian soldiery?"

Smith saw women's eyes widen; he saw some wince as they imagined what they had feared so many times in nightmares about the Shawnees and Miamis. He saw men stiffen their backs and clench their jaws. *Yes,* Smith thought, *now you are getting the picture of what it means to be a Texian family under the bootheel of Santa Anna.*

---

36 In the Battle of the Wabash in 1791, 39 officers, 593 soldiers and more than 200 women and children were butchered in the snow by a Shawnee attack. Of the 920 men who set out from Fort Washington in Cincinnati with General Arthur St. Clair, only 24 men came home uninjured. The bodies were left in the woods near Fort Recovery, Ohio. The Shawnee attack was led by Chief Little Turtle and Blue Jacket.

37 The battle against Irish volunteer firemen became so heated, Piatt was burned in effigy on his own front lawn by a violent mob of volunteers. He finally prevailed when the Latta steam fire engine was invented in Cincinnati. He persuaded the leader of the Irish volunteers to supervise use of the new steam engine and opposition melted away.

Smith summoned his strength, ignored the stabbing pain in his stomach and raised his voice again to almost shout, "Texas stands alone and fights for a constitution. She goes for liberty alone and will have it or sink in the contest. O fair and beautiful Texas, may I soon be with you!"

The crowd at the courthouse rose to their feet like a crashing wave of enthusiastic applause. The secret agent from the distant, sun-blasted land called Texas had captured their hearts and forged their resolve. The people of Cincinnati knew very well what the Texians were facing, what terror and suffering they had to endure in the cause of freedom, independence and security.

In fact, no other American city was still so close to its frontier past. In Cincinnati, the hardships and sorrows were as near as the family Bibles. The Queen City of the West had been built out of the wilderness with tears, sweat, blood, muscle, sacrifice and courage. Now the city was able to share its God-given blessings of wealth, power and resources. The crowd left the meeting determined: The brave Texians would not stand alone.

"Be it resolved," The Friends of Texas agreed in a resolution, "that from the best information we can obtain, the people of the State of Texas are justifiable in a Political and Religious point of view, in the resistance they have made to the usurpations of the despot Santa Anna."

Local attorney Edward Woodruff moved to form committees to help Texas, representing the five wards of Cincinnati. The motion passed and the committees were appointed:

1st Ward: David T. Disney, William M. Corry, James Saffin, Col. Charles Hale, James Wise.

2nd Ward: Nathan Seaman, Benjamin Chase, Henry L. Tatum, Joshua A. Perry, Dr. A.G. Smith.

3rd Ward: William Homes, Robert Reily, E.S. Naines, Septimus Hazen, John Armor.

4th Ward: David Griffin, Theodore Scowden, Andrew Patterson, Dr. William Price, A. Higbee.

5th Ward: Edward Woodruff, Col. E. Perry, Samuel Fosdick,
S. J. Kellogg, Pulaski Smith.

The men were determined to "cheerfully assist (Texas) with all the means in our power: and that they will have our most heartfelt hopes and fervent prayers for their final success."

One of those men, David T. Disney, a banker and speaker of the Ohio Senate, went above and beyond the means in his power. The following year, he liberated sixty-six muskets for Texas from the Federal Arsenal in Newport, Kentucky. At the time, he was chairman of all the Ohio groups sending aid to Texas. Disney, Israel Ludlow and Cincinnati industrialist Miles Greenwood were sued in 1839 by the state to recover the cost of the muskets: $1072.60 (about $16 each). But by then, Texas was able to replace the weapons and the lawsuit was dismissed.[38]

Disney's younger brother Richard Disney, publisher of the *Cincinnati Republican*, contributed far more. After the speech by Picayune Smith, he enlisted in the Texas Revolution, and was killed four months later in the Goliad Massacre.

Before Richard Disney left for Texas, however, he joined other local newspapers to squelch any news of The Friends of Texas activities. Thanks to E.C. Hammond and *The Gazette*, the leaders had quickly realized that aiding Texas could be as hazardous to them as it was for Picayune Smith to criticize Santa Anna.[39]

* * * * *

The journey to Cincinnati from Texas was more than a month of rough roads, harsh weather and bad food for Picayune Smith, whose stomach kept him in constant pain. His diagnosis was bleak, but his secret mission was a success that made the trip worth every mile of misery.

---

38   Clark, Kirk. "Origin of the Twin Sisters Cannon." Origin of the Twin Sisters Cannon, 2021.

39   Privately funded invasions of foreign countries, called "filibusters," had been tacitly allowed by the US government as long as they aligned with the young nation's policy of expansion and secure borders. But then in 1823, President James Monroe presented the Monroe Doctrine: The US would remain neutral in foreign conflicts but would not allow foreign colonization of the Western Hemisphere.

A resolution drafted by Robert Lytle stated, "We approve of and recommend to the citizens of this meeting a plan by which the citizens of Texas shall be supplied through their agent, Mr. Smith, by our contributions, with an amount of hollow ware as he may deem sufficient, to contain other provisions, by which they shall be fulfilled according to his judgment and sound direction."

On paper, The Friends of Texas had agreed to spend more than $600 to send "holloware" (cookware) to the people of Texas. But the crates marked "Holloware" were too heavy to contain pots and pans. Inside were two iron six-pounder cannons that were forged at Hawkins and Tatum Foundry on Plum Street in Cincinnati.

More crates for "other provisions" contained a supply of ammunition—six barrels of canister grapeshot from Eagle Ironworks—and two new gun carriages painted in bright red with blue wheels, made by Bruncia Cassett.[40]

The guns were finished by December 30 but sat on the docks for weeks before a ship's captain could be found who would dare to take the illegal contraband aboard. They were finally loaded onto the steamship *Splendid*, bound for New Orleans. They arrived on March 16, but the journey was just begun.[41] The meandering path to the Texians would take another month, through docks, various ships and boats—including the schooner *Ohio*—and then overland, through mud bogs and marshy bayous.

In New Orleans, the cannons were loaded onto the schooner *Pennsylvania*. Twin girls, Eleanor and Elizabeth Rice, age 9, happened to be passengers on the *Pennsylvania* with their father, Dr. Charles Rice.[42] As the cannons were unloaded in Brazoria, Texas, on the Brazos River southwest of Houston, the little girls were invited to join the ceremony. After that, the cannons became known as "The Twin Sisters."[43]

40　Woodrick, James. *Cannons of the Texas Revolution.* 2015.

41　The cannons arrived in New Orleans about 10 days after the fall of the Alamo. Even if they had arrived in time, the Cincinnati cannons would have been no help. The shortage was not cannons but men.

42　Dr. Rice, of Cincinnati, moved to Texas and joined the Texas Navy.

43　"The Twin Sisters: More Light on the Historic Artillery Pieces," *The Houston Post, Aug. 30, 1909.* Letter to the editor from C. B. Mitchel, granddaughter of Mrs. Elizabeth Stapp of Brazoria, who

Duffy told Nehemiah and Amos, "From Brazoria, The Twin Sisters—the guns not the girls—went to Galveston, then to Harrisburg, near Houston. The destination was uncertain. The whole bottom half of Texas was fleeing Santa Anna in what we called the 'Runaway Scrape.' Fearing Mexicans and Indian attacks, our families left everything behind, often burned their homes, stores and ranches, and ran north, starting in January when Santa Anna marched into Texas. Many died of disease, starvation and exposure.[44]

"The cannons were hauled by oxen across Texas until a notorious woman named Pamelia Mann found out Sam Houston was retreating and rode out to take back the oxen she had loaned him. Apparently, the lady could not abide retreat, and Houston preferred to fight Santa Anna rather than challenge Pamelia. She carried a Bowie knife and a pair of pistols. She was better than most men with pistol and rifle. A real Texas spitfire. They still call that blistering skirmish 'Sam Houston's Defeat.' Legend has it that a cloud of her curses still darkens the sky where they faced off. Not even a cactus could grow in that ground for years after."

Nehemiah asked, "By notorious, do you mean—"

"She was a very wealthy *hotel* owner," Duffy nodded with a wink. "Married four times and rumored to have... *consummated* countless more."[45]

The Twin Sisters were desperately needed by Sam Houston, Duffy said. He and his army had retreated to buy time, gather recruits and train them. "And then came the fateful day, April 17, 1836, when Sam Houston and his Texian army faced a fork in the road. One road led to Louisiana where they could flee to safety. The other led to Santa Anna in Harrisburg. He chose to fight Santa Anna."

"He must have felt all but abandoned by the Lord," Nehemiah said. Amos nodded.

---

died at 82 on Aug. 9, 1909. Elizabeth Rice died shortly after the Civil War.

44   Covington, Caroline Callaway, "Runaway Scrape," Texas State Historical Association, 1952.

45   Pamelia Mann eventually extracted $100 from the new Republic of Texas for the rental of her oxen. After the war, she moved to Houston and opened the Mansion House Hotel, a luxurious brothel popular with politicians and the military. Her story is told in *Houston Madam* by Gene Shelton, Pecos Press, 2016.

"That's true," Duffy said. "Like David fleeing King Saul, everything was going against him. Outnumbered. No cannons. Facing an unstoppable army that was leaving a wide swath of death, fire and destruction, led by the president of Mexico, who waved that terrible red flag."

"But their prayers were answered?" Nehemiah asked.

"Yes," Duffy said. "On April 11, The Twin Sisters arrived, truly an answered prayer. And then, a week later, the day after General Houston took the road to battle, his men captured a courier from Santa Anna's army. They were able to *persuade* the courier to tell them where Santa Anna was, and learned that he had divided his army and had less than a thousand men with him.

"Like the Israelites in the Bible, God had delivered the enemy into Sam Houston's hands. He would make a last stand for Texas at San Jacinto, just east of Houston, near Galveston Bay and Morgan's Point. The battle was on."

THE BATTLE OF SAN JACINTO

'Remember Goliad!'

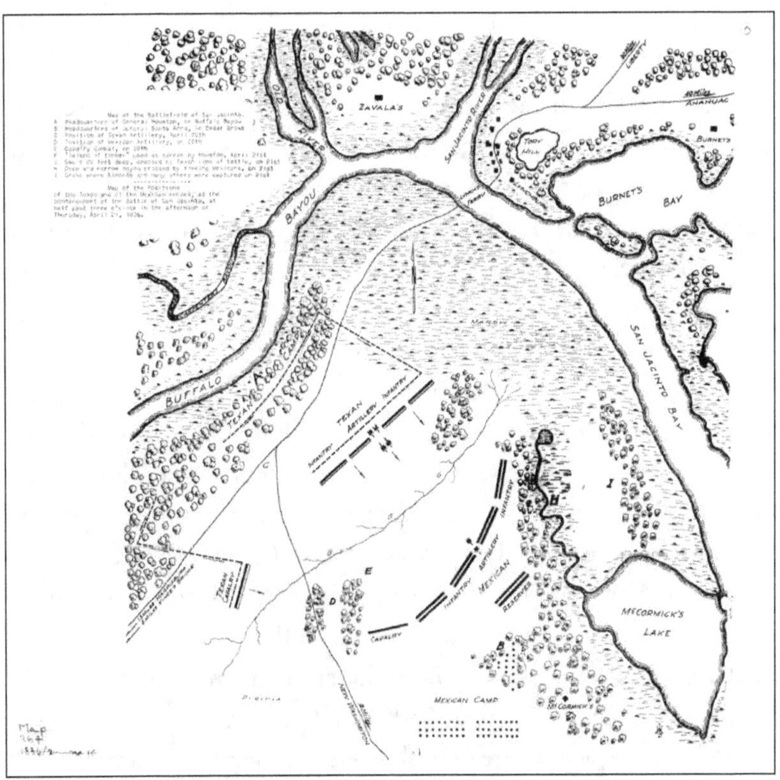

Battle map of San Jacinto, 1938, by Andrew Jackson
Houston, Military Maps of the Texas Revolution.

Pulling a pencil from his pocket, Duffy grabbed a napkin off the coffee
table and drew a map. It was a squarish shape with rounded corners;
rivers bordered the top and right side, and a dotted section labeled
"Marshes" was at the bottom. The left side had a smaller river, labeled
"Bayou."

"Sam Houston huddled with his officers and they set out, marching until midnight, then again early the next morning, to head off Santa Anna and cross Buffalo Bayou right here." Duffy pointed to the upper right corner of the map. "It was a near thing, but he got there first and was able to choose his ground. That made all the difference."

Houston and his army of 935 men camped in a line of woods along Buffalo Bayou, hidden from the approach of Santa Anna. They did not have to wait long. They had beaten the Mexican Army by only a couple of hours. At about noon on April 20, Santa Anna arrived with about 800 men.

The president of Mexico sent a detachment to probe the tree line where Houston's men were concealed. As the Mexicans approached, they were treated to a surprise. They believed Sam Houston had no cannons—until the first shots in the Battle of San Jacinto were fired by The Twin Sisters from Cincinnati.

The six-pounder smoothbore cannons had a range of more than 1,500 yards—nearly a mile. Loaded with canister or grapeshot, they were monstrous shotguns. Grapeshot was capable of mowing down infantry with a spray of twenty-eight balls in each shot. Canister, made from smaller metal scraps, hardware and other projectiles, was deadly to a range of 350 yards. At closer range, the cannons had terrifying lethal power.

There was one problem. The supplies of grapeshot sent by The Friends of Texas had been lost somewhere during the long journey from Cincinnati. But the Texians improvised.

Col. John Wade, one of the eighteen men who volunteered for artillery when the cannons arrived, told the story.[46]

"When the pieces were un-boxed, we found them to contain a pair of iron medium six-pounders, with all parts of the carriages, caissons, ramrods, etc., complete." But the grapeshot sent by Cincinnati was missing. Instead, the boxes contained only eighty rounds of round shot, which was good for knocking down walls but far less effective against infantry.

---

46 *The Galveston Daily News*, Feb. 28, 1878.

"Col. John A Wharton, who was adjutant general of the army, informed Colonel Neil in the presence of the artillerists that they [the cannons] were a present from the ladies of Cincinnati, Ohio, and had been shipped to the Texas army by a brother of the Hon. David G. Burnet, at the same time telling the boys that he knew they were being placed in the hands of those who would appreciate such a present from the fair sex.

"It is needless here to describe our march from this point to the battlefield of San Jacinto, over bad roads and with one pair of old, broken-down horses to each piece, but I will state that they were gotten there mainly by manpower.

"Upon arrival at Harrisburg, we found the place reduced to ashes, but finding some old tin and debris at a mill which had been burnt down, we improvised grape and canister shot by filling ten cases with screw nuts and other small pieces of iron, and by cutting bar lead into pieces about three-quarters of an inch in length and sewing them together into small bags of bed ticking.

"On the 20th of April, when Santa Anna made a demonstration on our camp with about 100 well-mounted, finely equipped lancers, the first shot was fired from The Twin Sisters, loaded with our homemade grapeshot."

The Mexican lancers who could still run scattered.

"Shortly after, the Mexicans opened up on our camp with a brass nine pounder, loaded with copper grapeshot, one of which took effect on the thigh of our brave Colonel Neil,[47] who had to return from the field dangerously wounded."

But The Twin Sisters' canister was too accurate and overpowering; the Mexicans pulled their only cannon back to their lines at the south end of the battlefield, where Santa Anna was backed up to a marsh, with a river on his right flank and to his left, a small bridge over a bayou—Vince's Bridge.

---

47   Col. James C. Neill. He was the first commander at the Alamo, but left to care for his family, who were seriously ill. He tried to bring 50 men to reinforce the Alamo but they were blocked by the Mexican Army.

Col. Sidney Sherman, commander of the Second Regiment of Texas Volunteers, urged Houston to turn the cavalry loose and attack as the Mexicans withdrew. He was sure they could turn the retreat into a rout. Like many in the Texian army, he was impatient with Houston's careful tactics, fed up with the long weeks of retreat, lathered up for action.

Houston shook his head and said "No." He ordered Sherman to scout but ordered him, "Do not engage the enemy."

Sherman and his men saddled up, rode out and almost immediately threw Houston's orders to the wind. The Texian Secretary of War, Thomas Jefferson Rusk, rode into the attack with Sherman's men, and reported on the action.

"Col. Sherman with sixty of our cavalry charged upon theirs, consisting of upwards of an hundred, killing and wounding several. Their infantry came to the assistance of their cavalry and opened upon us an incessant firing for ten or fifteen minutes which our men sustained with firmness.

"Too much praise cannot be bestowed upon those who were engaged in this charge, for never was one of equal peril made with more courage and terminated with less loss. Two of our men were severely wounded, but none killed. This terminated the movements of the day."[48]

Rusk had also sided with Sherman to impatiently urge Houston to be more bold. But he may have reconsidered that advice when he was unhorsed during the charge and found himself surrounded by Mexican lancers armed with long, needle-pointed stabbing spears like picadors at a bullfight.

As Rusk stood alone in the circle of lancers, Private Mirabeau Buonaparte Lamar came riding to the rescue. He charged his big stallion into the Mexicans and sent them flying like leaves in a gust of wind. He could see their astonished and frightened eyes as they looked up to see his horse's flaring nostrils, wild eyes and big square yellow teeth. At such close range, their seven-foot lances had no room to maneuver.

---

48   Texas State Library and Archives Commission, Sam Houston's copy of Secretary of War Thomas J. Rusk's Official Report of the Battle of San Jacinto, addressed "To His Excellency DG Burnet," dated April 23, 1836.

Lamar saw Rusk holding his right arm out and reached down, using his horse's momentum to lift him off the ground. Rusk swung himself up to ride just behind Lamar's saddle and off they went, furiously pounding away before the Mexicans could get organized.

The rescue was so gallant it drew cheers from the Texians *and* from the stunned Mexicans. Lamar, a superb horseman and fencer, risked his life to rescue two men that day, Rusk and Walter Paye Lane. For his gallantry, Lamar was promoted to colonel by Houston that evening and put in charge of the cavalry the next day. And after Sam Houston, he became the second elected president[49] of the new Republic of Texas in 1838.[50]

But while others cheered, Houston watched with bottled rage as more of his infantry disobeyed orders and rushed into the field. Sherman had "more zeal than discretion," he said. Such foolhardy recklessness made his carefully chosen high ground and small advantage in numbers meaningless.

And the premature attack by Sherman had shown Santa Anna all of his cards. He could no longer pretend to be outnumbered. Surprise would now be difficult or impossible.

The Texians, like Rusk and Sherman, were angry and frustrated that Houston held back. They wanted an all-out attack that first day. But Houston ignored them and spent the night planning the attack *his* way.

At the opposite end of the field, Santa Anna was now aware that he was facing a larger force than expected. He feared the Texians would attack any moment, before his reinforcements could arrive. He posted his

---

49   David Gouverneur Burnet of Cincinnati was the first president, unelected, serving as interim president of the Republic of Texas during the battle for independence, from March to October 1836. He was succeeded by his nemesis, Sam Houston, but became Lamar's vice president and secretary of state in 1838.

50   Lamar was elected almost unanimously when both of his opponents committed suicide before election day. Peter Grayson shot himself over a rejected proposal to a Louisville woman; James Collinsworth fell or jumped off a boat and drowned during a long drinking binge. Mirabeau Lamar went on to fight in the Mexican American War. Walter Lane became a Texas Ranger and fought in the Civil War as a Confederate with the Third Texas Cavalry. Rusk, a Christian Sunday school teacher, fought Indians and led the Texas militia. He committed suicide in 1857 after his wife died from tuberculosis while he suffered from a tumor in his neck. Rusk County and the town of Rusk, Texas, were named in his honor. Texas State Historical Association.

army at battle stations and put them to work building a flimsy defensive barricade of saddles, carts and brush. They worked all night and into the next day. As the Mexican soldiers tried to remain on guard for an attack at any minute, they lost their focus and grew weary, while their commander grew careless.

The next day at 9:00 a.m., General Martin Perfecto de Cos, Santa Anna's brother-in-law, led reinforcements over the only narrow bridge to the battlefield, bringing 500 men who had marched all night. Sam Houston and his Texians were now outnumbered, 1,250 to 935.

That's when Sam Houston burned his bridges.

He sent his scout, Erastus "Deaf" Smith,[51] to destroy the only bridge for either army, Vince's Bridge. They were all now trapped on the peninsula, surrounded by marshes, bayous and rivers. It would be a dog fight to the death.

The Texians who had questioned the resolve of their commander had to reconsider. There was no backing down, no retreat. Santa Anna had vowed no mercy, no quarter—and the Texians could not agree more.

In the afternoon, as his weary men waited and dozed, Santa Anna ordered them to stand down. Surely the Texians were just as tired, and now that they had seen his reinforcements there would be no attack. He retired to his tent for a siesta. Most of his men did the same.

But General Houston was just getting started. He had planned well. The battlefield was terraced by ridges from his high ground to the lower Mexican lines. Houston gathered his men and told them, "The army will cross and we will meet the enemy. Some of us may be killed and must be killed; but soldiers remember the Alamo. The Alamo! The Alamo!"

And with that, the Texians moved out through the tall grass, low and quiet, hidden by the ridges until they were just 200 yards from the Mexican lines. Their cavalry covered the flanks, hidden by trees along the riverbanks.

---

51   Smith had lost his hearing to a childhood disease. He was called "the bravest of the brave" by his commander at the Alamo, William Travis. It was Smith who captured the Mexican courier who revealed Santa Anna's whereabouts. He became a Texas Ranger and died in 1837. Deaf Smith County in Texas is named after him. Texas State Historical Association.

A small team of artillerymen in the middle of the lines hauled The Twin Sisters by hand, using rawhide ropes.

At 4:30, the Mexicans were caught completely by surprise with screams of "Remember the Alamo!" and "Remember Goliad." Once again, The Twin Sisters opened the battle with a deafening roar that shook the earth and ripped the Mexican barricades to shreds.

Colonel Roberts described how the artillery crews deployed The Twin Sisters, dragging them into point-blank range, loaded with devastating canister, ready to fire.

"We were not engaged more than twenty minutes. We fired eleven shots in that time, six from one piece and five from the other, but every one [shot] told. The last shot was fired seventy yards from the enemy's works, when we had to cease fire for fear of striking our own men, who were commingling with the enemy."

The newly promoted Col. Mirabeau Lamaar led the cavalry on the right, while the impetuous Colonel Sherman led his cavalry on the left. Not all of the Mexican Army was snoozing. "Upon arriving within reach of the enemy, a heavy fire was opened first with their artillery on our cavalry," Rusk wrote in his report the next day. "A general conflict now ensued, and the order was given to charge."

As the hot afternoon sun began to cast long shadows, the Texians overran the flimsy defensive wall and their withering fire drove the Mexican artillery crews into headlong flight. The Twin Sisters crews, meanwhile, hauled the cannons up to fire directly on the Mexican cannon "with great effect," Rusk wrote. "The cavalry under Col. Lamar fell on them at the same time with great fury and great slaughter. Maj. Gen. Sam Houston acted with great gallantry, encouraging his men to the attack, and heroically charged in front of the infantry to within a few yards of the enemy, receiving at the same time a wound in his leg."

At one point, Sam Houston was nearly killed by his own cannons.

"Then there were no percussion caps for cannons, and when Sgt. Ben McCulloch was in the act of firing his piece by touching it with a taper at the end of a rod, Gen. Houston, who had imprudently placed himself in front, passed in front of Ben's piece," William Physick Zuber recalled after the battle. "And, had Ben fired at that critical moment, he would have killed the general and his horse. But he saw the general just in time to jerk up the taper and let him pass."

Zuber, one of the artillery volunteers, recalled, "Our artillery charged to within ten feet of the enemy's breastworks and captured the Mexican cannon, which was loaded."

By then, the Texian infantry was "commingling" with the enemy in a surging tangle of howling Texians swinging rifles, stabbing with huge Bowie knives and taking their terrible vengeance for Santa Anna's "no prisoners" brutality. The Mexicans began to run and most never stopped until they were hip deep in the marshes or up to their necks in nearby Peggy Lake. Some of the Mexicans shouted, "No Alamo!" and "No Goliad!" Many had nothing to do with those massacres. They had been marched without mercy in the race to the battlefield. Some hated Santa Anna nearly as much as the Texians did. But the Texians had blood in their eyes and they shot them down as fast as they could reload.

Rusk described the scene: "Ten minutes after the firing of the first gun we were charging through the camps and driving them before us, who fled in confusion and dismay down the river followed closely by our troops for four miles. Some of them took the prairie and were pursued by our cavalry. Others were shot in attempting to swim the river, and in a short period the sanguinary conflict was terminated by the surrender of nearly all who were not slain in the combat."

El Presidente Antonio Lopez de Santa Anna, supreme dictator and the commander in chief who had given the orders to execute unarmed prisoners in cold blood, watched as his army collapsed all around him. He ran to grab a fast horse and rode it to Vince's Bridge, hoping to make his escape. But Deaf Smith had done his work well. The bridge was destroyed. The bayou there was not very wide, easily swimmable. But the supreme leader who ruled all of Mexico, who could command men to die for his slightest whim, could not part the waters and could not swim. He hid in the marshes that night—cold, wet, muddy, a raw feast for clouds of mosquitos and biting flies.

The next day the miserable, bedraggled president of Mexico was found and captured along with other prisoners. He had put on the uniform of a private, hoping to disguise himself and escape. All the gaudy gold braid, his ceremonial saber and medals were gone. He was filthy and utterly defeated. He might have slipped by unnoticed, but other Mexican prisoners laughed and pointed and gave him away.

San Jacinto veteran John Forbes was among the men who captured the dictator of Mexico. Santa Anna apparently changed his mind about being a private and threw himself in the way of the Texian patrol. He demanded to be taken to General Houston, Forbes said. He pulled out a letter and handed it to Forbes, pointing to the address: "Don Lopez de Santa Anna."

Forbes and the others were skeptical until they marched him past the Mexican prisoners and heard them call out, "El Presidente!"

They found Houston lying on a blanket outside his tent. He had been shot in the ankle while leading the charge in the middle of the battle lines. Houston was resting. "I put my hand on his arm to arouse him, he raised on his elbow and looked up," Forbes wrote. "The prisoner immediately addressed him, telling him who he was and surrendered himself to him as a prisoner of war. General Houston looked at him intently, but made no reply."

The secretary immediately confirmed it was indeed the president of Mexico. Santa Anna was given a seat in a chair beside Houston's blanket. His demeanor "was dignified and soldierlike but a close observer could trace a shade of sadness on his otherwise impassive countenance," Forbes recalled.[52]

Houston quickly realized the Mexican president was worth much more alive than dead. The Texians wanted to do to him what he had done to the prisoners at the Alamo and Goliad. A hanging would be too good for him. But Sam Houston played the right cards.

---

52   Texas State Library and Archives Commission, "Surrender of Santa Anna." Testimony of John Forbes. Forbes was from Cincinnati and moved to Texas with his wife Emily Sisson in 1835. In Texas he was elected as a judge and administered the oath of allegiance to new recruits, including David Crockett. He was put in charge of all the property captured from the Mexicans at San Jacinto and was later given 960 acres of land for his service.

He told Santa Anna that if he wanted to live, he must send orders to all of his commanders in Texas to immediately withdraw back to Mexico. And he would have to agree to a free and independent Texas. Santa Anna had no choice. He could see that only Sam Houston stood between him and the angry Texians who wanted to shoot him on the spot. So he traded a peace treaty for his own life.

The main Battle of San Jacinto on that second day lasted fewer than twenty minutes, but the slaughter of the fleeing Mexicans went on for hours into the afternoon. Those who fled into Peggy Lake on the right flank of the Mexican lines were killed and drowned in such numbers the water turned red. The Texicans had brothers, uncles, fathers and friends who were massacred at the Alamo and Goliad. They would have their revenge.

Unable to stop the killing until they were exhausted, Houston said, "Gentlemen, I applaud your bravery, but damn your manners."

San Jacinto veteran Lyman Rounds wrote, "In twenty minutes we had them on the run and before sundown we stretched eight hundred of [them] on the field never to rise."

His estimate was high but understandable. When all the killing was done, 630 Mexicans were dead, 208 were wounded and 730 were prisoners. Only nine Texians were killed or wounded so badly they would die within days. Another thirty of the Texians had less serious wounds.

The following day, Rusk filed his report: "Never in the annals of war was the interposition of divine providence so signally displayed."

The voice of providence sounded like The Twin Sisters from Cincinnati.

Among the spoils of war were "several hundred mules taken, with much valuable baggage."[53]

---

53   In 1895, relatives of Gen. Sam Houston sent Santa Anna's dagger to the City of Cincinnati "to show Cincinnati that Texas has not forgotten the prominent part the Queen City played in their struggle." The dagger had a solid-gold hilt with a pure turquoise scabbard. The dagger was part of Santa Anna's personal baggage that was given to Sam Houston in appreciation for sparing his life. The dagger was received by Cincinnati Mayor John A. Caldwell and was entrusted to the Cincinnati Art Museum. In 2024, a spokesperson for the Art Museum said the dagger could not be found and no images of it were available. In "A Dagger, the Famous Weapon Once Carried by Santa Anna," *Cincinnati Post*, April 6, 1895, the newspaper reported that the Twin Sisters cannons would be shipped to Cincinnati where they would be displayed at City Hall. That never happened.

Rusk singled out the valor of Wharton, Sherman, Lamar and others. "This glorious achievement is attributable not to superior force but to the valor of our soldiers and the sanctity of our cause," the Secretary of War reported. "It was freemen fighting the minions of tyranny. ... Hateful despotism cannot find a resting place for the sole of her foot upon the beautiful plains of Texas."

April 22, 1836 was one of those pivotal points in time that changed the world, when the river of time flooded its banks and changed the landscape of Texas and America forever—not only on the battlefield at San Jacinto but for all the generations to come.

Santa Ana, defeated and disgraced, met with Interim President David Burnet and signed the Treaties of Velasco. The first, made public, promised Mexico would withdraw from Texas, retreat below the Rio Grande and end the war. A prisoner exchange was arranged. And the new Republic of Texas agreed to send Santa Anna back to Mexico.

The second treaty was secret. Santa Anna would be released if he would work to make Mexico recognize the new independent Texas.

Both sides ultimately refused to honor both treaties. That led to the Mexican-American War in 1846.

Eager to expand and establish the border, President James K. Polk sent American soldiers into a disputed region of Mexico. When they were attacked, as expected, he used it as a pretext to declare war, telling Congress that the "cup of forbearance has been exhausted, even before Mexico passed the boundary of the United States, invaded our territory and shed American blood on American soil."

Santa Anna violated his promise and fought Texas again, but Mexico was defeated in 1848. The US won possession of almost a million square miles of land that would become California, Texas, New Mexico, Utah, Nevada, Arizona and parts of Colorado, Oklahoma, Kansas and Wyoming.

It was the first US war on foreign land. It opened the West to settlement in a vast territory that was almost the size of the rest of the country. And it staged an elaborate dress rehearsal for the American Civil War about a dozen years later. The generals and soldiers who would clash

North against South fought alongside each other, made friendships and learned their craft in the war against Mexico.

"One of them was General Lew Wallace," Duffy said to Amos and Nehemiah as he closed his story.

"And all of that was made possible by those cannons sent by Cincinnati?" Nehemiah commented.

Duffy nodded. "The man who persuaded the fine people of Cincinnati to send them was my grandfather. So you can understand, I hope, why I could not join the Confederates and wage war on the fine people who saved Texas."

"I had imagined something quite different when you offered to tell us an exciting story about twin sisters," Amos said with a wink. "But as a man who was long married, I can understand how those cannons came to be named after females. In my experience, they seldom lose a battle."

Nehemiah thought about it and replied, "In my recollection, the weapon I feared more than Martha's cannons was her silence."

"Leave it to a woman to believe she can punish a man by not talking," Amos laughed.

"And leave it to mush-head men like me to make it work," Nehemiah agreed.

August 1792

'Come ahead and try'

Replica of flatboat at Sharon Woods Heritage Village Museum, Cincinnati.

It had been Kenton's plan to scout the Shawnee camp, then go back and bring the other men to help rescue the prisoners, but once he reached the Shawnee campfire and saw that firelit horror, he could not wait. When he finally brought back the hostages, the rest of the rescue party grumbled about being deprived of their chance for revenge, but they were grateful to have the prisoners back—with one exception. The man burned at the stake was the brother of one of the men from Maysville, Kentucky. Simon and Bailey spared him the details and simply told him his brother had been killed—not how or by whom. Whatever scene his imagination painted would not be worse than the truth.

And as the Maysville man swore his vengeance through sobs, one more ruthless Indian fighter was made.

The next morning, they headed back to Covalt Station. It took them a long day and a half to cover the thirty miles back to the banks of the Little Miami. As they emerged into the clearing that surrounded the stockade, Bailey shouted, "Don't fire upon us! It's Reason and Simon Kenton. We have the hostages."

The heavy plank gates quickly opened, and they were swarmed by the families inside the station. They had shared their misery, grief and fear. Now they would share their joy.

Covalt Station was named after Revolutionary War Captain Abraham Covalt, who brought his wife and eleven children down the Ohio River in 1790 on big flatboats loaded with forty settlers and a menagerie of pigs, sheep, horses and cattle. Also packed aboard were various tools and implements and two millstones to establish the first flour mill in the Miami Valley. Like many settlers, they quickly began cutting trees to make a clearing in the wilderness for homes, crops and gardens. They broke up their flatboats for lumber to begin construction of a 100- by 400-foot stockade known in those days as a "station."[54]

Nearly all of the settlements were on land that was owned and sold by wealthy New Jersey lawyer John Cleves Symmes, a speculator and member of the Continental Congress. He had loaned the government a fortune to finance the Revolutionary War, then took his IOUs back in the form of more than 311,000 acres in the Miami Valley—the Symmes Purchase.[55]

Covalt Station was nearly as big as Fort Washington, which was finished just before the Covalt party landed, enclosing 40,000 square feet.[56] Also known as Bethany Town, Covalt Station was built with gun ports that allowed a crossfire to protect its walls from every direction. Land surrounding the fort was cleared of trees to give the men inside the

---

54 Early, Steven Jr. *Amid the Honorable Plenty: The Story of Covalt's Station and Ohio Frontier Settlement 1790-95.*

55 Also known as the Miami Purchase. Symmes sold land he did not own and sold land twice. He sold the Miami Valley with rosy promises to Revolutionary War veterans and left his name on Cleves and Symmes Township.

56 Fort Washington was at the west end of Lytle Park in downtown Cincinnati, near the northeast corner of East 4th Street and Ludlow Street.

fort an unobstructed field of fire, making it more difficult for Indians to surprise the settlers. But the Covalt stockade was so large it was difficult to defend without aid from the troops at Fort Washington.

By the time Kenton returned with the rescued hostages in the fall of 1792, it had been abandoned for several months, then reoccupied that spring. Cheneniah Covalt, a skilled Indian fighter like Bailey, brought Kenton up to date on the recent tragedies.

"First my brother Abraham Jr. was killed and scalped in January a year ago, along with Joseph Hinkle, our miller, who was tomahawked so severely his head was nearly removed from his neck. They were out hunting when they were ambushed. Then my father, Captain Covalt, was killed a few months later. And Abel Cook. And a man named Demitt was taken from Round Bottom station a few miles west of here. We believe he was burned. Hinkle left a widow and five young'uns.

"After that, we lacked men to defend the walls, and few were eager to hunt for the food we needed to survive. Losing my father, the Captain, was more than most could bear. So we marched to Fort Washington for protection."

Kenton nodded. It was a familiar story in Maysville, Boonesborough and other stations across the Ohio River to the south. *They arrive with flatboats full of children and dreams and quickly discover that the land of plenty is a dark and bloody ground that has no mercy,* he thought. *But the land lust is so strong they would die to get a piece of something they could never own in the Old Country.*

"My father often wondered," Cheneniah Covalt said, "how do we bring more men and families that are desperately needed to settle this wilderness, yet still prepare them for the savage attacks in summer and the black shadow of starvation in the winter?"

He reached into a jar and took out a folded paper that he opened and began to read from it: "Herds of deer, elk, buffalo and bear, turkeys, geese, ducks, swans, teal, pheasants, all in greater plenty than the tame poultry are in any part of the old settlements of America."

Covalt paused and looked up at Kenton. "This is from a handbill that was circulated widely, as far as Britain, Germany and France, but mainly in the eastern states. It was found on one of the bodies we recovered from the river after Shawnees attacked their flatboat."

"I reckon no mention of Miamis, Wyandots, rattlesnakes, copperheads, water moccasins, wolves, panthers, bears, ice storms, starvation and swamp fevers?" Kenton asked with a wry smile. "Or how those bears have a taste for man flesh since so many dead were left in the woods by Indian massacres?"[57]

"No, but you will find boasts of 80-pound catfish and rich soil that can produce wheat, rye, corn, buckwheat, oats, tobacco, indigo, silk, wine and cotton."[58]

The two were in Covalt's cabin, which formed a part of the station wall. It was the day after Kenton, Bailey and the hostages had returned. The Maysville group had agreed to stay a few days. The Indians would follow soon to retaliate. Every rifle, tomahawk and pair of hands to use them might be needed.

In a cabin nearby, Kenton could hear a child crying and a mother's heartbreaking comfort. The two men sat on crude furniture made of upright sawn logs for seats, with a small table made of planks and tree branches lashed together. In one corner was a bed of forked branches driven into the ground to support tree-limb rails covered with planks and a rough blanket. The settlers in Bethany Town had learned that furniture was disposable: a bed and table might be needed to feed fires through the winter.

"The children will be a long time troubled," Kenton said, tipping his head in the direction of the sobs and wails. "Nobody should ever see what they saw."

Covalt nodded. He understood. He had seen what was left after the Shawnees had a few days of sport with their prisoners. He got up and closed the cabin door, and thought again how Kenton had ducked his head and shoulders to enter. The ceiling beams were nearly as low, so that the giant woodsman also had to stoop when standing. It was dark

---

57 Doddridge, Joseph. *Notes on the Settlement and Indian Wars*, 1997.

58 Howells, William Dean. *Amazing Stories from the History of Ohio (Illustrated)*. Good Press, 2024.

inside, even at noon. The only window was small, covered in newspaper that had been oiled with lard to let in a thin, amber light. It could be used as a gun port, but if the Indians got inside the walls, it would probably be too late to save the settlement.

The Covalts, Baileys and others like them had arrived with nearly nothing and created a village in the wilderness with ingenuity, courage, determination, backbreaking work and sheer willpower. Everyone worked. Everyone shared whatever they had—including their victories and tragedies.

Outside, against the front wall, a crude ladder of lashed branches provided quick access to the lean-to roof that slanted up and outwards, making a platform for gun slits in stockade walls that were made from axe-sharpened poles anchored deep in the ground.

Kenton thought again about what Covalt had said earlier: How much should be told to settlers about that hazards they would find if they were lucky enough to make it to the new settlements in Indian country on the north banks of the Ohio? He had never considered it because he was kept too busy rescuing the flatboats full of pilgrims who could make it past Indian ambushes, and burying the families who did not.

He knew there were many like Benjamin Stites, founder of Columbia Station, and John Cleves Symmes, who were evangelists for the new frontier, with a firm belief that it was God's will to settle and civilize the new lands. Stites had 20,000 acres he had purchased from Symmes; Symmes had more than 300,000 acres. And both were eager to sell their land for a profit. They were not shy about spreading the word, even in newspaper advertisements about the "Eden" of rich lands and opportunities in the Miami Valley.

Stites and other men who established stations were also brave, gambling their own lives and the lives of their wives and children. Many new pioneer families were captured and killed before their flatboats arrived at Columbia, Fort Washington, North Bend Station or Covalt Station.

Kenton shook his head, and asked, "When was that handbill printed?"

Covalt replied, "It says it's from Reverend Manasseh Cutler,[59] Ipswich, Massachusetts, 1787."

"How is it someone from Massachusetts knows so much about the Northwest territory?" Kenton said. He stirred his pipe and relit it with a burning twig that Bailey pulled out of a small stone fireplace in his cabin. "Maybe best to just tell them the truth about the hazards," Kenton continued. "I see no shortage of pilgrims willing to come here. They have earned a share of this land by serving in the recent war. The way I hear tell, the government is too broke to raise fiddler's pay. All of us who fought to create this country will get naught but a thank-you, if that. Our only reward is land to be watered with our blood and a war against the Indians to keep it."

"True words," Covalt said. "If the attack on Dunlap Station[60] didn't discourage settlement, I guess nothing will."

The story of Dunlap Station, about twenty miles northwest of Fort Washington, was told and retold on the frontier. On January 8, 1791, a party of surveyors was attacked near the stockade. One was immediately killed and scalped, and Abner Hunt was taken prisoner. Two others made it back to the station. The men in the station prepared for defense while the women melted their spoons for bullets.

On January 10, several hundred Indians approached. It had rained and snowed five inches the night before, which saved Dunlap Station from being torched. The Indians used Hunt as a hostage, threatening to kill him if the gates were not opened. Lt. Jacob Kingsbury, in command, wisely refused.

A resident of Columbia Station near Cincinnati described what followed.

"The Indians had tied their prisoner to a sapling within sight of the garrison, who distinctly hear his screams, and built a large fire so near as to scorch him, inflicting the most acute pain; then as his flesh

---

59   Cutler, a Revolutionary War veteran, was part of the party that settled Marietta, Ohio. McCullough, David G. *The Pioneers*, 2019. He visited once, briefly, and did not return. His pamphlets were written before he saw any of it. McCullough, David G. *The Pioneers*, 2019.

60   Also known as Fort Colerain, it was on the Great Miami River, built in 1790.

from the action of the fire and the frequent application of live coals became less sensible, making deep incisions in his limbs, as if to renew his susceptibility of pain...."[61]

The siege lasted two days. One of the surveyors, John S. Wallace, escaped and ran to Columbia Station[62] for help. The Indians were gone by the time the rescue party arrived. The Indians lost about a dozen killed; Abner Hunt was the only settler killed.

Covalt stirred the fire and said, "My father and two brothers fought the British and took their payment in land. Few were better prepared for combat. And yet they are killed."

"The failure of Harmar and St. Clair have only made the Indians stronger and more bold," Kenton said, referring to the catastrophic punitive expeditions.

The first, led by Gen. Josiah Harmar in October 1790 had been such a spectacular disaster it cost the lives of 130 men—who could not be spared on a frontier where even a half-dozen men could mean the difference between life and death at a station under Indian attack.[63]

That disaster was put in the shade a year later by St. Clair's Defeat, when Gen. Arthur St. Clair, the governor of the Northwest Territory, led 2,000 regulars, militia and volunteers north from Fort Washington in Cincinnati.

"Harmar and St. Clair drew away all the soldiers we appealed to for protection," Covalt said. "The tales of the survivors who returned to Fort Washington were so bleak we thought all was lost. Did we fight and win the war for independence only to become such a feeble nation we cannot even protect our own families?"

"You have to take the long view, like the Shawnee," Kenton replied. He propped his long legs up on another piece of "furniture" that could have been a stump outside the stockade. "In the early days, they were

---

61 Spencer, Oliver M. *Indian Captivity in the Neighborhood of Cincinnati*, 1848.

62 Near Columbia Tusculum in Cincinnati, the city's oldest neighborhood, founded by Benjamin Stites in 1788.

63 The battle took place in what is now Fort Wayne, Indiana, where the St. Joseph's and St., Mary's Rivers meet to form the Maumee River.

almost willing to tolerate a few of us south of the Ohio River because that was their 'Middle Ground,' shared by the Shawnee, Miami, Wyandotte, Delaware, Iroquois, Potawatomi, Mingo, Ottawa, even Mohicans and others. It was their sacred hunting ground, shared by all.

"But this land here," Kenton pointed at the dirt floor. "This is Shawnee land. None of those other tribes would dare to settle here. Not even the Iroquois. The Shawnee are that fierce. But we did. And they intend to drive us out or kill every last one of us, man, woman and child. They are in for the long fight. If we intend to stay here, we have to fight until there are no Indians left to fight back."

Covalt nodded, but asked, "They would fight even without the British bounties on our scalps?"

"I reckon yes. I lived with the Shawnee for months—which even a minute was altogether longer than I would have liked. They have their own code of honor. They only respect a man who is strong enough to die without showing he cares. Sometimes, a man like that will be spared or adopted by the tribe, like I was."

"I think I'd rather die," Covalt said.

Kenton chuckled. "That's the spirit. The only way to live and survive capture is to welcome death and take the worst torture without a flinch. One of their favorite stories was told of a Miami warrior captured by the Shawnee, who mocked them as they burned him to death."

"But why the cruelty? They shot my father in the back. He fought like a panther, yet they still tomahawked him as he was dying. By the time we got to him I did not even know his face."

"If you are not Shawnee, the warriors consider you less than human and they can do whatever they wish to white people. They have been visiting the same cruel tortures on their captives from other tribes for centuries, as far as I can tell."

"It hardly seems that *they* are human," Covalt said. He told Kenton about the funeral for his father and Hinkle. It was attended by settlers from nearby stations—Round Bottom, Columbia and Gerard's Station.[64]

---

64   It was located on the east bank of the Little Miami near what is now Stanbery Park, west of Mt. Washington.

"Lt. John Gano brought fifty militiamen from Columbia to discourage attacks during the ceremonies. They tried to catch up with the raiding party but lost their trail."

As Covalt spoke, Kenton felt a troubling foreboding like a shadow across the moon. It was an instinct or sixth sense for danger that he had learned to respect. It had saved his life on many occasions.

"And then there was the schoolteacher at Columbia, John Newell," Covalt continued. "He was riding here to have some of his corn ground in the mill. Indian signs had been spotted in the area and along that trail, and he was warned, but came on anyway. We found him dead and scalped on the trail, his horse and grain gone. That was in September."[65]

Kenton stood suddenly, nearly cracking his head on the low, beamed roof. Covalt went silent as Kenton cocked his head to listen for a minute, then grabbed his rifle and ducked out the doorway with three words: "They are here."

Kenton was already climbing to the roof when Covalt emerged, banging an iron pot with the back of his tomahawk to alert the station. "Take your positions and prepare for attack!" he shouted.

As the men poured out of their cabins carrying rifles, the first shots came from the woods surrounding Covalt Station. They were followed by war whoops and high-pitched shrieks as the Shawnee raiders came running across the cleared ground in bright red, black and yellow war paint.

Behind the Stockade walls, men began to return fire as a few flaming arrows arced over the walls. One landed on a cabin roof, where an alert woman with a pail of water quickly climbed a ladder and put out the flames before they could spread.

Kenton waited until the Indians got close enough for a certain shot and put his sights on a warrior who was leading the charge. He pulled the trigger and immediately began to reload. As the smoke cleared he saw the man was down, writhing in agony, clutching his chest.

---

65   Early, Steven Jr. *Amid the Honorable Plenty: The story of Covalt's Station, an Ohio Frontier Settlement, 1790-95.* Steven Early, 2022.

The fire from the fort was thick now, almost steady as the men paced their shots, reloading and firing at a rate of about three shots per minute—some quicker, some slower, but all good marksmen. They had been attacked before. They knew what to do. Below them, many of the women in the fort stood by with axes, knives, frying pans and pistols, looking frightened but grim, prepared to do whatever it took to protect their children if the men should fail.

The Shawnee party was large, Kenton noticed. Something near fifty. Covalt Station was outnumbered two- or three-to-one. It would be a hot battle. He settled in and continued to load and fire, not even bothering to keep track of the warriors he killed and wounded. He knew his shots were true and deadly.

Another flaming arrow flew over his head and fell harmlessly in the middle of the station where it was quickly extinguished. Gradually, the Indians began to pull back. The firing slowed, then stopped. A single man stepped from the woods wearing a dark blue Continental Army coat over buckskin leggings and moccasins, with a single red-tailed hawk feather in his braided queue. His face and bare chest were streaked in stripes of blood-red paint.

Blue Jacket himself. *Red Snake must have had powerful medicine in the tribe*, Kenton thought.

When Blue Jacket got within thirty yards, Kenton shouted, "Stop and state your business. Talk small or I will put a ball through your eye."

Blue Jacket took one more step in defiance, stood, crossed his thick, muscled arms and looked up at Kenton. "Butlah. I hear you chirp. I will be happy to again see the hole I once put in your skull when I lift your hair."

"Come ahead and try," Kenton said.

"He talks good English," said Covalt, who was nearby.

"Some say he's a white man like us, but I disbelieve it," Kenton replied. "If he once't was, he ain't now."[66]

---

66   The legend that Blue Jacket was a kidnapped white boy named Marmaduke Van Swearingin has been disputed by historians and undermined by DNA testing.

Blue Jacket spoke again. "Butlah, yes. I will come ahead and try. I will hang your hair in a place of honor among many scalps in my wigwam. Or you can surrender. I will spare all but you. Maybe you, if you can run the gauntlet again in our village. We will see if you are still strong with your god's medicine."

"Go on and empty the bag, Blue Jacket. Tell the rest."

"If you wish. When we open your gates, your fort will burn and many in it. We will take scalps and prisoners for Detroit. Our women have not had good sport with prisoners in half a moon. They laugh when they burn feet and fingers. And when there is not pain left there, they cut off the feet and fingers and start burning again. A big man like you could last many sunrises. Would you like more from this bag?"

Behind him, Kenton could almost feel the fear of the women and children as Blue Jacket's words drew pictures in their imaginations.

"Bark at the moon," Kenton said harshly. "You have enough mouth for three faces. By my reckon, we have already taken a dozen of your warriors. We have plenty of shot and powder we would like to give to the rest of them. I have one ball I would like to give to you right now."

Blue Jacket took a step backward, then recovered his war face. "You could make a dog laugh, Butlah. I will have great pleasure when I watch you burn."

Kenton had lined up his shot carefully as Blue Jacket spoke. His target was the war club on Blue Jacket's waist—the same one Blue Jacket had used on Kenton. His shot knocked the man down. The top of the club—a smooth oval river stone attached to a hickory stick with rawhide—deflected the bullet, but the war club was broken. Blue Jacket was badly bruised but slowly stood again, showing no sign of the intense pain he felt. Kenton chuckled and said softly, "Now we're settling accounts."

"So it will be," Blue Jacket said.

"And so it will be you as dead and cold as a January cucumber if I see your hide again," Kenton replied.

As Blue Jacket walked back into the woods, Kenton turned to Covalt.

"Tell the men to make sure they are loaded and ready. Fill the water buckets. They are coming again."

This time the Indians were more careful. They used stumps in the clearing for cover and put shots into the gate, hoping to damage it or break the stout hinges. "West side!" a man in the blockhouse on that side of the stockade called out.

The new frontal attack was a diversion for a party of more than twenty who rushed the narrow end of the station where the livestock were kept outside the walls. Some of the men at the walls quickly shifted to the west side. Kenton jumped off the roof and loaded as he ran to that end of the fort. As he arrived, they let loose on the attackers with all they had. Four fell in the dirt and were dragged away. Two made it as far as the stockade and climbed over the sides of the livestock fence.

One put a hand over the top of the stockade, but had it quickly hacked almost off his arm by an axe. The other was shot point-blank by the man from Maysville, who leaned out over the side to make the shot and then lurched backward with a yelp, taking a ball in his shoulder.

After half an hour of furious gunfire, the Shawnee retreated again. *Just like Boonesborough and Dunlap Station*, Kenton thought. *Thank the Lord the Shawnee have not figured out how to defeat a stockade.*

In the corral at the west end, two of the settlers' cattle were killed, along with one sheep. One horse was wounded, two others stolen. But Kenton smiled. *We will eat well tonight*, he thought. *Beef and mutton.*

He shot one more Indian who poked his head up over a stump. The head snapped back and the warrior slumped sideways without a sound. He would be left there until dark. None would dare to retrieve the body under "Butlah's" gun.

As the fighting paused again, Kenton climbed down to take a look at the man from Maysville, who had already lost his brother. He saw that the ball had gone clean through, breaking the man's right collar bone. He would recover. But he would not wrangle a plow, pick corn, ride or shoot a rifle for weeks—a sentence of death on the frontier unless someone could be found to care for him.

There's that Hinkle widow with five children, Kenton thought. *And this man with no kin left.*

But that could wait. Blue Jacket had now lost about half of his raiding party, with more wounded and unable to fight. He was a smart leader. Kenton figured he would withdraw back to his village in Chillicothe and wait for another opportunity for revenge on Covalt Station or some other unlucky settlement that was not so well defended. It didn't matter to Blue Jacket, as long as he took two or three scalps for every warrior he lost.

Kenton was right. As the sun set, Blue Jacket vanished back into the wilderness just before a party of militia from Columbia Station came to Covalt Station, marching to the sound of the battle. They were led by Major John Gano, a man Kenton wanted to meet. At the time, Columbia Station was as large as Cincinnati, with about 40-50 cabins built with gun ports and heavy planked doors, clustered around the stockade like ducklings around a mother duck.[67]

He was impressed by Gano. As the men talked, Kenton learned that Gano's father had been a chaplain for George Washington's army. The chaplain's son, John Stites Gano, had left Morristown, New Jersey, and became one of the first to step ashore on the north bank of Ohio in November 1788, where he helped to build Columbia Station. John Gano had just been made major in command of the 1st Division of Hamilton County Militia.

"I heard you was with St. Clair last year when that butchery took place," Kenton said. They sat sharing some bark tea around a small fire to push back the autumn evening chill.

"Aye," Gano said. "St. Clair was no Captain Grand fool. Without his brass to call the last charge, not a one of us would have come back to tell the story. But he was so crippled by gout, he never should have led us."

"I've never had the misfortune to know it, but I hear it's like broken glass in your feet and knee hinges," Kenton said.

"Must be. During the battle, General St. Clair was so crippled he crawled about on hands and knees like Nebuchadnezzar eatin' grass,

---

67   Spencer, Oliver M. *Indian Captivity*, 1848.

shouting orders as the men were fleeing all around him. We finally got him up on a packhorse and from there he ordered the final bayonet charge. It was all clapper-claw in every direction, and gardyloo for your own arse."

"He was not brandy-faced drunk?" Reason Baily asked.

"Any who say that have mouths so big they eat with a coal shovel. They probably were not there to see it, as they were first to strap wings on their feet. No, the general was no beef-head. He was swearing like a bosun with a face like murder, but he got the men organized into a line with bayonets open for business, and that was our Jacob's Ladder out of hell. Otherwise, they would have made mice feet out of us. Which they did, anyway, survivors such as myself notwithstanding."

Kenton learned that there was talk in Philadelphia of forming an army to avenge the embarrassing defeats of Harmar and St. Clair, to finally put an end to what Major Gano called "the murderous invasions of numerous savages."[68]

Kenton said, "I was otherwise occupied and unable to join General St. Clair, but I lost some good friends from Kentucky there. And now I have the opportunity to learn more about it from two of the men who survived. You and Covalt, here, who I understand was the only one of his brothers who came back alive."

Covalt nodded. "It is still choking hard to speak of."

Together, they told Kenton the story of the Battle of Wabash, as they preferred to call it.

---

68   Gano, John Stites. Letter from the Gano family papers, Cincinnati History Library and Archive, Cincinnati Museum Center.

Fall 1791

'Skulking about in considerable numbers'

Gen. Arthur St. Clair portrait
by Charles Wilson Peale, 1782-84.

The Indians attacked at sunrise and they were everywhere.

Cheneniah Covalt was camped with the militia on the north side of the Wabash River, where the Indians hit first. He had not slept all night. As one of the scouts who was sent out the evening before, he had quickly encountered signs of a very large camp of Indians who were infiltrating the woods all around the army's positions on both sides of the river.

It was clear they would be attacked at dawn. This was reported to Maj. Gen. Richard Butler, but he did not want to disturb General St. Clair, who he believed was finally asleep in his tent across the river, resting from the agony of gout that plagued him.

Maj. Jacob Fowler, one of the founders of Newport, Kentucky, was with the Kentucky Militia. He had been through hell in the previous year's disaster known as Harmar's Defeat. And now he saw the same mistakes being made again.

"Excepting in a single instance, St. Clair kept out no scouting parties during his march," he recalled later, "and we should have been completely surprised by the attack when it was made, if it had not been that volunteer scouting parties from the militia were out on the evening before and the constant discharge of rifles throughout the night warned us to prepare for the event."

Lieutenant Ebeneezer Denny recalled, "The frequent firing of the sentinels through the night had disturbed the camp and excited some concern among the officers. The guards had reported the Indians to lie skulking about in considerable numbers."

The next morning, more musket fire crashed in the woods as St. Clair ordered his bugler to sound reveille and rushed to strap on his belt and painfully pull on his boots for battle. The shots were Little Turtle's signal to begin closing the noose around St. Clair's army. A wave of 1,000 Indians immediately overran the 270 members of the Kentucky and Ohio militia on the north side of the river, and many were killed as they tried to scramble up the steep riverbanks.

Cheneniah Covalt fled with the rest, running through the woods as men around him fell. He finally gained the higher ground, his rifle clutched in his right hand, tomahawk in his left, and ran for his life to get back to where the regular army should have formed a square of artillery, bayonets and muskets.

That was not what he found.

As St. Clair emerged from his tent, there was a crashing in the woods as Covalt and other men of the militia began to pour across the Wabash River into St. Clair's camp. As they emerged from the trees and undergrowth, wild-eyed men ran through the regular army, some wounded and bleeding, all of them blinded by panic in their headlong flight to escape the screaming Indians coming on their heels.

"Those men carried terror like a sickness," Lt. John Gano told Simon

Kenton as they smoked their pipes around a fire in Covalt Station. "It spread faster than fire on spilled lamp oil. The general never should have put the militia on the opposite side of the river. When they came back through our camp, many of the men on our side ran too."

Kenton pictured the scene: St. Clair's lines were broken almost as soon as the battle began. Kentucky Militia members who survived that terrible day had told him their camp was made foolishly on low ground, almost impossible to defend.

"The general was in poor shape. We tried to get him up on a horse. He could not stand on his own very long without aid," Gano continued. "And it seemed every time he got onto a horse, it was shot from under him. Later we counted eight holes in his hat and uniform where balls had passed through."

As St. Clair's men tried to meet the attack, the new-fallen snow was quickly churned into a mix of muddy, bloody red slush as the soldiers were cut down by gunfire from both flanks, from the front and back. Many rushed to huddle together in the middle of the camp, to find comfort and courage. But they only made themselves easier targets.

"Between the powder smoke from our own guns and the trees they hid behind, we couldn't see anyone to shoot," Covalt said. "The enemy was smart and disciplined, unlike anything I have seen before. They used the cover to advance and kept pouring lead, tomahawks and arrows into us. Every tree, fallen log or stump seemed to hide an Indian."[69]

Miami Chief Little Turtle and Shawnee Chief Blue Jacket had planned the battle well. They led the largest force of warriors that had yet gone to war against the white invaders in Ohio. They led warriors from several tribes. In addition to the Miami and Shawnee, Chief Pipe[70] led the Delawares, Chief Tarhe led the Wyandots, and warriors had

---

69 "They advanced from one tree, log, or stump to another, under the cover of the smoke of our fire." Major Ebenezer Denny. "The Battle of the Wabash and the Battle of Fort Recovery: Mapping the Battlefield Landscape and Present-Day Fort Recovery Ohio," National Park Service, Ball State University, Ohio History Connection and Fort Recovery Historical Society.

70 Chief Pipe was said to be seven feet tall. He said later he "slaughtered white men until his arm was weary with the work."

come from the Ottawas, Cherokees, Chippewas, Mingos, Kickapoos, Mohawks, Piankeshaws and Potawatomis.

The United States was in its first battle since the Revolutionary War, and it was flailing, overwhelmed, surrounded.

General St. Clair was a tough veteran of the brutal French and Indian Wars. Then he had crossed the Delaware with George Washington on a frigid December night in 1776, to fight the British at the Battle of Trenton. He was no stranger to the sound of screams and gunfire, the smell of sulfur and the clouds of choking, eye-stinging smoke from cannons and muskets. As the battle dragged on for hours, he realized his men could be annihilated.

All through a sleepless night of agony from his gout-swollen feet and ankles he had heard shots in the woods as his scouts fired at Indians. But the Chickasaw Indian scouts he had brought along had failed him. He had no idea that his poorly prepared army of 1,400 was facing an alliance of nearly 1,500 Indians.

His battery of artillery—deadly four-pounder and six-pounder cannons—could be devastating if they could only see the enemy. The cannons cut loose with round shot that felled small trees, then loaded canister that spread fans of deadly projectiles into the woods. But the trees provided a natural shield. And when the Indians crossed the river in front of his lines, the cannons could not fire low enough to reach them and fired uselessly over their heads. Once under the guns, the Indians advanced and the artillery crews were cut to pieces with rifles, arrows, tomahawks, warclubs and knives in hand-to-hand struggles.

"Concealed as the Indians were, it was almost impossible to discover them and aim the pieces to advantage; but a large quantity of canister and some round shot were, however, thrown in amongst them," Winthrop Sergent[71] wrote in his diary.[72]

---

71 A veteran of the American Revolution, Sergent was wounded twice in the battle but heroically led counterattacks, then retreat.

72 "The Battle of the Wabash and the Battle of Fort Recovery: Mapping the Battlefield Landscape and Present-Day Fort Recovery Ohio," National Park Service, Ball State University, Ohio History Connection and Fort Recovery Historical Society.

Little Turtle was easy to spot. He was a big man, leading his warriors in full, colorful battle dress. He flanked St. Clair's rectangle on the right and from behind, while hundreds more hit the left flank. As St. Clair ordered a bayonet charge to clear the woods in his rear, the Indians overran his camp on the left, and 200 unarmed camp followers—women and children—were slaughtered as they cowered helplessly alongside their husbands and fathers in the snow.

It was November 4, 1791. What began as a mighty expedition to punish the Shawnee and avenge the defeat of the army just a year ago, had gone terribly wrong.

*   *   *   *   *

When General Arthur St. Clair arrived at Fort Washington on January 2, 1790, it was as if the struggling settlers finally had their own George Washington to lead them out of the darkness to victory. The square-jawed general was elegant and imperious. He was a close friend of Washington, and a hero of the Revolutionary War, like Washington. He had served among the Founding Fathers as a delegate and president of Congress when the Constitution was written—also like Washington.

From a distance, he even looked like Washington—especially in his uniform of buff pants and deep blue tunic with gold lapels and epaulets.

But upon closer inspection, he was fat and old, limping and crippled.

Still, the Scotsman St. Clair was everything the beleaguered, terrorized pilgrims along the Ohio River could hope for. He was among the men who created the Northwest Territory with the historic Northwest Ordinance, after the Treaty of Paris in 1783 officially ended the American Revolution. The new United States had won its independence and Great Britain was forced to retreat into Canada and grudgingly give up its claims on all the new lands east of the Mississippi.[73] At least on paper.

---

73 When the British insisted that the Ohio River would be the western boundary of the United States, John Adams said, "No! Rather than relinquish our claim to the western territory, I will go home and urge my countrymen to take up arms again and fight till they secure their rights or shed the last drop of blood." The British gave in. McCullough, David G. *The Pioneers,* 2019.

The Northwest Ordinance was the first founding document to contain a Bill of Rights and prohibit slavery. That was partly because tobacco growers in the existing states feared competition from slave owners in the new states. But it was also because many of the men who drafted the Ordinance abhorred slavery. The Ordinance regulated surveying and land sales in a territory that doubled the size of the United States, with almost 266,000 square miles. In addition to banning slavery, it said that "education shall forever be encouraged" and promised absolute religious freedom.

The doors to the vast new territory had been flung wide open and settlers were pouring over the Allegheny Mountains down the Ohio River.

In a speech that year, Washington said, "May the same wonder-working Deity, who long since delivering the Hebrews from their Egyptian Oppressors and planted them in the Promised Land—whose providential agency has lately been conspicuous in establishing these United States as an independent nation—still continue to water them with the dews of Heaven and to make the inhabitants of every denomination participate in the temporal and spiritual blessing of that people whose God is Jehovah."

St. Clair was sent to save the Promised Land.

He was appointed by President Washington as the first governor of the Northwest Territory and given orders by the president: Punish and "awe" the Shawnee and Miami Indians and make the new wilderness safe for settlement.

One of the first acts of the new governor when he arrived at Fort Washington was to replace the homely name of the struggling little village that was clinging to the skirts of the stockade.

But it was an awkward name for a city that would tame the frontier. It needed something inspiring, that called forth the spirit of the Revolution.

St. Clair met with the men who had founded the small settlement[74]

---

74   Robert Patterson, Matthias Denman and Israel Ludlow.

and offered a new name to honor President Washington. Both St. Clair and Washington were members of the Society of Cincinnatus, named after the Roman hero who left his farm to save the republic, then declined to be emperor and returned to his farm—very similar to how Washington had declined to be king.

Washington, a founder of the Cincinnatus Society, was known as "The American Cincinnatus."

"Cincinnati," St. Clair suggested.

The other men were in no position to disagree. James Filson, who had chosen "Losantiville," could not object because he had disappeared three years earlier, probably taken and killed by the Shawnees. And the other founders thought that here at last was their own Cincinnatus to save their tiny new empire. "Cincinnati" sounded fine.

St. Clair also named the new county after his friend General Alexander Hamilton, and took command of Fort Washington, a solid, imposing, two-story stockade with sturdy blockhouses and high walls that represented what the earliest settlers desperately yearned for: safety, power and security.

The soldiers inside the fort were too few and badly demoralized. Most were survivors of Harmar's Defeat just a few months before, when Little Turtle had slaughtered their expedition. But now General St. Clair had orders to build a new army, with the support of President Washington, who owned a large parcel of land near Covalt Station and had nearly been killed in the Ohio River Valley during the French and Indian War.[75]

St. Clair planned to lead an army of 4,000 to Kekionga,[76] the large settlement that was the capital of the Miami nation. He would annihilate the Indians and burn their village and their crops. The Shawnee and other tribes would get the message: The Shemanese "long knives" were settling the Northwest Territory and they were here to stay.

---

75 Washington never forgot his days surveying and fighting in the Miami Valley, and probably had the beautiful, rich land of Ohio in mind when he spoke of the "Promised Land."

76 Now Fort Wayne, Indiana.

But his plans began to fall apart almost as soon as they were made, riddled by the termites that infested the new US government even from the start: corruption, bureaucracy, paperwork, stupidity and endless delays and more corruption.

President Washington ordered St. Clair to launch a summer campaign, when the weather would favor his troops with dry trails and plenty of grass for his horses. But Quartermaster General Samual Hodgdon, in charge of logistics and supplies, refused to leave safe Pittsburgh, where he wasted the summer months making deals with a crooked supplier.

General William Butler was assigned to recruit fresh soldiers. But the pay approved by Congress was so low, he was forced to resort to emptying prison cells to fill the ranks.

The supplies that arrived were late and shoddy. Uniforms were old and badly made; guns were outdated, poorly made, broken; and gunpowder was shipped months late or not at all. Axes were flimsy and defective, rations were terrible, the troops were sent very slowly on insufficient boats, and the horses and mules were far short of the contract agreement even before many died from incompetent handling.[77]

The quartermaster and recruiting general were supposed to report to Fort Washington by July 15. They did not arrive until September, when St. Clair, in frustration, had already left the fort and was marching his army north—only 2,000, not the 4,000 he had been promised.

St. Clair left Fort Washington on September 6, 1791. On their first day's march, his troops covered just one mile. And almost immediately, some of the men began to desert. As they trudged north in the warm September sun, the army carried "heavy baggage," which was the soldier's slang for women and children—camp followers.

---

[77] The investigation of St. Clair's Defeat by the US Congress in 1793 was the first congressional oversight investigation. It established a tradition that has been honored for more than two centuries: As congressmen bickered and dithered, the investigation dragged on for more than two years and was inconclusive. President Washington and his cabinet set the precedent for Executive Privilege by excluding any requests for documents that "might harm the public." The final report found "gross and various mismanagements and neglects in the quartermaster's and contractor's departments." Quartermaster Hodgdon was demoted. Everyone else was let off the hook.

The "Caterpillars," as the soldiers called themselves, moved at inch-worm speed, seldom making more than five miles in a day. As they made a path for the artillery, the crude trail had to be improved with axes and saws and bridges had to be built. By September 30, the army had covered just over thirty miles and St. Clair stopped to build Fort Hamilton.[78]

It was intended to be the first link in a chain of forts that would anchor new settlements. St. Clair named it after another friend, Treasury Secretary and future President Alexander Hamilton.

He left behind a few dozen soldiers he could not spare to garrison the fort and resumed the march north. Two weeks later, on October 14, he stopped and began work on a second stockade, Fort Jefferson.[79] Also called Fort Depot, it was intended to stockpile supplies—if and when the supply convoy ever caught up.

The desertions continued. At Fort Jefferson, men whom Gen. Butler had signed up for six months now had their enlistments expire and went home. As the army leaked away its muscle, it was watched closely by Indian scouts who reported to Little Turtle and Blue Jacket.

An early winter hit St. Clair's army as he left Fort Jefferson. A hard frost destroyed fodder for the pack animals and made the men miserable in their flimsy, poorly made uniforms. The nights were frigid. More deserted.

One night, a group of sixty militia not only deserted, but threatened to intercept and raid the long-missing supply convoy. After they disappeared, St. Clair ordered the 1st Infantry Regiment to follow and protect the convoy, losing another 300 regular army soldiers he could not spare.

Late on November 3, the army reached the banks of the Wabash River. They were worn out, wet, cold, surly and demoralized. Gen. St. Clair decided it was too late to dig rifle pits or cut logs for defensive fortifications. He thought he was much farther north, near Kekionga. In fact, he was in the jaws of a bear trap set by Little Turtle.

---

78   Now the city of Hamilton. Fort Hamilton was located near the intersection of High Street and Monument Avenue.

79   Near Greenville, Ohio. Fort Jefferson Memorial Park is at 3981 Wavers-Fort Jefferson Road, Greenville.

Ironically, St. Clair had made the same mistakes made by the British in the American Revolution. He formed his men in a rectangle in an open area with artillery along the sides, making them easy targets for encirclement by Indians who were shooting from cover; he divided his force on the way up and again when he arrived; he did not post adequate scouts on the journey, or protect his men with defensive fortifications when he arrived.

In a word, he had made the classic mistake of underestimating the enemy. Hubris.

As the battle raged on, St. Clair valiantly tried to rally his men, stumbling about on gout-crippled feet until he was finally crawling on his hands and knees. His troops hoisted him onto another horse, and he called for a retreat. But to escape south back to the trail they had made, they would need one more bayonet charge to clear the way. It was led by Lt. Col. Willaim Darke, whose Maryland Battalion and other units used their nearly 17-inch icepick bayonets—"long knives"—to clear

"St. Clair's Defeat," by Rufus Fairchild Zogbaum, in *Harper's New Monthly Magazine*, 1895, illustrating an article by Theodore Roosevelt.

just enough opening for the survivors to flee back to Fort Jefferson, thirty miles south.

They only escaped because the Indians stopped to loot their camp.

Cannons, supplies and weapons were left behind in the snow. So were nearly all of the wounded, including many helpless children and women, who joined their dead fathers and husbands in the next world as they were tortured, murdered and scalped.

General William Butler was shot twice and died in his tent—one of the first generals killed in what would become the new US Army. As the retreat began almost four hours after the battle started at 6:30 a.m., arrows were raining on the camp along with bullets, as the Indians ran low on gunpowder.

Major Jacob Fowler shot Indians until his rifle broke, then found another rifle that had been abandoned by its owner—presumably dead—and continued fighting. It was so cold his stiff fingers went numb so he fed bullets into the muzzle with his mouth.[80] Finally, when he saw that the battle was lost, he ran to find his cousin, Captain William Piatt of North Bend Station. "I told him that the army was broken up and in full retreat."

"Don't say so," Piatt replied, "You will discourage my men, and I can't believe it."

They argued briefly, and Fowler gave up. "Finding him obstinate, I said, 'If you will rush on your fate, in God's name do it.' I then ran off towards the rear of the army, which was making off rapidly. Piatt called after me, saying 'Wait for me.' It was of no use to stop, for by this time the savages were in full chase and hardly twenty yards behind me."[81]

As Fowler ran, he passed two Indians who fired at him almost point-blank, but both missed. Chased by dozens of warriors, he ran through a meadow that was littered with so many dead soldiers he had to be careful not to trip over them.

---

80   Howells, *Amazing Stories from the History of Ohio* (Illustrated). Good Press, 2024.

81   "The Battle of the Wabash and the Battle of Fort Recovery: Mapping the Battlefield Landscape and Present-Day Fort Recovery Ohio," National Park Service, Ball State University, Ohio History Connection and Fort Recovery Historical Society.

"Being uncommonly active in those days, I soon got from the rear to front of the troops, although I had great trouble to avoid the bayonets which the men had thrown off in the retreat, with the sharp points towards their pursuers."

Others later reported seeing Captain Piatt sitting near a tree, wounded. They tried to help him, but he said, "Go on and leave me. Save yourselves. I am too badly wounded." He was never seen again.[82]

By the time his straggling line of survivors limped into the safety of Fort Jefferson, St. Clair had lost nearly a thousand soldiers, including almost 200 of their wives and children. There were 918 killed and 276 wounded. Almost half of the army was dead or wounded.[83]

Only about thirty of the warriors in the allied tribes had been killed.

When President Washington heard of the defeat, he was furious. He demanded St. Clair's resignation and told Congress, "We are involved in actual war!"

Congress agreed to fund an army sufficient to avenge the defeat and formed the Legion of the United States,[84] to be led by Revolutionary War hero Anthony Wayne, at Washington's request.

An investigation by Congress exonerated St. Clair of misconduct.[85] He returned to Cincinnati and Fort Washington and served as territorial governor until 1802, when his scheme to divide Ohio into two states was rejected by President Thomas Jefferson and he was dismissed.

Men such as Major William Fowler, Lt. John Stites Gano and scout Cheneniah Covalt were undaunted by the slaughter at St. Clair's Defeat. They joined the next battle against the Indian nations with General "Mad Anthony" Wayne a couple of years later.

Another veteran Indian fighter who survived St. Clair's Defeat was

---

82 "The Battle of the Wabash and the Battle of Fort Recovery: Mapping the Battlefield Landscape and Present Day Fort Recovery Ohio," National Park Service, Ball State University, Ohio History Connection and Fort Recovery Historical Society.

83 Feng, Patrick, "The Battle of the Wabash: The Forgotten Disaster of the Indian Wars," The Army Historical Foundation.

84 The beginning of the US Army.

85 Buffenbarger, Thomas E., "St. Clair's Campaign of 1791: A Defeat in the Wilderness that Helped Forge Today's US Army," US Army Heritage and Education Center, September 15, 2011.

typical of the courage and grit that carved out homes in the wilderness. Col. Robert Patterson was one of the original founders of Losantiville before it became Cincinnati.

In 1776, he was returning to Kentucky from Fort Pitt (future Pittsburgh) when his party was attacked by Indians. He was shot twice through his arm, breaking the bone, then tomahawked in the back. He survived and four years later he joined George Rogers Clark in 1780 when Clark attacked and destroyed the Indian village of Chillicothe.

Colonel Patterson fought in the American Revolution as a Minuteman. In 1782, as the war was ending, a force of 300 Indians and fifty British Rangers attacked Bryant Station in Kentucky.[86] Patterson led his Lexington Militia to the rescue, driving off the raiders.

With the help of 130 men inside Bryant's Station, who were led by Daniel Boone and Col. John Todd, Patterson and his men chased the attackers and caught them at the Battle of Blue Licks.[87]

In a letter asking the governor of Virginia for 500 more men, Daniel Boone reported details of the battle on August 30, 1782:

> Notice being given to the neighboring stations, we immediately raised 181 horsemen commanded by Col. John Todd, including some of the Lincoln County militia, commanded by Col. Trigg, and having pursued about forty miles... we discovered the enemy lying in wait for us.
>
> On this discovery we formed our columns into one single line, and marched up in their front within about forty yards before there was a gun fired. Col. Trigg commanded on the right, myself on the left, Major McGary in the center, and Major Harlan the advance party in the front. From the manner in which we had formed, it fell to my lot to bring on the attack. This was done with a very heavy fire on both sides, and extending back of the line to Col. Trigg, where the enemy was so strong that they rushed up and broke the right wing at the first fire.

---

86   Now a neighborhood in northeast Lexington.

87   Southwest of Maysville on the Licking River in Robertson County, Kentucky.

Thus the enemy got in our rear, and we were compelled to retreat with the loss of seventy-seven of our men and twelve wounded. Afterward we were reinforced by Col. Logan, which made our force four hundred and sixty men. We marched again to the battleground, but finding the enemy had gone we proceeded to bury the dead. We found forty-three on the ground, and many lay about which we could not stay to find, hungry and weary as we were, and somewhat dubious that the enemy might not have gone off quite. By the sign we thought the Indians had exceeded four hundred; while the whole of this militia of the county does not amount to more than one hundred and thirty.

It was the last battle of the American Revolution in Kentucky. Patterson marched to fight with St. Clair as a colonel of the militia in 1791 and became Ohio Quartermaster in the War of 1812. He went to his grave in 1827 still suffering pain from his wounds in the Indian attack of 1776. He was a founder of Lexington, Cincinnati and Dayton.[88]

*   *   *   *   *

After hearing the stories from Covalt and Lieutenant Gano, Kenton thought about what could have been done differently if he had been there on the Wabash River as a scout. He would not have allowed St. Clair to blunder into such a trap. The Kentucky Militia and its Ohio brothers would have made a stand on better ground. But fighting the allied Indian nations on their ground in winter was a fool's errand.

"I'm for leaving tomorrow at sunup," he told the men. "Two days is more than I can abide behind walls."

"Many is the man who envies the ranger," Covalt said. "You are out there free, while we are in our stockades. These walls are a prison as well as protection. Our women cannot step outside the gates for months at a time, and even then, only with a guard of armed men. We are often like bait on a hook, attacked relentlessly with no opportunity to strike back. We lose our loved ones, our children, our wives and parents. Inside

---

88   Wright-Patterson Air Force Base in Dayton is named after Robert Patterson.

we starve, outside we are murdered and tortured."

Kenton had to admit to himself that he did not share the same bottled-up frustration, rage and fury at the Indians. He had his revenge wherever he found it. He took the battle to the woods, on their trails, in their hunting grounds and in their villages.

Lieutenant Gano asked if the men had heard of the preachers in the East who condemned the pioneer savagery against the Indians. "Columbia Station will pay thirty dollars for a scalp with the right ear attached, to prove it's an Indian," he said.

"I don't hold with that, but I understand how some do," Kenton said. "An eye for an eye, a scalp for a scalp. I might do the same if my own wife and son were taken. But I have not heard of any Indians burned at the stake or tortured for days. Except by other Indians."

"All well and good for the gospel shops in Philadelphia," Covalt said. "If their pastors are anything like their jaw-me-down lawyers, they have lungs like bagpipes and strangle the truth in its crib."

Kenton nodded, looked over both shoulders, and said softly, "If they could but see what those poor children saw...." He paused. "These lands around us fall far short of Eden. But the Shawnees could teach school in hell."

Secrets of the Knights

J.W. Pomfrey was a wealthy man. His stately brick home was on Second Street in Covington, just a block south of River Street, on the dog's ear of land where the Liking River marries the Ohio. A block away was Carneal House, the stately home of one of the founders of Covington, Thomas Carneal, who was a friend to senators, presidents and foreign leaders, including the Marquis de Lafayette.

Duffy lifted the large brass knocker at Pomfrey's creamy white door and dropped it twice. There were footsteps within, and the door was opened by a man whom Duffy thought resembled his mansion—brick-solid, wide and tall, with a bay window jutting over his belt.

Pomfrey wore an expensive tailored wool suit of dark gray, with a thick gold chain looping from a vest button to his watch pocket. As if to confirm the contents of the pocket as well as the hour of the meeting, he retrieved a fat gold watch, pushed a button to open the lid, peered at it and nodded as if he reluctantly consented to the time of day.

"You gentlemen are prompt," he said, stepping aside. "I've been expecting you."

"The general sends his regards," Duffy replied, extending a hand.

After introductions, Pomfrey led them past the parlor to his library while Nehemiah and Amos trailed behind as they gaped at the silk covered parlor furniture and Amos took a fright at his own image in a tall mirror over the mantel.

In the library, they were amazed again. Tall windows lit the room with shafts of sunlight that played gentle shadows on rose-pink walls, making echoes of the leaves dancing in the breeze among the tall oaks outside. It made Nehemiah think of his humble little log home in the forest—hardly bigger than Pomfrey's parlor.

They were waved to large, leather-covered easy chairs so soft that Amos wondered if he would sink right though the floor, then wondered how he would get back to his feet. Pomfrey took a seat behind a large desk on which his business was organized like a street grid, with perfectly squared stacks of paper making the city blocks.

What is it these people do with all that paper? Nehemiah wondered, remembering General Wallace's cluttered desk.

As if to answer, Pomfrey said, "I'm a trader, gentlemen." He pointed to the stacks in turn and said, "Molasses, boots, hides, tobacco, uniforms, powder. That's just one boat, the *Kenton*[89], which is between contracts for military transport. Before the war began, I would handle three or four steamboats a week like this one. But the *Queen of the West* and others have been drafted by the army. The war has been very hard on our local economy."

"Hard on many soldiers as well," Nehemiah rumbled.

"My apologies," Pomfrey said, "I had no intention to offend. You are right, of course. If my sons were not working for the quartermaster, they would be eager...." He noticed the look on Nehemiah's face, and the dark scowl from Amos, and let the thought go unfinished. "But enough about business. How can I help?"

"Our Friend Detective Reaney led us to believe you may have knowledge of a society known as the Knights of the Golden Circle," Duffy said.

Pomfrey drew back, cleared his throat and looked suddenly less assured. "Yes, I think I can help. But I need to be careful—and you should be as well. Let me explain. I was nearly aboard the *Moselle* when she exploded in 1838, at the Fulton boatyard across the river.[90] More

---

89 The sternwheel packet built in 1860, capacity 215 tons, was called into service for the Union and served off and on during the war as a troop transport. Nash, Francis W., *Georgetown Steamboats*, 2009.

90 The *Moselle* was among the fastest riverboats on the Ohio. The explosion happened as it was leaving the boatyard, just east of Cincinnati. All four boilers simultaneously blew up. Witnesses who survived said Captain Isaac Perin had caused the disaster by ordering excessive boiler pressure to race the *Ben Franklin*.

than half of the three hundred passengers were burned, scalded to death by steam or drowned. This endeavor could blow up in a like manner."

It was the first really fall-like day of September, with welcome relief from the heat of the previous weeks, but Duffy noticed drops of sweat crawling down into Pomfrey's bushy side whiskers that the soldiers called "sideburns," after Union General Ambrose Burnside. He thought of the young men who had died in the mud of Corinth and the cornfields of Kentucky and he lost his patience.

"We are well acquainted with hazardous duty, sir," Duffy said, waving a hand at Nehemiah and Amos. "I was assured you were already aboard this particular *steamboat*. But if you choose not to join us, I can talk to General Wallace about helping your eager sons get a good look at the elephant."

"That won't be necessary, I am aboard," Pomfrey quickly replied. He reached into a drawer and pulled out a pamphlet. "I published this last year at my own expense and have come to no end of grief for it."

Nehemiah cleared his throat with an ominous growl and Pomfrey hastily amended, "Not the personal grief of losing a son I cherish, but there have been elements hereabouts who have made things... more difficult. Some have made threats. Perhaps you have heard of the Vigilante Committee of the Knights of the Golden Circle? No? They are quite active on both sides of the river. Their commander is Sergeant Elmer Butcher of the Cincinnati Police. He is protected by Mayor George Hatch, who, if not a member, certainly likes to give the impression he is one."

Nehemiah's caterpillar eyebrows rose and wiggled and he winked at Amos as if to say, "Flummadiddle, if that ain't some pumpkins!"

Amos chuckled and thought, *Sergeant Butcher is going to get his timber sawed.*

The booklet Pomfrey handed to Duffy was titled, *A True Disclosure and Exposition of the Knights of the Golden Circle: Including the Secret Signs, Grips, and Charges, of the Three Degrees, as Practiced by the Order.*[91] At the bottom was "J.W. Pomfrey."

---

91   Published in 1861. J.W. Pomfrey lived in Covington.

"Might have spared some of that tragical personal grief had you not put your name in big letters on the front," Amos said dryly after leaning over for a peek.

"I confess that I underestimated their reach—as I fear too many have," Pomfrey said.

Duffy flipped through a few pages and said, "This may prove useful. Please tell us what you know."

The story began with Mexico and the attempted filibusters of Cuba and Central America, Pomfrey said.

"William Walker was able to set himself up as the ruler of Nicaragua in 1855 with only three hundred men," he said. "That was powerful-strong catnip to a man like George Bickley.[92] And not just Bickley. Private invasions of Mexico had support from Texas, most southern states, all the way to the White House."

As Pomfrey told it, a man who claimed to be a doctor showed up in Cincinnati in 1851 and became a professor of phrenology[93] at the Eastern Medical College in Cincinnati, and also a professor of medical jurisprudence in the Ohio Law School.[94]

"As I discovered too late, it was all bosh," Pomfrey said. "Bickley is a highly skilled hornswoggler, but he is nonetheless dangerous."

Bickley then married a widow who was an heir to a wealthy Cincinnati banking family, the Kinneys, but he was caught trying to put her fortune in his own name. "It was quite a scandal." Pomfrey said. "The brother-in-law, Eli Kinney, sent him packing, but they kept it out of the newspapers, of course. He was thrown out on his ample assets."

---

92   Southern California lawyer William Walker invaded Mexico in 1854, to create a Republic of Baja California. That failed, but he exploited a civil war in Nicaragua a year later and took over the capital, even winning recognition as president of Nicaragua by the US government in 1856. He was deposed and fled 10 months later in a dispute over shipping rights with Cornelius Vanderbilt but became an American hero. He was executed in Honduras in 1860 while attempting another "free-booting" private takeover called a "filibuster." Pruitt, Sarah, *Hundreds of 19th Century Americans tried to Conquer Foreign Lands. This Man Was the Most Successful*. History, 2019.

93   The 19th century "science" of predicting behavior by the shape of a person's skull.

94   Fesler, Mayo, "Secret Political Societies in the North During the Civil War," *Indiana Magazine of History*, September 1918.

Well aware of the success and fame of Walker's filibuster, and the national support for the Texas War for Independence, Bickley hatched an idea. It began with an emblem: A Maltese cross over a lone star. "And thus was born the Knights of the Golden Circle."

Duffy said, "In Texas we knew it as the Order of the Lone Star of the West. George Chilton, commander of the Texas Rangers, was a grand poohbah. So was Sam Houston, I was told, until he found out that Bickley was a fruit fly in a snuffbox. Which made sense, I reckon, seeing as how Texas was happy to have help to put hobbles on Mexican outlaws and push the border deeper into Mexico."

"Exactly," Pomfrey said. "If Bickley is any kind of doctor he is a doctor of chicanery. But the man is no short-wick candle. He is bright. His plan to invade Mexico drew more applause than the Dance of the Seven Veils. He even boasted of support from President Buchanan and members of his cabinet."

Nehemiah said, "Are you saying our own government gave the giddy-up to some shoddyocracy invasion of Mexico?"

"Yes and no," Pomfrey said. "When I was involved in the organization, it was well known that President Buchanan would not enforce the Neutrality Act if some private army was *invited* to civilize Mexico. Hell, his vice president, John Breckinridge, wore the KGC cross and star on his lapel.[95] But this was much more than one tinhorn. After the Knights of the Golden Circle merged with the much larger Order of the Lone Star in the South—Bickley's doing—they became the most powerful shadow society throughout the South and as far north as New York, Connecticut, New Jersey, Delaware and Maryland."

"And Indiana, Ohio and Kentucky," Duffy added.

"Correct," Pomfrey said. "The society had its founding in Cincinnati where there is still quiet but enthusiastic support. One of the most

---

95   Breckinridge, from Kentucky, was the Southern Democrats' candidate for president in 1860. He was accused by Kentucky Sen. John Crittenden of being a KGC member and wearing KGC jewelry. In 1861, Breckinridge was expelled from the US Senate, 36-0, as a "traitor." He served as a major general in the Confederate Army at Shiloh and other battles, then became the Confederate States Secretary of War. After the war he fled to Cuba and England, finally returning to Kentucky in 1869, to practice law.

ruthless leaders is in Indiana. And Kentucky has been among the most generous states."

Pomfrey told how he had been recruited by Bickley as a knight of the second degree, to provide financial aid and supplies. "As you can imagine, I was well chosen for this role with my resources as a river trader. Here's the card he presented to me."

Pomfrey reached into the drawer again and withdrew a business card that showed a Confederate flag with "KGC" in bold type across the stars and bars. At the bottom it said, "General George Bickley, Mexico and a United South."

Duffy whistled. "Very impressive."

"I was a second-degree knight," Pomfrey said proudly. "First-degree Knights were the most common—open to any white man between 21 and 50 who could carry a gun and pay a one-dollar initiation fee and monthly dues of five cents. They were recruited with extravagant promises."

"I have witnessed such vaporizing in person," Duffy nodded. "More promises than Dr. Feelgood's Liver Liquor. Recruitment from the ranks. A guarantee of six hundred and forty acres in Mexico. Seven dollars a month to go liberate the oppressed Mexicans from tyranny...."

Pomfrey nodded. "That was for the foot soldiers. The Knights of Second Degree would get much more land, and Bickley and his Knights of the Third Degree—politicians, military men—would have their choice of plunder. Bickley was most generous to Bickley. He promised himself three thousand acres of the best land in Mexico."[96]

"And by arranging to be *invited* to Mexico's party, it would be no violation of the Neutrality Act?" Duffy asked.

"Precisely. Bickley assured all of us that he had a personal invitation from Benito Juarez, leader of the opposition in the Mexican Civil War. He may have been right. General Juarez was losing, and needed reinforcements, even if he had to trade power and land. But when Juarez

---

96   Enlisted men were promised 640 acres; lieutenants, 960 acres; captains, 1,280, majors, 2,560; commander-in-chief (Bickley), 3,200. Fesler, Mayo, "Secret Political Societies in the North During the Civil War," *Indiana Magazine of History, September 1918.*

started winning and Presidente Miramon fled to France last year, Bickley realized he had the wrong pig by the ear and began to embrace a new cause, secession."

Nehemiah took an old clay pipe from his pocket, lit it and asked, "How is it so many popeyed gullibles were snookered by Bickley's promises? Couldn't they foretell he would never milk the pigeon?"

"Some caught on and called him a thief and a fraud. They pointed out how all those dues seemed to evaporate when they got near General Bickley. He couldn't turn water to wine, but he turned words into moonshine, and many were the fools who got blind-monkey drunk on his dream to create a new American empire from Canada to Patagonia. You're looking at one of them."

"I took the oath and kissed the Bible myself," Duffy said. "Nearly all of the Texas Rangers did. Having more Southern states to balance the power of the North sounded fizzing. They said it was no different than France joining our cause of freedom in 1777."

Pomfrey said, "I heard that comparison too, at an 1859 meeting at the Greenbriar Hotel in Tennessee. Senators, congressmen, governors— even President Buchanan's secretary of war and secretary of the interior were there. Bickley claimed he had forty-eight thousand members and promised to raise an army of a hundred thousand."[97]

"As I recall, fear played no small part in recruitment of men and gold," Duffy said.

"True, General Bickley played fear the way General Wallace can play a fiddle. And he had an orchestra of newspaper editors and a chorus of politicians following his sheet music."

Duffy turned to Nehemiah and Amos and asked, "Are you gentlemen familiar with the Texas Terror?"

They shook their heads. "No, but *you* might fit the description," Nehemiah said.

Duffy laughed and said, "A bad fire nearly burned the town of Dallas in 1860. The editor of the newspaper, a member of the Knights,

---

97   Keehn, David C. *Knights of the Golden Circle.* LSU Press, 2013.

quickly blamed it on a slave uprising and the fear spread faster than the fire. Everyone was palaverin' about St. Domingue in 1791, when a hundred thousand slaves burned more than a thousand plantations and killed twenty-five thousand whites.[98] Before long, the whole state was in a panic. Vigilantes killed more than a hundred Texas slaves, and the Knights spread word through their newspapers that the slave rebellion was directed by President Lincoln."

"I imagine they found fertile ground for those seeds of hysteria," Pomfrey said. "The South was eager to believe the worst about Lincoln and the North. Before the cause became abolition, it was the Tariffs of Abomination, designed to steal Southern cotton for northeastern textile mills with tariffs that strangled sales to Europe. As a trader, I can recognize truth in the claim by Bickley that the North has stolen more than a hundred million dollars a year from the South.

"It should not be surprising that cotton states like Texas wanted to even the odds by adding new slave states in Mexico. All the immigration went to the North, and with it went all the votes and power of the Congress. The South was no better than a serf, tilling the land for the Northern masters."

Duffy said, "So the plot to raise an army to invade Mexico was easily refashioned to support secession and raise troops for the Confederacy."

Pomfrey said, "With a few strokes of his purple pen. After the invasion of Mexico went tail down, Sam Houston turned against the Knights. Bickley needed new 'gullibles,' as Mr. Woods put it. He promised to use the Knights to shut down the Underground Railroad and create a slave empire that could triple cotton production.[99] He soon had new castles hatching like boll weevils."

Amos frowned, shook his head and said, "I can track a fish through water, but I cannot follow what Paddy-gonyah, France and all this

---

98   Present-day Haiti. The rebellion spread to a five-year race war, killing more than 100,000 French and British soldiers and 200,000 blacks. Statista, 2004.

99   Bickley promised in writing: "No more negroes will be spirited away on the famous Underground Railroad. There will not be a free negro in the southern States in 1870, and your cotton production will be fifteen instead of five million bales." Fesler, Mayo, "Secret Political Societies in the North During the Civil War," *Indiana Magazine of History, September 1918.*

gullyfluff about Mexicans and weevils has to do with us."

Duffy said, "Keep going, Mr. Pomfrey. Tell him how the Golden Circle comes back around our necks like a noose at a necktie party."

"Well, I will try," the trader said, raising a hand to show three fingers. "At the meetings I attended, we discussed three goals for the northern states. Encourage and protect Union soldiers to desert with their weapons; encourage and protect draft resisters and sabotage recruitment; and prolong or stop the war.[100]

"There have been murders of Union soldiers at home on leave—by the Knights. Recruiting has dried up like a creek in a drought in some counties of Indiana. Thousands of soldiers have deserted, and many have joined the Knights with their weapons. The recent victories by the Confederacy, the unpopular draft and the butchers' lists of the dead in our newspapers have all done their part to turn people against the war. But make no mistake, the Knights have been very active in Ohio, Indiana, Kentucky, Illinois and Missouri."

Duffy said to Nehemiah and Amos, "It is that third category that concerns us, gentlemen. 'Stop or prolong the war.' General Wallace's good friend Indiana Gov. Oliver Perry Morton has built an extensive network for espionage—"

"Can you put that in American?" Amos interrupted.

"Spying," Duffy replied. "Men like me, who are secret agents of the governor, pretending to be Knights of the Golden Circle so we can attend meetings and report their plots and plans."[101]

Pomfrey said, "So that is the origin of Governor Morton's investigation, and the grand jury report this past August?"

Duffy nodded. "General Wallace told me there were sixty indictments for treason and conspiracy."[102]

---

100 Fesler, Mayo, "Secret Political Societies in the North During the Civil War," *Indiana Magazine of History, September 1918.*

101 ibid.

102 From the grand jury report: "Said grand jury has abundant evidence of the membership binding themselves to resist the payment of the federal tax and to prevent the enlistment in the Army of the United States. In localities where the organization extensively prevails there has been a failure to furnish a fair proportion of volunteers. The meetings of the order are held in by-places,

Nehemiah blew a cloud of smoke and asked, "How do these scallywags hope to stop the war?"

"They have plots for that, as well," Pomfrey said. "Mr. Bickley and his moonshine circus are coming to Cincinnati soon—very quietly, according to my informants who attend meetings of Golden Circle Castles on both sides of the river."

Amos interrupted, "I have seen fine hotels and houses hereabouts, but I have not seen any castles. Do tell where are they? Do they have bridges that lift into the air and guards wearing pots and pans?"

"Castles is what they call their local groups," Duffy explained. "They are not as splendid as the name might suggest. The meetings are often held in abandoned buildings, barns or in the woods."

"As I was saying," Pomfrey continued, "there may be a meeting soon that General Wallace would like to *adjourn* before it gets started."

Duffy asked, "Something similar to the Greenbriar meeting?" He turned to Amos and Nehemiah. "You see, gentlemen, one of the topics discussed by Bickley and his inner circle at the Greenbriar Hotel was a plot to seize Washington and prevent the inauguration of President Lincoln. Am I right, Mr. Pomfrey?"[103]

"Yes sir. My informants tell me that the same group of men who nearly took the president's life in Cincinnati in January 1861, as he traveled by train to his inauguration, are meeting again to discuss another try."

Nehemiah said, "I cannot read the most recent newspapers where I live, but I would have expected to hear something about that."

"It was not publicized," Pomfrey said. "A bomb on the president's train car was discovered before it could blow him and the entire coach clean to Columbus. It was kept mum so as not to encourage others."[104]

---

sometimes in the woods, and at other times in deserted houses; its members frequently attend with arms in their hands, and in almost every instance armed sentinels are posted to keep off intruders. The credulous and unwary are often allured into the fold of the order upon the pretext that it was instituted for no other purpose than the better organization of the Democratic party."

103 Keehn, David C. *Knights of the Golden Circle*. LSU Press, 2013.

104 President-elect Lincoln's Inaugural Train arrived in Cincinnati on February 12, 1861. (In those days, presidents were not inaugurated until March.) He gave speeches and stayed at the Burnet House

"Regarding this meeting, do you have names?" Duffy asked.

"I trust this will not come back to me?" Pomfrey said.

"I don't think you will have trouble with Sergeant Butcher, if that's what spooks your donkey," Nehemiah said.

"We will practice discretion until it no longer avails," Duffy said.

Amos snorted. "Call me old rustyguts, but that sounds like bacon-faced hooey. Why all the shinning around? Nehemiah, are we still in company with the same mopus we found eatin' his toenails in the woods?"

Nehemiah laughed, Duffy joined in and Pomfrey finally asked, "Can someone tell me what that man just said?"

Nehemiah answered, "He said give us the names."

Pomfrey grudgingly reached into a drawer for a fresh piece of paper, dipped his pen in an inkwell and began to write.

"We've already discussed George Bickley, whose name is at the top," Pomfrey said, passing the paper to Duffy. "The second name is well known in Indiana. The third man is known only by his codename 'Brutus,' and his alias, J.B. Wilkes—"

"Well sit on my spurs, if that second hombre ain't Colonel Bowles!" Duffy interrupted. "General Wallace will be dash-fire pleased to see that." He turned to Amos and Nehemiah, "They have unsettled business."

Pomfrey continued, "The fourth name on the list is one of my best informants, Klaus Wolff."

"Scheisse!" Amos blurted.

Duffy stared. Amos laughed. Pomfrey said, "Yes, Klaus is German. Almost half of Cincinnati is foreign born and two-thirds of them are Germans. He is an excellent purchasing agent, which enables him to travel to many castles."

Hotel overnight. The next morning as he prepared to leave, "A grenade of the most destructive character" was discovered on his train car just before he boarded. The grenade had "force sufficient to have demolished the car and destroyed the lives of all the persons in it." *New York Times,* February 18, 1861. All along his route to Washington, Lincoln had death threats from Copperheads and the Knights of the Golden Circle. His chief of security, Alan Pinkerton, hustled him off the train in a disguise when they reached Baltimore. His guards offered him a pistol and Bowie Knife to defend himself, but Lincoln declined, saying, "I have no fears."

"I am grateful this wolf is on our side," Amos said. Then, turning to Duffy, "If you mistook 'Amos Breyer' for a Frenchman, you have saddled the wrong horse. My family came over from Battweiler in der Rhineland in 1795."

"You and half a million like you," Duffy said. "I thought all the Germans was in Texas."

"Those are the ones we told to keep on going," Nehemiah said.

"Achtung, grober mann," Amos said.

"Now *I* don't know what ack-tongues he's talkin'," Nehemiah said.

Duffy laughed and said, "I think he said, 'Watch out, big man.'"

"If we could get back to the business at hand," Pomfrey said. "Mr. Wolff can be found in the Rhineland neighborhood across the Miami Canal.[105] Look in the beer garden near Moerlein brewery.[106] He will be easy to find. He dresses smart as a carrot and carries a gold-topped walking stick."

"Did the man say 'beer'?" Nehemiah asked, standing up. "All these cramp words have made me as dry as a Baptist wedding."

---

105 The 'Rhineland' later became Over-the-Rhine; the Miami Erie Canal ran along Central Parkway before it was abandoned in 1906. When it was finished in 1845, it connected Lake Erie to the Ohio River, carrying cargo in canal boats towed by mules.

106 Founded in 1853. Christian Moerlein was a blacksmith in Over-the-Rhine who began brewing beer in his blacksmith shop. It became the biggest brewery in Ohio, exporting to South America and Europe. Shut down by Prohibition, Christian Moerlein Select Lager was revived in 1981 and returned to Cincinnati in 2004. "Our History," ChristianMoerlein.com.

SEPTEMBER 15, 1862

Sergeant Butcher meets his match

The three men left Pomfrey's house and walked west to the pontoon bridge. It was the first bridge across the river, made on orders from General Wallace by local architect Wesley Cameron, with help from riverboat captains who towed and lined up coal barges to support the planked surface. As the men crossed the river, the towering, unfinished piers for the new John A. Roebling Suspension Bridge loomed on their left like blockhouses.

"That won't never work," Amos said, tipping his head at the blocky stone bridge work. "Cain't hang a bridge with string. Any wagons that cross had better float."

Nehemiah made a doubtful sound. "Then again, they said this city could not defend itself."

A heavily loaded four-horse wagon passed them, making a thunderous drumming racket as the hooves and wheels pounded the planks over hollow barges.

"Noise enough to wake snakes," Amos said when it was gone.

Duffy said, "Gentlemen, we are being followed."

"You mean that skinny guttersnipe lollygagging back there," Amos said. As they reached the end of the bridge he said, "Excuse me while I absquatulate. I will join up with you gents later."

He headed east along the riverbank, while Duffy and Nehemiah continued north.

By the time they reached the beer garden a few blocks on, Nehemiah looked back down the street and saw no sign of their escort. They entered the dim, wood-paneled saloon and waited for their eyes to adjust from the September sunshine. Among the first things Duffy saw were the risqué painting hanging over the bar, and a well-dressed man leaning back against the bar beneath it, who was eyeing him back.

"I think we have found our Jim Dandy," he said.

Nehemiah was taking it all in. "This ain't no common doggery. If the beer's as good as the scenery, we are in for a treat."

"The specialty is lager," Duffy said. "Whatever that is."

"Amos will know. He is a deft hand at making antifogmatics."

"Lager is smoother than ales," Amos said, arriving silently behind them. They both looked at him, then at each other with raised eyebrows. Amos continued as if he did not notice, "It requires the cooler temperatures and ferments from the bottom of the barrel."

Then he added, "Us Germans know our beer the way the Irish know their taters."

The man at the bar pointed to a doorway, and led the way. He was of medium height and walked with an athletic confidence. His hair was tinged red, matching his thick beard that was trimmed short over a crip white shirt and black, bow-tied cravat. His suit was also black to match his hat and walking stick, making his white shirt cuffs flash in the dim light.

"Allow me to grab some largers," Nehemiah said.

"LAH-ger," Amos corrected.

"I intend to make mine LARG-er," Nehemiah replied. "What become of our guttersnipe?"

"I'm afeared he went for a swim in the canal."

Duffy laughed. "I guess that fixed his flint. Was it that soldier we saw with Captain Burnet and Sergeant Butcher?"

"None other," Amos replied.

"Is he feedin' carp?"

"No, he slapped water as if trying to fly until he stood up and found it was just four feet deep."

"The plot thickens," Duffy said. "Join me when y'all get them larger lagers." He followed Klaus Wolff through the darkened doorway.

Nehemiah and Amos found Duffy and Klaus already seated around a table with room for six, in a small room crowded with crates, growlers[107] and empty pint bottles.

"Now if that ain't cold coffee," Amos said. "I was expectin' to find that lady over the bar back here."

"If you are thirsty for horizontal refreshment, I provide such a place in Newport," Klaus said with a trace of his clipped German accent.

Amos replied in German and Klaus laughed.

"What did he say?" Duffy asked.

"Too long without practice for indoor sports," Klaus replied. Then he said something in German and Amos laughed. When Duffy and Nehemiah looked at Amos, Amos just shook his head with a smile. "Texians and bears would not comprendeevoo."

"You must be Mr. Breyer, and you are Mr. Woods," Klaus said, nodding at each.

"You cotton quick," Nehemiah said, brushing beer foam off his mustache.

"It saved my skin more than once," Klaus replied. "I see you enjoy my lager. It is good." He said good like "goot."

"Das ist deins?" Amos asked, holding up his nearly empty stein.

"Nein, it is brewed by Herr Moerlein across the street. I own this saloon, Blume des Rheins."

"Flower of the Rhine," Amos translated for Duffy and Nehemiah.

"I reckon no introductions are needed," Duffy said. "We have already done finished our secret handshakes and passwords. Mr. Wolff here is *autentico*, as we say near the border. He has invited me to attend a meeting of the Queen City Castle next week. I am to be introduced as you first knew me, a Confederate deserter from Morgan's Raiders. And a Knight of the Texas Lone Stars."

"Ja," Klaus said. "They roll out the red rug for you."

Klaus withdrew a folded paper from the inside pocket of his suitcoat and spread it out on the table. It was a list of states, followed by numbers:

---

107 Take-out bottles that could be sealed to carry draft beer.

Missouri: 100,000
Illinois: 100,000
Indiana: 125,000
Ohio: 40,000
Michigan: 25,000
Kentucky: 30,000

Jotted in the margins were "Democratic Invincible Club, Chicago"; "The Democratic Reading Room, Louisville"; then "Knights of the Mighty Host" and "Mutual Protection Society."[108]

"These membership numbers vas written by Dr. William Bowles of Indiana," Klaus said.

Duffy gave a low whistle of appreciation. "General Wallace will be grateful to have this. The numbers are much greater than we feared."

"And this," Klaus said, producing another smaller sheet with handwritten notes:

Prisoners – 50,000.
Relic to British – $50,000.
Brutus – $10,000.

"These notes are in the hand of George Bickley," Klaus said. "They reveal his latest schemes."

He explained. The South needed men. Nearly 500,000 captured Confederate soldiers were held in northern prisons such as Camp Chase in Columbus, Ohio. With most of the Union military was away fighting battles to the south, an uprising of state castles by thousands of Knights might easily overpower any prison guards and set those prisoners free to rejoin the Confederate Army.

"That's the second time today we've met Brutus," Nehemiah said, putting his finger on the last line.

---

108 Fesler, Mayo, "Secret Political Societies in the North During the Civil War," *Indiana Magazine of History, September 1918.*

"I'm sorry, I cannot help you with that. But the tablet, I believe, is something being sold to the British to raise $50,000 for the South. What exactly it is, I do not know. Yet."

Duffy said, "Maybe we can learn more at the meeting." He was about to say more when a crash of broken glass came from the barroom and Klaus shot to his feet. "Stay seated tightly," he said, drawing the top of his walking stick to reveal a 10-inch stiletto.

Another crash of glassware followed, louder than the first, this time with shouting. Then there was a shout by Klaus: "Halt! Stoppen!"

As the three men waited, the barman calmly delivered four more lagers, compliments of Klaus. They heard murmured voices… raised almost to shouts… then lower.

Finally, Klaus came back. "A sergeant of the mayor's Special Police is here, with a very wet boy who smells of dead animals and foul rubbish. The sergeant refused to leave until he finds the squirrel man he's looking for." He raised his eyebrows and looked at Nehemiah, whose face lit up in a smile that his eyes did not share.

"Big man with a face like raw beef?"

Klaus nodded.

"Stay seated tightly," he winked, rising.

As Nehemiah emerged from the back room, Butcher was standing near a puddle of spilled beer and broken glass, silhouetted by the light from the open door to the street. Both men paused to stare at each other. Butcher was a streetfighter, scarred across his knuckles from bare-fisted brawls and saloon prizefights. He could be mistaken for fat, but that would be a fatal mistake. He could move fast, and the extra weight around his middle padded the solid muscle beneath. His face was purple red again, except for a long white scar that started on his forehead, ran between his eyes and then curved down his left cheek.

Knife wound, Nehemiah thought. But the sergeant of Mayor Hatch's Special Police—a motley conglomeration of thugs, drunks and plug-uglies—was not holding a knife. Instead, his right hand gripped a wooden truncheon that was nearly two feet long.

Nehemiah reached over to his right, grabbed an empty spindle chair, flipped it upside down and effortlessly ripped a leg off with a tearing crack, keeping his eyes on Butcher.

And then Sergeant Butcher bull-rushed him.

Nehemiah bent at the knees and waited, expecting Butcher to swing at his head. When he did, Nehemiah stood taller, taking the swing at shoulder height and blocking it with two hands on the chair leg, which was cracked by the force of the blow. *This thing won't last. That club of his must be hickory.*

Butcher recovered surprisingly fast and swung his club again, aiming to bring it down to break a collarbone and disable Nehemiah's left arm. But Nehemiah was just as quick. He moved in on Butcher and blocked his blow by sweeping the chair leg up into Butcher's right arm, breaking its momentum and nearly cracking Butcher's forearm.

Nehemiah snaked his left arm in and used his height advantage to grab Butcher by his thick hair, pulling his head forward to meet the sledgehammer blow of his right fist which held the added reinforcement of the chair leg like brass knuckles. He felt the sergeant's nose crack and felt blood on his fist as he jerked the man's head to his left and whacked him again across the back of the neck, so hard he splintered the chair leg.

Butcher was stunned and dazed. He tried to swing his club back at Nehemiah, but he had no reach with his body turned. Nehemiah thought of using the splintered end of the chair leg to stab Butcher below the ribs, a killing blow, but dropped it instead and used his right hand to grab a fistful of Butcher's belt from behind. He lifted the man like a sack of grain, swinging him out to his left, letting the momentum of the man's 240 pounds carry the body in an arc back toward the open door to the street.

When he let go, Butcher flew through the air and bounced off the doorway, breaking his shoulder, then hit the floor and slid through the puddle of beer and broken glass as he tumbled into the street. He landed hard, facedown, knocking the air out of him like a punctured balloon. He laid there struggling, slowly rolled over onto his back and moved his mouth like a beached fish, gasping for a breath, desperate for even a spoonful of air, his eyes wide and wild like a horse in a barn fire.

A shadow fell over him and he looked up to see a man who looked a mile high, with cold eyes and a colder smile. Somehow, the man was holding Butcher's club now, and jabbed it into his gut, pushing out his last tiny gulp of air.

"Stand up," the tall man said. Butcher wondered if he would ever stand or breathe again. He had never taken such a beating. "Stand up and I will thump you cold as a wagon tire," Nehemiah said.

Butcher didn't move or speak. His wild, frightened eyes gave the answer. Nehemiah shook his head in disappointment, straightened up and broke Butcher's hickory club between his hands like it was no more than a chicken bone. He dropped the pieces on Butcher and said, "Not so chirk now? Know this. If we meet again, you will awaken in your eternity box."

He turned and saw Private Wheeds standing in the doorway, and his eyes went less flinty. The kid was trembling, and not just from his wet clothes that reeked of the offal and sewage that floated in the canal. His eyes were round, unblinking, terrified.

"Tell Detective Reaney that Nehemiah Woods has settled his business with Sergeant Butcher," he said. "He may find me at the Burnet House."

The kid nodded but didn't move.

"Go," Nehemiah said softly, and the young man started like a rabbit.

Behind him, Butcher groaned and very slowly pushed himself to his feet, using one arm. He gave a sideways, scared glance at Nehemiah. His face was a bloody mess from his broken nose and from sliding through the broken glassware he had smashed earlier. The front of his tunic and pants were darkened by spilled beer. *Or fear*, Nehemiah thought. One arm slumped low, the shoulder dislocated or broken. With shaking hands, Butcher slowly tried to pick up his club, looking at it in amazement, then came to his senses, realized it was useless and let the broken pieces clatter to the ground.

Nehemiah left him there and turned to go inside. Standing in the doorway were Duffy, Klaus and Amos.

"What'd I tell ye," Amos said. "Chawed that man up catawamptiously."

September 1792

'A Mighty Fortress'

The James Kemper Log House was Kemper's second home, built in 1804 in Walnut Hills on Kemper Lane. It was moved to Sharon Woods Heritage Village Museum.

"They are as a sleep: in the morning they are like grass which groweth up. In the morning it flourisheth and groweth up; in the evening it is cut down, and withereth..."

The man quoting scripture was slender and hawk-faced, Kenton observed, with piercing eyes over sharp cheekbones and the hard look of a no-nonsense, head-slapping schoolmaster or a tough veteran soldier, not a preacher. *Then again,* Kenton thought, *I have been in church so seldom, how would I even know what a preacher should look like?*

"...For all our days are passed away in thy wrath; we spend our years as a tale that is told..."

The preacher stood on a tree stump in a black frock coat, holding a thick and worn Bible that looked as if it had been through many battles. It probably had been. James Kemper, the first pastor in the new wilderness of Ohio, was like most of the men who were brave enough to bring their families into the new frontier: He had fought in the Revolutionary War.

"...for it is soon cut off and we fly away."[109]

Kenton recognized the Psalm comparing men to the oceans of wild grass that covered hills and meadows and died each winter to grow deep and thick again in the springtime. He had heard the same verses at services for other men killed in battle or families who were taken by the Indians, never to be seen again.

"...and let the beauty of the Lord our God be upon us, and establish thou the work of our hands; yea, the work of our hands establish thou it."[110]

Kenton smiled. *If hard work is a blessing, these people are blessed beyond measure.* Nothing could be done in this wilderness without sweat and backbreaking labor. Their very existence was sustained by relentless chores: fetching water, clearing the forest, breaking the ground for crops, planting, harvesting, hunting, storing up supplies for the cruel winters, cutting wood, building and repairing their homes and the stockade that stood between them and almost certain death by massacre. Even the clothes on their backs had to be spun and stitched by hand.

As if reading his thoughts, Pastor Kemper was reading from Genesis 3. It was Eden after the fall:

"... cursed is the ground for thy sake; in sorrow shalt thou eat of it all the days of thy life; Thorns also and thistles shall it bring forth to thee; and thou shalt eat the herb of the field. In the sweat of thy face shalt thou eat bread, till thou return unto the ground; for out of it wast thou taken: for dust thou art, and unto dust shalt thou return."

---

109 Psalm 90, King James Version.

110 ibid.

Gathered around the Reverend Kemper this morning were all the families of Covalt Station. The men held rifles across their shoulders or kept them within reach, loaded and ready. Two men had been posted on the stockades to keep watch on the woods. The rest of the men, women and children stood with their heads bowed, dressed in worn but neat homespun clothing in muted browns, grays and blacks—a sharp contrast to the vivid splashes of gold and red on the warpainted sugar maples in the surrounding forest.

Like Kenton, the men wore linen hunting shirts that came to their mid-thighs, wrapped around and belted over leggings. A few women wore shoes they had brought along to the wilderness, but the rest of the men, women and children who were not barefoot wore moccasins made of deerskin, with flaps that rose over the ankles, tied with thongs around their shins. The women wore loose skirts called bedgowns, covered with a long blouse that was belted around the waist. Some wore a brighter scrap of cloth tied around their necks. The women's bonnets had once been white, but were now gray and worn from many washings in the river.

As he looked over the stockade walls to the surrounding forest, Kenton favored the hickories that were starting to turn brilliant yellow, as if they had trapped the summer sunshine and were reluctantly letting it go.

If forced to explain his own faith, he would say he saw God in the flash of rainbow colors on a trout that rose from night-dark depths into daylight; or on a string of diamonds made by morning dew catching sunbeams in a spiderweb; in the vividly perfect, mirrored reflection of deep emerald, blazing scarlet and deep gold of autumn trees on a looking glass river; on lazy, swaying meadows of graceful prairie grass, purple thunderclouds, the effortless leap of a running deer, the sudden and awed silence of the winter's first fresh snow....

But he was a man of action, not given to much reflection. His cathedral was the forest; his hymns were sung by lilting bluebirds, trilling cardinals, operatic mockingbirds and the soaring hawks that called out like the angels of death.

"For God who commanded the light to shine out of darkness hath shined in our hearts," the preacher quoted, *"to give the light of the knowledge of the glory of God in the face of Jesus Christ."*

"Amen!" a strong male voice affirmed.

"But we have this treasure in earthen vessels that the power may be of God, and not of us."

Kemper closed the Good Book and looked up. "We are all like jars of clay. Fragile, easily broken. But that is where the light of God shines forth most brightly, through our broken places."

He looked down again, opened his Bible, found his place and read again: *"We are troubled on every side, yet not distressed..."*

Kenton nodded to himself. *Troubled on every side is about right for that last attack,* he thought. *But I'd reckon we were more than a little distressed.*

"...Cast down, but not destroyed..."[111]

Kenton looked around at the families. *True enough,* he thought. *They are strong. Not destroyed. Not yet.*

The service was for the man from Maysville who had died at the stake in the woods to the north. Kenton did not know his name when he took the man's life out of mercy, but now it was being spoken by the preacher:

"... a man named Gabriel Sullivan. His brother and his friends knew him as Gabe. But his Christian name came from an angel of the Lord, and it meant 'warrior.' By the grace of God, it was well chosen. Gabe and his brother marched north with General St. Clair one year ago, and he was among those few survivors that God spared."

Kenton heard sobs from beneath a woman's bonnet. *She likely lost a son there,* he thought. He saw the man named Gabriel again in his imagination, the look in his pleading eyes before the trigger pull released him from his agony in the flames.

"It was only one year ago that we all saw the darkness of defeat fall on us and began our long journey through the valley of death," the preacher said. "We all remember it very well."

---

111 2 Corinthians.

This blockhouse, similar to the one built by James Kemper for his family of sixteen children, was built during the Indian wars in the Pacific Northwest.

Kenton had heard how Reverend James Kemper had gone from family to family in Fort Washington to encourage them to stay after they had seen St. Clair's battle-torn, bleeding, dispirited troops straggle in on November 9, 1791. The new US Army that was supposed to punish the allied tribes came back wounded, whipped, scared and hopeless. The soldiers brought their fear with them like the lice they carried, spreading it throughout the settlements along both sides of the Ohio River. The most powerful army yet assembled by the new young nation had been thoroughly massacred. There was nothing to stop the Indian nations from annihilating all of them. Everyone was certain more attacks were sure to come.

That defeat of St. Clair was the darkest day in Ohio: November 4, 1791. When St. Clair returned, Kemper had only just arrived nine days earlier at Fort Washington on a one-year mission to carry the gospel into the wilderness. He could have easily used the shocking defeat as an excuse to return to Transylvania Seminary in Danville, Kentucky. Nobody would have blamed him. Instead, he visited each family and implored them to stay and stand strong. He told them it was their duty as Christians to stay.[112]

---

112 Preston, Steve, *Reverend James Kemper*, Southwest Ohio History, 2017.

And Kemper stayed too. He moved into a tiny blockhouse miles away from Fort Washington, where he lived with his wife and sixteen children, constantly threatened by Indians.

Kenton listened as Kemper continued. "Now we turn to the Book of Nehemiah, chapter four, verses thirteen and fourteen." He paused as Bible pages rustled through the tiny gathering like dry leaves in a breeze. And he began to read.

"Therefore set I in the lower places behind the wall, and on the higher places, I even set the people after their families with their swords, their spears, and their bows."

Simon Kenton turned to check the men on the walls and nodded to himself. They had their eyes turned to the forest, their muskets held ready.

"And I looked and rose up, and said unto the nobles, and to the rulers, and to the rest of the people, 'Be ye not afraid of them. Remember the Lord, which is great and terrible, and fight for your brethren, your sons, and your daughters, your wives and your houses...'"

The Reverend Kemper had volunteered to come along with Lt. John Gano and his soldiers from Fort Washington to rescue Covalt Station. He was warned that it could be dangerous, even fatal. Lieutenant Gano did now know what to expect. But the preacher was fearless. He trusted the Lord to protect him.

Now he was helping to "bury" a man whose remains were many miles away in an unmarked clearing in the forest. *Ashes to ashes*, Kenton thought, *dust to dust.*

Reverend Kemper was reading from the book of Isaiah:

"Fear thou not, for I am with thee; be not dismayed, for I am thy God. I will strengthen thee, yea, I will help thee; yea, I will uphold thee with the right hand of my righteousness."

Then he talked about the war of the flesh and the war of the Spirit. Settlers in the new Northwest Territory were Christian warriors, he said, bringing civilization and the gospel to lands that were ruled by principalities of evil: the dark gods of the heathen savages. The Christians would suffer pain, anguish, loss, grief and death, but the spirit of God would not be overcome. They had not survived so much, by the grace of the Lord, to surrender now.

Kenton's thoughts turned to the strange mounds just outside the stockade and all along the north banks of the Ohio River and into Ohio. Wherever the mounds had been excavated, bones were found. Some were from small children. Many had broken skulls as if they had been tomahawked. *Is that what he means by 'dark gods' from ancient times?* he wondered.

From his time in captivity, Kenton knew the Shawnee and Miami tribes feared the mounds and the "ghosts" of what they called the "Ancients."

"Do not be discouraged or defeated," Reverend Kemper said. "With God, all things are possible."[113]

Kenton liked this man. He was a Presbyterian, whatever that meant, but he was hitting the mark. Whether the rest of the country knew it or now, Ohio and Kentucky were at war. These pilgrims needed a man of God like Kemper who would tell it plain and give people a strong faith to lean on, a spiritual fortress to match the log walls around them.[114]

"The angel of the Lord encampeth around about them that fear him, and delivereth them," Kemper quoted. Then he looked up from his Bible and said, "Our Lord is merciful and mighty. He will not abandon his children in the wilderness. He has brought us across the sea, through rivers and tangled forests and winters of privation. He has favored us and blessed us with our independence as a new nation. Surely God's hand gave us victory over the world's greatest empire.[115]

"And He will not desert us now as we battle the merciless agents of

---

113   The motto of the State of Ohio. From Matthew 19:26.

114   Bailyn, Bernard. *The Barbarous Years*. Vintage, 2013. "The savagery of the [theological] struggle, the bitterness of the main contenders and the deep stain it left on the region's collective memory were driven by elemental fears peculiar to what was experienced … of what could happen to civilized people in an unimaginable wilderness … in which God's children were fated to struggle with pitiless agents of Satan, pagan Antichrists swarming in the world around them. The two were one: threats from within merged with threats from without…."

115   Kemper's own journey was fraught with peril, setbacks, depression, grief and failure. His sermon here is fictional, but reflects the beliefs of Christians at the time and is based on similar sermons in that period.

Satan who worship ancient gods of darkness. As it says in Psalm 37, '*The wicked watcheth the righteous and seeketh to slay him. The Lord will not leave him in the hands of the wicked. Keep His way and He shall exalt them to inherit the land.*'"

Murmurs of "Amen," came from the families of Covalt Station, who had risked their lives and worked themselves almost to death to create their tiny refuge of protection in a beautiful paradise that had hell lurking behind every tree.

The preacher's voice rose as he finished, "*When the wicked are cut off, thou shalt see it!*"

More "Amens," stronger, filled with spirit. Gabe's brother sobbed loudly, hiding his face in his bandaged arm.

"From 1st Peter," the preacher said, "*Be sober, be vigilant; because your adversary the devil, as a roaring lion, walketh about, seeking whom he may devour: Whom resist, steadfast in the faith, knowing that the same afflictions are accomplished in your brethren that are in the world.*"[116]

The Covalt families closed the service by singing "A Mighty Fortress is Our God."

> *"And though this world with devils filled,*
> *Should threaten to undo us,*
> *We will not fear for God has willed*
> *His truth to triumph through us.*
> *The Prince of Darkness grim,*

---

116 James Kemper came west in 1785 with horses, six children and a pregnant wife, Judith. By the time he got to Cincinnati in 1791 he had 10 children and would father 16. He established the first church in Ohio, the Cincinnati-Columbia Presbyterian Church. Men were required to bring their muskets to church for protection or be fined 75 cents. He founded First Presbyterian, which is now in Pleasant Ridge. A plaque in the church honors The Reverend James Kemper as "A Valiant Soldier of the Cross; He Being Dead Yet Speaketh." During his life, Kemper spoke through his many accomplishments as well as in the pulpit. He founded Walnut Hills, named after his farm that was courageously chosen nearly three miles outside Fort Washington. The little blockhouse where his family lived was so remote his daughters could not fetch water without an armed guard, and it would have taken soldiers at the fort three hours to reach him if they heard an attack. He established Walnut Hills Academy in 1807. Kemper was a circuit rider who risked his life to preach the Word, often escorted by his sons, who were armed. At one of his services, a man who was missing from church was later found murdered and scalped. Source: Preston, Steve, "Reverend James Kemper," *Southwest Ohio History*, 2017.

We tremble not for him.
His rage we can endure,
For lo, his doom is sure..."

Kenton lifted his rifle and turned to leave. Lieutenant Gano, Reason Bailey and Cheneniah Covalt opened the gate for him and bid him farewell with strong handshakes, nods and a few words. He set out east to cross the river and return to his own cabin "fortress" in the woods. Behind him, as he passed one of the biggest ancient mounds of the dark gods, the voices inside the stockade floated into the cloudless blue autumn sky, strong and undaunted.

"...The body they may kill,
God's truth abideth still;
His Kingdom is forever!"[117]

---

117   Written in 1529 by Martin Luther, known as "The battle hymn of the Reformation."

SEPTEMBER 17, 1862

Whittlesey's Earthworks

Newark Earthworks in Newark, Ohio is listed by UNESCO along with the Egyptian Pyramids and the Great Wall of China. It is one of the largest earthworks in the world, covering more than 3,000 acres.

Col. Charles Whittlesey was almost doubled over in the saddle as he rode to the Covington headquarters of Maj. Gen. Lew Wallace. The sharp, stabbing pains in his stomach and bowels made him nearly groan aloud. His joints were stiff and aching with rheumatism. He had a troubling hernia caused by a fall from his horse. And his gut was in a conspiracy with his nightmares to keep him from sleeping.

He tossed and turned all night with insomnia. If he did fall asleep, his dreams were often a dark and terrifying place, back on the battlefield at Shiloh with the torn bodies of the dead or wounded, bleeding soldiers who pleaded, moaned and screamed in agony.

He was pretty sure the stomach troubles had started with bad pork a year ago when he was stationed in Cincinnati. He had been mortally sick for days, and never quite felt the same again.[118]

The griping pain finally abated, and he straightened. A lieutenant riding with him nudged his horse closer and asked, "Sir, are you feeling poorly again?"

Whittlesey gave a brusque nod, then said, "I will be fine, thank you for asking, Lieutenant. But I would be grateful to visit a common house when we arrive.

"Yes sir. I know of a privy near headquarters, I will take you there."

Colonel Whittlesey looked across the river at the Queen City and he was pleased. The defenses he had designed the year before had served well. His network of batteries, forts and trenches had been left unfinished in 1861; work was called off when the waves of invasion-panic at the beginning of the war subsided. But under the command of General Wallace, he had returned a few weeks ago to reinforce his line of defenses for a real invasion by Confederate Gen. Henry Heth and his army of 10,000.[119]

Now that the siege had been lifted for nearly a week, he hoped he might soon be allowed to return to his home in Cleveland for the long overdue rest his mind and body craved. He had resigned from the Army last April because of his own illness and to help his ailing wife. Then he was called out of retirement by General Wallace. He could not say no to his country or refuse his good friend and revered commander, whom he had served under at the Battle of Shiloh.

---

118   Totten, Stanley M. *The Brilliance of Charles Whittlesey*. Kent State University, 2022.

119   Beginning in 1861 and reinforced in 1862 were 25 batteries and forts stretching seven miles across Northern Kentucky, in the hills south of Cincinnati: Battery J. L. Kirby Smith, Battery Coombs, Battery Bates, Battery Perry, Fort Mitchel, Battery Kyle, Fort Wright, Battery McRae, Battery Hooper, Battery Carlisle, Battery Burbank, Battery Hatch, Battery Buford, Battery Burnet, Battery Larz Anderson, Battery Wiggins, Battery Holt, Battery Harrison, Battery McLean, Battery Shaler, Fort Burnside, Battery Groesbeek, Battery Kearny, Fort Whittlesey and Battery Lee. Totten, Stanley M., *The Brilliance of Charles Whittlesey*. The Kent State University Press. 2022.

Colonel Whittlesey had led the Third Brigade of Wallace's Third Division through those awful two days in southern Tennessee. He recalled how Wallace paced like a caged tiger on that first day, when they were given no orders from Grant for six hours as they listened to the cannons rage seven miles to the south. Then, when the orders finally came, they were vague pencil scratches on stained paper, unsigned by Grant or any officer.

Wallace's Third Division marched as fast as they could for half a day that hot April morning—more than 7,500 infantry, cavalry and artillery. Then just as they were approaching the fringe of the battle on Sherman's right flank, with an opportunity to hit the Confederates by surprise and sweep them from the field, another officer sent by Grant rode up and ordered Wallace to turn around.

He said the Shunpike Road they were on was the wrong road, although Wallace had improved it in readiness for just such a battle. Wallace could not believe it. They were ordered to turn back to find a crossing through a swamp, then use the River Road, which was aptly named—spring floods had left it mostly underwater.

It was a miserable march through bogs, mud and water to their chests. The cannons got stuck repeatedly and required dozens of men and horses to pull them free from the sucking mud, only to get mired up to the axles again. The Third Division finally arrived on the battlefield in the evening, exhausted, soaked and covered in mud. By then, the fighting had ended for the day.

All because one of General Grant's nincompoop aides told us that's what Grant ordered,[120] Whittlesey remembered. *Balderdash! Grant could not have been such a fool.*

Whittlesey had become good friends with Grant's father the year before in Cincinnati, and he was sure Grant was raised better than that.

Leave it to some frig pig, dog booby, lickspittle aide to foul up a battle

---

120   President and General Ulysses Grant wrote in his memoir, "My order was verbal and to a staff officer who was to deliver it to General Wallace so that I am not competent to say just what order the general actually received."

and then hang the blame on an honorable and courageous general like Wallace.[121]

To protect Grant from being court-martialed for his mistakes on the first day, his staff wrote reports that shifted the blame to Wallace for being "lost."

Colonel Whittlesey was a lawyer, a West Point graduate, a nationally respected geologist, surveyor, cartographer, minerologist, archaeologist, inventor and engineer. He had nearly been killed several times exploring the wild lake country in Wisconsin and the ancient copper mines in the Upper Peninsula of Michigan—nearly drowned twice in storms on frigid Lake Superior.

He was known and loved by his soldiers as a fair and fearless leader with bedrock-deep Christian faith. He especially treasured the letter written by the men who served under his command at Shiloh. It lauded his courage and coolness in battle and said they "all felt ready to follow you unfaltering into any contest, and into any post of danger."[122]

But he was often rankled, like Wallace, at the incompetence and enstupidation of the "leaders" who commanded the Union Army in Washington, and the Ohio governor who commanded Ohio's regiments from the state capital in Columbus.

He had served in the Black Hawk War[123] as far west as Iowa Indian Territory in 1832. He had practiced law and helped publish the *Cleveland Herald* newspaper in Cleveland, then became assistant geologist for

---

121 In 1873 and 1875, Wallace wrote to Whittlesey asking him to help clear his name of the blame for Grant's mistakes a Shiloh. Whittlesey vouched for Wallace's courage and determination. Whittlesey responded with a report that quoted seven officers who marched with Wallace's Third Division that day, all testifying that Wallace followed orders "explicitly." Whittlesey wrote, "It would be very difficult to produce a statement wider of the truth than that which attributes the defeat of the first day at Shiloh to the tardiness of Wallace's division." He accused Grant and his staff of "an effort to shift responsibility at the expense of historical truth."

122 Totten, Stanley M. *The Brilliance of Charles Whittlesey*. The Kent State University Press.

123 Sauk Chief Black Hawk led several tribes in an uprising over a disputed treaty ceding land in Illinois. Abraham Lincoln also served in the Blackhawk War, along with Zachary Taylor and Jefferson Davis. Both sides took scalps and committed atrocities. It ended with Black Hawk's defeat at the Battle of Bad Axe in Wisconsin, which was "less of a battle and more of a massacre," according to one historian. Black Hawk surrendered and became an American celebrity.

Ohio. That led him north to copper mines in Michigan, west to Wisconsin and Minnesota and through all regions of Ohio.

As a veteran of one of the most recent Indian wars, he shared the majority opinion that America was the Promised Land, given to God's children who were willing to tame it. The primitive Indian culture had to give way to civilization and progress. Efforts to assimilate them had failed, often with terrible results. Hunter-gatherers had to make way for a new era of agriculture and industry. The land belonged to those who would use it best for the benefit of civilization.

Whittlesey wrote, "It may be impossible to save the savage races of the United States from annihilation," but believed the land should be purchased from the Indians "by upright means."

"What is the purpose of the earth—to produce game or the bread of life? To sustain one human being per square mile or one hundred?" [124]

As he had traveled the woods, lakes, rivers and ravines of Ohio, he became curious, then fascinated by other cultures that preceded the Indian tribes by thousands of years. Ancient engineers had left behind mounds and mysterious earthworks almost everywhere he went. Many of them were near Cincinnati, along the Ohio River, the Miami River and the Little Miami River.

As he looked north to the solid and modern city of Cincinnati across the river, he could almost picture the large mound he had seen there, twenty-seven feet high, near the original site of Fort Washington, before it was leveled to make way for Mound Street and new buildings. The city was growing like ivy, spreading up the hillsides away from the river in every direction. The mound was destroyed in 1841, he recalled. His friend Jared Potter Kirtland had told him a story about a curious artifact found when it was removed.

A man had come into Kirtland's office at the Medical College of Ohio in Cincinnati, carrying a small, rectangular tablet, about as big as a postcard, covered in strange hieroglyphics. He claimed he had just dug it out of the mound and offered to sell it for $50. But after examining

---

124 This echoes Alexis de Tocqueville's assessment of the "Indian Problem" in his book *Democracy in America*, published in 1835.

The Cincinnati Tablet, estimated to be about 2,000 years old, is in the collection at the Cincinnati Museum Center.

it, Kirtland scoffed and declared it was a fake.

A few months later, the Western Academy of Natural Sciences in Cincinnati examined the "Cincinnati Tablet" and declared it was genuine.[125] The debate escalated with salvos of arguments and papers declaring with absolute certainty that it was genuine—or that it was a hoax.

Whittlesey was not surprised either way. Flim-flam artists sometimes salted mounds with fake "treasures" they could sell to gullible collectors. But Whittlesey had excavated far larger earthworks along Round Bottom Road just northeast of Newtown. In fact, that site was called the Whittlesey Mound in honor of his work there.[126]

---

125 The Cincinnati Tablet was featured in the first volume publication by the Smithsonian Institution in 1848. It has been displayed in London and elsewhere and was among many artifacts discovered by workers as they leveled a mound near Fifth and Mound streets in downtown Cincinnati in 1841. The tablet is believed to be more than 2,000 years old, from the Adena culture during the Early Woodland Period (1,000-200 BC). Archeologists speculate that the sandstone artifact may have been used as a stamp design or as a template for tattoos. Swinney, Tyler, *The Story of the Cincinnati Tablet,* Cincinnati Museum Center Blog, 2019.

126 It was renamed the Turner Group of Earthworks in 1882 when the owner of the property, Dr. Michael Turner, gave exclusive permission for excavations to the Peabody Museum of Harvard University. Dr. Charles Metz of Madisonville was chosen to conduct the archeological digs that continued until 1908.

His discoveries had been mysterious and troubling.

Buried relics included beads, pearls, bear skulls, flaked-stone arrowheads, knives, axe blades and a wolf's jaw. Based on his background in geology, he was first to estimate that the mounds were more than 2,000 years old.[127] He wrote, "It is therefore reasonable to suspect that man existed in North America with the extinct elephant, mastodon, Megalonyx,[128] horse, beaver, and the peccary of the United States, which lived towards the close of the ice era."

"None were more difficult to explain than this," he wrote after visiting the Newtown site and its perfectly symmetrical earthworks that formed an exact circle, a bird-shaped mound, a huge oval with a gate and two sets of precisely parallel ridges more than a thousand feet long.

The structures sprawled over hundreds of acres, but somehow maintained nearly perfect symmetry. Whittlesey could not imagine how primitive ancient Indian tribes could accomplish such an engineering marvel, making bird and serpent effigy mounds hundreds of feet long, an exact circle that was 200 yards in diameter, and perfectly aligned earthen walls forty feet high—all without modern surveying tools.[129]

Whittlesey had also been among the first to explore the Newark Mound, which was soon called one of the wonders of the ancient world—the largest, most precise and best preserved that had yet been found.[130]

According to his own painstaking measurements with a transit and chain on a cold day in January 1838, the Newark works were spread over

---

127 Carbon dating has estimated that firepits found in Ohio may date to 17,000 BC.

128 A prehistoric tree sloth that could weigh 2,000 pounds and be up to 10 feet tall.

129 The Fort Ancient Earthworks in Oregonia, about 10 miles northeast of Kings Island, has two features that line up with the summer solstice, and two that line up with the winter solstice. Archologists estimate that 628,800 cubic yards of earth were moved to create the site, which has been compared to Aztec temples.

130 Since 1910, part of the Newark Earthworks has been part of a unique golf course that features greens and fairways among earthworks that are thousands of years old. In 2024, the Moundbuilders Country Club lost its legal battle in the Ohio Supreme Court and the state's Ohio History Connection was given permission to purchase the property by eminent domain for a public park. The Country Club site observed, "Won't archeologists 2,000 years from now be puzzled when they study the mounds and find all those lost golf balls?"

more than two miles and encompassed more than 3,000 acres.[131] In the center was a circle around another giant bird effigy more than 150 feet long, sixty feet wide and seven feet high.[132]

How did they build that? he wondered. *What was the purpose of such a huge symbol that could only be appreciated when drawn on paper or seen from above?*

As a military engineer, he was convinced that many of the mounds, like the ones found in Terrace Park, Newtown and Milford,[133] were "not designed either for attack or defense, under any supposed mode of human warfare."[134]

He wondered if they were used for ceremonial or religious purposes.[135]

And that was the troubling part. Along with the expected animal bones, trinkets and jewelry, he found copper that he believed came from mines near Lake Superior.[136] There were sharks' teeth, ocean shells—and human bones of all kinds.

The mounds in Newtown contained skeletons of women, men and children. Some had both legs broken below the knees. Some had been buried together, in postures that spoke from the grave across the centuries, and told of violent deaths, even perhaps burials alive. Some had

---

131 The Great Circle was used as the Licking County Fairgrounds from 1853 to 1933. From 1898 to 1924, it was Idlewilde Park, an amusement park with rollercoasters, a Ferris Wheel, a casino, hotel and restaurants. Totten, Stanley M. *The Brilliance of Charles Whittlesey.* The Kent State University Press, 2022.

132 Based on relics found at the site, some archeologists believe that ancient tribes made pilgrimages to the Newark Earthworks from across the continent.

133 The first mapping of the Milford Earthworks (between Garfield, Lila, Main and Cemetery) was done by Revolutionary War veteran and Cincinnati founder William Lytle in 1803. *History of Clermont and Brown Counties* by Byron Williams in 1913 counted more than 400 earthworks in southwestern Ohio and 200 in Clermont County. www.Earthworks.site.

134 An 1837 report by Whittlesey said the mounds and earthworks were not used for defense and should not be called fortifications, as they had been. By the end of 1838, he had mapped, sketched and described in detail more than 30 of the ancient works in Ohio, including the largest, the Newark Earthworks in Licking County. *The Brilliance of Charles Whittlesey.* Kent State University, 2022.

135 Archologists now say the mounds in Ohio and throughout the Midwest go back 2,000 years. *The Mounds and Mysteries of Ancient Ohio,* Archeology Ohio, 2023.

136 Archeologists concluded that the Ohio mound builders sent crews to the copper mines on Isle Royale in Lake Superior each summer.

crushed skulls, and some had perfectly round drill marks through their skulls. Others had been cremated on what appeared to be altars of some kind, where many human bones were mixed with ashes and charcoal.[137]

Were these skeletons the remains of human sacrifice? Were they prisoners taken and tortured the same way the Shawnee, Miami, Apache and Commanche Indians tortured and burned their victims centuries later? Were they killed in battles? Victims of cannibals? Could that explain how some skeletons were dismembered, with separated heads lying near the feet, with arms and legs removed, all showing evidence of being burned? What stories could those bones tell?[138]

The reports from Conquistadores in the 1600s had told how the Aztecs sacrificed thousands of children and adults and put people in cages to be fattened like livestock, their flesh sold in butcher shops like cuts of beef or pork.[139] There were many similarities in the mound relics to Aztec, Inca and Mayan discoveries: serpent worship, pyramids and mounds, giant effigies of birds and serpents. Those cultures all shared something else: cannibalism and human sacrifice.[140]

---

137 A report by the Peabody Museum in 1889 found a skeleton with its pelvis broken in three places, "the lower jaw was a foot from the skull, which was near the feet." The bones had been burned and laid on a bed of burned human bones. *Turner Group of Earthworks, Hamilton County, Ohio.* Corinthian Press, 1922.

138 In 1922, the Peabody Museum published an extensive study of the Turner Group of Earthworks. Among the conclusions: The Miami Valley was the center of a large prehistoric culture that stretched from Illinois to Tennessee, to Western Michigan. Post holes suggested the parallel earthworks were part of some kind of habitation, stronghold of council house. Obsidian was found from Yellowstone; shells and shark teeth from Florida; copper from Lake Superior region; mica from Appalachia; and ivory from mammoth tusks. The deity of the culture was a horned serpent (Aztecs, ancient Egyptians and Sumerians also worshiped serpent gods). Based on examinations of 90 skeletons, the men were estimated to be about five foot five. The researchers concluded that the Serpent Mound about 50 miles east was their chief shrine. *The Turner Group of Earthworks, Hamilton County, Ohio.* Corinthian Press, 1922.

139 Castillo, Bernal Diaz. *The Conquest of New Spain.* Penguin UK, 2003.

140 Ophiolateria (serpent worship) was common in many ancient cultures that also shared sacrifice and cannibalism. The Mayans worshiped a serpent god called Kukulkan; the Aztecs sacrificed to Quetzalcoatl, which means "precious serpent." "Historians have also noticed another common theme: Serpent gods and human sacrifice tend to go together," and have been found linked in many ancient cultures including Egypt, the Druids, the near East, Mesopotamia and Sumeria. At a mound near St. Louis that looks like Mayan and Aztec pyramids, evidence of human sacrifice was found. "In one gruesome discovery, the bones of 52 young women were found and are thought to have been sacrificed at the same time. In another find, 39 men and women were ritually beaten to death." Ungit, Lewis. *The Return of the Dragon.* Glome Press, 2022.

Whittlesey also knew from his well-worn Bible that there were other ancient cultures that worshipped serpents and sacrificed humans, especially children: The Canaanites, Philistines and Ammonites sacrificed children to Moloch and Baal. Even wayward Israelites fell under the wrath of God for sacrificing children to the old gods Molôch and Baal.[141]

Like many who were drawn to the mounds and earthworks, he was intrigued and mystified—and believed the mystery would never be solved in this life.[142]

* * * * *

When Colonel Whittlesey finally arrived at headquarters, the staff was in a flurry of paperwork and orders. He was surprised to learn that General Wallace was being transferred to Camp Chase in Columbus. The notorious prisoner of war stockade was intended for Confederate prisoners of war. But soon it was also used to confine Union soldiers who had been captured by the South and then set free on parole on condition that they could not rejoin the war.[143]

Wallace was already on his way north to Columbus, with orders to report to Camp Chase on September 19. Just a week after he was hailed as the Savior of Cincinnati, with proclamations from the mayor and the governors of Ohio and Indiana, he was once again being treated like the

---

141 Leviticus 20:2-5: "Say to the Israelites: 'Any Israelite or any foreigner residing in Israel who sacrifices any of his children to Molek is to be put to death. The members of the community are to stone him. I myself will set my face against him and will cut him off from his people; for by sacrificing his children to Molek, he has defiled my sanctuary and profaned my holy name."

142 In 1927, Willis F. Walker built a reinforced tunnel 350 feet into Spearhead Mound in Anderson Township, one mile east of Newtown (40 feet high and 625 feet in circumference). They revealed the skeletons of men who were estimated to have been seven or eight feet tall. That led to a popular mystery about the "Adena Giants," which were said to be described also by Indian legends. Walker and his partners did painstaking archeology at the site, but also sold tickets to view the skeletons. Agents of the Smithsonian who explored mounds also reported unusually large skeletons in the 1880s. The Spearhead Mound was destroyed and turned into a gravel pit in the late 1930s. Murphy, James L., *Hamilton County's Spearhead Mound*, Ohio State University Libraries.

143 The orders came in a telegram from the commander of the Army, Henry Halleck. Wallace wrote, "That the order was intended deliberately and with malice aforethought to put me to shame seemed glaringly plain. Not impossible there was a further intent behind it to drive me out of the army. Enough that I wrestled with myself all night before finally resolving to go to Columbus on the duty prescribed." Wallace, Lew. *Lew Wallace: An Autobiography: Volume 2.*

Scapegoat of Shiloh, punished by General-in-Chief Henry Halleck in Washington. "Old Brains" was all too eager to believe the worst about Wallace from Grant's lying staff, Whittlesey thought, because Wallace was not a West Pointer.

Like most who had seen Halleck's so-called leadership in action on the road to Corinth after Shiloh, Whittlesey had no respect for the plodding, timid West Point professor. Whittlesey was familiar, too, with degrading assignments. Although he was a West Point officer, engineer and Army veteran, he had been assigned by Ohio Gov. William Dennison to hand out equipment to new recruits at Camp Dennison, north of Cincinnati.

He could imagine how frustrated and angry Wallace would be, desperate to see action, fight for the Union and redeem his name after the slander at Shiloh. But "Old Brains" decided it was best to park him on the shelf, commanding the disgrace called Camp Chase. *May as well hitch a thoroughbred to a chuckwagon,* he thought. *The racehorse would pull the wagon, but its spirit would be broken. What a criminal waste.*

Whittlesey suspected that Old Brains probably hoped Wallace would fail in Cincinnati so he could be dismissed from service. *And now they don't know what to make of him and would rather drink lye than admit they were wrong, so they conjure this fimble-famble duty to make him resign. Lew won't do it. He will have the best of them yet.*

The headquarters staff handed Col. Whittlesey a sealed, handwritten letter from his friend General Wallace. It was typically direct:

> *"Please do whatever you can to assist my agents who are investigating a local Copperhead conspiracy involving the Knights of the Golden Circle. They will brief you on our progress. They have been sent a copy of this letter and will identify themselves with a line from Henry IV: 'Diseased nature often breaks forth in strange eruptions.' Your utmost discretion is paramount. — Major General Lew Wallace."*

Whittlesey read it again and thought, *He included no names. Discretion, indeed. This could be interesting.*

Inside the Castle

Amos was disappointed. The Cincinnati Castle of the Knights of the Golden Circle had no drawbridge, parapets, towers or damsels in distress. And no guards in shining armor "pots and pans." The meeting was held in a large room on the second floor of an old tannery on the riverbank. It reeked of lime, vats of sour, decaying oak bark that supplied tannins and, under it all like a dark family secret, the smell of death.

Decomposing flesh clung to the unwashed hides stacked in the tanning rooms downstairs, permeating the whole building with a background stench that seemed to seep from the woodwork, reminding Duffy of battlefields a day or two after the shooting was over.

Amos and Nehemiah had caught a whiff of the chutes that dumped offal into the river and agreed they would be more than happy to wait outside in the street.[144] The whole riverfront was the city's septic field and the river was its sewer. But the tannery was an entirely different level of perdition, they agreed, both longing for the clean air of the woods.

As Duffy and Klaus reached the top of the stairs, sentinels guarded the door. Two large, bearded men stood stiffly and held rifles as if they were itching to use them, or at least brandish the long bayonets that were fastened to the muzzles, making the guns as tall as the men.

A third man, well dressed in a topcoat and a black planter's tie, wearing a medal around his neck, recognized Klaus, but looked suspiciously

---

144 Cincinnati had cholera epidemics in 1850, 1851, 1852, 1866 and 1873. "The deplorable conditions of the city reservoir (drinking water)" were described by the *Cincinnati Commercial* in 1845: "dead animal carcasses floated on the surface; dirty water ran in, surrounded by dead and dying vegetation, and not 20 feet from the reservoir a chemical establishment chimney poured out 'poison gas.'"

at Duffy. He was a round man, with a middle like a bedroll and a face that looked as if he had fallen on his head from a tall building—eyebrows too close to his mustache, cheeks like he was holding air, and eyes like cuts in leather.

Klaus stepped forward and said, "Sir, this is Mr. Smith of the Order of the Lone Star of the West in Texas. A real Fire Eater."[145] The man's eyes widened and his eyebrows shot up. Duffy gave the required password, grip and handshake. "My pleasure, I reckon."

The guards relaxed. "Then it appears we have two special guests tonight," the greeter said. "General-in-Chief Bickley will be pleased to hear if it."

"Do y'all mean the *authentic* General George Washington Bickley is here in the flesh?" Duffy asked, sounding awed.

"The same," the man said. "I'm sure he will be most gratified to make your acquaintance."

Klaus beamed as if he had received an award. Duffy said, "Splendid!" as if he had just been invited to Buckingham Palace.

As they were ushered in, they saw that the room was well-lit by candles and oil lamps, revealing the crowd that filled the room. It was an unlikely conglomeration. Some had hands stained by honest work, with blackened, torn fingernails; others had worn, patched elbows in their shirts from clerking, counting and deskwork; one or two wore pants that were splashed in brown, dried blood that made a straight line near the knees where their slaughterhouse aprons had been worn. A few had the rounded bellies, storebought cigars, gold watch chains and tall hats of industrialists and entrepreneurs. What they all shared in common was a menu of grievances: sympathy with the South, a fervent desire for the war to end so they could return to profitable business as usual, and a loathing of President Lincoln and the Republicans.

There were also more than a few in the crowd who were lured by promises of adventure, glory, land and riches.

General Bickley was introduced by the well-dressed man at the door,

---

145   Fire-Eaters were the most extreme secessionists in the South.

who called him "The founding father of the Knights of the Golden Circle, a visionary who saw the future before this terrible war began...." He asked for a hearty welcome of the Queen City's Prodigal Son.

Duffy had seen Bickley from a distance at a rally in Texas. Now, upon closer inspection, he saw a well-groomed man who looked wealthy, with a florid face, long dark hair and a soup-cooler mustache that he chewed on with his bottom teeth to punctuate his sentences with a look of angry, bulldog determination. His face seemed stuck in a permanent scowl.

The man was below-average height, but was lean and stood straight, giving him the appearance of being taller. He wore a sort of uniform tunic in black, with brass buttons befitting a major general, all cinched at the waist with a polished black military-style belt.

As he listened, Duffy had to admit that in spite of himself, he was impressed again with the man's eloquence. He used words like a magician's wand to create misty abracadabra empires in the clouds—a happy, peaceful and prosperous kingdom that stretched from Tennessee and Kentucky to Central America, circling Mexico, the Caribbean Islands and Cuba in a bear hug of what he called the "divine institution"—slavery.

"I was thrown on the world penniless and friendless; yet with great energy I educated myself and rose to eminence in the profession of medicine," he said. "I have written many books, and vast quantities of minor essays on all conceivable subjects. I have built up practical secession and inaugurated the greatest war of modern times."[146]

So you started the war between the states all by yourself, Duffy thought. *So modest, too.*

Bickley talked of the valiant sons of the South who were spilling their blood for freedom from Northern tyranny "...on battlefields so close we can almost smell the dead."

Clever, Duffy smiled.

He encouraged the local vigilante committees to punish "submissionists, Lincolnites, abolitionists and anyone who dares to violate our

---

146 From George W. Bickley's biography, written by Bickley in 1862. He claimed his Knights of the Golden Circle incited secession and "inaugurated the greatest war in history." Keehn, David C. *Knights of the Golden Circle*. LSU Press, 2013

sacred oaths of secrecy." He spoke fast, pouring out words with great energy, moving quickly to serve a new dish of ideas before his listeners had time to digest what he had just laid on the table. As he spread his arms, a large medal that was pinned to his lapel flashed—a star over a Maltese cross.

Duffy and Klaus shared a significant look when Bickley alluded to "machinery already in motion" to accomplish what was nearly done "right here in my beloved Cincinnati" in 1860. He mentioned "the hero Cypriano Ferrandini," a Corsican Baltimore barber and KGC member who led a plot to assassinate Lincoln as he arrived in Washington for his inauguration.[147]

Bickley almost shouted, "I will not rest or sleep until Abraham Lincoln, now president, shall be removed out of the presidential chair, and I will wade in blood up to my knees, as soon as Jefferson Davis sees proper to march with his army to take the City of Washington and the White House."[148]

As the cheers subsided, he leaned forward, brought his voice to almost a whisper, and said he would share something that had never been revealed in public before, if they would swear on the Bible to absolute discretion.

A chorus of agreement and nods went through the crowd.

"Plans are afoot," he said, "to bolster the Confederate Army by thousands. As we speak, 50,000 good soldiers who are ready to fight for the South are languishing in stockades across Ohio, Indiana and Pennsylvania," he said, keeping his voice so low that the room became as silent as a cemetery. "Just imagine if these men can be freed and turned loose." The crowd murmured in awe. "Stand ready, Knights of the Golden Circle. When the time comes, fate may call upon *you* to save the South!"

"Hear, hear," some said as others stamped their feet, almost growling with eagerness.

---

147   Lincoln's chief of security, Allan Pinkerton, reported that an undercover agent had met with Ferrandini, who said Lincoln "must die ... if necessary, we will all die together." Ferrandini was not prosecuted in secessionist Baltimore. Pinkerton, Allan. *The Spy of the Rebellion*, 2017.

148   Taken from a KGC oath used in Marion, Ohio.

He told the men they were warriors, just like the valiant boys in butternut and gray, engaged in a great and noble battle for freedom from despotism, just as their forefathers battled and defeated King George and his hated British Redcoats.

"Gold is as valuable as guns," he said. "Your money is a weapon equal to all the muskets in the Union Army."

To close, General Bickley vowed, with visible emotion, "I will never desert the order or its arms as long as five brothers can be found who remain true to its work."

As a symphony of huzzahs shook the rafters, he waved an arm to introduce his traveling companion, Dr. William Bowles, a knight of the elite Third Order who had come from southern Indiana. Bowles stepped forward to recite the oath:

"Do you swear to obey our laws, rules, and regulations, and to execute, if in your power, every lawful commission entrusted to you; that you will do all you can as an honorable man to promote the best interests of the 28; and that you will deal justly by every brother twenty-eight as if he were your natural brother, so help you God!"

Several new recruits shouted "Yes!" together, and stepped forward, one by one, to kiss a Bible held by Dr. Bowles. When the last one bent to the Bible, straightened up with squared shoulders and saluted General Bickley, there was more applause and cheering. Hats were passed and soon overflowed with dues and contributions to the cause.

"What's this 28?" Duffy asked quietly.

"The man speaks numbers as a code," Klaus replied softly. "That is the number for Knights of the Golden Circle."

As a drill team marched and shook the floor, led by one of the guards at the door, the greeter touched Duffy's elbow and said, "My apologies sir, but General Bickley must hurry away to escape discovery and regrets he cannot meet you. He is in constant peril, as I am sure you understand."

Duffy nodded and said, "I reckon even Mr. Bickley has no appreciation of the peril he is in now."

The man nodded enthusiastically, then drifted back into the crowd. Duffy turned to Klaus and said softly, "I don't reckon General Bickley was in such haste as to leave without the generous dues and donations he collected."

Klaus laughed and replied, "Ja, enough to buy himself a clean new soul when the devil takes the one stained by blood. Let's leave. I can no longer abide the odor."

"The rotting hides?"

"That also."

It was Duffy's turn to chuckle.

• • • • •

Around the corner and upwind from the tannery, Amos said to Nehemiah, "Look yonder at that sawed off skulker slopin' off like a coyote stealin' a chicken." He pointed to one of the side doors, where a small moon-faced man in a dark suit was looking over his shoulder both ways as he emerged from the meeting place carrying a bulging carpetbag.

"That man ain't even knee high to a bar stool," Nehemiah said. "That bag is nearly dragging the ground. Are you inclined to give him a hand?"

Amos only nodded without taking his eyes from the man, then eased off into the shadows. A short time later, he returned, carrying the satchel. "This seemed to be a prodigious heavy burden so I offered to carry it for him," Amos said.

"Is the man fit to be measured for the sheet and box?" Nehemiah asked.

"No, he won't be planted in the bone orchard. But he will not be chirping merry."

"What do you reckon the baggage contains?"

"From the jingle, I speculate coins," Amos said, giving the bag a shake that produced a heavy metallic clinking.

"I think I know that tune. It sounds like several lagers at Mr. Wolff's saloon," Nehemiah smiled. "And here he is now in his roast beef outfit, with our new friend Buck MacDuffy."

"I told y'all I am not yer Buck," Duffy said.

Wolff looked down at his shirt and protested, "Nein, I am not wearing roast beef."

Nehemiah replied, "That's how us country folks talk when we see someone dressed for Sunday church—what we call roast beef day."

Ammos said, "Perhaps we can stand you gentlemen a beer to make amends." He gave the carpetbag another shake.

Duffy's eyes went from annoyance to a smile. "Now who do we reckon made this generous gift to our cause? Could it be Generalissimo Bickley?"

"With his compliments," Amos said, adding a slight bow. "This should dash his plans to flinders."

"I know a place to spend that geld," Klaus added.

"Lead the way, sir," said Duffy. Then, turning to Amos and Nehemiah, "Along the way I would be obliged if y'all would share the latest news of your adventures."

"It will be a short story," Amos said. Nehemiah laughed as Duffy and Klaus looked at each other in puzzlement.

"Pray tell," Klaus said. "We are all of us ears."

'Beware of surprise'

Gen. Anthony Wayne portrait by Trumbull and Forest.

The hickories, maples and sycamores were blazing with bright red, yellow and orange in the woods north of Fort St. Clair[149] as a convoy of twenty wagons loaded with grain and supplies made its slow, creaking journey to Fort Jefferson, about twenty miles farther north.[150]

---

149 Present-day Eaton Ohio, west of Dayton and about 60 miles northwest of Cincinnati.

150 Just south of Greenville, Ohio.

As dawn lit the morning sky, the dense forest beside the road suddenly erupted with war whoops and rifle shots, and the convoy came under attack. Within minutes, the scarlet maples were echoed in splashes of bright crimson on the uniforms of two young officers. The leaders of the convoy detachment, Lieutenant Lowrie and Ensign Boyd, were targeted first by the Indian raiders and shot dead.

News of the attack came to Cincinnati on the pages of the first edition of the first newspaper in Ohio, *The Centinel of the North-Western Territory,* on November 9, 1793:[151]

> Many reports have been circulated with respect to the attack made by the savages upon a convoy of provisions, some little time ago, between Fort St. Clair and Fort Jefferson, the following is an authentic account of that affair.
>
> Lieut. Lowrie of the Second, and Ensign Boyd, of the First sub-legions,[152] with a command consisting of about ninety noncommissioned officers and privates, having under their convoy twenty wagons loaded with grain and commissaries stores, were attacked between daylight and sunrise, seven miles advanced of Fort St. Clair, on the morning of the 17th. These two gallant young gentlemen, with thirteen noncommissioned officers and privates, bravely fell in action. It would appear that, after the fall of the officers, the party did not make much resistance, which was naturally to be expected.
>
> The Indians killed or carried off about seventy horses, leaving the wagons and stores standing in the road, and they were brought into the camp, six miles advanced of Fort Jefferson, on the 20th, with scarcely any other loss or damage, except what is before related.

---

151   Hughes, Timothy, *History's Newsstand Blog*, Rare & Early Newspapers, 2011. The Centinel was published until June 1796, when it was sold and became *Freeman's Journal*. The second oldest newspaper in Cincinnati and Ohio was the *Western Spy and Hamilton Gazette*, 1799.

152   The 1st Sub-Legion, also known as the First American Regiment, was formed in 1784 to protect the western frontier. It's first commander was Lt. Col. Josiah Harmar and it became known as "Harmar's Regiment." The First Regiment fought in all three campaigns in the Indian War in Ohio: Harmar, St. Clair and Wayne. After the War of 1812, it was consolidated into the US Army's 3rd Infantry Regiment, which still carries the colors assigned to it by General Anthony Wayne: black and white.

Cincinnati's first newspaper was welcomed with pride, but the news it contained spread dismay, alarm, fear and anger. Once again, the American military seemed helpless against the ruthless Shawnee and Miami tribes. And adding insult, this latest attack was identical to one that happened in the same place almost exactly a year before, when Major John Adair and 100 Kentucky Militia were attacked by Miami Chief Little Turtle almost under the walls of Fort St. Clair.

That convoy was looted and lost 100 horses and fifteen men: six killed, five wounded and four missing—presumably taken captive to be tortured and killed later for the entertainment of the Indian villages.

Both attacks happened at dawn. Both convoys had been taken by surprise. Both were timed to remind settlers and their soldiers of the anniversary of St. Clair's Defeat in 1791. To the residents of Cincinnati, Covalt Station and other stockades along the Ohio River, their back-breaking work to plant the seeds of a city in the wilderness seemed hopeless. American military leaders sent to protect them had been humiliated again. First the doomed Josiah Harmar expedition in 1790; then the horrifying massacre and defeat of General Arthur St. Clair in 1791. Now even armed supply trains escorted by more than 100 soldiers of the regular army were routed and plundered.

The beleaguered new outpost at Fort St. Clair could not even be resupplied without surprise attacks and huge losses of men and horses. The Indians ruled the Northwest Territory, and the Americans would never learn.

But one man greeted the news with determination, not despair. He was certain that the Americans would learn and would soon win. The future of the new nation depended upon it. If the young United States could not control and safely settle the new lands won in the 1783 Treaty of Paris, after defeating Great Britain, everything west of the Ohio River could fall back into the hands of the colonial superpowers, France, England and Spain.

America's bright future would be dimmed, its growth stunted like a tree in poisoned soil; it would be a feeble nation, clinging to the Atlantic coastline, withering without room to spread its roots.

All of that rested heavily on the shoulders of General Anthony Wayne, the new commander of the nation's first standing army: The Legion of the United States.

Known as "Mad Anthony" Wayne for his hot temper and daring heroics in the American Revolution, he would prove to history and his many critics that he was made for the job. But at first, he looked like a poor choice. Even President George Washington, who selected him, wrote a dubious profile of General Wayne: "...more active & enterprising than judicious & cautious. No economist, it is feared. Open to flattery—vain—easily imposed upon, and liable to be drawn into scrapes. Too indulgent (the effect perhaps of some of the causes just mentioned) to his Officers & men. Whether sober, or a little addicted to the bottle, I know not."[153]

Yet Washington's second option was worse. Gen. James Wilkinson was suspected by Washington's cabinet of being a spy for Spain—and they were right. So Wilkinson was passed over and assigned as second in command under Wayne. Wilkinson was so bitter he tried to sabotage the mission to embarrass Wayne. The men came to loathe each other.

Wayne, it turned out, was by far the best choice for Washington.

Anthony Wayne was tall, handsome and dashing. He had been raised on dreams of military glory,[154] hearing tales from his Irish father, who had fought in the French and Indian War. Growing up, he played war constantly with his schoolyard friends, acting out glorious victories over the Indians. He was trained as an engineer and like so many adventurous young men, he chased fortune and excitement as a surveyor in the wilderness.

In those days, surveyors were glamorous. They were the daring young men who risked their lives to plant stakes, measure acres and draw maps

---

153 George Washington, "Memorandum on General Officers, March 9th, 1792." Letter. From Founders Online, National Archives. The Wayne Museum, Wayne Township, Passaic County New Jersey.

154 The creator of the Batman comics, Bill Finger, named his hero's secret identity Bruce Wayne. According to the comics, Bruce Wayne was a direct descendant of Anthony Wayne and lived in a mansion that was a gift from George Washington. "Anthony Wayne: Wayne State's Namesake and Batman's Ancestor," *Ethnic Layers of Detroit, Wayne State University*.

that put a saddle and bridle of ownership on the wild country. Once mapped, it could be sold; once sold, it could be settled and tamed.

Wayne's natural warrior spirit was forged in blood at his first battle of the Revolutionary War in Quebec, where he was first to attack and last to leave the battlefield. The Battle of Trois-Riviéres was a defeat for the Americans, but a victory for Colonel Wayne, who put to shame his rival American officer, Col. Arthur St. Clair.

Wayne had survived through America's bleakest winter at Valley Forge (1777-78) with his friend and commander, General Washington. Mad Anthony had been valiant during that bitter winter, when so many men died of frostbite and disease and others deserted. It was Wayne who had recommended the campsite, not far from his boyhood home. Wayne fed the starving men by leading foraging parties to bring in beeves and grain.

And when that frostbitten, demoralized Continental Army finally emerged from Valley Forge the next spring, General Wayne was the man chosen by Washington to lead the attack at the Battle of Monmouth. After a brutal day of fighting, the British slipped away in the night and abandoned the battlefield. It was the first victory over the British after months of defeat and despair.

Bayonets at midnight

Later in the war, Wayne was awarded a Congressional Gold Medal for leading a daring midnight surprise attack that routed the British in the Battle of Stony Point in New York.

The British were in an island fortress that was believed to be as impregnable as Gibraltar.[155] Their cannon batteries and several companies of troops covered the steep hillside, and a swamp had to be crossed to even reach the foot of the cliff. In the river were British warships with cannons trained to protect the fort.

On July 16, 1779, Brigadier General Wayne was ordered by General Washington to do the impossible: Take Stony Point by leading 1,200 handpicked light infantrymen "with fixed Bayonets and Muskets

---

155   On the Hudson River, just north of New York City.

"Storming of Stony Point" by J. Rogers.

unloaded."[156] Wayne told the men to put their entire trust in their bayonets.

In the middle of the night, his men scaled the steep, rocky cliff, which was bristling with sharpened logs and defensive earthworks. They moved in complete silence.

When they got near the top, the British were alerted and responded. Savage, hand-to-hand combat broke out. Wayne was shot by a ball that creased his head and he lost consciousness. When he woke, the battle was still raging. He called out, "March on, boys. Carry me to the fort! For should the wound be mortal, I will die at the head of the column!"[157]

He suffered from his wound for weeks. It would be the first of a half-dozen battle wounds he sustained in the war. But his best medicine was always glory and acclaim. Inspired by Wayne, his men took the fort at Stony Point and captured 500 British prisoners. They turned the fort's cannons back on the British.

---

156   The muskets were unloaded to prevent an accidental discharge that would give away the advantage of surprise. Maly, Mark, "The Battle of Stony Point," American Battlefield Trust.

157   Ibid.

"The fort's our own," he reported to Washington. "Our officers and men behaved like men determined to be free."

Their victory lifted the spirits of the Continental Army and inspired the new American nation.

After Stony Point, Wayne's proven blueprint for command relied on tough discipline, constant training, bold action, personal courage and one of the infantry's most terrifying weapons, the bayonet.

So, ten years after the end of the American Revolutionary War, when President Washington desperately needed a fearless, experienced and effective general to defeat the allied Indian nations in the Northwest Territory, he turned to Mad Anthony Wayne.

Washington was a man whose emotions were sealed as tight as a coffin. But he had exploded in rare anger when he heard the news of St. Clair's horrible defeat.

"St. Clair defeated… routed! The officers nearly all killed, the men by wholesale, the rout complete," he stormed when the news was delivered by one of the soldiers who barely survived, Major Ebenezer Denny. "Too shocking to think of. A surprise in the bargain!"[158]

Before sending St. Clair to "awe" the Indians and pacify the Northwest Territory, Washington had warned him specifically:

"Yes! Here on this very spot, I took leave of him," he said in his Philadelphia parlor. "I wished him success and honor. 'You have my instructions,' I said, 'from the secretary of war. I had a strict eye on them and will add but one word: Beware of surprise! You know how the Indians fight us.'

"He went off with that as my last solemn warning thrown into his ears, and yet, to suffer that army to be cut to pieces—hacked by a surprise—the very thing I guarded against! Oh God, oh God, he's worse than a murderer!"

When he had finally paced up and down his parlor and vented his final curses on St. Clair, Washington took a breath, collected himself and told Secretary of War Henry Knox that St. Clair would get complete

---

158   Hogeland, William. *Autumn of the Black Snake. Farrar,* Straus and Giroux, 2017.

justice and a fair hearing. "Angry George Washington" was back in the box and the lid was nailed shut.

But secretly, he cursed himself for the choice of St. Clair. St. Clair had been courageous and even heroic in the war against the British. But he had become obese, with rolls of his belly bulging over his belt; and he was almost crippled by the "gentleman's curse" of the times, the gout. Washington had sent a limping fat man to tame the fiercest warriors in Ohio.

But it was no time for doubts and second thoughts. The coolheaded George Washington who had kept his wits amid roaring cannons and flying lead took control of himself and the future of his country. More than half of his nation's military had been annihilated. The beautiful Promised Land he had explored as a young man was now terrorized, held hostage; the gates to Eden were blocked by bloodthirsty demons.

Ben Franklin had famously told a bystander that the US Constitutional Convention had made "a republic, if you can keep it."

Washington had won a war to make a nation out of the wilderness in the Northwest Territory—but the question was again, "Can you can keep it?"

The US Army is born

Washington needed a new, professional army to keep it. And he knew he might not get another chance if the next campaign against the Indians failed.

After St. Clair's defeat, Cincinnati and its neighboring stations were plunged into chaos and gloom. The surviving soldiers who staggered back to Fort Washington were out of control, lawless and drunk if not suffering and wounded or slowly dying. The Indian Confederation that almost wiped out St. Clair's army could attack at any time, and there was nothing to stop them from burning everything in their path like an grass fire, all the way back to Pittsburgh. Every raid felt like the beginning of the final attack that would overwhelm their stockades, eradicate their sparse settlements and return the vast wilderness to the Indians.

In November 1792, a year after he led a raid that provoked the Indians' brutality at St. Clair's Defeat, Lt. Col. James Wilkinson wrote from Fort Washington:

"We are vulnerable to the Enemy at every point, the moment we step beyond the walls of our little fortresses; and the Enemy, if he knew our real situation, would greatly embarrass, if not cut off, all communications from post to post.... Should they act with vigor, there will be no security for any escort."[159]

But the Indians paused.

The winter of 1792-93 was one of the hardest in memory, which was almost welcome to the settlers as a relief from Indian raids. And the tribes could not maintain their alliance for long after a victory. The warriors took their plunder and returned to their villages to dance with the hundreds of new rifles and dried scalps they had taken, then go hunting to sustain their families through the long winter.

Washington used that pause to prepare for war.

He decided that undisciplined militias and soldiers recruited from the dregs of the frontier would not do. He wanted a standing army. He was convinced that the young nation could not survive and thrive without it. The European powers had laughed in disbelief when the Americans disbanded the Continental Army in 1784.

But the US Congress was made up of veterans, also, who had fresh memories of the insults and injuries when they were forced to quarter troops by the British standing army. Many were leery of a centralized government that could lead to the same tyranny they had just sacrificed so much to escape.

To those members of Congress, a standing army meant taxes, more central government power, less independence and more wars. In return for their grudging votes to establish an army, they demanded negotiations for peace with the Indians.

---

159 "The Indian Confederation failed to take advantage of the strategic opportunity following St. Clair's Defeat in 1791. The United States had suffered a tremendous military disaster and was incapable of any offensive action at all." Blair, Bryce Dixon Jr., "The Battle of Fallen Timbers and the Treaty of Fort Greeneville: Why did Anthony Wayne Win Both and Could He Have Lost?" Master's Thesis, University of Toledo, 2005.

Washington agreed and ordered Secretary of War Henry Knox to send two men to negotiate with the Miami and Shawnee tribes: John Hardin and Major Alexander Truman, both survivors of the terrible St. Clair defeat. The Indians answered the peace overture by scalping and killing both men. The tribes were winning the war and saw no reason to negotiate. And after Hardin and Truman were murdered, Washington saw no reason either.

General Wayne's response to the murdered peace mission summed up the new resolve of Americans: "There can be little expectation of an honorable and lasting peace with a victorious, haughty and insidious enemy."

President Washington played his cards skillfully. He used the trump card of St. Clair's defeat and horrifying news of continuing Indian depredations in Ohio and Kentucky to rally the votes he needed. He prepared lengthy, detailed reports that showed how Congress contributed to the desertions and failure of St. Clair's army with skinflint pay and corrupt contractors who left the men without supplies.

It worked. Five months after St. Clair's defeat, Washington won approval by Congress to create America's first professional, permanent military. On March 5, 1792, the Legion of the United States was established. More than 5,000 troops were authorized to go to war against the Indians, at a cost of nearly $1 million—which was nearly equal to the entire national budget at the time.[160] The new army was financed in part by land sales in the new frontier.

To lead it, he called on his old friend and warrior, Mad Anthony Wayne.

General Wayne was grateful for the reprieve from retirement. His life had become a self-made swamp of financial flummery, legal lunacy, domestic duncery and political putrefaction. He had disgraced his marriage and was being held in contempt by Congress for election fraud. His huge debts stuck to him like mud from his failing, mismanaged rice plantations in Georgia that produced nothing but headaches.

---

160 Hogeland, William. *Autumn of the Black Snake.* Farrar, Straus and Giroux, 2017.

He was more than happy to buckle his sword on again and ride off to seek glory.

Given a choice between lawsuit-happy lawyers and bloodthirsty Indians, he chose the Indians.

He resolved that this time would be different. He would not warn the Indians he was coming and lead an army of "old men and boys," like Gen. Josiah Harmar. And he would not go to war with a motley militia of malcontents and deserters who ran when the first shots were fired, leaving the wounded and their families at the mercy of the scalping tomahawks, like St. Clair's army.

His men would be trained, fairly paid, disciplined and as sharp as the points of the bayonets they would carry into combat.

"The bayonet is the most proper instrument for removing the film from the eyes and for opening the ears of the savages that has ever been discovered," he said. "It also has another powerful quality! It's glitter instantly dispelled the darkness and let in the light."

Little Turtle and Blue Jacket would soon discover that Mad Anthony Wayne was a new kind of enemy: relentless, fearless, effective and deadly. After watching Wayne and his army, some Indians called him Black Snake. Little Turtle called him the "black snake who never sleeps."

Wayne prepared by studying the earlier defeats. He was a creative and innovative strategist who had the support of two heroic Revolutionary War veterans, Secretary of War Knox and President Washington. And his mission had a personal motive: He had a low opinion of General St. Clair, whose defeat had cost the life of Wayne's good friend Maj. Gen. Richard Butler, who was left behind, mortally wounded, bleeding to death against a tree while his two brothers fled.

As soon as they were recruited with the lure of decent pay, his men were trained every day in "open order drill." They would not clot together in rigid columns to make easy targets. They were instructed to spread out and maneuver, to follow whatever lines the ground and the battle required.

General Wayne dressed them in new uniforms, with bearskin covers for their hats. They had to shave and bathe regularly and keep their uniforms clean and in order. Soldiers caught sleeping on guard duty were executed. The men had heard about Wayne's reputation. When he was commanding Fort Ticonderoga in the Revolutionary War, he stopped a mutiny by personally facing down 262 men and ordering first their leader, then the rest of the men, to kneel on the ground. When one threatened him, Wayne beat the man severely.

But his men got regular whiskey rations—with extras for the units that won mock battles and shooting contests. He made sure their muskets and powder were the best that could be found,[161] and the men were taught to reload on the run, just as Simon Kenton had done for years to survive gunfights even when he was outnumbered. The Indians were excellent marksmen, but new US Legionnaires who could load faster would have the tactical advantage of throwing more lead on their targets.

In mock battles, some of Wayne's men played the role of the Indians so they would learn how the enemy fought. The Sub-Legions each had their own colors: 1st was black and white; 2nd, red and white; 3rd, buff and black; 4th, green and white. As they competed against each other, each unit developed an esprit de corps; morale was as high as their certainty of victory.

General Wayne also made sure he had cavalry and scouts to be his eyes and ears in the field. As President Washington no doubt warned, "Beware of surprise." He would not be caught in an ambush like St. Clair and Harmar.

Finally, he made plans to build forts along his march to ensure an adequate supply chain—another mistake made by St. Clair, who lost many troops to desertion because they could not be fed and supplied, and then sent another detachment of valuable regulars to search for a missing supply train.

As a great admirer of Julius Caesar, General Wayne adopted the Roman Legion's strategy: a string of fortified positions to support his attack, cover retreat and defend the territory. The convoy that was

---

161 Wayne invented an improved firing mechanism that was adopted for his men's rifles.

attacked in October 1793 had been sent to supply those forts ahead of his march. The Indian raid defeated the escorts—but they did not defeat General Wayne's plan. What others saw as a humiliating defeat, he brushed off as a setback.

He ordered troops in the forward forts to come out and guard the convoys. It put them at risk and stretched the men and their horses to the limit, but it worked.

One of his newest outposts, Fort Recovery,[162] would play a decisive role in the war.

General Wayne never got the 5,000-man army he was promised by Congress. But when he left Fort Washington and marched north on October 7, 1793, he had 3,500 well-trained soldiers in uniform under his command.[163]

He had only one major worry: Would the British who stubbornly held onto their forts in Detroit and northern Ohio join the Indian Confederation to outnumber him and deploy the cannons and tactics the Indians lacked?

162　Fort Recovery, Ohio, is just east of the Indiana border, southwest of St. Marys.

163　Compared to about 1500 for Harmar and 2300 for St. Clair.

Summer 1794

'*Pick up the tomahawk*'

Stone tomahawk or warclub.

While General Wayne prepared to march north, the British were doing all they could to pour fuel on the bonfire of war without burning their own fingers—observing Shakespeare's admonition, "Heat not a furnace for your foe so hot that to singe yourself."

The Indians were "stimulated by British emissaries to a continuance of the war or to dictate terms of peace perhaps disgraceful to the American character," Wayne wrote at the time.

He was right. The governor of the Province of Quebec was British officer Sir Guy Carleton, also known as the 1st Baron of Dorchester, a title created for him in 1786. Lord Dorchester believed the 1783 Treaty of Paris was a colossal blunder that gave away a continent to end a troublesome skirmish with misfit colonial rebels. He wanted to fix that by starting another war—but Great Britian was already going to war against France, so he had orders from London to avoid provoking America.

But news took months to reach London. He had an ocean of latitude to hatch schemes to punish the upstart colonists and block American expansion westward. If he could not start a war, he would incite the Indians to be the proxy army for Great Britain. His agents Alexander McKee and Simon Girty supplied weapons, paid bounties for scalps and prisoners, and went from village to village to encourage raids, depredations and havoc. Both agents led raids against the settlements.

Their message wherever they went was as clear as the black beads that signaled war to the tribes: "Pick up the tomahawk."

Girty was especially terrifying to the settlers. A white man who had gone over to the Indian life, he was known to be more brutal than the worst of the Indians when it came to rape, torture and cruelty. He had presided over four days of torture of Col. William Crawford in 1782, who was slowly burned, mutilated, beaten and shot seventy times with powder to inflict agonizing burns. Girty laughed as Crawford begged to be put out of his misery.

Girty had at one time been a friend of Simon Kenton, but became the dark shadow that crept into nightmares on the Ohio River. If Kenton was hailed as an avenging angel who rescued settlers from certain death, Girty was the Lucifer of wilderness Hell.[164]

Early in 1794, Lord Dorchester gave a speech to the assembled Six Nations chiefs of the Indian Confederation. He told the gathered tribes—Shawnee, Delaware, Miami, Mingo, Wyandot, Ottawa, Iroquois and others—that the British would go to war against the Americans by the end of the year, and the tribes would get back all the land in Ohio that rightfully belonged to them.

---

164   Girty was indicted for treason by the US government but fled to Canada and never was caught. The British gave him a 164-acre farm in Canada near Detroit in 1798. He died there in 1818. British soldiers fired a salute over his grave. Doddridge, Joseph. *Notes on the Settlement and Indian Wars,* 1997.

More incendiary words could hardly have been found to recruit warriors throughout the Northwest Territory and as far away as Tennessee, Michigan and Missouri.

The Indians already felt invincible. Now they had a promised alliance from the most powerful empire in the world.

The British justified their "secret" war against the Americans behind legal claims. Two British forts, Fort Miamis[165] and Fort Detroit,[166] were on United States land that was granted by the Treaty of Paris. But the British said they would not leave until the Americans paid restitution for British land that had been seized by Americans in the Revolutionary War.

Ironically, those seized properties included both Georgia rice plantations owned by General Wayne.

President Washington, Wayne and the rest of Congress knew very well what the British were doing. Wayne would get his chance to humiliate Lord Dorchester and the British by the end of the summer.

But the opening battle for General Wayne in the Indian War would come first.

---

165 Maumee, Ohio, southwest of Toledo.

166 Fort Detroit enclosed less than a half-acre, with blockhouses at the corners. It had a drawbridge and bristled with cannons, including 24-pounders called "The British Lions." Spencer, Oliver M. *Indian Captivity, 1848.*

St. Clair's revenge

Reproduction of Fort Recovery in Fort Recovery, Ohio.

On a cold, snowy Christmas Eve in 1793, Gen. "Mad Anthony" Wayne and 300 soldiers of his First Legion halted their march on the banks of the Wabash River, laid down their packs, rubbed aching shoulders and rested their tired feet. Then they got back to their feet and went right to work building a stockade. Wayne named it Fort Recovery.

Wayne had deliberately chosen the blood-soaked ground where Gen. Arthur St. Clair's army was massacred in 1791. That gave the name two meanings: the recovery of the American military after its humiliating defeat two years before; and the recovery of the remains of the men who died there.

Before they could build the new fort, pitch their tents or even find a place to sit or lie down, Wayne's men had to clear away the bleached bones of nearly a thousand men, women and children who were butchered in St. Clair's Defeat.

Everywhere they swept away the snow, dug footings or cut trees to build the stockade, they found more bones from the tragic victims who were left behind in the greatest Indian victory over the American military in US history.[167] Many showed evidence of grisly torture and mutilation. The trail of skulls and skeletal remains, often still attached by decaying flesh, stretched for miles down the trail of the fleeing army.[168]

General Richard Butler's skeleton was found by his brother, Edward. It was mostly intact, still sitting under the tree where he had been left behind, bleeding to death.[169]

General Wayne had no respect for General St. Clair, who still lingered as governor of the Northwest Territory. But he had an eye for history and a heart for the men who had died there. He ordered his men to gather all the skulls they could find, then buried them with a reverent ceremony in the center of the fort as a memorial and a warning: Beware of surprise.

The fort location was also a warning to the Indians, who had marked each anniversary of their victory over St. Clair with deadly attacks. Wayne wanted them to know that America was determined to recover its security, its hope and its honor.

And Fort Recovery would play a pivotal role.

When the 15-foot stockade walls were finished, Wayne returned to Fort Greeneville and left Captain Alexander Gibson in charge of the fort, which was garrisoned with 250 men and six cannons that had been left behind by St. Clair.

Six months later, on the morning of June 30, 1794, a band of Choctaw and Chickasaw scouts who served with the American army rode up to the fort and reported a large mass of Indian warriors nearby. A patrol was sent out, but found nothing unusual, so a large supply convoy set

---

167 By comparison, 260 were killed at Little Bighorn; almost a thousand soldiers and their families were killed at St. Clair's Defeat.

168 "...the now silent, contorted forms provided mute evidence of the Indians' unbelievable vengeful depravity." Van Trees, Robert V., "The Military History of Fort Recovery, Ohio. Van trees, of Fort Recovery, was a military pilot who one day found himself in the cockpit with a copilot who was a direct descendant of Blue Jacket.

169 Hogeland, William. *Autumn of the Black Snake. Farrar,* Straus and Giroux, 2017.

out to return their empty wagons south to Fort Greenville, while their 100-man escort finished breakfast.

The convoy was still in sight of Fort Recovery and its escort was still at breakfast when the Indians struck. A mounted company of dragoons led by Major William McMahon rode to the rescue, but the Indians were waiting in ambush. There were more than 2,000 concealed in the woods, including warriors from all the Confederated Tribes and a company of British soldiers led by Alexander McKee and Simon Girty. It would be the greatest force of Indians ever assembled for a battle in the Northwest Territory.

The Indians were reluctantly led by Miami Chief Little Turtle and Shawnee Chief Blue Jacket. Both had argued against attacking the fort and wanted to instead raid supply lines to starve out the chain of forts, but they were overruled. The Indians waited until the dragoons were within easy musket range and opened fire with a devastating volley.

About half the men outside the walls of the fort were killed, including the commander of the dragoons and convoy escort, Major McMahon. Riflemen were deployed with bayonets to cover the retreat, and the remainder were able to get back inside as the gates were slammed shut.

That left about 250 Americans inside the fort, outnumbered by ten to one. Once again, the Indians had pulled off an ambush that took the Americans by surprise. But the battle was not over. This would not be another rout of St. Clair. The Indians faced tall, solid stockade walls, and they had no cannons to breach the log fort.

After the first attack, Little Turtle and Blue Jacket wanted to leave and attack General Wayne's main force at Fort Greenville. But again, they were overruled, and the most eager warriors launched a direct assault on Fort Recovery. Among the warriors who fought in the battle was a future Shawnee chief who would lead another Indian Confederation in the War of 1812: Tecumseh.

The battle continued through the night and lasted three days. Inside the fort, supplies were running low. But the men were safe behind the walls of Fort Recovery and used their rifles and cannons effectively.

After the third day, the Indians left, defeated and demoralized. Little Turtle and Blue Jacket were proved right: Without cannons, their vast numbers, even with British help, were useless against General Wayne's forts.

In the initial attack, the First Legion lost thirty-five dead, forty-three wounded and twenty captured or missing. Among the horses used for convoys and cavalry, forty-six had been killed. The Indians captured more than 200 horses and thirty cattle.

The Indian Confederation lost about fifty killed and 100 wounded. As they returned north, warriors in some tribes accused their traditional tribal enemies of shooting them in the back during the battle.[170] The confederacy was beginning to fall apart.

America's new standing Army—General Wayne's First Legion—had its first victory in its first battle. Their training and discipline had paid off.

And the ghosts of the men and families whose bones littered the battlefield of St. Clair's Defeat must have cheered at last.

---

170 That may have happened, or it may have been Chickasaw scouts who flanked the Confederated Tribes and fired on them from behind. Or both.

The Kentucky rebellion

"Needles," Nehemiah said. "My pappy always carried a leather pouch of needles. He said they was worth more than all the gold a mule could carry. Saved his life, he claimed."

"Needles?" Amos asked, looking skeptical.

"Think on it," Nehemiah said.

They were riding east along the Wooster Pike, looking for Colonel Whittlesey, who had taken an afternoon away from the avalanche of paperwork at headquarters to return to his earthworks on Round Bottom Road, near Newtown.

"That little sliver of steel was never seen by the tribes until traders came. They had to sharpen bird bones, sticks, whatever came to hand. They would trade almost anything for a needle and thread. And a small pouch with no more weight than a dog's ear could carry hundreds."

"I never thought of that," Duffy said, nodding. "Just a little thing that never crosses my mind. But it must be nearly a miracle to them. How did it save his life?"

"He was half froze to death on the trail to Cincinnati after St. Clair's Defeat—"

"Is that the Battle of the Wabash?" Amos interrupted.

"Yes," Nehemiah nodded, "also called Little Turtle's Victory." He paused, gave a sidelong look at Amos, as if expecting another question, then continued. "He was able to trade a handful of his needles to one of the Indian scouts for a bear pelt that spared him from leaving a trail of toes and fingers in the woods."

As they arrived at the earthworks, they found the colonel up to his waist in a trench that was dug into the side of what looked like the raised track of a goliath gopher. Whittlesey glanced up briefly as they approached, held up a hand to signal "Wait," then bent to pick up a clump of clay. As he picked away the dirt with his blackened fingers, a shape emerged.

"Pipe?" Nehemiah asked.

"You have a good eye," Colonel Whittlesey replied.

"I've seen the like near Chillicothe," Nehemiah replied. "How old, you reckon?"

"At least a thousand, maybe two thousand years," Whittlesey said. He extended his hand up for an assist, and Amos dismounted and hoisted him up out of the trench. Whittlesey carefully laid the relic down next to a small stack of what looked like bones.

"Judging from those ribs, they were hardly bigger than children," Duffy said.

"Many of these *were* children," Whittlesey nodded. "If only they could speak to us…" He gave his head a quick shake, then said, "Forgive my meanderings. You gentlemen are here to discuss a matter that was left in my hands by General Wallace. I am curious to learn more."

As they described the recent events, Whittlesey's eyes lit up and his eyebrows raised at the mention of Bickley and Bowles. When the impromptu outdoor briefing was finished, he said, "That explains a recent letter from the general. I am somewhat familiar with these Knights of the Golden Circle."

The colonel then told them how he had been stationed at Camp Dennison in December 1861 when a party of angry citizens arrived from Kentucky to meet with the commander, Gen. Melancthon Smith Wade. They reported that lawless Copperheads were terrorizing Boone, Owen, Gallatin, Grant and Carroll counties.

"Men who were outspoken for the Union were shot and hanged," Whittlesey said. "And Lord help anyone who openly supported President Lincoln. The Knights or Secessionists or whatever they called themselves openly recruited for the Confederate Army and threatened to burn entire towns that leaned to the north."

General Wade ordered Colonel Whittlesey to take the 20th Ohio Volunteer Infantry south to restore order and protect loyal Unionists from the marauding Secessionists. Whittlesey and his men arrived in Warsaw, Kentucky by riverboat on Christmas Day. Within two hours, the leaders of the Knights of the Golden Circle were arrested and put on a riverboat, shipped off to prison at Camp Chase in Columbus, Ohio.

"But then the good citizens of Warsaw protested," he said, emphasizing "good" in a way that made it sound worse than a curse. "They supported the Union as long as they did not have to oppose the Confederacy."

"That's Kentucky in a peanut shell," Duffy said. "I suppose the Knights had strong political influence?"

"You suppose correctly," Colonel Whittlesey said. "But I had my orders to protect the Union loyalists in Kentucky not only from violence, but from the fear of it, against anyone who threatened them on account of their adhesion to the Government of the United States."[171]

"Whatever happened next?" Nehemiah asked.

"I continued to arrest anyone who was conspiring to overthrow the government or who put peaceable and loyal men in fear for their persons or property. I announced that anyone who had Secessionist sentiments but took no action would not be molested but would be protected.

"After that we had trouble with a group called the Eagle Home Guards. We were pleased to discover that they had foolishly circulated a list of their officers and seventy-two others who had pledged to resist the Union to the death. Their commander was a wealthy man, Nash Sanders, who lived about ten miles south of Warsaw. We did not find him at home, but we discovered a letter from the adjutant general of the state of Kentucky, promising them arms and support."

Duffy said, "I am flummoxed by how Kentucky has been able to take both sides at once."

Whittlesey chuckled and resumed his story. "We finally cornered the Knights in New Liberty, surrounded the town and searched their

---

171 *The Brilliance of Charles Whittlesey.* Kent State University, 2022.

homes. We confiscated enough small arms to outfit a small company. But this time, instead of arresting the men, I gave them the option to sign an oath that they would refrain from injuring or harassing anyone for their loyalty to the Union and promise not to participate in any efforts to overthrow the government."

"It worked?" Amos asked.

"Much to my surprise, yes. More than 150 men signed it, and nearly all of them honored it. We had to occupy Owenton, also, for the same purpose. But within the passage of three weeks, we had subdued the rebellion in Kentucky and we were able to return to Camp Dennison, leaving behind a detachment of two dozen cavalry."

"I heard you got crossways with General Buell," Duffy said. "How did that come to pass?"

"Some of the Knights of the Golden Circle who were incarcerated at Camp Chase hired lawyers."

"Lawyers," Nehemiah said, and spit on the ground.

Whittlesey nodded agreement. "General Buell seemed more in sympathy with the Secessionists than with their unfortunate Union neighbors. He wanted the prisoners released, but I would not. Eventually, my position was becoming so ineffectual to protect Union men, and uncomfortable to myself, that I applied to be relieved from that duty. But I was satisfied that we had done our small part to save Kentucky for the Union."

Duffy nodded. "I believe President Lincoln said, 'We hope that God is on our side, but we must have Kentucky.' Well done, sir."

"Yes and no," Whittlesey replied with a rueful shake of his head. "My request for reassignment took me to the battle of Fort Donnelson, where I was under the command of General Wallace. I went from General Buell's kettle to General Wallace's bonfire at the Battle of Shiloh."

"I was honored to serve there with him as well," Duffy said.

As Nehemiah and Amos listened, Duffy and Colonel Whittlesey compared notes on the battle, on General Wallace and on his Third Division commanders. Duffy agreed with Whittlesey that, "You could scarcely find a better man in a hot battle than Lew Wallace of Indiana or Col. Manning Force of Cincinnati."

"So you are all too aware of how General Wallace was ill-treated?" Whittlesey asked Duffy.

"Tell it for those of us who are not," Amos said.

Whittlesey did. Once they had finally overcome General Ulysses Grant's vague, garbled orders and arrived on the battlefield, General Wallace and his division held down the right flank and swept the field of Confederates on the second day at Shiloh. Duffy and Whittlesey expressed their disgust at how Grant's staff used their reports to blame Wallace for Grant's mistakes.

"But enough war stories," Whittlesey said. He reached into his jacket pocket and said, "General Wallace asked me to pass along this letter to you." He handed it to Duffy. "As you may be aware, the general knows a great deal about Dr. Bowles and likes none of it."

Duffy nodded. "Remember Buena Vista," he quoted.

"Yes," Whittlesey said. "General Wallace has never forgotten."

'Cease firing and retreat!'

Lew Wallace was deep in Mexico, closer to Guatemala than to Texas. He was riding a wave of patriotism that he believed was certain to deliver him to the golden shores of battlefield glory.

Back in Crawfordsville, Indiana, Wallace had been treading water as a mediocre attorney who detested the tedious work. But it provided enough reputation to form and command a company called the Marion Rifles in the 1st Indiana Volunteer Regiment. Everything he knew about tactics, training and war was self-taught from the pages of books.

The Mexican-American War had flared up like kerosene in a cookstove nearly a year ago. According to the newspapers, Mexican President Antonio Lopez de Santa Anna was still bitter over his humiliating capture at the Battle of San Jacinto and set out to take back the independent Republic of Texas to punish the Americano gringos.

Santa Anna did want revenge. But the cause of the war was complicated. President James Polk had baited Mexico into a border confrontation so he could declare war and spread the stars and stripes over Texas and grab land along the Rio Grande that Mexico claimed.

To Wallace, that hardly mattered. His country was calling with a chorus of trumpets that sounded like triumph, action and adventure.

The 1st Indiana had come more than a thousand miles to get near the battlefield at Buena Vista, only to find it was nothing like their recruiting dreams. Gen. Zachary Taylor's headquarters were filthy and shabby. As they marched past on review and saluted, Wallace and his men were disappointed that the gallant commander known as "Old Rough and Ready" did not even poke his head out of the stained tent where his flag flew. Instead, they saw a fat, tattered man in a dirty, mangy uniform, wearing a scrofulous wool slouch hat low over his unshaved stubble.

That tramp, Wallace learned later, was General Taylor.

By the time they arrived, Second Lieutenant Wallace's regiment of Hoosiers had lost more than 500 men to dysentery, smallpox and other diseases. But he was still eager for battle.

He got what he wished for in a huge cloud of dust on the morning of February 22, when the Mexican Army arrived on the battlefield. Santa Anna led more than 15,000 men; Taylor, with fewer than 5,000, was outnumbered three-to-one.[172]

But when Santa Anna sent a demand for Taylor's surrender, Old Rough and Ready refused and called out all the troops under his command—except Wallace's unit of Hoosiers.

While the battle raged that day, Wallace was trapped behind the lines in an old adobe hacienda with several other soldiers, fighting furiously to survive a Mexican attack.

But it was the fate of the 2nd Indiana Regiment that would change his life.

In the heat of the battle, the 2nd Indiana was under heavy fire when it was ordered to charge. Instead, their commander, Col. William Bowles, ordered, "Cease fire and retreat!"

Wallace wrote later that Colonel Bowles was "too confused to consider anything but escape in the quickest possible time ... Only the company nearest heard what he said, and they turned and gazed at him in wonder."

So Colonel Bowles yelled again: "Cease firing, and retreat!"

It nearly cost them the battle. Many good men and horses were killed because of Colonel Bowles's poltroonery. A court of inquiry considered charges of incompetency, ignorance of tactics, misbehavior and cowardice, but thanks to his friends, he was exonerated. To spare Bowles, General Taylor blamed the 2nd Indiana Hoosiers for running from battle when they were clearly ordered twice by Bowles to retreat.

---

172 The United States won the battle with about 267 killed; Santa Anna lost nearly 600 killed and Mexico lost the war that ended in 1848.

"Now no man shall say this was not an order," Wallace wrote in his letter to Duffy. "It was an order, and by one in authority. And at once all the shame of the flight that followed attaches to him who gave the order—the gallant Colonel Bowles."

Duffy shared the letter with Nehemiah and Amos. Wallace wrote:

None of the men who followed him dreamed that under his order the ultimate martial issue to which they looked forward so ardently would turn out a lifelong provocation of tears and shame."[173]

If you want to understand why Bowles betrayed the Union with the Knights of the Golden Circle, know this: After he ordered his men to retreat, he abandoned his command and concealed himself by pretending to be a private soldier among the Mississippians led by Col. Jefferson Davis. Yes, the same Jefferson Davis who now is president of the Confederacy.

It was Davis who vouched for Bowles in his trial for cowardice. And now Bowles is repaying his debt of dishonor by leading the KGC in Indiana to overthrow the Union and replace President Lincoln with President Jefferson Davis.

Duffy closed the letter and said, "You gentlemen should also know that General Wallace recruited troops in Indiana with the battle cry, 'Remember Buena Vista.' They were all edacious hungry to recover their honor at Shiloh, and they did."

Nehemiah said, "So General Wallace redeemed them at Shiloh, but lost his own reputation. And now he has restored his own reputation by saving Cincinnati."

Duffy nodded. "His letter also gives us our orders. We are to do whatever we can to frustrate the efforts of Bickley and Bowles, and endeavor to discover the identity of the man who is known by the Knights of the Golden Circle as Brutus."

---

173 Wallace, Lew. *Lew Wallace; an Autobiography*. New York; London, Harper & Brothers, 1906.

October 4, 1794

'I defy all the devils of hell'

Anthony Wayne allowed himself a rare and private smile as he opened the report from Captain Gibson. He was alone in his tent. It was a moment to savor.

News of the victory had come from a courier who rode into Fort Greenville[174] with Gibson's written report. Wayne immediately wanted to ask the man for details but held back. He wanted to project the impression among his officers and men that it was no less than he had always expected.

And now he opened the letter and began to read. For an hour, he forgot his painful gout and all the constant frustrations of moving an army through wilderness, maintaining discipline, keeping his men fed and supplied....

His contractors were, as always, corrupt and incompetent. The supplies ordered and paid for never arrived on time if they arrived at all— and when the wagons were finally unloaded, the moth-eaten uniforms, shoddy shoes and moldy flour only brought anger and disappointment.

The military contractors sent gunpowder that fizzled and rag-water whiskey so raw it could melt the brass off a soldier's buttons.

His army was made of men a lot like himself—failures at civilian life, drunks and borderline criminals. One member of Congress had scoffed that his recruits were "purchased from the prisons, wheelbarrows and brothels of the nation at foolishly low wages ... enlisted because they could no longer live unhung any other way."[175]

---

174 Greenville, Ohio: originally named after Revolutionary War hero Nathanael Greene. The fort was first named Fort Greene Ville, later changed to Greenville.

175 Robb, H.L., 'Mad Anthony' Wayne's Campaign Against the Indians in Ohio, 1792-1794 *The*

And yet he had sharpened them on the grindstone of discipline into a razor-edged bayonet, which was now stabbing deep into the heart of Indian Territory. From Fort Washington they had marched, on average, twelve miles a day.

He had faced nearly all the same obstacles that were blamed for St. Clair's Defeat—even the relentless gout that made walking feel like stepping on bear traps. And yet he had bested his old rival completely. He pictured St. Clair's lemon-sucking face when he got the news of the victory at Fort Recovery, on the same ground where St. Clair was humiliated. It made him smile again.

In his younger days, St. Clair had the looks of a patrician—slim, elegant, gray at the temples, aristocratic. But he was a mediocrity, Wayne thought. All his courage came from a glass of whiskey or bowl of rum.[176]

He thought, *And here is Anthony Wayne, doing what the sainted St. Clair could not—what all those critics in Congress said could never be done, especially by that rogue Mad Anthony.*

He chuckled. He would never admit it openly, but he liked the nickname. It kept his enemies off balance. They would never know what to expect from "Mad Anthony." All the nabobs who had warned Washington he was making a mistake—who insisted Wayne was a scoundrel, a failure, a fool....

Now they could eat their powdered wigs. Mad Anthony was winning. His training, his discipline, his strategy and tactics had just humiliated the largest force of Indians ever assembled in the Northwest Territory.

And now it was time to advance to the next step. It would be done with his own brand of reckless caution: relentless marches, constant vigilance, meticulous preparation and devil-may-care, bayonet audacity in battle.

As Wayne and his army moved north ever deeper into the wilderness, closer to the Indian power and danger, they would build careful defenses every day before they could camp in safety. It was hard on

---

Military Engineer, November-December 1921.

176 Pennypacker, Samuel W., "Anthony Wayne," *The Pennsylvania Magazine, 1908.*

the men, but it kept the army from the fate of St. Clair and Harmar: Beware of surprise.

He had his dragoons[177] riding on the flanks, always there, with scouts in front and behind, giving Little Turtle and Blue Jacket no chance to steal horses, loot supplies, kill men, spread fear or spring an ambush.

Congress had come around—finally. All the antiwar dithering had made Wayne wonder how a republic could ever survive when its military is at the mercy of civilians and politicians. But now, after months of being told to wait, Secretary of War Henry Knox was urging him to attack, attack.

Wayne reached into his stack of correspondence on his portable camp desk and pulled out an earlier letter from Knox near the start of his march, right after he moved his men to Fort Hobson[178] outside Cincinnati to get them away from the whiskey and debauchery of that muddy little village. There it was: "The people are adverse in the extreme to an Indian war," Knox cautioned. "It is still more necessary than heretofore that no offensive operations should be undertaken against the Indians."[179]

And now he was told he could not attack fast enough. He laughed.

No, he had nothing to worry about from that direction, but his mind turned to another threat from the rear. This one was closer: His own second in command, Gen. James Wilkinson.

Letters from his friends in Philadelphia hinted that Wilkinson was writing anonymous letters to undermine him and had even expressed his intentions to file charges against his commander. Now it became clear: the source of backbiting, malingering, discontent; the sudden silences and conversations that stopped in midair when he joined his officers: That was all Wilkinson. Bitter about being passed over for command, perhaps. Or was there more to it? The man was charming, efficient, eager to please when they were together, but it was all a charade while Wilkinson plotted to sabotage Wayne and their mission.

---

177 Cavalry.

178 Named after Hobson's Choice—meaning there was no better choice.

179 Pennypacker, Samuel W., "Anthony Wayne," *The Pennsylvania Magazine, 1908.*

But Wayne smiled again. He was warned, and therefore armed against Wilkinson's plots.

On July 28, a cannon salute was fired, drums boomed and rattled, and Wayne led his army out of Fort Greenville. He rode at the front, leading his army to a new stockade that would be built, Fort Defiance,[180] north of Fort Recovery, at the place where the Auglaize and Maumee Rivers joined together.

It would be named by Kentucky Militiaman Charles Scott,[181] who was riding with Wayne's army. Scott said, "I defy the English, the Indians and all the devils of hell to take it."

But before Wayne could get his men there to begin building Fort Defiance, he was nearly killed. On the afternoon of August 3, as he rested after a long day's march, a tree suddenly crashed down on his tent, narrowly missing him, but painfully pinning his leg and ankle.

Wayne was revived with smelling salts and surprised his men by mounting up again as soon as he was able to walk. Privately, he believed it was no accident. He immediately suspected Wilkinson of attempted murder.

But he was determined that he would not be stopped.

Many miles to the north, there was another new fort in the Northwest Territory. This one was built by the British: Fort Miamis.[182] It was a British chess piece placed strategically to block the Americans, not far from the site of Fort Defiance.

The British Lieutenant Governor of Upper Canada, John Graves Simcoe, sent troops to build Fort Miamis in the spring of 1794, to supply and encourage the Indian Confederation in their war on the Americans. Simcoe was also worried that Wayne might march his army of Americans all the way to Detroit.

After Little Turtle and Blue Jacket were defeated at Fort Recovery,

---

180   Now Defiance, Ohio, southwest of Toledo and northeast of Fort Wayne, Indiana.

181   Scott was a fierce warrior and veteran of the American Revolution. He fought alongside Anthony Wayne at the Battle of Stony Point. His son was killed in the doomed Harmar expedition. Scott survived St. Clair's Defeat to again lead his mounted militia into the Battle of Fallen Timbers. He was elected governor of Kentucky in 1808.

182   Near present-day Maumee, Ohio.

those worries increased. Before long, Little Turtle visited Fort Miamis to ask for help. He had been assured that Fort Miamis was there to protect the Indians. Now he asked for cannons and British soldiers to man them, so he could launch another attack on Fort Recovery.

The British, for all their talk of support, refused. And now Little Turtle began to worry.

Meanwhile, Wayne advanced to the site of Fort Defiance, which was finished on August 17. He rested his men, then issued orders: They would move out again soon. And this time they would lighten their packs by carrying only enough rations for a few days. But they were issued extra ammunition.

The battle was near.

NOVEMBER 13, 1862

'Et tu, Brute?'

"I wished I had one of them needles you was runnin' on about," Amos said to Nehemiah.

"Which one?"

"The one named Brutus. It must be lost in forty acres of haystacks."

They sat in the backroom at Blume des Rheins saloon owned by Klaus Wolff, commiserating over steins of lager. For weeks they had checked hotels and questioned customers at every tavern in town. It was thirsty work. Even Detective Rainey was unable to offer any information. Nehemiah's friend who worked as a porter at the railroad station, Moses Williams, had also agreed to keep an eye out for someone named Brutus.

But all their efforts had come up as empty as their drained beer steins.

When it finally came, their first clue arrived from an unexpected direction.

Klaus sat down to join them and spread open a copy of the *Cincinnati Enquirer*. As Klaus read about the defeat of Gen. Ambrose Burnside at the Battle of Fredericksburg, Nehemiah's eye was caught by a small notice on the back page. Under the headline "Amusements," it announced a play at the National Theater on Sycamore, between Third and Fourth streets.[183]

It was a comedy called "Money."

Not very comical to them that lacks it, Nehemiah thought. But it was the name of the leading man that drew him to take a closer look.

He jabbed the back of the paper, startling Klaus into an eruption of German curses that made Amos laugh.

---

183   The *Cincinnati Enquirer*, November 13, 1862, page 3.

"Isn't that the famous actor who does Shakespeare?" he asked.

Klaus flipped the page over and studied it. "Nien, you mistake him for his brother. This man is not so famous. But he is well known at my business across the river, where we provide the horizontal refreshment, as you gentlemen like to call it."

Duffy returned from the bar with fresh beers, sat down and asked, "Now what are y'all on about?"

"I've heard this name before," Nehemiah said, pointing to the newspaper. "Something to do with Shakespeare. Gets me to cogitating about *Julius Caesar.* There's a scene... somethin' like 'Et tu, Brute.'"

"No I have not et too, don't mind if I do," Amos said.

Duffy picked up the paper and studied it. He looked at Klaus. "You say this hombre is a regular in your Corinthian temple?"

"Ja," Klaus replied.

"Well, I might not know Julius Caesar from a bull's foot, but Nehemiah could be accidentally right."

"Even a blind acorn can find a squirrel," Klaus said.

"And we might as well go look for a horse ladder or pan gold in a privy," Amos said.

Nehemiah nodded. "It's a longer shot than plinking a small squirrel from a tall tree, but we done looked everywhere else. I'd like to clap eyes on the actor. I ain't never been to a real stage play."

"I can obtain tickets," Klaus said.

"And here I thought we was going to visit the School of Venus," Amos said. "Now you've done ruint my day."

Klaus laughed. "A fine new name for my establishment! School of Venus."

Duffy asked Klaus, "Do you reckon you can collect any details about him from your, ahh, hostesses?"

"Ja. The man talks enough for two sets of teeth, I am told. And always about himself. The curtain never drops on his playacting."

"Then it's settled," Duffy said. "Amos and Nehemiah go to the play, and Klaus and I will visit the School of Venus and see what we can learn."

"Consarn it," Amos said. "I was afeared of that. You scallywags get to visit the ladies and we get the gullyfluff."

"Pay him no nevahmind," Nehemiah said. "The dog barks loudest what has no teeth."

"Is that the same dog that barks in the wrong tree?" Klaus asked.

*   *   *   *   *

When they met the next day, Amos offered his review of a night at the theater.

"Lots of tongue-tangled words. Them actors talk like an apothecary. Couldn't hardly make sense of it. All them ladies and gentlemen in their church-goin' finery was laughing like lunatics. If I didn't know better I'd guess they was drunk as Davey's sow. Then old surly boots here keeps a-jabbin' me in the ribs so I could not get two winks of sleep. I'd druther hunt rabbits with a dead weasel."

Klaus said something in German that made Amos nearly choke on his lager. Duffy raised his eyebrows and Klaus answered, "I told him I would have gladly traded places."

Duffy laughed and told Amos, quoting Shakespeare, "There is nothing either good or bad, but thinking makes it so."

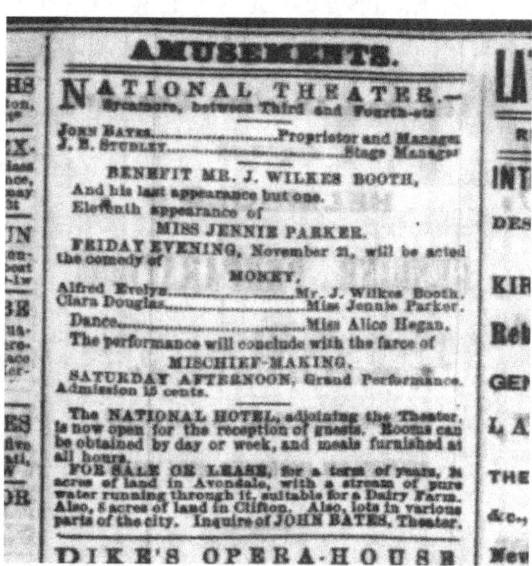

From the Cincinnati Enquirer, Page 3, November 13, 1862.

"Then I'd say it was badder than sticking my head in a beehive," Amos replied. "I'd swear on the Good Book that boy was wearing lip rouge and lady slippers."

"The play was not in the same county with Shakespeare," Nehemiah agreed, "but our man on stage was dashing spry. He cavorts like a rooster on a red-hot griddle."

He turned to Klaus, "And do tell, Herr Wolff, how did you spend your evening and what did you learn that might be shared among refined gentlemen such as Mr. Breyer and myself?"

"Not so much rooster," Klaus said. "He is more peacock."

Duffy added, "The man's favorite role is the hero of his own imagination. Second favorite is Julius Caesar," he said with a nod at Nehemiah. "With the help of Emmaline, we were able to shuck enough peas from the pod—"

"Emmaline?" Amos asked.

"German girl, born Agnes," Klaus answered.

"If I may be so bold as to continue," Duffy said with a sharp look at Amos. "He is the son of a British actor of some reputation. His father was named Junius Brutus—"

"Hah!" Nehemiah slapped the table, making the beer steins bounce.

"His brother Edwin is said to be a far better actor," Duffy continued. "Another brother is named Junius Brutus Jr.—all of them perpetrators of make-believe in the acting trade. Our man is also a proud second-degree Knight of the Golden Circle in Maryland, and boasted that he once put on the costume of a private in the Maryland Volunteer Infantry so as to attend the hanging of the abolitionist John Brown. He posed as one of the guard detail."

"Sounds like we have treed the cat," Nehemiah said.

Duffy nodded. "John Wilkes Booth, alias J.W. Wilkes and Brutus, is almost certainly our man."

"I'd like to hear more about Miss Emmaline," Amos said.

FORT DEFIANCE

Backbiters and malcontents

Before he became an American hero and opened the West for America, William Clark was a 24-year-old lieutenant serving under Anthony Wayne in the Indian War. Ten years later he would join Meriwether Lewis on the Lewis and Clark Expedition, sent by President Thomas Jefferson to find the great river highways that would expand the United States from sea to shining sea.

But on the trail north with General Mad Anthony Wayne, Clark was a callow malcontent, constantly finding reasons to complain and criticize his commander. He had fallen under the spell of the second in command, the jealous and bitter Gen. James Wilkinson.

Clark did not know then that Wilkinson was a spy for the Spanish, who were still jealously guarding their own lands in North America. Wilkinson sent them intelligence and schemed to sabotage Wayne's mission, even willing to sacrifice victory to embarrass his rival.

Years later, as Clark met Meriweather Lewis in Louisville to start their historic Lewis and Clark expedition, Wilkinson also betrayed his friend Clark and alerted the Spanish to his mission. Spain sent soldiers to intercept Lewis and Clark but failed to stop them. Like the scorpion in the Aesop's Fable, Wilkinson had once again betrayed his country and stung the men who trusted him because that was his venomous nature.

If Clark had only known.

Lieutenant Clark kept a journal during his 1794 service with General Wayne, parroting his idol Wilkinson. *"His Excellency* thought proper to order a halt for the coming up of the baggage," he wrote about General Wayne the day after they marched north from Fort Greenville. "By which time the day was far spent and obliged us to camp for the night about a mile from the fort." [184]

General Wayne was too slow, then too fast. Too timid, then recklessly bold. Clark wrote in his journal that General Wayne did not post adequate scouts and sentries—a false claim disproved by the accounts of other officers, such as Gen. Thomas Posey. [185]

In fact, General Wayne had sent out his scout, William Wells, who captured Indians and searched the land ahead of the march for signs of attack. Wells, who had been captured by Miami Indians at age 12 and adopted by Little Turtle, had joined Wayne's army. His knowledge of the land and the tribes was as valuable as Simon Kenton had been on previous campaigns.

As the men slogged through swamps, deep ravines and fields of waist-high nettles that stretched for miles, there was no inconvenience or challenge that Clark could not blame on Wayne. When a large beech tree nearly crushed his commander, Clark treated it as a lark, an "unaccountable prank," and implied that he would have been happy if the tree had landed "a few feet more to the right or left."

"His Excellency was more scared than hurt," he wrote. In fact, Wayne was in great pain from the injuries.

And when Wilkinson proposed a reckless attack that would have been ambushed and massacred like previous expeditions by Harmar and St. Clair, Lieutenant Clark insinuated that Wayne was too timid, even too cowardly "to embrace so probable a means for ending the war."

As the inevitable battle drew closer, Wayne tried to offer peace if the Indians would negotiate. The tribes replied by telling Wayne that if he stopped where he was, they might consider talking to him after ten days... perhaps. But they refused to consider any treaty unless the border of Indian land was pushed all the way back to the Ohio River.

Unknown to General Wayne, British commander John Simcoe had drafted a plan to lead three regiments all the way down the Ohio

---

184 William Clark's Journal of General Wayne's Campaign.

185 Thomas Posey was an Indian fighter and veteran of the Revolutionary War who became a US Senator from Kentucky. He saw through Wilkinson's schemes and despised the man.

River from Fort Niagara, and capture Fort Washington. His goal was to destroy Cincinnati and cut off Wayne's supplies.

But Wayne knew there would be no peace with the Indians as long as the British had a vote.

By the time General Wayne reached Roche de Bout Island[186] in the Maumee River, he was just six miles from the British Fort Miamis. He had led his army 400 miles through mud, swamps, briars, dense undergrowth, rain, baking sun, swarms of mosquitos, no-see-ums, biting flies and chiggers.

He had cut roads the entire way and built bridges, including one that was 210-feet long over a swamp. He had kept the spigot of supplies flowing against all odds and constructed three new forts in the wilderness that would form a chain of military defense no matter what came next.

His entire march had been shadowed by Shawnee and Miami scouts and raiding parties who followed his steps, always watchful, looking for the slightest weakness or mistake to steal horses, plunder supplies or ambush the army.

A few men who deserted were captured by the Indians and gave up details of General Wayne's plans. But William Wells, scouting for Wayne, captured Indians who revealed that the tribes were waiting in ambush with thousands of warriors, just behind Fort Miamis, under the protection of British cannons.

General Wayne could hardly ignore the backbiting and disrespect that radiated from Clark and others, whose morale had been poisoned by the charming, handsome officer they followed like ducklings. But he would not allow them to undermine his mission.

On August 18 at Roche de Bout, he ordered the men to build a makeshift stockade that he named Fort Deposit. Most of their equipment would be left there. They would travel fast and light. And they would attack the next morning, August 20, 1794.

---

186 Waterville, Ohio, southwest of Toledo.

'Charge the damned rascals'

"Charge of the Dragoons at Fallen Timbers," painted by R. F. Zogbaum
for *Harper's Magazine*, 1895, shows the cavalry charge led by
Capt. Robert Campbell, who was shot from his saddle and killed.

The next morning dawned under a close, smothering sky that was as dark as gunpowder. The rain fell as if it were poured from a pitcher. It did not cool the men or the thick air they breathed through a wet blanket of humidity. The downpour made a sound like bacon sizzling in a frying pan.

The men checked their weapons and did their best to keep their powder dry. General Wayne mounted his horse and looked back over his columns that stood ready to march, bayonets bristling from shouldered guns.

Wilkinson and his petulant underlings were bellyaching again about the order of march. Nothing would do but for General Wilkinson to lead the army. Anything else was *unacceptable.*

Wayne smiled. *You will fight in spite of yourselves,* he thought. *Let's see who wants to lead the army when you have a real enemy in front of you.*

The march set out at seven o'clock. For the first hours, the thick woods seemed to be allied with the Indians, fighting to stop them. They sweated and struggled, sodden and hot, down through muddy ravines, then up along slick hillsides. Near 11:00, scouts rode in and alerted General Wayne that the enemy was close. Then shots rang out, soon swelling to a rolling sound of crashing rifles that kept building like some huge angry beast.

As Wayne and his army emerged from the forest, they had the Maumee River on their right, protecting that flank where Wilkinson's 1st Legion troops would fight. On the left was General Robert Todd, leading the 3rd Kentucky Mounted Volunteers. In the left center was a column of infantry commanded by Col. John Hamtramck, a veteran of the Revolutionary War and survivor of St. Clair's Defeat.

As Wayne looked to his front, he saw the flashing muskets of the enemy and a massive tangle of fallen trees, as if a mighty hand had ripped a forest out by the roots and hurled it to the ground. The Indians had chosen their ground well. The snarled bird's nest of logs and branches caused by a tornado earlier that year was a natural defense.

The mounted Kentucky Militia led by Major William Price led the army into the battle and was first to be hit by an Indian ambush. They took withering fire before they began to fall back through the ranks of the Legions. Brig. Gen. Thomas Posey reported that the survivors of the ambush "retreated in the utmost confusion through the front guard of the regulars," with most "either killed or wounded."

Wayne saw that Little Turtle and Blue Jacket were using the same tactics that had been so successful in the massacre of St. Clair's army: An ambush, followed by a pincer movement to encircle the enemy.

He was prepared. He ordered Gen. Charles Scott to flank the Indians with his Kentucky Militia by moving left—where the fighting was heaviest—as Price and his men fell back through the ranks of the 1st Legion regulars led by Wilkinson.

Then Wayne ordered Capt. Robert Campbell to charge his cavalry right into the fallen trees. Confronted by the waving swords and huge warhorses leaping over logs and branches, the startled Indians began to break in the center. Then Captain Campbell went down, killed as he was shot from his saddle.

Wayne spurred his own horse closer to the front and ordered the infantry to form two lines to follow up the charge. General Wilkinson also sent his men in behind Campbell to support the charge.

The Indians were falling back. They had tried to cover the entire front and were spread too thin. Wayne turned to his aide, Lt. William Henry Harrison,[187] and shouted, "Charge the damn rascals with the bayonet!"

Wayne looked so eager to join the fight that Harrison warned, "General Wayne, I am afraid you will go into battle yourself."

Wayne grinned and said, "And if I do, recollect the standing order of the day is 'Charge the damned rascals with the bayonet!'"

As the bullets cracked and flew, men around him fell, but Wayne saw that the Indians were only able to fire one volley before the First Legion was upon them with bayonets. The long ice picks of steel had the same effect Wayne had seen at Stony Point: They were terrifying. The Indians ran, while his men kept pressing the bayonet attack at double-time, just as they had been trained to do.

Some of the Indians began throwing away their British rifles. Wayne saw white men in their ranks, too—Canadians and British. Now all of them were breaking, running, fleeing the bayonets.

For two hours the battle raged. The second hour was a rout, as Wayne's men chased their enemy for miles, ran them down and killed them as the Indians fled back to Fort Miamis.

There were more than 1,400 Indians in the battle, plus about seventy Canadians and British soldiers, according to their British commander,

---

187 Elected as the ninth president of the United States in 1840, the hero of the Indian Wars and the War of 1812 served only a month in office before he died of pneumonia. He was buried on his family farm in North Bend, Ohio.

Maj. Alexander McKee—the same Indian agent who had incited war and raids by encouraging the tribes to "Pick up the tomahawk."

There could have been more than 2,000, but General Wayne had learned from his scout William Wells and from his own experience fighting Indians, that warriors often fasted before a battle. So he wisely waited two extra days before the attack to make sure they would be weakened, while his own men would be fresh and rested.

On the eve of the battle, about 400 Indians of the Confederated Tribes had left the ambush site and returned to their camps at Fort Miamis for food. Those who remained for the battle were weakened by hunger.

Little Turtle had advised, again, to avoid the battle. The British had refused to provide cannons. The Iroquois had refused to join the alliance. And Little Turtle was alarmed about the new general who never slept. He predicted defeat, but he was overruled. Military leadership by committee would be their fatal flaw.

Wayne and his army followed the fleeing Indians to Fort Miamis, where he set up his camp defiantly under the fort's fourteen cannons.

The Indians appealed to the commander at Fort Miamis, Major William Campbell, to open the gates and let them in, as they had been promised. But Campbell refused. The fort was on US territory. Allowing the Indians to come in would have provoked Wayne to attack and would be a declaration of war.

Great Britain already had its hands full in a war with France. Starting another one was a decision for Parliament, not one minor officer in a remote fort in the wilderness.

Campbell could defy his country or betray his Indian allies. He chose to lock out the Indians. Little Turtle, Blue Jacket and the rest had to be turned away. He had a formidable fort, manned by 120 British soldiers, with four big blockhouses, plenty of cannons, row upon row of sharpened logs around the perimeter and trenches 25-feet deep to make attacks almost suicidal. But all of it was useless.

The Indians also had no choice with General Wayne on their heels. They fled back into the forests and disappeared. Their Confederation was shattered.

Major Campbell sent a message to General Wayne, demanding to know what his intentions were and threatening to fire on him.

Wayne replied by ordering his men to surround the fort. Then he rode out of the woods alone, and casually approached the fort within a few dozen yards, close enough to be shot by a pistol. He took his time inspecting the British fort, taunting Campbell, daring him to start a war.

It was a legendary act of courage. British riflemen in the fort begged their commander to let them kill the insolent American. Wayne must have felt their eyes on him behind rifle sights that were lined up on him. But he rode on, leisurely, until he was satisfied.

Then he sent a bold written message back to Campbell: Take your garrison and get off American land and you will not be molested.

For the next three days, Wayne's men ranged over the country-side, burning Indian villages, crops and even the homes of Campbell's Indian agents who had incited so much bloodshed and terror. Major Alexander McKee, who had caused years of torture, grief, misery and murder, watched helplessly from the fort as his own home was looted and torched.

Finally, Wayne took his army of volunteers, militia and First Legion regulars back to Fort Defiance. In September he marched again, this time to the capital of the Indian Confederation, the Miami Tribe village of Kekionga. He built another fort there. When it was finished, General Wayne invited the oldest serving soldier in the army to choose a name.

The man chose "Fort Wayne."[188]

Meanwhile, Gen. James Wilkinson was apoplectic. As he sat and stewed in Fort Defiance, he wrote a letter to a friend in Kentucky. It was framed as a private letter, but Wilkinson clearly wanted his friend to share it.

The smarmy, histrionic screed accused Wayne of misconduct, disorderly command, marching too fast or too slow, neglect of the wounded and dead and failure to take Fort Miamis.

---

188 Fort Wayne, Indiana.

Wayne "deserves to be hanged, damned he certainly will be," Wilkinson wrote—all the while patting himself on the back for his courage and valor, disavowing "any imputation of vanity or malice."

"I stand behind the armor of truth, integrity and true patriotism," said the man who lied, spied and betrayed his country.

He called Wayne "Old Horse," "despotic, vainglorious and ignorant."

He insisted the whole Wayne expedition was a failure. "We destroyed prodigious quantities of corn, but we have in truth done nothing which might not have been better done by 1,500 mounted volunteers in thirty days."

He was egregiously wrong.

As Wilkinson's pen poured venom on August 28, nine days after the battle, Wayne was also in his tent at Fort Defiance, writing his report to President Washington.

He congratulated his First Legion and all of his volunteers and militia troops on their "brilliant success in the action of the 20th against the whole combined forces of the Hostile Savages aided by a body of Militia of Detroit."

He passed out praise for his officers—even Clark and Wilkinson, which must have burned like coals on their heads. He had a special commendation for a young officer who would one day be president, Lt. William Henry Harrison.

Three Chickasaw scouts were awarded medals for their courage.

And he showed that he grasped what Wilkinson and his malcontents never understood: Fallen Timbers was a historic strategic victory for the Northwest Territory and the United States.

General Wayne wrote that the Indians now understood that "the British have neither the power nor inclination to afford them that protection which they had been taught to expect, but on the contrary a numerous garrison well supplied with artillery have been compelled to remain tacit spectators to the general conflagration around them and their flag displayed at that post insulted with impunity to the disgrace of the British and honor of the American arms."

Blue Jacket and Little Turtle, the terrors of the territory, were finished. They had been defeated twice: First by Wayne's First Legion, and second by the British betrayal. Their Confederation was finished.

The tribes would eagerly sign the Treaty of Greenville a year later, finally ceding the Northwest Territory to the settlers. A decade of peace had come at last, and the news was greeted with balls, celebration and jubilation at the stations near Fort Washington along the Ohio River.

More settlers began to pour in. In 1794, the entire white population of Ohio was probably less than 40,000.[189] By 1820, there were more than 581,000 whites in Ohio.[190]

Because of his brilliantly engineered tactics, Mad Anthony Wayne had won the greatest victory since the Revolutionary War, with the lowest loss of life: fewer than fifty killed on each side.

The Indians went into the battle with 1,300-1,400 warriors and seventy British and Canadians. They lost fifty killed and more than 100 wounded. General Wayne led 3,500 and lost thirty-three killed, eleven who died of wounds later and ninety wounded who survived.

To the British, the victory at Fallen Timbers was a warning: Get out of America. They soon hauled down their Union Jacks, abandoned Fort Miamis and Fort Detroit and did not return until the War of 1812.

France and Spain, coveting US territory, also got the message and decided the cost was too great. The new little nation would not be bullied. Americans would fight and win. Spain responded by inviting the fiercest tribes in the Midwest to move west, as a buffer to discourage settlement near their lands. It was the British policy in duplicate. And it would fail again.

The victory at Fallen Timbers proved the effectiveness of a well-trained, disciplined standing Army. President George Washington's all-or-nothing gamble to win the Indian War was vindicated; the $1 million cost was justified. The previous defeats had proved that state

---

189 An estimate in 1790 put the Indian Population of the entire United States at 60,000. By 1822, another estimate that included Texas put the Indian population at 471,000. Today it is almost 5 million.

190 Blair, Bryce Dixon Jr. Thesis, *The Battle of Fallen Timbers and the Treaty of Fort Greeneville: Did Anthony Wayne Win Both and Could he have Lost?*, University of Toledo, 2005.

militias could not defend and protect areas as vast as the Northwest Territory. The victory by Washington's new army bonded the states into a nation—the *United* States.

The nation's first debate over expansion of the US government at the cost of state autonomy had been settled. But the argument was not over. It would flare into a raging bonfire of blood and tragedy half a century later in the Civil War.

The tactics Wayne adopted for the 1st Legion became the foundation for the new US Army: Vigilance, reconnaissance, rigorous training, esprit de corps and freedom of movement by individual units.

His offers of peace[191] to the Indians—scorned by General Wilkinson—became a hallmark of US policy: Avoid war if possible, but never back down. For the first time in the long-running Indian War, the United States sent an army to conquer, not to punish.

The victory and the treaty that followed opened the gates of the West from the Ohio River to the Pacific Ocean.

Finally, General Wayne's victory at Fallen Timbers settled the question raised by history, phrased by Col. Charles Whittlesey when he wrote an open letter to Gen. James A. Garfield in 1872 on the "Universal Indian Problem."[192]

"What is the purpose of the earth? To produce game or the bread of life? To sustain one human being per square mile or one hundred?"

The same question had been raised by others such as Alexis de Tocqueville, who concluded that the land belongs to those who use it for the greatest benefit. The American settlers brought technology and advanced civilization that enabled surplus production. Farming fed not just one family or village for a winter—it would feed hundreds and thousands. Whereas the seasonally nomadic Indian tribes had to

---

191   As late as August 13, General Wayne sent a captured Indian to offer peace to the Confederated Tribes, saying he would rather negotiate than meet them in battle. The Indian never returned with an answer. William Clark's Journal of General Wayne's Campaign, 1794.

192   At the time, Garfield was negotiating a treaty with a tribe in Montana. He would be elected president in 1880 but served only seven months before he was assassinated. He grew up in poverty in a log cabin near Cleveland, Ohio, served as a brigadier general in the Civil War and was elected to Congress. Whittlesey's letter was published in the *Cleveland Herald*.

regularly move their villages as they used up the land by hunting it dry, the new settlers planted permanent towns and cities of wood, brick, steel and cement.

It was a battle between the Stone Age and the Industrial Age. The Stone Age lost.

The Indian wars continued in the West through the next century, but the future was inevitable: The Promised Land belonged to those who were willing to fight for it, tame it and use it best.

In 1795, when he signed the Treaty of Greenville, Blue Jacket said: "Our hearts and minds are changed, and we now consider ourselves your friends and brothers."

Presenting Mr. John W. Booth

**Photo of John Wilkes Booth in 1865
by Alexander Gardner.**

Amos not only heard more about Miss Emmaline, he was privileged to meet her at the lavish "men's club" that Klaus owned on Monmouth Street in a tall and stately redbrick home in a quiet, tree-shaded neighborhood of Newport.

It was cool and dim inside. The heavy floor-to-ceiling red drapes were always drawn, day and night. But the low lights flashed off buttery gold wall sconces, a glittering crystal chandelier and a large polished black piano. Deep couches and club chairs covered in dark leather and deep blue velvet were placed around the large parlor, arranged around a polished walnut bar that filled the back wall.

Beneath their feet was a lush carpet of ornate patterns in red, blue and gold.

"If'n I was a member in a club like this I would never go home," Amos said. "This must be nicer than the White House."

"Given the business that goes on, I'd reckon it's closer to Congress," Nehemiah said.

"Then call me senator, I'm hell-bent for election." Amos said.

"You haf my vote," said a lilting voice with a German accent.

"Allow me to introduce Miss Emmaline," Klaus said.

Duffy bowed deeply, Nehemiah scraped off his tattered hat and Amos stood slack-jawed, unable to speak. She was a tall woman, with blond hair wrapped in braids that were pinned up. As her flashing blue eyes sized up the men, she smiled, showing deep dimples and even white teeth.

She wore a deep green gown the color of magnolia leaves in August and seemed to walk in a cloud of apple blossoms.

Amos was so stricken he spoke in German. "Mein Gott," he spluttered. "Es ist ein engel...."

"Nein," she replied laughing, "God in heaven knows I am no angel."

Amos replied with a paragraph of German that ended in a question.

"Ja!" she replied, delighted, her face lighting up. She turned to the other three men: "We are almost—what you call... nachbarinnen—"

"Neighbors," Klaus supplied. "Agnes—Miss Emmaline—apparently comes from a village only a few miles from the town where Amos was born in Germany."

"Whatever all that parlayvoo was about it was worth it for that smile," Nehemiah said.

"Ahh... if we might get to our business—" Duffy said.

Miss Emmaline looked surprised and he hastily shook his head and added, "Nein, I mean no, not that business. We're here to learn more about one of your, ahh... acquaintances, Mr. John W. Booth."

Her face darkened like a cloud had passed over the sun. "That one," she said. She spoke briefly in German to Amos, whose own face darkened like a tornado sky. Nehemiah saw the look and raised his eyebrows. *Someone's gonna get his timber sawed*, he thought. *I would not trade places with Mr. John W. Booth for a barrel of Cincinnati lager.*

Amos growled, "Miss Emmaline says she will be pleased to help us set a snare for that lizard in lady slippers."

As they expected, Booth had boasted extravagantly. From Miss Emmaline they learned that he had been named after a radical English member of Parliament who had incited a massacre, named John Wilkes—hence his alias "J.B. Wilkes." Booth had claimed John Wilkes was a man of the people, a true "Republican Democrat."

"I've aheared of a catfish and a cow horse, but a Republican Democrat sounds like a crime against nature," Nehemiah said.

Booth's namesake Wilkes was also a member of the infamous Hellfire Club in London and kept a pet monkey dressed like Lucifer in a cape and horns. And even worse, he wrote for a newspaper.

"That's all I need to know," Duffy said, shaking his head. "It appears Mr. Booth idolized a man who held the lowest profession, even lower than acting."

"Danke," Miss Emmaline said.

Duffy looked puzzled, but she continued. Booth's father had died on a riverboat on his way to perform in Cincinnati. John Wilkes Booth was the youngest of three brothers. His mother was his father's American mistress.

"Der bastard," Klaus said.

"Ja!" Miss Emmaline agreed. "He carries a clipping from a newspaper that called him the most handsomest man in America." She saw Amos wince and added, "Like silk ribbons on a box of snakes."

"Did he speak of the Knights of the Golden Circle?" Duffy asked.

"He was bold about his support for the Knights and the Confederates. He would laugh often about Yankee fools who applaud his stage acting while he is destroying the Union. He talked of men named Bickley and Bowles... as if he plans to meet with them before he leaves town."

"Anything else you recall?" Duffy asked.

"He talked of an old tablet from Cincinnati. He said it came from an ancient race of abbey originals."

"Aboriginals?" Duffy asked.

Emmaline nodded, but Amos looked confused.

"Indians," Duffy explained.

October 15, 1795

'Henceforth all hostilities shall cease'

The first time he floated down the winding Ohio River, Oliver Spencer was only nine years old. He never forgot the ominous menace that lurked behind the towering oaks, maples and elms that lined the riverbanks like ancient sentinels. That was 1790.

"There seemed to be blended with the beauty and the lovely scenery of the Ohio a wildness and a solitude which struck the beholder with mingled fear and awe," he wrote in 1834. "Indeed, there was with us a prevailing sense of loneliness; a feeling of apprehension."[193]

Now it was 1795, and he was drifting down the Ohio River again. The riverbanks were even more lovely, lit with brilliant scarlet, yellow and orange, the mid-October warpaint of Ohio. His spirits soared to the treetops and beyond the cotton clouds. He was going home at last. After three years in captivity, the boy who was taken by Indians on July 4, 1791, was eagerly looking ahead to the landing near Columbia Station where his mother and father and family waited to shower him with love and grateful tears of joy.

They had never expected to see him again. And he had long ago given up hope of being set free by the Shawnees.

He had been walking home from Fort Washington to the family cabin a few miles east when he was captured. He was bored with the July 4th revelry of Independence Day and left without telling anyone.

At first, he took an offered ride in a canoe with three adults. But one of the men was so cross-eyed drunk he nearly tipped them all into the river. Oliver could not swim, so he asked them to set him on the shore,

---

193 Spencer, Oliver M. *Indian Captivity*, 1848.

where he walked barefoot alongside his Columbia Station neighbors as they paddled home.

It was a lovely summer day and for once he was free from the endless chores of life on the frontier.

"I walked along the beach, a little below the canoe, now listening to the merry conversation of my companions, and now amusing myself by skimming small flat stones over the surface of the water," he recalled later in a memoir that became popular.

Then suddenly two shots rang out and one of the men in the canoe slumped over. "I saw, through the thick smoke of their guns, two Indians, with faces black as midnight, rushing toward the canoe. One Indian rushed from the woods into the river to tomahawk and scalp the dying man. The other man and an old woman jumped into the river and swam for their lives.

Oliver ran but did not get far. Before he had covered a dozen yards, he almost collided with a second warrior who blocked his path. "Instead, however, of seizing me violently, approaching within a few feet, he extended his hand in a token of peace. I took it."

That day he was forced to walk forty miles, mostly without shoes until the Indians saw he could not keep up on his bleeding feet and gave him a pair of moccasins. Over the next six days, they would cover 180 miles from Cincinnati to northern Ohio near the Auglaize and Miami Rivers.

Most of the time he would have to almost run to keep up with the men. At night he would be tied to a tree with a rawhide rope around his neck as he sobbed himself to sleep, thinking about his family, sure he would never see his mother again.

For a while, when he had trouble walking on swollen feet, they put him on a stolen horse. But then the horse got sick and could not walk no matter how much the Indians beat it. They left it behind to die.

One day on the journey they went hunting and left him tied to a tree. He pulled and twisted the rawhide ropes until he managed to free himself, ran as far as he could and hid in a hollow log. When they found him they beat him without mercy, until they wore out the thick branches they used as clubs.

That night he was tied to a tree with his elbows pinned so tightly behind him he wished for death. "My head, bruised and swollen, pained me exceedingly, but this was trivial when compared with the torture I suffered from the violent straining of my arms behind my back. My ribs seemed every moment as though they would be torn from my breast and my shoulder blades felt as if they would separate from my body."

He was left there all night. For days he was beaten again and again. Yet he found that his new "master," a Shawnee named White Loon, could sometimes be almost "humane and benevolent." When the other Indian wanted to kill and scalp him, White Loon claimed Oliver as his property.

He was finally given to an old Indian woman who healed his bleeding, swollen feet and damaged toes and took him in to live in her bark cabin. She was a tribal princess and shaman who told the future by calling on the spirits.

During his years in captivity, Oliver met Blue Jacket: "This chief was the most noble in appearance of any Indian I ever saw. His person, about six feet high, was finely proportioned, stout and muscular, his eyes large, bright and piercing; his forehead high and broad ... his countenance open and intelligent, expressive of firmness and decision. ... He was dressed in a scarlet frock coat, richly laced with gold and confined around his waist with a party-colored[194] sash, and in red leggings and moccasins ornamented in the highest Indian fashion."

And he met the monster of the frontier, Simon Girty: "His dark, shaggy hair, his low forehead, his brows contracting and meeting above his short, flat nose; his gray, sunken eyes, averting the ingenuous gaze; his lips thin and compressed and the dark and sinister expression of his countenance, to me, seemed the very picture of a villain."

He met a chief wearing the blue officer's coat he had taken from a soldier he scalped and killed in the massacre at St. Clair's Defeat.

---

194 Multi-colored or checkered.

He quickly learned to hide from the random, murderous rage of warriors when "fire water" was passed around the campfire. He worked hard as a slave for the shaman woman who kept him. She was sometimes kind and sometimes cruel. He believed she was possessed by evil spirits.

He survived attacks by a wildcat and rattlesnakes, and regular beatings. And throughout it all, he was tormented by imagining his mother's fears, grief and anxiety, and yearning for his family.

His rescue began when he met another captive, William Wells, who had been taken many years before and was adopted by Chief Little Turtle. Wells got permission from the chief to leave the tribe and became a scout with General Wayne at Fallen Timbers. But he remembered the little boy in the Shawnee village, suffering as he had suffered himself, and took pity on him.

Wells persuaded the British to buy Oliver's freedom so he could be returned to his family.

"I was like a bird loosed from its cage, or a young colt from his stall; to suppress my feelings or restrain my joy would have been impossible."

But his troubles were far from over.

The British officer sent to rescue him and take him to Fort Detroit hated Americans. He abandoned Oliver on the way to Detroit and gave him to another tribe. Oliver was forced to fight an older Indian boy, who stabbed him after losing the wrestling match.

After he was delivered to Detroit, a surgeon treated the wound.

"He found it about three inches deep ... fortunately, he said, the knife in entering has struck the lower, posterior point of the right shoulder blade. ... Had it entered either an inch lower, or nearer the spine, it would probably have caused death."

After recovering in Detroit, he was put aboard a sailing ship leaving for Fort Niagara in New York. As they crossed Lake Erie, volent storms nearly capsized the ship. After weeks of travel, he arrived in Pittsburgh and took a riverboat down the Ohio River to Cincinnati, where his astonished family and neighbors were waiting at Columbia Station.

Oliver Spencer grew up to become a pastor and devoted his life to Christ in gratitude for his deliverance.

"Nearly forty years have since passed away," he wrote in 1834. "Our rivers teem with commerce; their banks are covered with farms, with houses, villages, towns and cities; the wilderness has been converted into fruitful fields. Temples to God are erected where once stood the Indian wigwam, and the praises of the Most High resound where formerly were heard the screams of the panther or the yell of the savage. O, 'What hath God wrought?'"

His Indian "father," White Loon, "paid me an annual visit" for several years until he "was gone to the land of his fathers."

Oliver Spencer's happy homecoming was living proof that the Indian War—also called the Ohio War and Little Turtle's War—was finally over.

Many others soon followed. The Treaty of Greenville required a prisoner exchange. Among them were captives from families that were torn apart for fifteen years, since the raid of Ruddle's Station and Martin's Station, northeast of Lexington, Kentucky in 1789.

Both stations were attacked during the Revolutionary War by British Capt. Henry Byrd, who brought six cannons and about 1,200 soldiers and Indians.

Byrd had assured the people in the forts they would be safe. Their wooden walls, built with help from Simon Kenton, were defenseless against cannons, so they surrendered. But the Indians ignored Byrd's promise and massacred twenty of them. The survivors were marched 600 miles to Detroit or left as captives of the Indians. Those who made it to Detroit were held as prisoners and slaves in Canada until they were released.

Their freedom, the security of Ohio and the creation of five new states were all made possible by the Treaty of Greeneville in August 1795. It said, "Peace is hereby established, and shall be perpetual; and a friendly intercourse shall take place between the said United States and Indian tribes."

Ohio (1803), Indiana (1816), Illinois (1818), Michigan (1836) and Wisconsin (1848) were born in the woods of Ohio in August 1795. And peace prevailed, mostly, for seventeen years—until the British returned to incite Indian raids that triggered the War or 1812.

Summer 1795

'Free passage by land and by water'

"Indian Treaty of Greenville," 1795, by an officer on Gen. Anthony Wayne's staff. Wayne, standing in foreground, listens to Chief Little Turtle. The interpreter, kneeling, is Capt. William Wells. Future President William Henry Harrison is among the officers.

Gen. Anthony Wayne was almost rubbing his hands with confident anticipation when he arrived at Fort Greenville in June 1795. He held all the high cards for his negotiations with the Indian Confederation.

His first ace was the fort itself. It was the largest wooden stockade built in Ohio, covering more than fifty-five acres, with walls ten feet high. Eight blockhouses reached 250 yards outside the stockade to provide a deadly perimeter defense with overlapping fields of fire in every direction. Attempting to attack Fort Greenville without cannons would be suicide—and the only cannons were inside the fort.

A town was rapidly growing inside the walls, and it would be named after the fort: Greenville, Ohio. The pioneers were spreading their roots fast and deep, getting stronger every day.

As General Wayne watched the tribes arrive, he knew they were awed by the imposing footprint of the United States Army. Fort Greenville was the massive battleship in a fleet of smaller forts that stretched north from Fort Washington, into the heart of what had been the perilous wilderness of Indian Territory.

A second ace in his hand was his victory just a year before at Fallen Timbers. The tribes had not just been beaten by the most disciplined army they had faced. The defeat had been like a splitting axe—it cleaved their alliances at the weak points. The tribes had no appetite for war. And their strongest ally was gone. When Wayne's army chased them to Fort Miamis, the British locked the Indians out and proved they could not be trusted.

Each year on the anniversary of St. Clair's Defeat, the tribes had taunted the Americans with devastating attacks. Now they were arriving on the anniversary of their own greatest defeat at Fallen Timbers— forced to accept peace on Wayne's terms.

General Wayne's third ace was a document that the British were desperate to keep from the Indians. He had the Jay Treaty.

Negotiated with the British by John Jay, chief justice of the US Supreme Court and one of the nation's founders along with Ben Franklin, Thomas Jefferson, George Washington and John Adams, the treaty erased any shred of hope among the Indians that they could rely on the British.

Article 2 said: "His Majesty will withdraw all His Troops and Garrisons from all Posts and Places within the Boundary Lines assigned by the Treaty of Peace to the United States. This Evacuation shall take place on or before the first Day of June 1796."

The British were given less than one year to get out of the Northwest Territory and surrender their forts in Ohio and Michigan that had been the source of so much murder and mayhem against the Americans. The defiant British violation of the Paris Treaty of 1783 had come to an end.

The Jay Treaty was signed on November 19, 1794, not long after the Battle of Fallen Timbers, when the British lost their proxy war against the Americans and had to abandon their Indian allies. It was ratified by the US Senate on June 24, 1795—just in time for the Greenville negotiations.

The British were forced to pack up and move north to Canada. Lord Dorchester's "freelance" attacks on the Americans were being investigated in London, where politicians in Parliament would officially censure him for urging the tribes to "pick up the tomahawk" against the Americans.

The British would try again to take back Detroit and Ohio in the War of 1812, but in the summer of 1795, the Jay Treaty would spell it out plain to the gathered tribes: They had no ally, no source of guns, knives, trade and tactical training. The British were gone.

When the negotiations began, Wayne read aloud to the Indians from the Jay Treaty: "The United States in the meantime at their discretion extending their settlements to any part within the said boundary line...."

Little Turtle was there. He was among the last to arrive, bitterly opposed to the negotiations. But his longtime ally Blue Jacket was enthusiastic for a treaty. He came dressed in his finest ceremonial uniform, leading a procession of warriors. He had been busy for months, visiting all the tribes to make his case. Heh ad done the same many times before—but this time it was for peace, not war.

Finally, Wayne had a fourth ace in his hand: He had been authorized by the US government to shower the tribes with almost $25,000 in gifts, with the promise of $10,000 to follow each year.

More than 11,000 Indians came to Fort Greenville to listen and witness the historic negotiations. They represented Wyandots, Delawares, Shawnees, Ottawas, Chippewas, Pottawatomis, Miamis, Eel Rivers, Weas, Kickapoos, Piankeshaws, and Kaskaskias.

By the time all the peace pipes were smoked and all of the chiefs were heard, the conference lasted almost two months—from mid-June to mid-August.

General Wayne adopted the approach that would become the maker's mark of US diplomacy for generations to come: tough but fair; respectful but resolute; patient but persistent.

He demanded an end to all attacks and depredations against the white residents of the Northwest Territory. The tribes would be required to accept that the US was sovereign.

"All prisoners shall, on both sides, be restored," he read from Article 2, as the gathered tribes sat on the ground around him and listened to translators repeat the words in their own languages.

"The Indians, prisoners to the United States, shall be immediately set at liberty. The people of the United States, still remaining prisoners among the Indians, shall be delivered up in ninety days from the date hereof, to the general or commanding officer at Greenville, Fort Wayne, or Fort Defiance; and ten chiefs of the said tribes shall remain at Greenville as hostages, until the delivery of the prisoners shall be effected."

With those words, General Wayne cut the bonds that held hundreds of captives.

And he promised that the Americans would step in to fill the trading vacuum left by the departing British. In a letter to Secretary of War Henry Knox, Wayne outlined his thinking. British agents "furnish the Indians with every necessary supply of arms, ammunition and clothing in exchange for their skins and furs," he wrote. They Indians were "dependent upon them until the United States establishes trading houses in their country."

Without such trade, "We can never expect permanent peace. ... I am confident that we should draw them over to our interest, notwithstanding every effort of the British to prevent it."

Knox agreed. And the Secretary of the Treasury authorized Wayne to spend $20,000 on "shirts, cloth, axes, wire, blankets, shoes, thread, thimbles"[195] and other gifts for the tribes, as well as another $9,500 of similar gifts each year, including livestock.

---

195   Hogeland, William. *Autumn of the Black Snake.* Farrar, Straus and Giroux, 2017.

And there was a cash payment for land access: Seven tribes were paid $1,000; five tribes received $500.[196]

From Article 7 Wayne read: "The said tribes of Indians, parties to this treaty, shall be at liberty to hunt within the territory and lands which they have now ceded to the United States, without hindrance or molestation, so long as they demean themselves peaceably, and offer no injury to the people of the United States."

And he included a warning to the settlers who would soon flood into Ohio: Anyone who went west of the Northwest Territory was going into Indian land at their own risk. "If any citizen of the United States, or any other white person or persons, shall presume to settle upon the lands now relinquished by the United States, such citizen or other person shall be out of the protection of the United States; and the Indian tribe, on whose land the settlement shall be made, may drive off the settler, or punish him in such manner as they shall think fit."

Nobody had to wonder what manner the Indians would "think fit." They had already seen it too many times. Proof was hanging in the lodges of every Indian village and on the belts of many warriors: dried scalps.

When the talking was finished, representatives from the dozen tribes signed or put their mark on the treaty—with one exception: Little Turtle refused.

He had been right with his strategy to defeat two previous American expeditions led by General Harmar and General St. Clair. He was right when he advised against attacking Fort Recovery, but he was ignored. He advised against fighting at Fallen Timbers but was ignored again. And he would be proved right about the Treaty of Greenville.

In the coming years, the Indians would be pushed west again and again until a new warrior chief, Tecumseh, formed another alliance. The same tragic story of raids, murder, depredations and defeat would play out in 1812. With the same result. The British and Indians lost again.

Chief Little Turtle was ignored again by his tribe, which agreed to the treaty.

---

196   In 2024 dollars, $35,000 and $17,000. The value of all the gifts today, adjusted for inflation, would be $683,000.

During the negotiations, a party of about twenty men came from Fort Detroit and offered to assist Wayne and advise the Indians, the *Centinel of the North-Western Territory* reported in Cincinnati.[197] "The general heard their story with a degree of attention ... then gave directions to an officer instantly to take them into charge and confine them in the guard house on bread and water, till further orders."

General Wayne believed they were British spies or agents, sent to sabotage the treaty. When it was signed and there was nothing they could do, "they were discharged with an injunction to depart immediately, for if they were found in or about the camp, they should be apprehended and treated as spies."[198]

197   November 28, 1795, edition.

198   Spies could be executed by a firing squad.

Fall and winter, 1795–1796

An assassin in Cincinnati

Gen. James Wilkinson was seething with bitterness and jealously that gnawed at his thoughts like a dog on a bone. The man he hated was being hailed as a hero again for the Treaty of Greenville. All of Cincinnati, where Wilkinson commanded Fort Washington, was celebrating the peace delivered by "Mad Anthony" Wayne.

Wilkinson picked up a pen and began writing. His letter would be anonymous, of course. But he would set the record straight and let everyone know the truth about Wayne.

"Drunkard, liar, fool, incompetent," he wrote. "Feckless ignorance." He stabbed at the paper as if he were driving a knife into the heart of his nemesis. "Coward, hypocrite."

With every word, Wilkinson was more accurately describing himself. He could have added "traitor," "back-stabber" and "spy." He was all of that and much worse. James Wilkinson could not even think of Wayne without breathing murder.

He put his quill pen down and thought: *If Mad Anthony's investigation finds I have been working for our enemies, I will be executed. It's him or me. Murder? Why not? If he dies, my career and my life are saved. I will take his place as commander of the Army. How much more will it be worth to Spain to have its own commander of the US Army rather than just a spy?*

Wilkinson sent his poison-pen letter to the newspaper. But it bounced off Wayne like a blunt arrow launched at Fort Greenville. General Wayne was a hero in all of Ohio and the Northwest Territory. He had ended the Ohio War.

Even Wayne's old rival Arthur St. Clair was forced to admit it.

The news of peace was made official in Cincinnati on September 8, 1795, when the *Centinel of the North-Western Territory* published a proclamation from the governor of the Northwest Territory, Arthur St. Clair.

It commended "His Excellency" General Wayne for the Treaty of Greenville—words that must have been excruciating for St. Clair, whose humiliation and defeat by Little Turtle was all the more galling now that Wayne had forced Little Turtle's Miami tribe to sign the peace treaty and surrender their lands.

"All the inhabitants of the Territory," St. Clair wrote, "are strictly enjoined and required to keep and observe peace with the said Indian tribes."

When he saw the proclamation, General Wayne had to smile. Even his most bitter enemies had to concede his historic victory and success.

Well, not quite all. He had sent General Wilkinson back to command Fort Washington, where he could cause no more trouble. Or so he thought. But Wilkinson was still scheming to weaken the new US Army and destroy Wayne.

Wayne returned to Philadelphia for the greatest hero's welcome since George Washington won the Revolutionary War. He was feted

Portrait of spy Gen. James Wilkinson, by Charles Willson Peale, 1797.

in the nation's capital with balls, parades and ceremonial dinners, where everyone wanted to hear his stories of glory at Fallen Timbers. The nation's leaders, including President Washington, all shook his hand as they congratulated him on the treaty he had brought back—signed, sealed, delivered to the president.

A year later, in December 1796, General Wayne was given another mission by his commander in chief. It was especially satisfying. He was sent to Fort Miamis and Fort Detroit to inspect them and take control of both forts from the British.

The same "Mad Anthony" who had recklessly ridden alone under the British guns of Fort Miamis, now rode through the front gate to take possession.

In Detroit, the British had to hand him their flagship fort in the Northwest Territory.

His joy was clouded, though. General Wayne was suffering again from severe gout during his final mission, aggravated by the many toasts to victory as he toured the battlefields and visited soldiers and officers who had fought by his side. He also had fevers that were probably malaria transmitted by mosquitos that infested the swamps of Michigan and northern Ohio.

Then his symptoms got much worse as he was returning aboard a ship sailing across Lake Erie from Detroit to Pennsylvania. He arrived in Presque Isle, Pennsylvania, on November 17 with severe joint pain. Then on December 3, the joint pain was replaced by "extreme torture" in his stomach.[199] He died that night. His last words were, "Bury me under the flagpole, boys." He was 51.

Ironically, he was replaced as commander of the US Army by General James Wilkinson, despite Wilkinson's suspected spying for Spain.

In Cincinnati, the land rush was on. The doors to the Promised Land were thrown wide open, and property values soared overnight. Ohio was free, safe and ready for plows, farms, roads, riverboats, towns and trade.

But the fate of the man who made it all possible is still a mystery. Ever

---

199 Letter by Capt. Henry DeButts on December 15, 1796.

since General Wayne's excruciating death, historians have speculated that he was poisoned by James Wilkinson. General Wayne was about to bring charges and court-martial Wilkinson, who could be executed as a spy. The previous summer, officers sent by Wayne had nearly captured papers in Kentucky that would have put Wilkinson's neck in a noose. He was betraying American secrets to the Spanish.

Wilkinson had the motive and opportunity to assassinate Wayne. He also had the means: He had gone to medical school and practiced as a doctor before he became a soldier. His training in pharmacology gave him extensive knowledge of poisons.

General Wayne had already suspected Wilkinson of trying to kill him with a falling tree on the march to Fallen Timbers. He called Wilkinson "a vile assassin" and "the worst of all bad men." In a letter to Secretary of War Henry Knox early in 1795, Wayne wrote, "I have a strong ground to believe, that this man is a principle agent, set up by the British & *Demoncrats* [sic] of Kentucky to dismember the Union."

Wayne was off target: Wilkinson was spying for Spain, not the British. But he was right that Wilkinson was a traitor.

Wilkinson's vitriol could not be contained. It leaked out like sour wine from a cracked decanter. While he was commanding Fort Washington, he wrote a letter that called Wayne "a liar, a drunkard, a fool, the associate of the lowest order of Society, & the companion of their vices, of desperate Fortune, my rancorous enemy, a coward, a Hypocrite, and the contempt of every man of sense and virtue."

General Wayne had graciously commended Wilkinson's role in the Battle of Fallen Timbers. But Wilkinson refused to give Wayne any credit for victory. He insisted the battle was won by "injudicious Conduct of the enemy."

And Wilkinson boasted in writing to his Spanish spymasters that he would soon "secure myself the commandant of the army."

A soldier who was with Wayne when he died described his symptoms: "...for on the morning of the 3d. [Dec. 3, 1796], it appeared that the gout had taken possession of his stomach, where it remained with unconquerable obstinacy and extreme torture, until it put a period to his existence. His remains will be interred tomorrow within this fort with military honors."[200]

Gout is seldom fatal. When it is, the causes of death are heart problems or kidney failure, not extreme stomach pain—which is more consistent with poisoning, such as arsenic.[201] And Wayne's excruciating, lingering death is exactly what a bitter enemy such as Wilkinson would arrange.

Did Wilkinson use one of his toady officers whom he had turned against Wayne to administer a fatal dose of poison?

Historian and author Hugh Harrington concluded, "If one does not accept that Wayne was murdered then one must accept that his natural death was one of the most extraordinary coincidences in history, as Wilkinson would almost certainly have been exposed as a traitor had Wayne lived."

There is no smoking-gun or autopsy roof. But the circumstantial evidence led President Theodore Roosevelt to say: "In all of our history there has been no more despicable character" than James Wilkinson.

That was the commander of Fort Washington in Cincinnati during the late 1790s: a back-stabbing spy, a traitor and a likely assassin described by historian Frederick Jackson Turner as "the most consummate artist in treason that the nation ever possessed."

In 1807, Wilkinson was involved in Aaron Burr's conspiracy to overthrow the US government and set up a new nation with help from Spain, Great Britain and Mexican revolutionaries. And typically, Wilkinson turned on Burr to save his own neck. Burr was eventually acquitted in the "Trial of the Century," but was personally destroyed.

Wilkinson did not escape justice. He was court-martialed by President Thomas Jefferson for conspiring with Burr. He died in Mexico City in 1825, where he was working another land scheme. He is buried

---

200 *American Mercury* (newspaper), Hartford, CT, January 9, 1797, 2, quotes letter of Captain Henry DeButts to James McHenry, December 15, 1796.

201 "Wayne's medical symptoms, and death, may be explained by the presence of poison. Poisons may mimic natural medical conditions. Arsenic, for example, could account for vomiting, diarrhea, convulsions, stomach pain and death." Harrington, Hugh, *Journal of the American Revolution,* "Was General Anthony Wayne Murdered?" August 20, 2013.

there—long forgotten by Mexicans and Americans.

In 1805, Aaron Burr visited Cincinnati, probably plotting with Wilkinson. "He at once was known to be a stranger," wrote Cincinnati resident William Stanley Hatch. "His appearance was elegant, extremely well dressed, a fine light olive cloth coat, then fashionable, with his hair, which was light chestnut color tied in a neat queue behind the neck, lightly powdered, with delicate side whiskers. ... It was the celebrated Aaron Burr, then vice president of the United States, who in the month of July of the preceding year had slain his great political rival and opponent [Alexander] Hamilton in a duel in Hoboken.

"And from thenceforth, to the end of his life, had like Cain, become a wanderer on the face of the Earth!"[202]

History was more kind to "Mad Anthony" Wayne. His grave can be found behind a low stone wall in an old churchyard cemetery on Valley Forge Road in Wayne, Pennsylvania, just west of Philadelphia—on a road named for one of his finest hours, near a town that was named for him.

The man who won the war and forged the peace treaty that was a Declaration of Independence for the Northwest Territory is honored with three streets in Cincinnati.[203]

Although few remember why, his name is everywhere in the Midwest, on hundreds of towns, counties, townships and cities, streets, highways, hospitals, schools, colleges, parks, forests, town squares, bridges and hotels. Wayne was no saint. His favorites might be Mad Anthony Brewing Co. in Fort Wayne, Indiana, or Mad Anthony's pub in Waterville, Ohio.

A half-dozen statues honor him in Fort Wayne, Valley Forge, Philadelphia and as far south as North Carolina. The best is at the site of the Battle of Fallen Timbers, dedicated in 1929 by the Ohio State Archaeological and Historical Society, when Americans and Ohioans

---

202 William Stanley Hatch papers, 1740-1888, Cincinnati History Library and Archives, Cincinnati Museum Center.

203 Wayne Avenue in Norwood, Anthony Wayne Avenue in Carthage and Mad Anthony Street in Northside.

**The monument at Fallen Timbers Battlefield near Toledo.
Photo by Victoria Stauffenberg, 2017.**

still appreciated what "Mad Anthony" Wayne meant to our nation's history.

It shows Gen. Anthony Wayne in battle dress, resolutely clutching his sword, looking into the distance as if surveying the battlefield... or turning his thoughts to home. On his right is an Indian chief holding a peace pipe, proud, defiant but defeated. On Wayne's left is a tough, determined, bearded pioneer holding a rifle—looking into the distance with Wayne, where the Promised Land has been tamed.

More than 5,000 attended the dedication of the bronze and granite monument on September 14, 1929. Distinguished guests in jaunty bowlers and fedoras sat in cane chairs on the speakers' platform, holding walking sticks, pipes and cigars as they listened to Arthur Johnson, the president of the Ohio State Archaeological and Historical Society, describe Anthony Wayne:

Here on this ground where we now stand, after his long and painstaking preparation for the supreme test in which others had met with disastrous failure, he broke the strength and humbled the spirit of the Northwestern Indians for all time, contributed largely to the transformation of the Treaty of Paris from a scrap of paper into a vital instrument, helped push back the international boundary from the Ohio River to the Great Lakes, made safe for American settlement this vast empire lying west to the Mississippi, and restored a waning public confidence in the administration of the First President....

No general officer of the Revolution served longer, was more often in the thick of the fray or suffered as many wounds. No general officer of the Revolution saw service covering so great an extent of territory....

If that bronze pioneer could take voice and preach the gospel of a sane true Americanism he would urge us to emulate the integrity of a Washington; to cherish the precious gift of human rights and personal liberty enunciated by a Jefferson; to practice the thrift of a Franklin; to strive for the solvency of a Hamilton; to develop the ruggedness of a Jackson; to pray for the faith and the patience and the understanding of a Lincoln; to be ever alert to the necessity of the rational preparedness of a Roosevelt, but above all, that we may preserve our God-given heritage for ourselves and for those who are to come, to have in such measure as we may, the SUBLIME COURAGE of an Anthony Wayne.[204]

The director of the Archaeological Society, Arthur Shetrone, used his remarks to honor the first Ohioans:

"Shall we not remember that they, like ourselves, were the sons of man, with all his vices and many of his virtues; that they differed from ourselves only in that they had not yet achieved the background of cumulative experience which makes for so-called civilization? ... It was not in the scheme of things that such a vast and fertile country

---

204 *Ohio History Journal,* The Ohio History Connection.

should remain the abode of a handful of savages—perhaps never more than 50,000 in number; the advance of civilization demanded the change, and the Indian gave way to civilization and today. But he was an Ohioan, just the same, who lived, loved, fought and died on Ohio soil, even as we. Let us give him belated recognition.

If the bronze pioneer on the statue could reply, he might have said, "That 'so-called civilization' was the whole shootin' match." The Europeans had better weapons, tactics, discipline, tools, communication, education, farming, housing and resources. The best chance the Indians had was Ohio. After Wayne at Fallen Timbers, it was just a matter of time.

The base of his monument has bronze relief scenes on each side:

"The Battle of Fallen Timbers" has soldiers from Wayne's Legion advancing with muskets and bayonets over fallen and running Indians.

"Onward in Peace" shows a pioneer family: mother in bonnet, barefoot little boy, faithful dog and dad carrying an axe.

"The Greenville Treaty" scene has General Wayne speaking with one hand raised as Indians listen and a chief in headdress extends a peace pipe.

The most dramatic is "Indian Warfare," dedicated "In Memory of the White Settlers Massacred 1783-1794." It is fraught with action and sadness. A hatless frontiersman holding a musket dodges an Indian warrior on horseback, who stoops for the kill like an angel of death, his shield making a dark wing that echoes Gustave Dore's illustrations of Satan for John Milton's *Paradise Lost*. Clutching the frontiersman's leg at the bottom of the scene is a little girl in a dress, her face buried against her father as he sacrifices his life to protect his family.

As visitors approach the monument along a walkaway between columns of old Ohio hardwoods, the figures on the pedestal seem to have turned their backs. They are facing the Maumee River and its valley that stretches out to the horizon for miles of beautiful rivers and forests.

General Wayne is looking south. All of Ohio is in his eyes.

ON THE OHIO RIVER

'Be he ne'er so vile'

John Wilkes Booth woke up just before noon in a deep featherbed in the royal suite at the Burnet House. He had spent the previous night—as much as he could recall—carousing in Newport, sampling Kentucky's finest whiskeys. His admirers refused to let him buy a drink, and a gentleman could hardly refuse such kindness.

Some flattered him about his acting. Others slapped him on the back and whispered their support for his other role as a crusader for Dixie. A few shook his hand with the secret signals of the Knights of the Golden Circle.

As he climbed out of bed, he shook his head to clear the cobwebs and uncaged an angry headache that made his skull feel like it was full of sharp stones and broken glass. He was forced to sit back on the edge of the bed.

He had to stop and think. *Cincinnati. Yes, we nearly killed that baboon Lincoln here with a bomb a couple of years ago. One of these days...*

But what am I doing today. Tomorrow, a riverboat to Louisville with another week of performances. With any luck, Gen. Braxton Bragg might march in and take the city while I am there to see the stars and bars fly over the Mississippi.

But today... Yes, that pestiferous little man Bickley... calls himself a general or some such. And his friend, Dr. Bowles. Does he pronounce it like the intestines? Maybe I will, just to annoy him....

There was a soft knock at the door. "What is it?" he shouted before clutching his head.

"Sir, a note was left at the front desk for Mr. John W. Booth. It is marked 'Urgent' on the front."

"Please slide it under the door," he said, speaking more softly.

"Yes sir."

"And bring me a pitcher of cold water."

"Yes sir."

"And a bottle."

"A bottle, sir?"

"Yes, whiskey!" he shouted, then clutched his head again to keep it from falling in two halves like a sliced melon.

"Yes sir," the voice said, already retreating.

Imagining the sliced melon made him queasy so he went to the door and retrieved the note, shuffling to an easy chair to read it. It was on sparkling white paper, crisply folded in the middle.

"Mr. Booth,

We have not met but I am an admirer of your role as a lead-ing man on stage and also behind the curtain where a battle is being waged in the shadows to set our states free from northern oppression.

You and I are among the band of brothers whose thespian talents are in service to a better cause than playacting.

Meet me tonight at Blume des Rheins on Vine Street. I have what you're looking for.

The note was signed by "St. Crispin."

Booth was interested. He liked the references to Shakespeare's *Henry V.*

Act IV, Scene 1, he thought.

He recited the lines in a voice that tiptoed around the distempered beast in his head:

"We few, we happy few, we band of brothers;

"For he to-day that sheds his blood with me

"Shall be my brother; be he ne'er so vile,

"And gentlemen in England now a-bed

"Shall something-something hold

"Their manhoods cheap whiles any speaks

"That fought with us upon Saint Crispin's day."

There was only one thing Booth wanted besides cold water for his parched tongue and whiskey to warm his mind again: He wanted that artifact from the ancient Indian mounds.

Bickley had explained it all. A British collector wanted the Cincinnati Tablet for the British Museum, which had already purchased most of the best artifacts from the Ohio earthworks.

And that same collector—"Sir Boiled Beef" or "Lord Satinpants" or some such—was close to Lord John Russell, the English foreign minister.

The way Bickley and his sidekick "Bowels" described the plan, they could steal the tablet and sell it to Lord Satinpants for $50,000. But even more valuable than the income to outfit whole regiments was the goodwill of Lord Russell. Great Britain needed only a nudge to cross the dance floor and join the war on the side of the South.

Booth looked at the note again. Nine o'clock at a saloon on Vine. That should give him time to recover. He tried to remember what Bickley had told him about the tablet they wanted.

Something like 3,000 years old. About the size of a playing card, etched with doodle designs like Egyptian hieroglyphics.

Balderdash. Probably as phony as a stage-prop dagger. But if the British Museum wants it, who am I to say no?

There was a knock at the door.

"Yes?" he asked, his dry voice creaking.

"Your water and bottle, sir."

"Just leave them by the door," he said.

"Yes sir," the voice said, disappointed. There would be no gratuity. Booth smiled.

NOVEMBER 15, 1862

'All the world's a stage'

"I not only know what it is, I believe I know where it is," Colonel Whittlesey had told Duffy and Klaus.

As soon as they learned from Miss Emmaline about the tablet that Booth wanted, they had gone to his headquarters. Whittlesey told them he believed it was fake, but others insisted it was real.

"I was working in the chemistry laboratory with John Locke at the medical college here in 1841," the colonel had explained. "A man came in and offered to sell it to us for $50."

Duffy told him the Confederates believed it was worth $50,000, according to notes written by Dr. Bowles of the Knights of the Golden Circle.

Whittlesey shook his head in disbelief. "That would buy a lot of cannons and rifles for Jefferson Davis," he said.

"Yes sir, we believe that is their intention," Duffy said.

"The original tablet is likely in the custody of Ephraim Squier, but I would not trust the man as far as I can throw him, and I would dearly like to do that. We had some disagreements over his use of my work without attribution. Squier has sold most of the artifacts we uncovered to the British Museum. He partnered with Dr. Edwin Davis in his early work, then plundered Davis's scholarship just as he plundered the earthworks."

"This Squier man sounds like what you call a skunk," Klaus said.

"Worse, he is a journalist,"[205] Whittlesey said. "But you won't need

---

205 Squier was editor of the *Scioto Gazette* in Chillicothe when he met the amateur archeologist Edwin Davis. Davis financed the excavations and contributed the artifacts. Squier wrote papers claiming all the credit without mentioning Davis or Whittlesey, who also contributed to their

his help."

Whittlesey reached into a bag near his desk and pulled out a stiff-sided leather case. Inside was a rectangle that looked like stone, five inches long, three inches wide and about a half-inch thick. It had elaborate carvings on the front, and grooves on the back.

"Those carvings are supposed to represent some kind of bird," the colonel said, "but I have never been able to make it out."

"This is the tablet?" Duffy asked, his eyebrows raised.

"For your purposes, yes," Colonel Whittlesey said. "To untrained eyes, it is indistinguishable from the original. And I would hazard to say you will be dealing with the exceptionally uneducated eyes of Mr. Booth, Dr. Bowles and *General* Bickley." He said "general" like a man spitting out a watermelon seed.

Duffy raised his eyebrows again and started to ask, but Whittlesey spoke first: "A casting. We made several on the day it was brought to us. I kept one so I could study it."

"My eyeballs have not gone to school, either," Klaus said, "but it looks very real and quite old."

"The result of being carried in my satchel for more than twenty years," the colonel said. "Until you mentioned it last time we met, I had forgotten about it entirely."

And now Klaus and Duffy waited in the backroom at Blume des Rheins for their guest, John W. Booth, a.k.a. "Brutus."

"That hombre walks like a cat in a dog pound," Duffy would say later. "And those men with him made me want to take a hot bath."

Booth was accompanied by Bowles and Bickley, both in civilian clothing, dressed like any businessmen on the riverfront, in dark suits, with fresh white neck stocks, black ribbon ties, walking sticks and bowler hats. Bickley chewed his mustache, revealing his nerves. Dr. Bowles looked down on them the same way he seemed to look down on

---

catalogue of earthworks, *Ancient Monuments.* Whittlesey wrote to Squier: "A reader not otherwise acquainted with the fact, would infer that before you there were none worthy of notice . . . that you are the original and principal source of information." Barnhart, Terry, "A question of Authorship," *Ohio History Journal*, Ohio History Connection.

everyone, even sitting down. He had a high forehead, receding white hair and a narrow face with thin lips that looked as cold as his piercing eyes.

Duffy spoke the password. Bickley nodded but looked unconvinced until Duffy shared his Knights of Golden Circle bona fides and flattered the general by complimenting his recruiting speech Duffy had attended in Texas.

Klaus ordered a round of drinks from an exceptionally large bartender with a beard like a possum pelt. The bartender winked and said, "Yes sir. Does that include a lager for me?"

"I am Klaus, not Santa Klaus," the German replied with a laugh. "But serve yourself. You will anyway."

The big waiter left with a wink. "At your service," he said.

Duffy waited until they were alone, opened the black case and asked, "Is this what you gentlemen are looking for?"

Bickley's face turned red. Booth smiled and looked at the others as if to say, "What did I tell you?" Dr. Bowles reached for the tablet but Duffy slapped his hand hard, making a loud crack like a breaking stick and leaving a red welt.

The doctor yanked his hand back and rubbed it, giving Duffy a squint-eyed, angry stare.

"I reckon that means the answer is yes," Duffy said. "The only question left is how much do you gentlemen reckon this gewgaw is worth?"

Before they could answer, the giant bartender returned with two fists full of lager steins and beer foam on his gray beard. As he set them down, he lurched spilled one on the front of Bickley, then used his towel to wipe it off so violently he nearly knocked the man out of his chair.

"That is all now!" Klaus barked with the hint of a smile.

When Bickley had recovered, he said, "That man should be shot!"

"Many have tried," Duffy replied. "About our business?"

"I was under the impression that you were of a like mind in sentiments about the South," Bickley said. "If you understand the importance of this... *object* to our cause, you would understand that we cannot put a price on victory for those who have already given the ultimate sacrifice."

"Vat das he say?" Klaus asked.

"I ain't entirely sure. I think he said he wants us to give it to him for nothing," Duffy answered. "Is that how y'all do business here in the East, General Bickley?"

"I would be more than willing to pay you handsomely, but our collection was taken by ruffians last week." He paused, then turned to Booth, who was busy soaking up his lager like parched soil in a drought.

"But the celebrated Mr. Booth, here, has had a very successful run in the city," Bickley said. "Isn't that right, Mr. Booth?"

Booth looked up, his face quickly showing surprise, then annoyance, then resignation. "Yes, very successful," he said grudgingly. "The reviews were most generous with praise and flattery, as they always are."

"And the income?" Bickley prompted.

Dr. Bowles rubbed his stinging hand, took a drink and smiled as if he was enjoying Booth's discomfort.

"Yes, that too," Booth said. He quoted, "Whiles I am a beggar, I will rail and say there is no sin but to be rich; and being rich, my virtue then shall be to say there is no vice but beggary."

"Vat ist he saying," Klaus asked Duffy again.

"Shakespeare," Duffy answered. Then, turning to Booth, quoted, "If money go before, all ways do lie open."

"The Merry Wives of Windsor," Booth replied. "Like an ass whose back with ingots bows, thou bearest thy heavy riches but a journey, and death unloads thee."

Now Bickley looked confused, but Duffy smiled. "General, he means the money means nothing to him."

Booth gave Duffy an angry look, then pulled out a wallet from the inside pocket of a richly tailored suit jacket. As the others watched, he shuffled bills from a stack into a neat pile, counting in a whisper.

He said, "That's more than $5,000, nearly all I have. I will keep $400 for my travels to Louisville."

"Y'all are getting warmer," Duffy said, turning back to Bickley.

"General Bickley?" Booth asked.

Now it was Bickley's turn to look uncomfortable. He emptied his wallet and produced more than $2,000. When Duffy looked at him with raised eyebrows, he replied, "Not *all* the collection was taken. I had the foresight to *reserve* a share for my personal expenses."

Then all eyes turned to Dr. Bowles, who put his hands out as if he was pulling out his empty pockets. Duffy looked him over.

"That's a fine watch you carry," he said, pointing to a big gold pocket watch displayed from a short chain on the doctor's vest. Bowles looked as if he would protest. He turned to Bickley, then to Booth. He found no sympathy, only stares as cold as a Judas kiss.

He unclipped the watch and started to hand it to Duffy, then jerked his stinging hand back and slid it across the table.

Just then, the big bartender returned with another round of beers, but only three this time. As he put them down carefully over the shoulders of Booth, Bickley and Bowles, he winked at Klaus.

Duffy caught the signal and said, "This here belongs to you gentlemen." He pushed the case across the table to Bickley and scooped up the cash and the watch.

"Enjoy your beers," he said, standing.

"They are upon our house, special for you," Klaus said as he stood, following Duffy.

Booth was never sure what happened after that second stein of beer.

The next morning he awoke on a riverboat in a cramped berth, with bruises that seemed to cover every inch of his body, an aching jaw, a split lip and another headache that felt like the broken glass of the day before had been joined by nails, razors and sharks' teeth. He fumbled for his jacket to find his wallet and found a note pinned to the front:

"The fool doth think he is wise, but the wise man knows himself a fool. – St. Crispin."

The wallet contained a ticket to Louisville and $10.

He tried to remember the previous night. He vaguely recalled being carried like a sack of grain over the shoulder of that huge bartender... *two men speaking German... one very angry, looked like a bearded scarecrow in a suit... something about someone named Agnes....*

He groaned and gave up.

Bickley and Bowles were not seen or heard from for weeks.

1863-1865

Killed, captured and convicted

William A. Bowles

On May 20, 1863, just weeks before the decisive Battle of Gettysburg, more than 10,000 antiwar Copperheads gathered in Indianapolis to protest the war and the "tyranny" of President Lincoln.

It was a disaster for the Knights of the Golden Circle. Republicans mocked it as "The Battle of Pogue's Run." And the fiasco had the fingerprints of the Indiana's foremost KGC poohbah, Dr. William Bowles—the founder of French Lick, owner of the town's first hotel and a snake-oil salesman of magical "Pluto Water" from the mineral springs on the hotel property.

The antiwar protest rally began with speeches lamenting the recent arrest of the nation's most famous Copperhead, Congressman Clement Vallandingham, a Democrat from Dayton, Ohio. Vallandingham had been dragged out of his home by federal troops in the middle of the night, still in his pajamas, on the orders of Cincinnati's military commander, Gen. Ambrose Burnside.[206]

The arrest was a "base usurpation" of "rights and the Constitution," one fiery speaker said. The crowd was lathered and angry. Many were

---

206 Vallandingham, a Democrat, was eventually handed over to the Confederates, then fled to Canada, where he ran for governor of Ohio in absentia. The *Cincinnati Enquirer* reported a plot by the Knights of the Golden Circle to import 50,000 voters to vote for Vallandingham in 1863. He lost the election. But Vallandingham, calling himself Supreme Commander of the Sons of Liberty, a KGC offshoot, planned a triumphant return to Ohio so he could be arrested again and trigger an uprising. His return was enthusiastically ignored, and his plot fizzled. He eventually returned to practicing law. In 1871, Vallandingham was demonstrating his defense of a murder suspect to friends at the Golden Lamb in Lebanon, Ohio. He argued that the victim shot himself while pulling a pistol from his waistband. As he showed how it could happen, Vallandingham accidently shot himself in the stomach and died. According to local legend, his ghost still haunts the Golden Lamb.

members of the Knights of the Golden Circle, who had been called out by Dr. Bowles and others. Their plan was to seize a federal armory and then attack a local prison to set free thousands of Confederate prisoners held at Camp Morton.

But the KGC had been infiltrated by spies sent by Indiana Gov. Oliver Morton,[207] and a company of paroled Union troops was sent to police the rally.[208]

At about 4:00 p.m., the Union soldiers had seen enough. Fed up by insults to President Lincoln and arm-waving bloviating about overthrowing the federal government, ten of them waded into the crowd with bayonets fixed and rifles cocked.

That sent a wave of panic through the mob. The speakers hastily adjourned the meeting and scuffles broke out. Many of the assembled "Peace Democrats" and KGC members were arrested and hauled off to the nearest guardhouse.

As thousands boarded trains to leave Indianapolis that evening, shots were fired from the trains. Union troops responded by placing a cannon on the tracks to block the trains and boarded the cars to seize all weapons.

More than 500 pistols and knives were taken. One woman who was searched carried seven weapons. Many of the war protesters on the trains tossed their guns and knives into a nearby creek called Pogue's Run, named after blacksmith George Pogue, whose body had been found floating in the creek in 1821, killed by a renegade Indian called "Wyandot John."[209]

The soldiers found many of the weapons they seized on a train that was bound for Cincinnati, which had sent a large delegation of KGC members.[210]

---

207 Dr. Bowles's brother, Thomas Bowles, later plotted to kidnap Gov. Morton, but failed.

208 Gov. Morton, speaking in Cincinnati, pointed out how Gen. US Grant had disbanded the 109th Illinois Regiment on April 10 because it was infested with disloyal members of the Knights of the Golden Circle. Fesler, Mayo. "Secret Political Societies in the North during the Civil War." Indiana Magazine of History, 1918.

209 Taylor, Stephen J., "The Intriguing Tale of Pogue's Run," *Hoosier State Chronicles*, May 7, 2015.

210 Republicans in the Indiana House tried to launch an investigation of the Knights of the Golden

Democrat newspapers condemned the affair as more tyranny by President Lincoln, while Republican newspapers lauded the soldiers for stopping a rally of traitors.

The derisively named "Battle of Pogue's Run" was a defeat for the KGC. Dr. Bowles was plotting to recruit 10,000 men to rise up and join Confederate Gen. John Hunt Morgan's Raiders, who terrorized Indiana and Cincinnati that July. Like many of his schemes, it came to nothing. After Pogue's Run, the recruits lost their enthusiasm for insurrection.

Bowles was well known for his support for the Confederacy in French Lick. He was a close friend of Confederate President Jefferson Davis. And before the war, Bowles's wife caused a scandal when she brought her household slaves from New Orleans to the free state of Indiana. It had taken a court order to force Bowles to return them to Louisiana.

In June 1864, a year after the failed rally in Indianapolis, Dr. Bowles was arrested for treason. He was convicted by a military tribunal and sentenced to be hanged on May 19, 1865. But three days before his execution, his death sentence was commuted to life in prison by President Andrew Johnson.

On April 12, 1866, Dr. Bowles was set free from prison and returned to his home in Paoli, near French Lick. In a landmark ruling called *Ex Parte Milligan*, the US Supreme Court, led by Chief Justice Salmon Chase of Cincinnati, ruled that his conviction was unconstitutional. Civilian courts were available at the time of the trial, and the US military had no jurisdiction, the court ruled.

But by then, two years in prison had taken the starch out of the Fire Eater rebel doctor. There was not enough Pluto Water to restore his vitality. He declined steadily and died in 1873. More than $40,000 in unpaid alimony was seized from his estate for one of his three wives who had divorced him on grounds of his "improper conduct."

Circle in 1863, but it was blocked by Democrats, who feared too many politicians in their party would be exposed as members. Fesler, Mayo. "Secret Political Societies in the North during the Civil War." *Indiana Magazine of History*, 1918.

**George Washington Bickley.
Photo taken in the 1860s.**

A 1904 history of French Lick described Dr. Bowles as a man of "captivating influence."

"His personality, his eccentricity and his magic power over his fellow man was remarkable…. Everybody seemed to admire and almost reverence this remarkable man." After being expelled from the local Baptist Church, Dr. Bowles became "a most popular Baptist preacher." As a doctor, "his name was a household word in Southern Indiana."[211]

Dr. Bowles is still credited as the father of French Lick, who turned the local mineral springs and "Pluto water" into a casino and resort that has drawn tourists from all over the Midwest to the site where his wooden three-story French Lick Springs Hotel was built in 1845.[212]

George W. Bickley

Union Gen. William Rosecrans had a curious visitor at his headquarters in Tullahoma, Tennessee in July 1863. The man claimed to be a surgeon from the Confederate Army and introduced himself as George W. Bickley. He said he had been forced to join the Confederates and asked for permission to pass through the lines to go home to Cincinnati.

---

211 Rhodes, A. J., *French Lick and West Baden History and Story From 1810 to 1904*, 1904.

212 The French Lick Springs Hotel and casino is on the site of the original wooden hotel. About a mile away is West Baden Springs Hotel, built in 1902, a luxurious Jazz-age treasure from the pages of *The Great Gatsby*. It had the world's largest free-standing dome (200 feet) for 50 years.

The man insisted he was certainly not the infamous George W. Bickley of the Knights of the Golden Circle, only his nephew. Rosecrans listened, and gave him permission to travel on the condition that he would make no stops and go directly to Cincinnati.

But General Rosecrans was not fooled. He assigned a man to trail Bickley and report back.

The detective followed Bickley to Louisville. That's where things got interesting. Instead of getting on a train to Cincinnati, as he promised, Bickley set out for New Albany, Indiana, just over the Kentucky border—only about fifty miles from his good friend Dr. Bowles and numerous active castles of the Knights of the Golden Circle.

That was proof enough. Bickley and his wife were arrested in New Albany and taken back to Louisville where he was put in solitary confinement. His trunk was opened and found to contain KGC pamphlets, opium and letters that proved he was *the* George W. Bickley, who was on his way to meet with other leaders of the KGC, probably including Bowles. His wife's luggage was found to contain Bickley's Great Seal of the Knights of the Golden Circle—a Maltese cross surrounded by a star.

In one of the letters in the trunk, addressed to the Confederate Secretary of War, Bickley offered to form a mounted brigade.[213] He was probably going to Indiana to recruit help for Morgan's Raiders.

The man who bragged that he singlehandedly started the Civil War was finally caught.

The *Cincinnati Enquirer* published a long letter by Bickley later that year, in which he claimed he was forced to take an oath of allegiance to the Confederacy against his will, and only wanted to return to Cincinnati to see his family.

He had asked General Burnside to investigate his innocence, he wrote, "but behold! I was ironed [shackled] and ordered to the Ohio State Penitentiary and placed in *solitary confinement*. From the 18th of

---

213 Fesler, Mayo. "Secret Political Societies in the North during the Civil War." *Indiana Magazine of History*, 1918.

August till the 20th of October, I was locked in a cell seven by three and a half feet, when I was allowed no exercise."[214]

He insisted his secret society was not treasonous but merely an "offspring" of the Monroe Doctrine—as if he had never led rallies for secession with speeches inciting the Civil War. The Knights of the Golden Circle were only interested in "filibustering" to seize land for America, he wrote.

A report by the army's judge advocate general said Bickley was "the chief of the treasonable association known as the Knights of the Golden Circle, an officer in the rebel army, a conspicuously disloyal individual and a most mischievous as well as dangerous character."

"His personal restraint is, for these reasons, advised."

He was never given a civil or military trial but remained in prison until October 1865. He died two years after he was released, in Baltimore.

Many agreed that his Constitutional rights were abused. The *Cincinnati Enquirer* compared his treatment to the abuses of the notorious French Bastille prison.

But most people thought his treatment was slight punishment for the man who claimed to have instigated a war that took 750,000 lives. Most thought prison was too good for the scoundrel who founded the Knights of the Golden Circle to enshrine slavery in half the Western Hemisphere. It was especially rich that Bickley claimed Constitutional protections from a government that he had tried to overthrow.

John Wilkes Booth

The "handsomest man in the world" died after being cornered in a burning barn, where Union soldier Boston Corbett shot him through the neck. Paralyzed and bleeding to death, the actor, spy and assassin died after a few hours of agony, surrounded by the posse that tracked him down in the biggest manhunt in US history at that time. Booth was killed on April 26, 1865, 12 days after he assassinated President Abraham Lincoln at Ford's Theatre in Washington, DC, shouting "Sic

---

214 Keehn, David C. *Knights of the Golden Circle.* LSU Press, 2013.

temper tyrannis" ("Thus always to tyrants") as he leaped from Lincoln's private box to the stage below.

Booth had spent the early months of the year recruiting a gang of conspirators who plotted to murder the leaders of the government.[215] Booth first proposed to kidnap Lincoln and take him to Richmond, Virginia, the Confederate capital, to be bartered for Union concessions. But when Richmond began to fall, he decided to kill the president, even as the war was coming to an end with an inevitable Confederate defeat.

He was assisted by John Surratt, Lewis Powell, David Herold, George Atzerodt, Mary Surratt and others. Powell, like Booth, was a member of the Knights of the Golden Circle. John Surratt fled to Europe. The rest were hanged following a tribunal that was presided over by Gen. Lew Wallace, among others. The prosecutor was Henry L. Burnet, who practiced law in Cincinnati.

Booth's burial became a mystery. He was buried in an unmarked grave along with the other assassins, in the Old Penitentiary in Washington where they were executed. But then government officials staged a phony burial at sea to misdirect curiosity seekers.[216]

Later, Booth's body was exhumed twice before being reburied in 1869 in another unmarked grave in a family plot in Green Mount Cemetery in Baltimore. Near an imposing monument to his father, Junius Brutus Booth, a blank white headstone is often decorated with Lincoln pennies left by visitors—giving Abe Lincoln the last word.

---

215 Vice President Andrew Johnson and Secretary of State William Seward were also targeted by the Booth gang. The assassin assigned to kill Johnson got drunk and lost courage. But Seward was attacked and slashed severely in his home. He survived. Booth may have also planned to kill Ulysses S. Grant, but Grant did not attend the play that night. Greenspan, Jesse. "The other Targets of John Wilkes Booth's Murder Conspiracy," *History*, 2020.

216 "John Wilkes Booth 'Buried at Sea,'" *Remembering Lincoln*, A Project of Ford's Theatre.

1812-1815

The forgotten war

"Battle of Lake Erie" by Francis Christian Muller.

William Hatch woke up with a jolt at 2:00 a.m. His bed was lurching like the deck of a ship in a storm. The windows rattled and his furniture was jumping and walking around the room. Then as fast as it started, it suddenly stopped.

A few hours later at 8:00 a.m., it began again—this time, much worse. Hatch was outdoors near his Cincinnati house and staggered in shock as the ground began to roll and ripple like waves on the ocean. As he tried to run to the Ohio River he was pushed backward, "the same as when attempting to run upon the deck of a vessel when running against a stiff breeze."

As he looked over a cliff to the river, the whole surface of water rose to meet him. Although the river was low, "The waves were quite high, and rolling water moved and dashed fearfully against the gravel beach. ... Every flatboat or boat of any kind was forced up to the bluff. The water of the river was suddenly raised at least eight feet by the motion of the earth alone."[217]

It was December 16, 1811, the first day of the New Madrid Earthquakes that rattled Ohio and the Midwest. Until March 1812, more than 2,000 earthquakes rippled the landscape like a sheet on a clothesline.

The first one was 8.1 on the Richter Scale. Others were as high as 8.8.[218] The shocks were felt as far as Boston and in the White House. Near the epicenter in New Madrid, Missouri, the Mississippi River ran backward, new waterfalls suddenly appeared and wild animals suddenly acted tame while livestock went wild.

Huge cracks in the earth opened up, some as long as five miles. People, animals and property were swallowed up, never seen again. Homesteaders learned to cut down trees when the tremors began, then use them as a bridge they could cling to across the gaping abyss. Sometimes the dark fissures were lit from within by flashes like lightning as quartz crystals were crushed.[219]

The skies were filled with loud cracks of thunder as continental tectonic plates shifted and crushed against each other.

The early 1800s were a time of frightening cataclysmic events. Before the earthquakes, there was a solar eclipse in 1806. Then in 1811, a huge comet lit the skies at night for seventeen months. In America it became known as "Tecumseh's Comet"—a bad omen for the pioneers and their families in the Ohio.

Tecumseh and his shaman brother said the "Black Sun" eclipse, the comet and the earthquakes were a sign: The gods wanted them to go to war again and take back their land. And Tecumseh, whose name meant "Shooting Star," was clearly the one to lead them.

To the pioneers, it must have felt like the end of the world was near. As it turned out, 1811 was indeed the End Times—for peace.

---

217 Papers of William Hatch, Cincinnati History Library and Archives, Cincinnati Museum Center.

218 By comparison, the 1906 San Francisco Earthquake was 7.9.

219 Called "seismoluminescence." "Strange Happenings During the Earthquakes," New Madrid Missouri website.

· · · · ·

Books about the Civil War and World War II could fill entire libraries. Books about the War of 1812 might fill one shelf. Called the "Forgotten War" even before Americans gave that name to the Korean War, the War of 1812 is best known for producing America's National Anthem. But other than that, little is known or remembered. Something about Andrew Jackson… The Battle of New Orleans… the White House burned?

The war really began before 1812 and lasted into 1815. The battle described in "The Star Spangled Banner" took place at Fort McHenry in Baltimore. But the war started in Canada and spread south into the Northwest Territory and Ohio as the British dusted off their blood-stained strategy to use Indians in a proxy war against Americans.

The best-known cause of the war was impressment—or kidnapping—of American sailors by the British, who were desperate for manpower in their war against France and Napoleon. But there was a second cause named in the United States' declaration of war: The British supported Tecumseh and his new First Nation alliance of tribes that dragged Ohio back to the Dark Ages of the Miami Slaughterhouse.

In his speech to Congress urging war, President James Madison cited impressment, blockades and "British involvement in Indian warfare."

After being defeated by the Americans in 1776, and again in the 1790s, the British once again tried to stop the westward expansion of the United States by giving weapons and support to the Indians, urging them to "pick up the tomahawk" and follow the charismatic Shawnee Chief Tecumseh.

In Cincinnati and the rest of Ohio, the return of the nightmare was met again with resolve. Militias were raised and reinforced.

As early as 1809, as tensions rose and the Indian attacks increased, Maj. Gen. John S. Gano, a veteran of the doomed St. Clair Division, was sounding the alarm. As commander of the 1st Division of the Ohio Milita, he warned about the "gloomy aspect" of "belligerent powers."

"From every appearance, they wish to involve us in WAR," he wrote. He called for citizens of Cincinnati to show their "patriotic ardor and zeal."[220]

He was right. On November 7, 1811, while pretending to negotiate, hundreds of Shawnees attacked a force led by Indiana Territorial Governor William Henry Harrison, near Tecumseh's village along the Tippecanoe River.[221] Harrison was prepared and counterattacked, scattering the Indians and destroying their village.

By 1812, the war was official. Major General Gano was notified that the president was calling for 1,200 men to march with US Army regulars to Detroit to battle a "murderous incursion" by the British and Indians. Meanwhile, Tecumseh took his warriors north to join the British in Canada.

Then came disaster. "Dreadful News," *The Ohio Centinel* reported on August 22, 1812. "...Detroit was taken and [American] General Hull and his army had surrendered without firing a gun." The British had again seized the fort that had been the source of so much misery and grief in Ohio during the Indian War.

"Our frontier is now completely exposed to savage depredations and we must, for the present, rely upon our own means of defense for security," the Dayton newspaper reported. "...Your wives, your children, all you hold dear are in danger of being destroyed by savage violence, instigated by our semi-barbarian enemies."

American militias, including the Cincinnati Light Infantry Company and soldiers from Ohio and Kentucky, marched north to fight the battle they thought was won at Fallen Timbers. What followed was a disaster that nearly matched St. Clair's Defeat, and was equally discouraging to Ohio and the Northwest Territory.

General James Winchester was in command of fewer than 1,000 Americans. They met about 1,400 British and Indians at the Raisin River near what is now Monroe, Michigan, just over the Ohio Border from Toledo.

---

220 Papers of John S. Gano, Cincinnati History and Library Archies, The Cincinnati Museum Center.
221 Northwest of Indianapolis, near Lafayette.

Like St. Clair, Winchester did not send out pickets to give warning of an attack. On January 22, 1813, the Americans were caught sleeping.

The Americans put up a fight, but the British cannons and numbers were too much. Winchester surrendered. A few hours later, his Kentucky volunteers ran out of ammunition and also surrendered.

And then the massacre began.

Maj. Gen. John S. Gano's brother, R.M. Gano, was one of the few survivors. His January 25th letter to General Gano was published in Cincinnati's Western Spy newspaper on February 1.

"What shall I say or how to begin. My God, my God, my God, has thou forsaken us. ... Totally defeated. Did I say totally, yes. Out of 1,050 officers and men, not more than thirty have escaped the British savages. ... Mourn, mourn, mourn, America. Your history does not furnish an equal. Arouse, unite and march to avenge your loss."[222]

The Americans lost 934 men killed, wounded and taken prisoner. The British and Indians lost only 182.

Those were dark days for America. But when Napoleon was defeated by the British at the Battle of Waterloo in 1814, things got worse. Now the British could turn the full power of the greatest superpower in the world against the Americans.

It seemed the earthquakes, "Black Sun" and comet omens were right: America was doomed.

But the hand of Providence intervened.

William Henry Harrison—the young aide to General Anthony Wayne at Fallen Timbers and hero of the Battle of Tippecanoe—was put in command of the American Army in the Northwest Territory. He marched out and took back Detroit.

Then Capt. Oliver Hazard Perry defeated the British in the Battle of Lake Erie in September 1813, and announced the news with the stirring words, "We have met the enemy, and they are ours."

British troops laid waste to towns and villages as they marched to burn Washington in August 1814—but then the British Army was

---

222 Papers of John S. Gano, Cincinnati History and Library Archies, The Cincinnati Museum Center.

struck down by a violent tornado and lightning storm that put out the fires in Washington and scattered the British.

A shell that would have obliterated Fort McHenry during a bombardment on September 13, 1814, failed to ignite in the fort's powder magazine, and Baltimore was saved. By the next dawn's early light, the huge star spangled banner over Fort McHenry still waved. The British armada sailed away.

In early January 1815, a powerful British army that invaded New Orleans was sent running by a vastly outnumbered motley collection of American soldiers and frontiersmen led by Maj. Gen. Andrew Jackson.

Again and again in key battles, British officers in command were among the first to fall in combat, leaving their armies leaderless and lost.

The British had already given up and agreed to a peace treaty before the Battle of New Orleans. But Andrew Jackson's victory underlined the message sent to the world by the United States in 1776: "Don't Tread on Me."

Major General Gano summed up the attitude in a letter he wrote in 1813: "Be ready to right the wrongs and adopt the motto of the first volunteers in the American Revolution: God and our Rights; Freedom or Death!"[223]

---

223 Papers of John S. Gano, Cincinnati History and Library Archies, The Cincinnati Museum Center.

NOVEMBER 20, 1862

'Vaya con Dios'

Lew Wallace cleaned out his desk and packed his bags when the last Union soldier "absquatulated" from Camp Chase in Columbus, Ohio. He had deliberately encouraged the desertions by posting the men on guard duty far from the prison, unsupervised and unseen. They quickly caught on to his game and walked away home.

Union soldiers were held as prisoners in a northern City because they had the misfortune to be part of a company or regiment that had been captured—usually by no fault of their own. Rather than feed and guard the prisoners, the Confederates paroled them to the North on the promise that they would not rejoin the war.

Union officers did the same and paroled Confederate prisoners to the South.

But Camp Chase did not want to feed the paroled Union prisoners either. They were starved and neglected, given no pay, no fresh uniforms. They lived in appalling squalor amid a stench that stung the eyes, wasting away in the shadow of disease and death.

After the war, Gen. Wallace supervised the trial of the Confederate officer who commanded notorious Andersonville Prison in Georgia.[224] In his memoir, Wallace said the conditions at Camp Chase were nearly as horrible as Andersonville.

"Such a sight I had never seen nor imagined—men long-haired and bushy-whiskered, their faces the color of green cheese; most of them

---

224 Capt. Henry Wirz was hanged for the brutal murders and starvation deaths of 13,000 prisoners at Andersonville. Nobody was held accountable for Camp Chase. During the trial of Wirz, Lew Wallace sketched "Deadline," depicting the death of a prisoner. It became one of the most well-known images of Andersonville.

without head-covering of any kind, or coats or shoes; some in dirty cotton drawers and wrapped in old blankets in lieu of shirts. Looking down upon them—God help me speak the truth—I could see vermin crawling over their unwashed bodies, while the smell with which the mass thickened the air about me is in my nostrils as I write, it was so pungent and peculiar."

Thousands of paroled Union soldiers were imprisoned at Camp Chase. In another section of the prison, thousands of Confederate prisoners were locked up, and many died and were buried there, often in mass graves, victims of even worse abuse, neglect and disease.[225] Some were Confederate soldiers who were wounded at the Battle of Shiloh. They were brought to Camp Dennison in Cincinnati. The ones who died were buried near Camp Dennison, then dug up and reburied at Camp Chase.[226]

As he boarded a train for Cincinnati, General Wallace was glad to leave the prison camp behind him, but hardly thrilled about his next assignment: He would preside over an investigation of Gen. Don Carlos Buell, who had been relieved of command after the Battle of Perryville, Kentucky.[227] It was another stinging insult for Wallace, who knew he belonged on the battlefield. He had proved his skill and courage in battle at Fort Donelson and Shiloh. But now he would be just a cog in the threshing machine that would grind up Buell.

Buell's crime was his reluctance to pursue and destroy the Confederates.

There's poetic irony, Wallace thought. The General-in-Chief of the Union Army was "Old Brains" Henry Halleck—who dawdled

---

225 Today, the graves are marked with headstones, although no one is sure what bodies are there. Camp Chase was named for Salmon P. Chase of Cincinnati, former Governor of Ohio. The cemetery is on Sullivant Avenue in Columbus. Neff, Lois, Hilltop Historical Society "History of Camp Chase."

226 An old general store near the Camp Dennison cemetery has been the source of many stories about hauntings.

227 Buell, of Lowell, Ohio, near Marietta, was accused of being a traitor because he failed to win a decisive victory although his troops outnumbered the Confederates 60,000 to 16,000, and because he did not obey orders to follow and destroy the Confederates. The five-month investigation was inconclusive, but his career was finished.

and allowed the Confederate Army to escape after Shiloh, wasting three months to cover nineteen miles to Corinth that the Rebels had marched in four days. Wallace had begged to follow and attack them as they were routed on the second day at Shiloh. He was ordered to stand down.

And now those Confederates had come back in early October to fight another bloody battle in Corinth, Mississippi. Nearly 7,000 men were killed and wounded because of Halleck's gormless incompetence. Where was the machine to hold Halleck accountable? It was enough to make a man wonder why he fought to save a government that was so infested with incompetence, corruption and stupidity.

Wallace knew he was being used to destroy the reputation and career of Halleck's old rival, General Buell.[228] Wallace smiled at the assessment of Halleck by Secretary of War Gideon Wells: "He originates nothing, anticipates nothing, takes no responsibility, plans nothing, suggests nothing, is good for nothing."

But for once I got the best of Old Brains, Wallace thought. When Army officials refused to pay the men in Camp Chase what they were owed, he ordered a burley officer to break the paymaster's neck if necessary. The paymaster reconsidered and the men were finally paid, fed, cleaned up and given fresh uniforms and new tents—then set free to walk off. "This was wholesale desertion, and, to say truth, exactly what I had anticipated," Wallace wrote later.

Maybe I will join Buell on trial as a traitor, he thought. *The Army never has enough scapegoats to sacrifice.*

He was reminded of Shakespeare: "Some rise by sin, and some by virtue fall."

---

228 The judge advocate/prosecutor was Donn Piatt of Cincinnati, who immediately informed Wallace and the other presiding officers that "we are here to convict." But Major General Halleck did not get the conviction he demanded from Piatt. The commission exonerated Buell—and its report mysteriously was "lost" in Washington before Congress could read it. But Wallace had kept a copy. And his disfavor with Halleck increased. Wallace was ordered to stay in Cincinnati for months, then finally sent home to Crawfordsville, Indiana.

Colonel Whittlesey asked, "Please indulge my curiosity, sir. I would admire to know the secret of your ability to extricate yourself so quickly from such an unwelcome assignment."

"I have also wondered," Duffy said, "if I may apply your method the next time you toss me into a pit of treasonous vipers, sir."

Wallace smiled. They were sitting in the library at Burnet House Hotel. Wallace had summoned the two men for a report on their assignments. "Gentlemen, I would not wish to incite insubordination. I can only say I followed orders as I read them. To be perfectly straightforward, my own soul was in rebellion against indignities."[229]

"There must have been a lot written between the lines in those orders," Duffy said with a smile.

Whittlesey laughed, then said, "You were wise to avoid the troubles in Minnesota. I've seen that part of the country. It is as raw as Ohio fifty years ago. I would not want to be in the vicinity with the Sioux on the warpath. They may not be Blue Jacket and the Shawnees, but Little Crow is formidable."

Duffy said, "I find it hard to believe the army intended to send half-starved Union prisoners to fight Indians in Minnesota."

"Well, they had made no promise not to battle Indians," Wallace said. "And Little Crow and his warriors had to be stopped. They have killed more than 500 settlers and nearly 100 soldiers. More than 2,000 refugees were forced to flee their farms and towns."

"I read Governor Ramsey's message to Minnesota in the local papers," Whittlesey said.[230] "The horrors of the Miami Slaughterhouse

---

229 Wallace, Lew. *Lew Wallace; an Autobiography*. New York; London, Harper & brothers, 1906. When Wallace arrived at the prison, the angry inmates mobbed him and might have tried to kill him if he had not boldly stood his ground.

230 *Cincinnati Daily Enquirer*, September 19, 1862. "Hundreds of every age and sex perished by the hands of these remorseless butchers. ... But massacre itself had been mercy if it could have purchased exemption from the revolting circumstances with which it was accompanied.... Nothing was omitted from the category of their crimes. ... Infants nailed alive to doorposts to linger out their little life in mortal agony ... women held in captivity to undergo the horrors of a living death, whole families burned alive...."

are repeated—and families left helpless while their men are off to fight the Rebels."

"I reckon we will have the same problems in Texas when this war is finished," Duffy said. "Each state must fight its own war, just as Ohio did."

Wallace nodded. "The Indians will soon discover that this recent war has refined and perfected our brutality."

Whittlesey sipped a glass of milk and agreed. "Many will die and many will suffer. But the Indian problem will be resolved or they will be eradicated."[231]

Duffy said, "The railroad has opened the settlement of the West. It is all but inevitable. A man I have recently learned about, Simon Kenton, would understand this."

"Was he an associate of your companions, Mr. Woods and Mr. Breyer?" Wallace asked.

"No," Duffy shook his head. "But those hombres would have gotten along passing fine."

Whittlesey smiled. "I know of the man Kenton. Probably the best frontiersman and Indian fighter in Kentucky and the Northwest Territory. But before he died in 1818, he had to leave the land he tamed and go west. The Northwest Territory was 'too much crowded,' he said. As I look around this city, I sympathize."

Wallace asked Duffy, "Where are Mr. Woods and Mr. Breyer?"

"Nehemiah—he's the bearish one—has returned to his home on the Mad River, northeast of Dayton. And Amos has moved to Bethel, east of Cincinnati, with his new bride, a German girl named Agnes."

Wallace raised his eyebrows in surprise. "The man I met looked only partways human. And now married. Astonishing. Is this Agnes a lion tamer?"

---

231 More than 2,000 Dakota and Sioux Indians were captured. President Lincoln commuted most sentences of death, but 38 Dakota men were hanged in Mankato, Minnesota on December 26, 1862. The soldiers who escaped Camp Chase were spared the duty of participating in the largest mass execution in US history.

Duffy smiled. "In truth, Amos spiffed up quite nicely. After he was introduced to soap, razor and a hot bath, I would assay he was at least half human."

"Bethel sounds Biblical," Whittlesey added. "I believe the prophet Amos was called to preach in Bethel to confront the king."

Duffy laughed. "If there's a king of Bethel today, he had better cross the street to avoid our Amos or he may wind up like the Philistines, thrashed with the jawbone of a jackass."

"You gentlemen know your Good Book," Wallace said. "Maybe someday I can say the same.[232] Were Woods and Breyer compensated?"

"Yes sir," Duffy said. "They were handsomely paid by Mr. Bickley."

Wallace leaned back, surprised. "Did I hear you say *Bickley* paid them? There must be a good story behind that. Pray tell me more about your investigation."

When Duffy had reported how they flimflammed Bickley, Bowles and Booth and sent them limping away, Wallace asked Duffy, "Am I to assume then that you believe these men were involved in the 1860 plot to blow up the president's train car in Cincinnati?"

"I believe Booth was at least aware of it if not involved. The others are likely involved—if not directly, at least around the edges."

"And what of the gold you confiscated from that blatherskite Bickley and his bushwa Knights of the Golden Circle?"

"We offered a share to Klaus Wolff for repairs to his saloon, but he refused. He said he would have gladly spent as much for the entertainment of seeing Sergeant Butcher get all boogered up by Mr. Woods."

"Perhaps I can meet Mr. Wolf, now that I am posted in Cincinnati indefinitely to do the Army's laundry."

"Sir, I am not an admirer of General Buell," Whittlesey said, "but that is bad business. A shabby way to treat an officer. But no less than

---

232 After the war, Wallace sat on a train next to well-known atheist who challenged his faith and knowledge of the Bible. Wallace was embarrassed and resolved to read and study the Bible. The result was that he became a believer and follower of Christ, and he wrote the American classic *Ben-Hur: A Tale of the Christ*.

I would expect from a moral mud fence such as Old Brains Halleck."

Wallace suppressed a smile and turned to Duffy, urging him to continue his report.

Duffy said, "Another small share covered various expenses—mostly a substantial layout for enough lager to float a riverboat. The rest I divided between Woods and Breyer. Mr. Woods used part of his share to buy property and a moonshine still from Mr. Breyer, and that set up Mr. Breyer with enough to get married and buy a small farm."

"In Biblical Bethel," Wallace said.

"Yes sir."

Wallace turned, "Colonel Whittlesey, I must thank you for your outstanding service, as always. Now that General Bickley is euchered, our business is concluded, and you can return home to your wife in Cleveland and take care of that stomach."

Whittlesey smiled, rose and saluted. "Yes sir. I will miss the earthworks, but not much else. This is a fine city but take my advice and avoid the pork." He tapped his stomach with an exaggerated wince.

Wallace and Duffy chuckled as Wallace returned the salute.

When Whittlesey was gone, Duffy looked up with worry written on his face, like a man about to be told his barn has burned. "Sir, why do I have the feeling that this affair is not entirely finished?"

Wallace smiled and lit a small cigar, passing one to Duffy.

"Captain Smith—"

"Sir, I am a lieutenant."

"No longer. I have promoted you, Captain Smith. And I am giving you a month of leave. That should be sufficient time to visit that young woman you have been pining for and sweep her off her feet with a lasso, or whatever is the custom in your territory of tumbleweeds called Texas."

"Thank you, sir," Duffy said with a grin, almost rising out of his chair to leave. General Wallace held out a hand to stop him.

"That should also be enough time for Bickley, Bowles and Booth to recover from their recent misadventure in Cincinnati and get back into mischief. We have clipped their horns for now, but I have no doubt they will be back with another bag-of-nails conspiracy. I have communicated with Governor Morton, and we have decided to assign you to Indiana, where you can keep a close watch on Mr. Bowles and his secret society. As far as Dr. Bowles knows, you are still a Knight of the Lone Star, even if you did lift his gold watch."

Duffy grimaced. "Yes sir. Indiana suits me until I can go home to Texas."

"Like a crutch suits until the leg is healed?" Wallace asked.

"Exactingly."

"Meanwhile, I will write a report and alert Washington about the treasonous Mr. Booth. Bickley will be unreachable behind the skirts of the Confederates for now, but I think the dandy actor needs to be watched. What Washington does about it will probably come to nothing like so much they do there. But they will be warned, at least."

"Is that all, sir?"

Wallace could see that Duffy was on the edge of his chair, itching to run like a colt in a spring meadow.

"Yes, you are dismissed. Perhaps I will visit you in Texas one day. There are times when I feel as fenced as your hero Simon Kenton. It seems all the worst vices of our government are multiplied wherever people are too much crowded."

"I reckon that's what this war is about, sir. Are we so foolishly free as to allow slavery in the South and scalping in Texas? But if not, then how much liberty must we sacrifice for protection from such evils?"

Duffy put out his cigar in a crystal ashtray, stood and picked up his hat. "Left to me, sir, I choose the freedom of the West, where a man can stretch his legs under an open sky without scuffing the toes of another man's boots. Given my druthers between Comanches and lawyers, I am less afeared of the Indians."

Wallace laughed. "And when the Indians skedaddle, the last open prairies will be bridled, saddled and civilized," Wallace said. "There will be no frontier left for Mr. Kenton."

Duffy shook his head. "I reckon what we now call civilization will one day be looked upon as an agglomeration of cesspits, politicians and poverty. I pray there is still room enough in Texas to shirk it in my lifetime. We hold liberty more dearly there because we won it so recently."

He stood and saluted. "Until we meet again, sir. Vaya con Dios."

ACKNOWLEDGMENTS

In 1992, Cincinnati City Manager Gerald Newfarmer welcomed me to Cincinnati with a book about local history: *The Frontiersman*, by Alan Eckert. That led me to many other books about the fantastic history of the Miami Valley. Some of those are listed on the next pages for readers who would like to continue this journey into the past.

I thank my wife, Kathy, for her patience while I have been cloistered in my office for months of research and writing; my daughter Liz, for her excellent copy editing and suggestions; my son James, who loves history as much as I do and is always a source of encouragement; and my son-in-law Greg, for being a great dad to a new generation of enthusiastic readers, my wonderful grandchildren Audrey and Robbie.

My friend Ren Egbert urged me to explore local German history, and Russ Thomas, author of *Operation: Valkyrie*, inspired the use of German idioms in this book.

A huge thanks to Bill Branson, who read *The Man Who Soved Cincinnati* and called to tell me about The Twin Sisters.

And to my friend Chip Eberle, who brought me a great primary source history, *Notes on the Settlement and Indian Wars* by Joseph Dodderidge (1824).

Thanks also to Jill Beitz and Mickey deVise at the Cincinnati History Library and Archives in the Cincinnati Museum Center. As always, they graciously shared their extensive knowledge and goldmine of resources.

Jenny Shives at the Loveland Historical Society Museum generously provided original, handwritten pages from Daniel Boone's diary.

Steve Kramer of the Greater Cincinnati Police Historical Society Museum sent his research on the history of Detective William Henry

Reany, who fought, chased and helped capture Confederate Gen. John Hunt Morgan, leader of Morgan's Raiders.

Finally, thank you to all the readers who have encouraged me to keep writing books on our mutual passion, local history.

> "Either write something worth reading
> or do something worth writing."
> –Benjamin Franklin

BIBLIOGRAPHY

Bailyn, Bernard. *The Barbarous Years*. Vintage, 2013.

Boone, Daniel, and Francis Lister Hawkes. *Daniel Boone's Own Story & The Adventures of Daniel Boone*. Courier Corporation, 2012.

Castillo, Bernal Diaz. *The Conquest of New Spain*. Penguin UK, 2003.

Cozzens, Peter. *Tecumseh and the Prophet*. Vintage, 2021.

Doddridge, Joseph. *Notes on the Settlement and Indian Wars*, 1824.

Eckert, Allen W. *The Frontiersmen*. Jesse Stuart Foundation, 2011.

Fesler, Mayo. "Secret Political Societies in the North during the Civil War." Indiana Magazine of History, 1918.

Hämäläinen, Pekka. *The Comanche Empire*. Yale University Press, 2008.

Hogeland, William. *Autumn of the Black Snake*. Farrar, Straus and Giroux, 2017.

Howells, William Dean. *Amazing Stories from the History of Ohio (Illustrated)*. Good Press, 2024.

Keehn, David C. *Knights of the Golden Circle*. LSU Press, 2013.

McCullough, David G. *The Pioneers*, 2019.

O'Donnell, Patrick K. *The Unvanquished: The Untold Story of Lincoln's Special Forces, the Manhunt for Mosby's Rangers, and the Shadow War That Forged America's Special Operations*. Atlantic Monthly Press, 2024.

Pinkerton, Allan. *The Spy of the Rebellion*, 2017.

Preston, Steve, *Reverend James Kemper, Southwest Ohio History*. Heritage Village Museum, 2017.

Scamyhorn, Richard, and John Steinle. *Stockades in the Wilderness*, 2015.

Spencer, Oliver M. *Indian Captivity*, 1848.

Totten, Stanley M. *The Brilliance of Charles Whittlesey*. Kent State University, 2022.

Ungit, Lewis. *The Return of the Dragon*. Glome Press, 2022.

Wallace, Lew. *Lew Wallace; an Autobiography,* New York; London, Harper & brothers, 1906. *Lew Wallace; An Autobiography. Vol. II - Scholar's Choice Edition,* 2015.

Wilbarger, John Wesley. *Indian Depredations in Texas*. Eakin Press, 1889.

Willoughby, Charles C. *Turner Group of Earthworks, Hamilton County, Ohio.* Corinthian Press, 1922.

Turner Group of Earthworks, Hamilton County, Ohio. Corinthian Press, 1922.

Woodrick, James. *Cannons of the Texas Revolution,* 2015.

ALSO BY PETER BRONSON

The Man Who Saved Cincinnati (2023) The adventures of Lew Wallace, who went from being the Scapegoat of Shiloh to the Savior of Cincinnati. He rescued the Queen City from a Confederate attack, formed the first Black Brigade in the Civil War, saved Washington DC, captured Billy the Kid, stopped the worst range war in US history and wrote one of the most popular books of all time, *Ben Hur: A Tale of the Christ.*

Not in Our Town: The Queen City vs. The King of Smut (2022) The shadow war between Cincinnati and Organized Crime, and the battle against porn tycoon Larry Flynt. Find out how Flynt got bankrolled by the Mob and why he was shot; read about the curious case of Jerry Springer, the city's worst police scandal and the men who fought to keep the Mafia out of Cincinnati.

Forbidden Fruit: Sin City's Underworld and the Supper Club Inferno (2020) The 40-year empire of the Mob in Newport and Northern Kentucky, leading up to the Beverly Hills Supper Club Fire in 1977, called "the biggest mass-murder cold case in US history." Find out what was in the FBI vault of classified files about the mob and "The Las Vegas of the Midwest" in Newport.

Behind the Lines (2005) The stories the press never reported about the 2001 race riots in Cincinnati.

Signed copies at www.chilidogpress.com
Also at local bookstores and Amazon.com